THE HEIR OF THE FIRST TOWER

NICHOLAS P. ADAMS

Written by Nicholas P. Adams.
www.nicholaspadams.com

Cover & interior design by Brian C. Hailes.

The Heir of the First Tower

Paperback ISBN: 978-1-951374-70-9
Hardback ISBN: 978-1-951374-71-6
Ebook ISBN: 978-1-951374-72-3

Second Edition Printed in 2022 by Epic Edge Publishing

www.epicedgepublishing.com

Printed in the United States of America

10   9   8   7   6   5   4   3   2   1

DEDICATION

First and foremost, I dedicate this work to God, my Father in Heaven, who gave me ideas more often than I asked for inspiration. It is my sincere hope and prayer that this story will remind the reader that He is ever-present and always mindful of the day-to-day comings and goings of His children on Earth.

I dedicate this novel to my wife for believing in me and supporting my dreams to become more than a hobby writer.

I also dedicate this book to the readers who, like me, are eager to become swept away into another realm. I hope you forget your troubles for a time while you enter the world I discovered.

Finally, I dedicate these words to my critics and detractors: I honestly don't care what you think.

—Nicholas P. Adams

THE HEIR OF THE FIRST TOWER

NICHOLAS P. ADAMS

Contents

Foreword 8

Chapter 1 - **Adversary Or Ally?** 21

Chapter 2 - **Ears to Hear** 31

Chapter 3 - **The Healer's Art** 36

Chapter 4 - **Neb to Neb** 53

Chapter 5 - **Voices of Smoke** 62

Chapter 6 - **Confessions** 70

Chapter 7 - **The Question** 74

Chapter 8 - **R'Venin's Shadow** 80

Chapter 9 - **Sisters** 89

Chapter 10 - **A New Trust** 98

Chapter 11 - **The Deadly Sleep** 105

Chapter 12 - **Western Crossroads** 119

Chapter 13 - **The Whispering Woods** 132

Chapter 14 - **Gha'Barahat** 139

Chapter 15 - **The Master Alchemist** 151

Chapter 16 - **The Unnatural** 159

Chapter 17 - **Homeward Flight** 169

Chapter 18 - **Secrets** 185

Chapter 19 - **Nesting** 196

Chapter 20 - **The Seer of Willowlimb Bazaar** 203

Chapter 21 - **The Vision** 211

Chapter 22 - **Bargaining Favors** 222

Chapter 23 - **Prepare and Purify** 235

Chapter 24 - **The Hearts of Ch'Hotee** 248

Chapter 25 - **High Road to Ruin** 259

Chapter 26 - **Wind and Ash** 269

Chapter 27 - **Ka'Ala's Vow** 283

Chapter 28 - **No Turnng Back** 290

Chapter 29 - **The Night Raid** 307

Chapter 30 - **Gha'Barahat's Apprentice** 321

Chapter 31 - **Shadowed Hearts** 336

Chapter 32 - **The Heir Returns** 345

Chapter 33 - **Scattered Leaves** 357

Chapter 34 - **The Council of Nine Towers** 367

Chapter 35 - **Divided Branches** 379

Chapter 36 - **Alchemy and Treachery** 391

Chapter 37 - **The Tears of Vi'Jeet** 408

Chapter 38 - **Weaving Branches** 427

Chapter 39 - **The First Dawn** 442

Foreword

Nicholas Adams and I have been friends for several years. I see his kids trick-or-treating at Halloween, and I visited with his in-laws regularly a couple of years back. Reading and writing both runs in the family. It's always fun to help out a friend with something like this, and it's an honor to write an introductory foreword for The Heir of the First Tower. He asked me for a couple of reasons beyond being friends. First, I'm the 2020-2021 president of a state-wide writer's organization. Second, I have a fantasy trilogy with strong ties to magic and animals but done in a completely different style.

Nicholas and I have experience with both novels and short stories. I've read other books by him, and we've got a lot of shared experience with short story markets. We've submitted short stories to the same contests a few times. Rather than viewing Nicholas as a competitor, writing this foreword is a chance to cheer on a fellow author as we both pursue our dreams. The challenge helps us to try harder and learn new things. That's one of the hallmarks of a healthy writing community, and I'm happy to say that the League of Utah Writers is such a place.

Architecture may seem like a random tangent at this point, but I bring it up for a reason. Architecture relates to planning, outlining, and creating a final product, whether a building or a story. Nicholas is an architect by trade and uses that sense of structure to give each story a uniform feel. In addition to the form and feel, you have to add interesting characters and conflicts. A construction blueprint doesn't have heroes and villains, but a healthy dose of imagination can help both buildings and stories. Four walls and a roof can be dull if done wrong or generate awe when done right. It's the same with a story.

There are rewards for the careful reader in The Heir of the First Tower; little tidbits of conversation hint to things not outright stated. Ideas you may not have thought of yet as a reader. This book will help you to escape the mundane world for a while, but it can do more than that. It can teach you the importance of love and the joys of serving others. It can do this all in the background while the story entertains you with its complex societies and a range of emotions to keep you reading.

I'm confident you'll enjoy it!

—John M. Olsen, 2020-2021 President of the League of Utah Writers, Author of the Riland Throne trilogy: Crystal King, Crystal Queen, Crystal Empire

* * *

R'Venin Character Portrait by Yassine Sey

Ka'Ala Character Portrait *by Yassine Sey*

Ba'Jai *Character Portrait by Yassine Sey*

Ja'Naam Character Portrait *by Yassine Sey*

Kar'Nevala Character Portrait *by Yassine Sey*

Gha'Barahat *Character Portrait by Yassine Sey*

K'Marot *Character Portrait by Yassine Sey*

K'Rawin Character Portrait *by Yassine Sey*

__P'Vrit__ Character Portrait by Yassine Sey

Part One

Chapter One

Adversary or Ally?

Maybe this wasn't such a good idea, after all. R'Venin clawed his way through the crimson maize fields of the central plains as the battle raged a thousand wingspans overhead. Ripe corn ears blooming with silver silk fell against his broken wings with each agonizing handspan of ground. Wisps of silk snagged at his fractured helmet, threatening to pull it off and reveal the ruby-encrusted crown hidden underneath.

Three thousand spans beyond the warring clans, R'Venin imagined his father watching the battle from the white cliffs, their last conversation haunting his thoughts.

* * *

"Remember, R'Venin, show no mercy. No remorse." K'Rawin's juniper eyes reflected the rising western suns. "Show only cruelty to those who defy our destiny. We are the chosen flock of the great Windfather. The Ch'Hota will submit to the light or perish to our might. The V'Jeeta will one day rule over all Pirth'Vee Grah!"

R'Venin bowed and stretched his wings to reveal their undersides, transferring his helmet to his left arm to pound his right fist across his chest plate. The squad of V'Jeeta royal guards behind him copied his reverential gesture in unison. The silver and ruby crown atop his head glinted in the morning sun.

"This is wrong. Why must we conquer? Why can't we just negotiate for the Silver Silk?" R'Venin thought, his eyes flitting to the army assembling across the valley.

King K'Rawin stepped to the cliff's edge overlooking the plains, wrapping his armored talons over the lip. Spreading his wings upward, he winced as the joints cracked. His right wing spasmed and shuddered before stretching out to its full reach. He shook the dust off his feathers before pulling them back, cloaking his body.

R'Venin stepped forward, away from the royal guard. "Is it the White Claw again?" he asked, retracting his finger claws and massaging his father's wing joints.

K'Rawin's eyes flared, but his face remained hard as the Granite Spires of home. "No one can know," he snapped under his breath.

Everyone already knows. Who do you think you're fooling?

"May I take a look?" R'Venin whispered, leaning forward.

"You're a warrior, R'Venin," he sneered. "What would my generals think if they saw the high prince doing a frail-wings work?"

R'Venin sighed, closing his eyes. "I'll make it look like I'm adjusting your armor."

K'Rawin gave a slight nod as he stared across the fields below.

R'Venin placed his helmet on the dusty outcropping and closed the gap between them. Raising his wings, he offered some privacy from the royal guards' sharp eyes. K'Rawin opened his right flank again, fighting off another twitch, as R'Venin unlatched the hinged joint plating covering his father's wing claw. A chalky powder fell from within the sheath as R'Venin removed the bracelet-like armor from the wing's leading edge. The hook-shaped talon, dulled by disease, looked like a weathered tree trunk left to bleach in the sun. Hairline cracks ran the length of the shaft. The claw, black and shiny at the base, tapered to papery-thin snakeskin at the tip, as if ready to slough off at the slightest breeze.

R'Venin held his breath as the charcoal feathers across his back and calves splayed. The bitter smell of rotting leaves wafted across his nasal slits with the cloud of powdered bone.

"Not as bad as you thought, is it?" K'Rawin sneered, looking away from the exposed claw.

R'Venin replaced the armor plating, retrieved his helmet from the ground, and set it over his crowned head. "Perhaps you should have your healers take a closer look, Father," R'Venin bowed his head. "Your talons smell worse."

K'Rawin snorted. "Once we win this battle, I'll get my treatment for the next breeding cycle."

"If we bartered with the Ch'Hota for the silk," R'Venin leaned in, "we wouldn't have to fight over the harvest. There would be enough for both sides. We could treat all V'Jeeta with White Claw."

"I'll not share with those mongrels," K'Rawin spat. "There's not enough for all. If we don't defeat them today, there will only be enough Silk for the First Tower. And we need to breed more warriors if we're to crush our enemy to dust."

There's never enough because we destroy half the valley fighting over the Silk. Why it only grows here, I'll never understand. But if we didn't need it anymore, the war would end.

"I've been studying alchemy, Father," R'Venin whispered. "Mother has been teaching me. I believe if we had help, we could find a cure."

"We need help from no one," K'Rawin snorted. "And, alchemy is for crazy Pra'Acheen mystics, not a V'Jeeta prince. You're the eldest son of my first wife, and a V'Jeeta warrior, R'Venin." K'Rawin's eyes darkened. "Never forget that."

R'Venin nodded. "Yes, Father."

K'Rawin waved R'Venin away as an adolescent V'Jeeta warrior in gleaming obsidian armor swooped down from the clouds. The king's chest expanded as a younger version of himself came to a stop a wingspan off the cliff's face. He beat his wings against the updraft, hovering in place. "Ah," the king beamed, "K'Marot, my youngest son and best scout. What did you find?"

"Father," he shouted as dust billowed across the ledge. "The Ch'Hota are assembling at the edge of Needleleaf Forest. They have a hundred squadrons perched in the lower branches and dozens of ground artillery units moving into position between the Bluewoods and the Copperleaf Forest. I estimate we outnumber them five to three. It will be a slaughter."

R'Venin raised his spear in salute toward the boy. "Hello, little shadow."

Barely past a hatchling, and Father sends him out as a spy.

"Hello, brother," K'Marot's smile widened, bowing his head as his eyes locked on R'Venin. "I look forward to watching your skills in battle. Father says I can learn much from your example. I've wagered with the others that the field will be stained yellow with your kills."

K'Rawin's eyes narrowed as a wicked grin crossed his lips. "We will end them," he growled. "They will subject themselves or die."

"We may have more warriors, father," R'Venin leaned in, "But their armor and weapons are superior to ours. This battle will be costly," R'Venin paused then turned his head to look directly at his father. "On both sides."

K'Rawin spun away from the precipice, flaring his wings and backhanded R'Venin in the face. "I don't care what it costs," the king roared. "I'll send every last V'Jeeta to their deaths, as long as the Ch'Hota end up in bondage or extinction."

K'Marot drifted down, landing a wingspan from the king. "Father, R'Venin meant no disrespect. I'm sure he's only concerned about the lives of our army. Right?" He asked, looking into his eldest sibling's eyes.

R'Venin's eyes flitted between the faces of his father and youngest brother. "Yes, of course," he muttered. "I'm just worried about losing more soldiers in this war."

K'Rawin stared hard into R'Venin's averted eyes.

R'Venin bowed low, exposing his wing's undersides as wide as his joints would allow. "Praise to the King," he shouted toward the ground.

The royal guards drew swords or raised spears to the sky and opened their wings, chanting, "PRAISE TO THE KING!"

K'Rawin turned in a slow circle, touching each shouting warrior's chest plates before standing next to K'Marot at the cliff's edge. Drawing twin swords from their sheaths, he pointed them toward the Bluewoods in the distance and took a deep breath.

"TO BATTLE!"

The sky darkened as thousands of V'Jeeta warriors, led by K'Marot, took flight from the plateau, screeching like lightning.

R'Venin pulled the helmet over his head and raised his spear, screaming into the dawn as he stepped off the precipice and dove toward the cloud of Ch'Hota guardsmen rising from the branches below.

Death will be my only escape from this nightmare. At least I'll no longer be at the mercy of his talons.

R'Venin pulled in his wings, building speed. The wind whistled through his helmet's ear holes, rising in pitch with his descent. Wingspans above, metal clanged against metal as the V'Jeeta Army grappled with the Ch'Hota guardsmen. Screams of agony erupted as warriors on both sides ripped, sliced, and tore at the wings of their enemies. The bodies of adversaries and allies fell lifeless from the sky, skewered on spears or pierced by arrows, to the red fields below.

R'Venin spied a quintet of Ch'Hota, flanking him on the right.

I'd better make this look good, so Father retains his honor. Taking on five at once should give him reason enough to exalt my death.

R'Venin spun around, beating his wings faster and aiming his spear at the center guardsman. The rustling wind stilled like a frozen river as each flap took longer than the last.

Goodbye, Mother. Goodbye, B'Luren, my sister. I go to join Be'Tee, the Mother of All, in the Eternal Tree.

R'Venin banked left and right, preventing anyone who may be watching from knowing his true intent. Ten wingspans away, two of the Ch'Hota guardsmen broke formation and swooped upward, tilting their spears to the sky just as a V'Jeeta warrior pummeled them with a crash of steel. "My Prince!" he choked as the spears impaled him. "Fly!"

R'Venin tucked his wings and spiraled just as the three remaining guardsmen launched their spears at him. His spin snapped off three spearheads, still lodged in his wing joints. As R'Venin fell, his executioners drew their swords in unison and wheeled through the sky, searching for another V'Jeeta target.

Flailing against the stabbing pain in his shoulders, R'Venin clawed at the air. With nothing to grasp, the battling flocks above grew smaller as he plummeted toward the ground.

* * *

Did Father see me fall? If he discovers I'm still alive, he'll have me healed and then send me right back into battle.

R'Venin glanced back along the blood trail to the fallen warrior, the spear shafts holding him off the ground like a carcass over a roasting pit. A veridian pool collected at the dead warrior's knees, soaking into the ruddy soil, chasing R'Venin further from the chaos of war.

He clawed through the soft, tan dirt with his functioning arm, stretching the open wounds of all three spearheads still lodged in his wing joints. His armor plating failed to protect him against the squadron of Ch'Hota guardsmen that swooped out of nowhere.

With a broken ankle, shattered femur, and dislocated hip—all on one side—R'Venin's vision blurred from the pain. The Copperleaf forest seemed forever away as his driving thought pulled him forward.

I never wanted to be a warrior.

A flock of midget dovehawks erupted from the red maize to his right, followed by soft footfalls moving in his direction. His black armor, accented with bright scarlet crystals to match his plumage, blended against the shadows and red stalks.

His emerald eyes scanned between the rows of corn, watching for the noisemaker's colors.

Ally or Adversary?

The dovehawks circled above, squawking displeasure at their interrupted feast, and then darted northward.

R'Venin watched, bleary-eyed, toward the south, as he unsheathed his small dagger from a chest scabbard. An irregular rhythm of multiple footfalls approached at a slow pace; only the carbon-feather armor kept his hearts from erupting out of his chest.

Forcing his cotton-covered tongue to swallow the remnants of moisture in his mouth, R'Venin rolled onto his punctured shoulder to prepare for his final defense. The spearheads tore at his open wounds like a runnerhound digging for sweetroot.

The sounds of faltering footsteps and a cry of agony penetrated through the thick maize stalks before the body of a wounded V'Jeeta warrior landed a few feet away from R'Venin's trembling blade. He spotted the fractured, double-spear insignia on the motionless V'Jeeta's helmet.

Heavy Cavalry, Second Class. Fresh from The Branch.

"Ch'Dee," a dark shadow called from behind the rows. "Are you still alive?"

R'Venin gaped into the blank stare of the fallen soldier, green blood oozing out of his mouth and nose as the other warrior stepped into the swath of trampled corn. "Prince R'Venin?" the warrior donning a Wing Commander's sash exclaimed. "We thought you were dead."

"I'm not sure if that wouldn't be better than my current state," R'Venin groaned, reaching up while still clutching his small weapon. "What's your name, warrior?"

"I am D'Atch, of the Third Tower." The warrior tightened the grip on his spear and saluted R'Venin with a small bow. "I have the high honor of leading your father's Obsidian Battalion. I have learned much from his battle tactics. He speaks very highly of you, your highness."

Just wonderful. R'Venin grimaced inwardly as he sheathed his dagger. *Another death-worshiper.*

D'Atch looked over R'Venin's injuries. "You need to see a healer, your majesty," he said, keeping his wings open and vulnerable. "Your brother's camp is not far. I can take you to him."

R'Venin turned his gaze toward the distant battle of two great flocks in a heated conflict. The crash of metal on metal faded to tinkling cymbals where he lay injured on the ground.

If I refuse his aid, he's sure to tell K'Marot that I'm still alive. Then I'll never escape.

The Ch'Hota squadron that left him butchered and broken flashed behind his eyes. R'Venin shuddered, then fluffed his blood-soaked plumage as if attempting to shake off the stains.

"I'll be alright," R'Venin sighed. "You should get back in flight. The king will need all the warriors he can muster to defeat the Ch'Hota. Go."

D'Atch puffed out his chest, standing tall. "Forgive me, your majesty. But, I'll not leave the King's first son to die in a field. With your permission—" D'Atch leaned forward, planting his spear and extending his arm.

"Thank you, D'Atch," R'Venin reached up, taking the warrior's outstretched hand. "Aargh!" Open wounds tore apart, letting his loathed royal blood seep to re-stain his armor with a fresh coat of green.

R'Venin wrapped his working arm under D'Atch's wing, unable to help the uninjured soldier; he could do no more than express his gratitude. "I'm sorry about your fallen comrade," R'Venin grunted between agonizing steps through the rows of red stalks. "Were you close?"

D'Atch kept his stoic eyes on the path between the rows as they inched closer to the sounds of battle. "He was my father's first son. And though I am his youngest, Ch'Dee was my best friend."

R'Venin felt a stab of guilt. *The first son of the king and the devotee of his youngest brother.* "Small flock," he said between steps. "It seems we have a little in common."

Suddenly, D'Atch spread his arms and wings as a spear burst through his chest armor. Collapsing onto the ground under the weight of his fallen aide, R'Venin looked up to the crystal sky from the flat of his back, only to find a Ch'Hota guardsman readying another pike from high above.

The Ch'Hota guardsman dove, pulling in his wings tight to build up speed before plunging the spear at R'Venin's helpless form. *This is the end*, R'Venin thought to himself. *Thank the great Windfather.*

Just as the spear left the guardsman's hand, a V'Jeeta warrior dove into the Ch'Hota soldier. The V'Jeeta's talons dug deeply into the Ch'Hota's back as he tore at his wings with a guttural battle cry.

The spear pierced through D'Atch's wing and into R'Venin's no-longer-good shoulder, pinning him to the soil a mere second before the tumbling aerial combatants blasted into the ground like meteors a wingspan away from his feet. A cloud of feathers, browns, and tans, splattered with blood, plumed into the air. Bits of fallen compatriot, mixed with his father's enemy, floated on the wind and landed on R'Venin's face.

Unable to move, D'Atch's dead body pinned him on one side. The spear on the other. R'Venin let his head fall against the soft, loamy soil. His final pillow.

Creamy clouds swirled in the azure sky, the colors blurring together with each exhausted breath. The red corn stalks painted silvery trails as they swayed in the breeze.

R'Venin half-closed his unfocused eyes to watch the dance of light and shadow.

Free from war. Free from hate.

A muffled voice, like distant thunder, shouted indecipherable words.

Dazed and sleepy, R'Venin ignored the crunching footfalls getting louder. A blurry silhouette hovered upside down into view.

Just let me die. I can't go back.

The misshapen shadow grew as the newcomer leaned down. The sensation of the soft, earthy bed suddenly left him as a lungful of dusty air, distinct with the odors of corn and sweat, filled his nasal slits.

A stabbing pain pierced his left shoulder as the blurry shape rolled his body onto its broken side. In a brief moment of clarity, a green-soaked spearhead came into view. Bits of meat and feathers dangled from the barbs.

Those look a lot like mine.

The stranger's hand dropped the bloody mass, which disappeared under R'Venin's head. His body floated off the ground and spinning amid the stalks, drifted sideways through the rows of corn, whose silvery hairs brushed his brow. No longer able to keep them open, R'Venin closed his eyes and drifted away.

Chapter Two

Ears to Hear

A hooded figure nestled deeper into the branches, her onyx feathers and umber tunic with matching leggings blended into the shadows of Copperleaf. Her pearly eyes spied on the Ch'Hota guardsman struggling to carry a wounded V'Jeeta warrior. Gripping the bark, she leaned her twiggy frame out as the Ch'Hota stumbled. He had dropped his spear and then crashed into the trunk with the V'Jeeta twenty wingspans below. The V'Jeeta moaned, and the Ch'Hota sucked air in between his teeth.

"I'm here, Windfather," she whispered, ignoring the grunts emanating from below. "I found the place you showed me. But why? What is it you desire of me?" She closed her eyes, pulling back onto her perch.

A gust passed by, carrying a hint of maize with the rank of death into her nasal slits. She covered her mouth and nose, holding her breath with pinched eyes. Her stomach convulsed from the stench: blood and gore.

She peered back over the branch at the sound of fabric tearing to find the Ch'Hota kneeling and ripping strips of cloth from his uniform. He wrapped the pieces around the unconscious V'Jeeta's misshaped limbs. The V'Jeeta rolled his head around, muttering, but never fully conscious.

"Did you send me here to help one of them?" she mumbled.

The Ch'Hota stood and looked around their small clearing. She followed his gaze as his head turned abruptly. Ten paces away, a spring bubbled from a rock. He flapped his wings, hovering to the fresh water, and pushed his face into the fountain. His noisy slurps rose to her ears. After a deep sigh, he pulled a wineskin from underneath his armor and sunk it into the shallow pool.

The Ch'Hota pulled the full bladder from the spring and flew back to the V'Jeeta laying broken on the forest floor. The V'Jeeta swallowed the drops poured into his open mouth. The Ch'Hota repeated the process a few more times, then wiped the dirt and blood from the V'Jeeta's face and neck.

Her eyes softened as the V'Jeeta's features emerged from the grime. *He's not as hideous as I expected. He's quite handsome; I suppose—for a bloodthirsty V'Jeeta. Probably wouldn't be a tragedy if he died—one less monster in the world.*

She tilted her head. Quiet music tickled her ears like distant armies announcing their quest for battle. Two musical battalions grew, resonating inside her skull until all but two instruments suddenly faded to silence. Two horns of different timbre wove a harmonic tapestry that danced in her mind.

The Windfather has destined them to be allies. Friends. Brothers!

Movement in the brush behind them caught her attention. Low branches parted, revealing a wild runnerhound slinking through the grass. Twice as tall as the Ch'Hota, its four legs tapered to wide six-toed paws with claws as sharp as razor-briar. Tawny scales bristled as it crouched, coiling for the attack. Three rows of fangs glinted in the waning sunlight.

A swift demise.

Ka'Ala, Windfather's voice spoke in her mind. *Help your brothers.*

What? Are you kidding? That's a full-grown runnerhound. I can help the Ch'Hota, but I don't know if I can save the V'Jeeta. You know what his people did to mine.

The Ch'Hota spun around, freezing in place. His gaze locked on the creature; its growl now rising to meet Ka'Ala's ears.

Ka'Ala, Windfather whispered again, *Help your brothers.*

"But I'm not a warrior," Ka'Ala whimpered. "I can't fight off a beast that size."

The runnerhound began circling. The Ch'Hota kept himself between the V'Jeeta lying at the tree's base and the snarling animal. The Ch'Hota yelled and jabbed his spear toward the predator, but the feral brute just swiped at it with massive paws.

"*Ka'Ala*," His voice pierced her twin hearts. "*You have the gifts necessary to save both.*"

A vision appeared in her mind as clear as a winter sunrise.

Reaching into the black leather pouch hanging from her belt, she retrieved a handful of smooth stones. With the other hand, she uncoiled a sling tucked behind her back and cradled a rock in the thong. Whipping the sling over her head Ka'Ala launched a stone toward the ground, striking the runnerhound in the face.

The beast recoiled, wiping its bleeding muzzle with its foreleg. The Ch'Hota lunged forward with his spear but missed as the hound reared back, clawing at the lance. Again, the Ch'Hota advanced, jabbing at the air and herding the animal around the tree. The unmoving V'Jeeta lay helpless between exposed roots as the Ch'Hota and runnerhound parried further away.

Ka'Ala took a deep breath and dove, plunging to the ground with wings tucked. The damp forest air whipped past her ears. Her hearts pounded against ribs, threatening to escape and let her fend for herself. At the last second, she opened her wings, landing hard on the soft bed of a hundred autumns. Cocooning the blacked-out V'Jeeta with her wings, she scrunched up her face and held her breath. Her wings shimmered from deep black to match the browns, reds, and greens of the root-bed around her helpless charge. From the outside, she may have looked like a simple leaf-drift.

The bedlam between the Ch'Hota and the runnerhound grew closer. Ka'Ala pressed her body tight against the V'Jeeta's armor; her face bowed into folded hands. "Please, Windfather," she trembled, "hide us."

Unable to see, she heard the stomping of giant paws, deep guttural roars, snapping jaws, and the clangs of struck metal. The Ch'Hota screamed out with a grating cry, followed by a thud a few wingspans around the trunk.

Heavy sniffing approached, moving from side to side. The runnerhound growled low as its footfalls closed in. Ka'Ala squeezed her eyes tight.

Great Windfather, I did as you asked. Please. Save us!

Suddenly, the monster yelped, followed by the paws' commotion stomping across the ground and a sound like metal dragging through the soil. The forest grew still as the chittering of tiny animals resumed their conversations.

Ka'Ala peeked around her wing, catching a glimpse of the Ch'Hota on hands and knees. He breathed heavily as one wing hung grotesquely limp and partially detached before he collapsed face-down in the dirt.

Her wings shimmered back to midnight black as she unrolled the V'Jeeta from her embrace. She looked at his face, examining his features. High cheekbones. Wide neb. Strong chin. Full lips.

A warm breeze kissed her cheek. "*Leave your provisions,*" He whispered. "*Follow, but do not yet make yourself known.*"

Ka'Ala stood up and shook the leaves and dirt from her wings before leaping into the air. She flew back up to her hiding branch and gathered the satchels hanging from a knot. Drifting back down, she lit softly between the two soldiers. She dropped one bag by the V'Jeeta's inert form and carried the other toward the Ch'Hota. She pulled a bundle of gauze from inside and knelt. The runnerhound left a deep bite mark in the wing joint as a souvenir. Gashes covered his back and arms. She stuffed a handful of gauze into the joint and splinted the wing to his body.

The Ch'Hota stirred, moaning, and pushing against the ground.

Ka'Ala hopped up and dashed into the air before the Ch'Hota could look around. From the branches above, she watched him regain his feet, wincing at his bound wing, his face a mask of confusion. Spotting the satchels, he searched through them by the V'Jeeta's body. He pulled out a small vial of clear liquid and uncorked it with a sniff.

"That's my healing potion," she breathed. "It'll help him."

Satisfied, the Ch'Hota poured the entire vial into the V'Jeeta's mouth. Dropping the spent container on the ground, the Ch'Hota slung both satchels over his shoulders and picked up the limp V'Jeeta like a sleeping child. Upon standing, he gazed around the forest and started walking.

Ka'Ala followed—her sling loose in her hand—hopping from branch to branch. She kept one eye on the forest, with the other on the soldiers, searching for the wounded runnerhound.

He may be hungry enough to take another chance.

Chapter Three
The Healer's Art

R'Venin awoke with a start, groaning against the pain, as a million daggerflies raged war under the skin along his left side. He tried to sit up, but the assault increased with every attempt to shift his weight. With gritted teeth, he clawed at the cotton-like bedding, trying to reposition as his eyes darted around the room. With bleary vision, he took in his surroundings.

He found himself on an oval-shaped mattress suspended from a domed ceiling by four, thick braided vines, a half-wing above the ground. The round walls tapered upward until they met a circular shaft rising into the only visible source of light.

From directly overhead, a shaft of light gleamed down, casting a warm glow across his exposed skin. He looked down to find himself naked save for his breechcloth.

Moss-stained bandages squeezed his wounds. He tilted his head toward his gauze-encased shoulder and winced. Unwelcome tears filled his eyes from the scent of moldy vomit.

My clothes! My armor! My crown!

Panicked, he searched around the room until his eyes found a pile of black and red crumpled against the wall. Trails of dried green blood streaked the ebony surfaces.

The walls, at first glance, seemed to be made out of sun-bleached tree bark. But as R'Venin's eyes focused, an interwoven root system coated with a layer of clay resolved from the blur. Rolling onto his side, he caught a glimpse of a lush grassy floor dappled with wildflowers reaching for the sunlight. R'Venin took in a quick breath as the daggerflies protested their nests' disturbance, while the woody scent of forest decay and pollen filled his nasal slits.

R'Venin went limp. He collapsed on the soft padding, kicking up puffs of dust that swirled and danced in the pillar of light. Relaxing, he let the fiery swarm go back to a dull buzz. Tipping his head against the mattress, he spied the portal to his little egg-shaped universe. A thick tapestry of purples and greens inlaid with dozens of four-pointed stars of varying sizes covered the entrance. The different points of each star displayed a unique symbol, four of which he recognized.

Mountain. Tree. Fire. Rain. The four elements of Alchemy. But, what's that fifth symbol in the center?

R'Venin closed his eyes and took a slow breath through his nose, filling his lungs with dusty air. Forcing his hearts to slow, he focused his ears on the sounds coming from beyond the tapestry. Metal clanging on metal. Wood clunking on stone. Mumbled, barely audible voices. Chanting.

"Where am I?" he whispered.

"You're awake," a raspy voice replied from beyond his view. "Good. We can finally begin."

R'Venin's head swiveled in every non-painful direction he could, looking for the one from which the voice had come but he spotted no one. The sound of stones dumped onto lush turf arose from underneath his suspended perch, followed by a grunt and the cracking of joints.

"Who are you? Where are you?" he called as his pulse raced. He returned his focus toward the tapestry again, watching for the fabric to move and reveal his visitor.

"I'm Kar'Nevala, and I'm right here!"

"Ah!" R'Venin jumped at the kindly voice suddenly coming from his left. His head spun while his body recoiled. "AUGH!" he screamed as the daggerflies renewed their sub-dermal warfare. He winced as he reached across with his right hand to grasp his other shoulder.

"Where am I?" He hissed through gritted teeth and watery eyes.

"You're in the sanctuary of The Three Mothers," said the maternal voice as he felt a light cloth wiping the sweat from his face. "Just relax. No harm will come to you here."

R'Venin obeyed and let himself nestle back into the soft mattress. A few deep breaths later, the warring insects called a truce. He turned his head and reopened his eyes. Next to his swinging bed stood a round-headed woman with large lilac-colored eyes surrounded by moss and pear-colored feathers. No taller than a V'Jeeta child, her wizened chin barely cleared the mattress. She gave R'Venin a disarming smile and shuffled away toward the tapestry.

"You're Pra'Acheen!" R'Venin called, staring at the stubby gray-colored plumage along her wings.

"You're observant," Kar'Nevala chuckled as she pushed through the tapestry. The voices and commotion behind the curtain doubled in volume for a moment, then silenced again as the fabric swished back over the portal.

"How did I get here?" R'Venin yelled toward the ceiling.

Several lonely moments passed before the noise beyond the veil returned with Kar'Nevala. R'Venin heard the soft tapping of wood on stone and looked over to find the Pra'Acheen female carrying a tray with four wooden bowls, ceramic mortar and pestle, the short stump of a lit candle, and a large silver kettle with long spindly legs.

"Somebody brought you here," she said as she placed the kettle on the ground.

"Huh?" R'Venin asked, distracted by the kettle.

"You wondered how you got here. Maybe you damaged your brain too," the stumpy woman chuckled. "Or have you always been slow?" She set down the tray and laid a trembling hand on R'Venin's forehead. She closed her eyes and cocked her head as if focusing on a hushed conversation. "Nope. Not slow. Just a little addlepated. Good thing for you. I heal bones. I don't fix stupid."

"WHO ARE YOU?" R'Venin hollered directly into her face. "WHAT ARE YOU DOING?"

"I told you who I am," Kar'Nevala smiled in a greatmotherly way. "And I'm going to heal you, my young prince."

R'Venin swallowed hard and licked his lips. "How do you know who I am?"

Kar'Nevala patted his forehead and shuffled to the pile of blood-stained armor lying just beyond his feet. Finally able to see more than her head, R'Venin took in her full appearance in flowing linen robes. The hem sparkled with lavender-colored leaves, and a belt of braided rosewood vines around her plump waist threatened to cut her in half.

Knocking pieces of armor over as if stoking a fire, she unburied the helmet and reached inside. Out with her hand came the silver ring of rubies. "Your mother had this made for you," she tottered back toward the kettle. "We'd never crafted for a V'Jeeta before her. She was a sweet one. Hoped you'd turn out more like her than your father."

Kar'Nevala closed one eye and tossed the crown on R'Venin's chest as if playing a ring toss game. R'Venin just stared, wide-eyed, at the glittering circle.

The symbol of my status. My priceless prison.

R'Venin propped himself on his working elbow, balancing between sitting up and setting off the daggerflies' nest again. The crown slid into the crook of his broken arm. "When?" he grunted as he felt shooting pains rake across his body. "When did she have this made? How do you know my mother?"

Kar'Nevala groaned as she sat down on the grass. She placed a sapphire crystal from the first bowl into the mortar and ground it into a dusty periwinkle powder as she muttered to herself. R'Venin couldn't make out the words until she tipped the mortar over the kettle and tapped it with the pestle and uttered "Hadd'yon ko sud'harane." The kettle emitted a faint blue-white glow as the old Pra'Acheen repeated the process four more times.

R'Venin's fixed his eyes on the silver pot, mesmerized.

"You had just branched. Not yet flying," Kar'Nevala mused as she placed a chunk of Red Pine root into the mortar and began grinding. "She came to me, asking for a special gift for your coronation. Something to give you wisdom. She had the gift. She would have mastered Pra'Acheen alchemy if K'Rawin hadn't taken her as a wife when she was barely a fledgling."

She poured the chestnut powder into the kettle, repeating the same process as before. "Hadd'yon ko sud'harane." The peaty scent of bark filled the chamber as the pot glowed from within as if filled with cooling embers. "How is your mother? Still barraging the elders with too many questions?" she asked with a smile.

R'Venin's face fell. He swallowed and stared at nothing behind Kar'Nevala's head. "No. She doesn't talk much," he mumbled. "At least when Father's around. He prefers silence when he's among his wives."

I always wondered where I got my talent for alchemy.

The old lady poured a bowl of crystal-clear water into the kettle and began stirring the mishmash with the pestle. "Sad to hear," she sighed. "She was such a delightful chatterbox. I can't tell you how many times I had to ask her to let me finish answering her question before she spat out another."

R'Venin laid back, focusing on the slow grinding sound of the ceramic pestle against the metal pot. "She was a fine V'Jeeta Alchemist," he grumbled. "For a female."

Kar'Nevala's chuckle caught him off guard.

R'Venin looked over and saw her shaking her head. "What's so funny?" he barked.

Kar'Nevala clicked her tongue. "Those are P'Phet's words. Not yours."

R'Venin wrapped his good arm around his chest. "How do you know those aren't my words?" he growled. "How?"

"You sleep-talk," Kar'Nevala chortled as she tapped the pestle against the kettle's rim five times. "Hadd'yon ko sud'harane," she repeated with each tap causing the glow within the pot to build its light, like blowing on coals. She set the pestle down, sliding the tray and bowls up against the wall before picking up the fluttering candle.

"What's that language you're speaking?" R'Venin's eyes narrowed. "It sounds familiar, but also like gibberish."

"Oh, what do they teach hatchlings these days?" Kar'Nevala laughed deep in her throat. "It's the ancient tongue. It's the root language of all life on Pirth'Vee Grah. Your mother spoke it too."

Holding the teetering candle with one hand, her joints popped as she stood, then she disappeared under the swaying platform. R'Venin heard more sounds of stones clunking together and felt something poke against the small of his back. "What are you doing down there?" he shouted.

Kar'Nevala emerged from under the bed, singing to herself with muddled words. Her stubby wings swayed like curtains as her little frame bobbed in time with an atonal melody. She picked up the silver kettle with a grunt and lugged it back underneath the bed.

The sound of the kettle clanging against stone rang out from below. R'Venin's head swiveled back and forth, searching for her reemergence. He startled as her wrinkled hands rested on either side of his skull, gently pulling him back to the mattress. "It's best if you lie still now," she whispered.

"How do I know I can trust you?" R'Venin licked his lips, eyes darting around the room.

Kar'Nevala patted his head. "Trust in your mother," she soothed. "As soon as you've healed, I'll help you talk with her."

"How?" R'Venin almost jumped out of bed, but the buzzing in his side protested against his sudden movement.

"All in good time, my young prince," Kar'Nevala chortled. "All in good time. Let's begin."

R'Venin relaxed into the soft padding and took a deep breath.

Kar'Nevala shuffled around the bed to R'Venin's damaged side using the ovoid frame as a handrail. He turned to watch as she closed her eyes and started chanting the same short phrase five times. Each time she spoke, he could hear the slurry growing to a rapid boil. Steam rose from the roiling sludge carrying the smell of hot mud across his nose. The glow from underneath increased until the light from below matched that coming down from the oculus above. The dark mist swirled like a miniature tornado around the bed as Kar'Nevala chanted a new song.

The ceiling descended, inching closer until R'Venin realized he could no longer feel the bedding against his back. He became light-headed as if flying in the thin air above the northern mountains. Turning his head, he found Kar'Nevala outside the swirling maelstrom. Her eyes were closed as she stretched out her hands and stirred the pot with an invisible spoon.

Pressure coiled around his limbs like vines starting at his feet. Invisible ropes slithered up his legs, across his torso and along his arms and wings until every inch of his body became wrapped by ethereal tentacles.

R'Venin tried to shout, but his voice never left his throat. His body spun lazily in the air like a leaf caught in a stream. The whirlwind seemed deafening until he felt the coils tighten, and he could hear the snapping of twigs. He looked down and watched in numb astonishment as his misshapen bones snapped back into alignment. First, his broken leg turned away from its skewed angle. Then his hip popped back into place, followed by his broken arm.

He watched in awe, expecting to feel excruciating pain with each sudden jolt to his frame. But no ache arose with the dull impact of bones reconnecting perfectly. His wing snapped and cracked as it healed, returning to its proper shape as if watching the breaks in reverse.

R'Venin tried to reposition his newly mended body, but he found himself limp, unable to move.

Kar'Nevala's eyes met his as he floated around to face her. She gave him a warm smile while changing her hand gestures from pot-stirring to something akin to basket weaving.

R'Venin watched in amazement as the bruises across his body faded. Bandages uncoiled and sloughed away as deep cuts closed in on themselves before vanishing without a trace.

Torn and broken quills fell away, replaced by new feathers over his arms and legs. Finally, his wings opened, brushing against the rough-textured walls while the torn joints sealed together, as if a potter were filling in a broken piece of art with unfired clay.

R'Venin's body lowered from the ceiling as the mist swirled and twisted upward into the oculus as if escaping through an inverted drain. Finding his footing on the swaying platform, his wings remained outstretched and he balanced on the oval trapeze. Looking over his outstretched wings, his budding talons glinted like obsidian in starlight.

If only Father's talons were so healthy. Then we wouldn't be in this eternal war.

"Feeling better?" Kar'Nevala asked with tired eyes.

R'Venin looked over his body from tips to talons and nodded. "I've never experienced anything like that before," he muttered, "How did you do that? How did you mend my bones, while I felt nothing?"

Kar'Nevala turned, hobbling slowly toward the wall, and pulled a small lever next to the covered portal. The platform rose. R'Venin flapped and jumped from the rising mattress onto the ground. "Ancient Pra'Acheen secret," she chuckled in her throat. "The body wants to be whole. We just help it along the path."

She pulled the curtain to the side and whistled a lilting melody into the unseen commotion. Moments later, another Pra'Acheen female entered carrying a bundle of linen. She gawked at R'Venin, wide-eyed with jittery hands, and she crept forward and held the garments above her head with her finger-talons extended.

R'Venin looked from the clothing to Kar'Nevala. "What's this?"

"We don't allow armor here. You will wear this while in the sanctuary," Kar'Nevala replied, gesturing to the trembling woman. "This is Nar'Sahayak. She will gather your possessions."

R'Venin reached down and took the package from Nar'Sahayak's shaking hands. "Thank you," he mumbled and took a half-step back, putting some space between himself and the frightened Pra'Acheen.

Nar'Sahayak backed away slowly, turning only her body toward the exit and stared into R'Venin's eyes as she exited the room.

"She's afraid of you," Kar'Nevala sighed. "You're the first V'Jeeta she's ever been nib-to-nib with."

R'Venin opened the bundle to find a simple linen robe. "Why shouldn't she be afraid of me?" he asked. "We don't exactly have a reputation for gentleness."

Kar'Nevala chuckled. "When you've dressed, come out. I'll show you around and then help you speak with your family. Let them know you're safe." She stepped past the threshold and let the curtain fall behind her.

Do I even want them to know?

R'Venin's stomach knotted. He lifted the robes, letting them unfold while examining the same coarse linen fabric. It looked like someone had cut a hole in the center of a sheet. The hems, interwoven threads of cerulean Bluewood needles along the two short ends, shimmered as he backed up to stand in the column of light. He flipped the robe over his head, letting the material fall across his wings like a drape in the back. Drawstrings sewn into the edges allowed him to secure the frock on both sides. He tugged at the hems, barely reaching his mid-thighs.

If I'm lucky, I'll die of embarrassment before Mother and B'Luren see me in this.

* * *

R'Venin pushed through the star-laden drape, ducking to clear the short portal's opening, and finding Nar'Sahayak flattening herself against the wall across from him in a spacious—but low-ceiling— alcove. She stood between one of the five tapestries and a broader opening that led to a brightly-lit hall. She directed R'Venin toward her left with a raised arm, holding a linen sack in the other. Her amethyst pupils widened as he made his way counter-clockwise around the circular antechamber. Matching him step for step across the turfy floor, she edged along the wall—slinking behind tapestries—until he arrived at the hall's threshold.

R'Venin kept his keen eyes on Nar'Sahayak's wary face until she slid behind the same curtain from which he emerged. "Hoo!" he shouted as the cloth barrier swished back into place. A shrill squawk pierced through the dense fabric followed by a tirade of high-pitched muttering and the cacophony of metal against metal.

"So, that's what Pra'Acheen profanity sounds like," he muttered.

"Did you expect it to sound poetic?" Kar'Nevala's voice mused from behind him.

Turning around to face the hall, R'Venin jerked back a half-step finding Kar'Nevala flapping toward him at eye level. "The young are so skittish," she snickered. "So afraid of what they don't understand." She flitted around him, touching down as softly as a wishflower petal in front of the curtain.

The muffled clatter of armor broke through the cloth, along with Kar'Nevala's muted words.

"Sha'anti uva'ek ho." Kar'Nevala's voice soothed. "Vah tum'hen c'hot na'hin ho'ga."

If Mother knew the ancient tongue, why'd she never teach me? I wish I knew what they were saying.

"Va'hek ra'akshas hai," Nar'Sahayak's piercing shrill rang out. "Ve'sabhee ra'akshas hain. A'ap un'par bha'rosa kaise'kar sa'kate hain?"

"Ek ra'akshas ke'val ap'anee kal'pana ke'roop mein dara'avana hai." Kar'Nevala's words came through the curtain softer than a whisper, followed by an audible sigh.

"Pa'vrit geet pu'stika," Nar'Sayahak's voice became contrite. "Das'aveen dhun. Ikkee'saveen sta'anz."

R'Venin stared at the woven artificial night-scape, willing the fabric to become as transparent as the evening sky itself. The clangs of metal softened, and a few moments later, Kar'Nevala emerged from behind the drape. He glimpsed Nar'Sahayak briefly pause her chore to wipe a hand across her bowed face.

Kar'Nevala pulled R'Venin from the curtain by the arm. "Is she alright?" he asked, turning to face the sunlit hall.

"We all understand the Windfather's will at the pace we can handle," The aged Pra'Acheen smiled. "The real magic comes when we allow His will to become ours."

R'Venin's brow furrowed at the same time his free arm rose to shade his eyes against the light. Squinting from the bright glare above, he peered up and around the spacious chamber. Intricately carved wooden benches in spiraling rows filled the hall. Perches and swings of glistening silvervine protruded from the arching dome of white-washed trunks and branches. Cylindrical shelves stuffed with aging parchment scrolls rose and spread outward like upside-down root systems searching for ethereal waters.

"This is a library," R'Venin whispered to himself.

At his side, Kar'Nevala lifted off the ground, hovering just above his shoulder. "All truth leads to healing," she beamed. "Come." Her graying wings flapped, pulling her towards the light. Her shadow crossed over his eyes long enough for him to spot healthy feathers lining her wingtips.

Not as old as she looks.

R'Venin opened his wings full span, launching into the air with a jump off a bench ornamented with the Mountain symbol. Dust billowed and trailed around his feet as he beat his wings against the warm breeze wafting through the perforated canopy. Flakes of bark drifted in swirls as he pounded his wings to catch up with his guide.

Kar'Nevala banked and arched around the room as if distracted by the shiny reflections glittering against the walls. With one eye on the zig-zagging Pra'Acheen, R'Venin scanned the cavernous repository with the other.

Pra'Acheens in linen robes with hems of every shade of purple sat, flew, and perched in groups ranging from duos to dozens. The soft murmur of a hundred whispered conversations echoed throughout. Lavender eyes stared, gaped, and smiled into R'Venin's as he soared past them following Kar'Nevala through the parchment forest.

Emerging from the columns, Kar'Nevala swooped downward through an oval-shaped tunnel, five wingspans tall and three wide.

R'Venin followed, barely dodging a small flock of Pra'Acheen children coming from the other side. The channel opened up into another domed chamber, enormous compared to the last.

Clouds like a blanket of winter's kisses drifted high above the primary oculus in the azure sky. The column of sunlight beamed down as Pra'Acheen, Ch'Hota, and V'Jeeta cut through the shaft like dust mites. The cavernous walls, pock-marked with platforms and alcoves, buzzed with life like a great hive. Far below, the sod-covered floor spread outward like a green sea speckled with wildflowers of every color and shade. Fragrant pollen filled every breath with new life.

Kar'Nevala soared through the pillar of daylight, catching an updraft and rising higher toward the dome's apex. "Where are we going?" R'Venin shouted to the deceptively agile Pra'Acheen leading the chase.

She threw out her wings, coming to a halt in mid-air. R'Venin veered, banking left to circle his hovering guide.

Kar'Nevala turned around on the spot, flapping out a fast beat to keep her face toward his. "I told you," she huffed between breaths. "I'm helping you talk with your mother. Now, don't make me lose my stride again. If you can't keep up, tell me, and I'll slow." She gave him a wink and dove into another nearby updraft.

I have no trouble keeping up. I just like to know where I'm going.

R'Venin scowled, looking around the vast dome. All eyes were on him. The sporadic Ch'Hota gawked at him with wary eyes as they gave him a wide berth. After one particular Ch'Hota woman's fiery glare bore into his skull, he gave a few extra flaps to close the gap between himself and the healer.

Kar'Nevala glided down, landing on a narrow outcropping—too small for two—before an equally cramped vestibule. "Welcome to my home," she waved him over as she cleared the tiny platform and shuffled into the portal less than half R'Venin's height.

"Sorry about the entrance," she chuckled as she cleared the entry and disappeared behind another star-strewn curtain. "I never expected to add so many to my family."

R'Venin got on one knee, craning his head about to glimpse beyond the veil and into the chamber. "So," he cleared his throat. "You've only had relatives—other Pra'Acheen—in your home before?"

Kar'Nevala's hearty cackle burst from behind the drape. "All Pra'Acheen are family," she crowed. "And anyone invited to my home becomes family. Now, come in and meet the rest of them."

R'Venin crawled on all fours, stretching his wings behind him like a cape, to squeeze through the narrow opening. The curtain brushed against his head, neck, and feathers until he spilled down a short flight of steps and onto the hard-packed dirt floor. Grunting, he stumbled to his feet, knocking over every piece of art and furniture within his wingspan during the effort. Rising to less than his full height, he crashed into a crystalline chandelier, raining amethyst shards.

He gaped around the room, looking for Kar'Nevala, and to get his bearings, but spotted no trace of her whereabouts. "We're up here," her voice called from beyond the furthest point he could see.

The dwelling had several levels; he stood on the lowest one. A series of platforms rose toward the lush green forest, and sunlight peeked in from across the nest. He stepped up, following the light, onto the next platform. The ceiling brushed his pate without crushing the crystal-dusted plumage. Two gossamer curtains concealed storage chambers on either side of him. Drawing back one sheet, he spotted the lumpy sack into which Nar'Sahayak had stuffed his armor amid bags of grain, baskets of nuts, and jars of fruits.

Gave me the scenic tour, eh?

He dropped the shroud and crossed the threshold of a pointed arch, onto the final and largest platform. The terrace extended to the dense canopy of Copperleaf Forest. Blades of shimmering yellows, reds, and grays danced in the breeze. Invisible creatures chirped, howled, scampered, and scurried amid the shaded leaves.

R'Venin sniffed in the honeyroot pollen with a deep lungful of air, breaking into an unbidden smile. He scanned the foliage, pausing every few degrees, taking in each minute detail.

I've heard stories of Copperleaf, but no tale compares to seeing it for myself. This is nothing like home.

R'Venin closed his eyes, taking in the fragrant air with a ten-second breath. "Stunning," he said to himself.

"I had the same reaction when Kar'Nevala brought me here for the first time," a mournful feminine voice said, erupting his thoughts.

R'Venin spun around. Three figures, hidden from his view at the archway, crouched around a fourth. Kar'Nevala and Nar'Sahayak painted a squirming male Ch'Hota's left wing with an ashy paste. The man rested prone on a wooden bench inlaid with mercurial etchings of Rain. Rivulets of dandelion colored blood oozed from slashes on his arms and back. His upper body armor lay in a pile at his feet while his legs and feet remained sheathed in gleaming chain-mail.

At the head of the bench sat a Ch'Hota woman massaging a pinkish oil into the man's hands while fanning air across his back. She wore a draping floor-length linen tunic hemmed in topaz-encrusted vines that matched her golden eyes. Her face turned toward R'Venin though her hands continued to rub, revealing the wetness brimming in her eyes.

"R'Venin," Kar'Nevala said, nodding at the man on the bench. "This is Ba'Jai. And that's Ja'Naam, his sister. She is an apprentice here." Kar'Nevala made eye contact with the Ch'Hota woman, giving her a kindly, wet-eyed smile.

Ba'Jai jerked away from the Pra'Acheen's gray-stained hands, stifling a grunt.

"You must lie still, Ba'Jai," Kar'Nevala soothed. "Or the graft will not take. Do you wish to be ground-cast?"

R'Venin edged closer. "What happened to him?" He watched the two Pra'Acheen continue to rub the whitish paste along Ba'Jai's feathers. "What's wrong with his wing?"

Ja'Naam's eyes followed R'Venin as he stepped closer. "It was torn half-off by a wild runnerhound," her voice caught in her throat. "Just on the fringe of the maize fields."

R'Venin caught Nar'Sahayak's piercing glare next to Kar'Nevala's, who merely went about applying the paste to Ba'Jai's wing joint. "What was he doing on the ground?" he mumbled. "Why didn't he just fly away as soon as it appeared?"

Nar'Sahayak opened her mouth to speak, her face twisted like the gnarled branches of a dying tree.

"He was trying to save you," the Ch'Hota woman whispered, tears spilling over her lids to fall onto Ba'Jai's hands.

"Why would he try to save me?" R'Venin croaked. "He doesn't even know me. You don't even know me."

Ja'Naam wiped the tears away with the back of her hand. "It's who he is," she sniffled. "He's always reached out to anyone in need. Even those who would kill him for trying." Her icy glare froze him in place.

R'Venin knelt a half-wingspan from the bench. "I'm so sorry," he mumbled, unable to return her gaze. "I—I didn't expect—I never thought—."

Kar'Nevala began chanting, joined by Ja'Naam and Nar'Sahayak. Tiny billows of olive-colored smoke grew from the graphite coat like blossoming seaweed.

"How can I help?" R'Venin asked, his voice barely audible.

Nar'Sahayak and Ja'Naam continued chanting. Kar'Nevala reached across Ba'Jai's body and ripped a feather from R'Venin's left wing.

"We'll need more," she said, pressing it into the mushy coat.

R'Venin lifted his wing and reached for another feather, hesitating.

"What are you waiting for?" Nar'Sahayak snapped. "He carried you 400 leagues on foot so Kar'Nevala could heal your broken bones. He almost had his wing ripped off, protecting you from that runnerhound. Are all V'Jeeta so spiteful that you would deny him a few feathers after he saved your life?" The young Pra'Acheen's voice trailed off. She shrunk back, though her burning eyes locked with R'Venin's.

R'Venin's head bowed, eyes darting between Nar'Sahayak and Ja'Naam. Kar'Nevala ignored the outburst. "He should have just left me to die," he mumbled. "I never wanted to be a part of my father's crusade."

"Where you were is less important than where you're going," Kar'Nevala said, yanking out a handful of feathers. "What you do moving forward is all that matters."

The older woman placed the feathers lengthwise along several of Ba'Jai's open gashes and sealed them with the gray paste. She looked up from her work and opened her hand.

R'Venin looked down at the patch of featherless skin.

Perhaps if I can help save his life, mine will have meant something, he thought as he tore quills one by one and handed them to the Kar'Nevala.

Kar'Nevala smiled as if a beloved greatchild gave her a love note. "Now," she whispered, "Paste your feathers across his back while we continue the incantation."

Chapter Four

Neb to Neb

The sun hung low in the sky, painting the rolling clouds with pastels of autumn. Leafhoppers chirped out a twilight symphony as R'Venin watched a pearly maelstrom spin away into the leaves. Ja'Naam and the Pra'Acheen alchemists ended their mournful chant as Ba'Jai's left wing fell limp, draping over the bench, clinging to the joint by sinewy threads and shredded muscles. The tendons melted like icicles in summer as the wing slowly tumbled into a pile of feathers and flesh. The smell of burnt skin rose as the wing joint closed under the sizzling white mush.

Kar'Nevala pulled a large feather from R'Venin's wingtip and covered the closing wound. Ba'Jai's golden blood seeped through, transforming the damage into an embossed scar along with the others glittering across his back.

"I'm sorry, Ba'Jai," Kar'Nevala whispered into his ear. "We couldn't save the wing. We'll have to fashion you a proxy. You're ground-cast now."

Ja'Naam pressed Ba'Jai's hands against her forehead, her shoulders shaking with hushed wailing. He freed his hands and placed them on Ja'Naam's bobbing head. "Be still, sister," he croaked. "All is as the

Windfather designs. Take hope."

Ja'Naam knelt forward, wrapping her arms around Ba'Jai's neck and wept. Tears poured from her closed lids as her body convulsed. Ba'Jai whispered inaudible words as he stroked her wing. She took a deep breath and released her grip, nodding to his private instruction. "Will you help me up?" Ba'Jai asked, keeping one hand on her shoulders while pushing against the bench with the other.

"Let me help you." R'Venin stood, grabbing Ba'Jai's arm.

Ba'Jai nodded and pulled his legs toward his torso, letting them flop over the edge while R'Venin and Ja'Naam steadied him upright. Ja'Naam slid next to him on the seat, keeping his arm draped across her shoulders.

R'Venin tried to pull himself away, concentrating on the floor. Ba'Jai kept hold of R'Venin's arm, gripping his hand to keep him close. The three remained stone-still as Kar'Nevala and Nar'Sahayak gathered the fallen wing and carried it away with the reverence of a funeral procession.

"My gratitude to you," Ba'Jai broke the silence, his gaze intense but warm. "For giving up a part of yourself."

R'Venin, humbled, raised his bowed head, eyes flitting from Ba'Jai to Ja'Naam. She avoided R'Venin's gaze, but gave her brother a sidelong glance. "It was nothing compared to what you sacrificed," he muttered. "I don't know how I'll ever repay you."

In Father's court, if you were in my place, you'd be expected to swear your life to me.

R'Venin suddenly stood, backed up a few steps, and got down on hands and knees. "It's the custom of my people to make a spirit-oath to someone who saves their life," he said to the floor. "I now pledge to serve you and your family until the end of my life. I only ask that my people never know I survived the battle."

"Why wouldn't you want them to know you're alive?" Ja'Naam

asked. "Aren't you the high prince? Don't you want to go home? Don't you want to rule? Continue your crusade? Wipe us out?"

R'Venin shook his head. "It's a three-sun story," he sighed, keeping his eyes on the ground.

The bench creaked as the weight upon it lifted, and two sets of footfalls—one light-stepped and the other halting—came to stand directly in front of him. "If you reject my oath," R'Venin said huskily, "I beg for you to finish me. It would've been better if I died on the battlefield than—."

R'Venin heard a grunt as a strong hand grabbed him by the arm and pulled him up to a standing position directly in front of Ba'Jai. "Why?" he asked softly. "Why would it have been better if you died?"

R'Venin had to look up slightly to see into Ba'Jai's face. Ja'Naam, maintaining Ba'Jai's balance under his arm, stared at R'Venin from just below his eye level. R'Venin seemed unable to withhold the truth. "Because if anyone ever discovers that I tried to kill myself at the hands of my adversary, dishonor will come to my father. His rivals would exploit it as a weakness, and it could lead to a war between the houses."

Ba'Jai tilted his head. "Some might say 'what's bad news for the V'Jeeta, is good news for everyone else.'"

"Some might also say..." R'Venin half-smiled, "'Better the monster in front of me, than the one I cannot see.'"

"That can't be the only reason," Ba'Jai peered into R'Venin's eyes. "The hope of staving off war isn't a good enough reason to kill yourself in battle. No single person, V'Jeeta or Ch'Hota, could ever have that kind of influence."

R'Venin's shoulders slumped. He looked down, feigning captivation by a leaf dancing across the floor. "Because I'm a coward," he exhaled. "Even though I believed that P'Phet foresaw the V'Jeeta as the destined rulers of Pirth'Vee Grah, I hate the idea of killing another. I've spent my life training as a warrior but always managed to avoid direct conflict by overseeing the transport of provisions. But, when the harvest of Silver Silk was in jeopardy, my father committed our entire army to your defeat. I saw no other way out of killing."

The wind gamboled through the branches as R'Venin, Ba'Jai, and Ja'Naam stood in silence, their shadows reaching for the door as flower petals gathered at their feet and performed a swirling choreography of movement to the evening songs of Copperleaf fauna.

"Can I share a secret with you?" Ba'Jai broke the lull, his eyes brightening with a thin smile.

R'Venin's brow furrowed as he lifted his head and gave a quick nod.

Ba'Jai took a deep breath. "I have to admit I didn't *want* to save you," he muttered, "when I found you in the maize fields. Not at first, anyway."

Ja'Naam's jaw fell, her eyes widening as she lightly punched Ba'Jai in the ribs. "That's an awful thing to say," she hissed.

R'Venin's stomach twisted.

Here comes the loathing my people have earned, he thought.

"I saw one of my fellow guardsmen launch a spear at you and that other V'Jeeta," Ba'Jai continued. "I watched it impale him, and then another V'Jeeta warrior collided with the guardsman in mid-air, taking him to the ground while ripping his wings off. I flew down to help my kinsman, but I could see there was nothing I could do as I landed. I was about to launch back into the air when I heard a voice. It said, 'Help your brother.'"

"I turned back around and ran over to the guardsman; checked him for signs of life but found none. His eyes—I'll never forget them—had rolled back in his head, and his entrails had spilled out onto the ground."

"Again, I was about to return to the battle when I heard the voice whisper, 'Help your brother.' I scanned the field for signs of another fallen Ch'Hota. I even yelled for the speaker to make himself known, but I heard no reply."

"Then my eyes crossed over you," Ba'Jai whispered. "I spotted you, with that other V'Jeeta lying on top, pinning you down. It was right when I looked at you and thought, there's one less murderer I have to deal with. Then I heard the voice again. But, this time, it wasn't a whisper. The voice pierced me in my hearts. *Help your brother.* I knew right then it was the great Windfather."

R'Venin swallowed hard, unable to move his eyes away from Ba'Jai's tender glare. From the corner of his vision, he saw Ja'Naam brush tears from her face.

"I have more to share; my brush with the runnerhound," Ba'Jai groaned, wrapping his free arm around his waist. "But, I think I should lie down now. Will you help me?"

R'Venin nodded and wrapped himself on Ba'Jai's side, helping Ja'Naam guide him to the hammock of vines near the platform's edge. Kar'Nevala returned with a candle on a long iron pole, lighting torches along the walls. The sun winked its last rays, leaving the balcony bathed in dancing firelight. She walked to the platform's edge, leaning on the railing and gazing out into the trees. She stood, muttering inaudible words for a few moments before turning away and dousing the flame.

Nar'Sahayak followed seconds later, hefting a large woven basket laden with bread, fruits, nuts, roasted strips of meat and vegetables. Ja'Naam hurried over and helped the young Pra'Acheen carry the load. The women set the basket in front of the hammock, and all but Ba'Jai sat on the floor. R'Venin reached for a bunch of ripe berries, but Ja'Naam slapped it away.

"Do you not offer thanks before meals in the spires?" her eyebrows knitted together.

Kar'Nevala held her hands up as if holding a scroll. The others sitting around the basket followed suit. R'Venin matched their gesture, straightening his back in the process.

"Ba'Jai," Kar'Nevala closed her eyes. "Would you petition for us?"

Ba'Jai nodded, closed his eyes, and raised his head toward the stars appearing above the canopy. R'Venin watched as the women all bowed their heads.

"Great Windfather," Ba'Jai's hushed voice rose with emotion. "The day has ended, and we gather as friends, new and old, to partake of the bounties of Pirth'Vee Grah. All things blow from your presence. Eternal is the wind that gave us life. Eternal is the wind that encircles the world. Let this bounty strengthen our wings, sharpen our eyes, and enlarge our hearts. As the wind blows."

"As the wind blows," all but R'Venin intoned.

Ja'Naam picked up the berries and handed them to R'Venin. "Now, we can eat," she said, a tiny smile struggling to appear.

Ba'Jai grabbed up a cluster of beans and tossed them into his mouth one by one. "Now," he mumbled. "Let me tell you about the runnerhound."

* * *

Ka'Ala watched from the shadows above Kar'Nevala's home. Her stomach growled as she listened to Ba'Jai, telling the others about the runnerhound attack. Ja'Naam snuck glances at R'Venin throughout her brother's tale.

"The runnerhound got between us," Ba'Jai pointed at R'Venin. "I shoved my lance in his face and tried to squeeze between him and the tree, but when I caught sight of where you had fallen, I froze. You'd disappeared. It looked like the roots wrapped around you and were about to pull you into the ground."

"In the split second I lost my focus, the hound slashed at my back and caught my wing in its fangs. It picked me up and tossed me over its head like a child's toy. I fell a few paces away. My head spun, and I could barely stand. I just made out the hound sniffing the ground; I assumed he'd caught your scent. I still had my spear, so I charged and stuck it into his flank."

"He dragged my spear through the brush as fast as he could go!" Ba'Jai howled. "I swear I could probably track his furrow and get my spear back."

R'Venin caught Ja'Naam looking at him while both of them, overflowing with laughter, had to hold onto their bellies.

Looking at R'Venin, Ka'Ala heard his horn-song build again. Then the sound of a flute whistled a delicate melody, harmonizing with the clarion call. She looked over at Ja'Naam, and the trill grew in volume to match R'Venin's song.

They must become one, Windfather's voice penetrated her hearts.

Relief, followed by frustration, rose in her throat.

Why would you play me his melody, and then tell me he's to be with another?

"*Trust in me, my daughter*," The voice soothed. "*All will be made clear in due time.*"

"I've been alone for so long," she moaned quietly, wiping tears from her face. "I admit I was scared at first because of what happened to my people. Now you tell me I saved his life for him to be with someone else? Am I to remain alone—in the shadows—until I die? And when will that be?"

All will be well, Windfather hushed. *You see a seed; I see a Forest. I will not leave you discomforted.* A whirlwind of leaves danced from above, coming to rest on Ka'Ala as if patting her back.

Ka'Ala hugged herself. "I'm sorry, Windfather. Thank you." She looked back to the enrapt group as Ba'Jai finished his story.

The older Pra'Acheen woman picked up the basket still laden

with a few untouched items and carried it to the balcony's edge. The younger Pra'Acheen hurried to catch up and reached for the basket. "Shall I put these away for tomorrow?" she asked, trying to unload the older woman's burden.

Kar'Nevala chuckled. "No, I think we should leave these out here for tonight. Perhaps some lonely creature will take some comfort in a morsel or two." She bent over and poured the contents on the floor, stacking them neatly into a pile, and turned away without a second glance.

Nar'Sahayak's eyes scrunched as she spied the mound of food going to waste. "Very well, Mistress." She took the empty basket from the older woman, wrapped her arm around the older woman's waist, and helped her off the balcony.

Ka'Ala's mouth watered while her stomach churned the emptiness.

"You need your rest, Ba'Jai," Ja'Naam's voice pulled Ka'Ala's attention off the food. "Let's get you inside. You can have my roost for the night. Tomorrow, I'll help you get home to Bluewood Cove." She took Ba'Jai's arm and pulled him forward in the hammock.

"I'll go with you." R'Venin stepped forward, taking Ba'Jai's other arm. "I've sworn a spirit-oath. I will remain at your side until you refuse my pledge or kill me."

Ba'Jai's eyes turned hard. "Then I guess I'll have to kill you."

R'Venin swallowed hard. His hearts sunk to his feet. He knelt in front of Ba'Jai and Ja'Naam and bowed his head. "Do as you please," he breathed. "Either way, I can't go back home."

Ka'Ala gripped her dagger and poised to lunge herself onto the balcony.

Suddenly, Ja'Naam punched Ba'Jai in the stomach. "Ba'Jai," she scolded. "Don't tease him. He doesn't know your macabre sense of humor."

Ba'Jai belly-laughed and pulled R'Venin up by the shoulders. "I won't kill you," he chuckled. "I could never kill you. Not after hearing the Windfather's voice telling me to save you." He wrapped his arms around R'Venin and Ja'Naam, who steadied him as they all walked off the balcony.

Ka'Ala released her weapon, jumped from her perch, and glided to the food waiting on the balcony. Just as she lit on the wooden floor, Kar'Nevala appeared at the archway. Their eyes locked.

"*Don't scream,*" Ka'Ala willed as she gathered the fruit into her arms.

Kar'Nevala winked and pulled a cord hanging from the wall. Small pots of water hanging over each torch tipped over, extinguishing the light with a hiss. The old Pra'Acheen turned without making a sound and shuffled back into the house.

Ka'Ala, standing like an ebony statue in a darkened museum, slowly turned back toward the canopy and exhaled into the night. Gliding down to a lower branch, she tucked herself into a crook and offered a short devotion before munching her bounty.

Ka'Ala cocked her head in thought. "Why in the world did that Pra'Acheen not lose her feathers after seeing me on her balcony?" she breathed.

Many flocks have I, Windfather whispered in the air. *And they are mine.*

Voices of Smoke

R'Venin hunched over and tucked his wings as he followed Kar'Nevala's shuffling figure through a squat hallway. The fire crystals embedded in the low ceiling emitted a soft honey glow, casting marigold shadows on the curved walls. Turning, he caught a glimpse of Ba'Jai nearly doubled over to avoid scraping his head against the ceiling. He kept one hand on Ja'Naam's shoulder while brushing the walls with his other. Ja'Naam stooped, giving Ba'Jai the extra space he needed to duck.

"Why didn't the smoke heal him completely, as it did for me?" R'Venin asked, looking into Ja'Naam's gilded eyes as he followed Kar'Nevala into a doorway.

"Just the nature of Alchemy," she shrugged, bonking Ba'Jai's head into the lintel as they crossed the threshold. She hissed an apology through her teeth as Ba'Jai rubbed his scalp. "Different combinations of elements and incantations have different purposes. We were trying to re-attach his wing. Sometimes, the Great Windfather doesn't answer in the way we would like."

R'Venin sidestepped as he entered the chamber and backed against a wall, finding himself in another dome-shaped room. Stars peeked through the intertwined branches of greens and grays. Heat emanated from the sandstone quarry tiles under his feet, the off-white grout lines spiraling outward like a spinner's web from the room's center. Heavy drapes of midnight blue embroidered with flecks of silver hung on either side of the archway. "Except for the chanting, V'Jeeta medicine is the same as yours." He cocked his head. "What does the Windfather have to do with Alchemy? He gave us the elements to use them as we will, right?"

"Your mother caught on much faster," Kar'Nevala chuckled. "I thought we wouldn't have to start at the roots with you."

R'Venin turned as Kar'Nevala finished unrolling a three-cornered hammock of woven vines. She looped the straps to hooks embedded in the plastered walls. "This should support your weight, Ba'Jai." She pushed against the suspended bed. "If not, the floor will have to do."

"Thank you, Kar'Nevala." Ba'Jai fell into the net and sunk until his body floated a handspan from the tiles. "It'll be just fine."

Kar'Nevala patted his head as she shimmied from behind the hammock. "Ja'Naam," she beamed, "you may stay here with your brother instead of returning to the initiates' house. I'm sure you'll want to chatter away the night, but he needs rest."

"Thank you." Ja'Naam knelt and wrapped the old woman in her arms. "For everything."

Kar'Nevala took Ja'Naam's face with both hands and kissed her cheeks and forehead. "Good night, dearest child."

Ja'Naam stood as Kar'Nevala strolled toward the door, pulling R'Venin by the hand. "Good night, Mistress," Ja'Naam pulled a rolled-up hammock from a wall niche. "Good night, R'Venin. Thank you—for your feathers." His eyes followed her as she dislodged the thick curtains from either side of the archway.

"This way," Kar'Nevala called from further down the low passageway. "I'm sure your mother is anxious to speak with you."

"What?" R'Venin's head banged against the ceiling. "My mother is here?" He closed the gap in three paces to find her at another peaked archway blocked by dark, starry-night curtains.

"Come along, child," Kar'Nevala pulled the drape aside, gesturing for R'Venin to enter.

* * *

R'Venin dashed through the archway, a smile ready to burst on his lips. Crossing the threshold, he entered the dim, circular chamber, illuminated only by the rays shining from high above Kar'Nevala's head. More tan sandstone warmed his feet as he spun in place, searching non-existent corners. An intricate mosaic, resembling the four-pointed stars from the healing chamber, lay centered on the single opening directly overhead. Four wall niches embedded at each point held a different object, a small, brass pot with stubby legs; a dark leather pouch embroidered with a silver tree element; a clay vase; and a bundle of lightning sticks.

"Where is she?" his face fell. "You said I'd get to talk to her."

Kar'Nevala entered behind him, casting the room into darkness as she let the drape swish to a close. Dust motes danced like stars in the column of moonlight trickling from above. "I said I'd help you talk to her." She shuffled around the room, gathering the pot and other objects, and then sat on the Mountain symbol. "Please join me." She pointed to the Tree symbol across the star.

R'Venin sat in silence as she placed the brass pot on the central symbol and poured a viscous, honey-colored oil from the vase. She then took a lightning stick and rubbed it against the sandstone until it burst into flame. A trail of smoke rose into the moonlight as she lifted the rod above her head—chasing away the floating specks—before dropping the fiery twig into the bowl. The oil caught fire, brightening the room with a soft orange glow. He took in a lungful as vapors of cinnamon and rosewood swirled throughout the chamber.

"What are we doing?" R'Venin shifted his crossed legs. "How will an oil fire help me speak to my mother?"

Kar'Nevala smiled, crow's feet bunching around her eyes. "This is my prayer room," she said, raising her arms and wings together. "My sacred place."

R'Venin followed her eyes around the blank walls, catching glimpses of shadows playing inside the four niches. Kar'Nevala's wings spread flat to the floor as she placed a palm next to the glowing pot. "This is the fifth element of Alchemy," her words lilted like a prayer. "This is the symbol for the Great Windfather. It is his voice that brings power to the infusion of mountain, tree, fire, and rain."

"I've never heard of a fifth element," R'Venin scoffed. "Not even from my mother. You said she was an apprentice here. So, why did she never teach me about this?"

"You ask a fair question," she answered, giving a slight bow. "Why do you think she would not teach you about *all* the elements of alchemy in your father's house?" Kar'Nevala's piercing gaze locked onto his eyes.

"I don't know." He bowed his head, staring into the dancing flames. "You tell me."

Kar'Nevala gently fanned the pot with her wings, nudging the smoke toward R'Venin. "Knowledge is not the same as wisdom," she answered. "All flocks on Pirth'Vee Grah have been taught the same knowledge. Yet some choose to ignore certain truths. Why would that be?"

R'Venin shrugged again. The guttering flames became the only break in the silence for several minutes. "I suppose some just don't like or accept all truths. They want to pick and choose. Like at a great feast."

"Wisdom comes from accepting immutable truth," Kar'Nevala beamed. "From wherever it comes. If one does not accept *all* truths, they are forgotten. And those that re-discover truths are often in danger from those not willing to hear and understand."

R'Venin continued to stare at the flames, nodding, but with distant eyes.

"Now," the old woman's smile broadened, "if you're ready to be taught, you'll speak with your mother."

R'Venin straightened his back, resting his hands on his knees. "What do I need to do?"

Kar'Nevala put her fingertips on the edges of the brass pot, the short claws scratching along the rim. R'Venin noted for the first time the etchings around the lip.

"What are those?" He pointed at the strange markings.

"All in good time," she chuckled. "This is my k'tora, the speaking bowl. Your mother has one similar to it. During this ceremony, we will create a connection between the two that allows us to see each other."

She reached into the leather pouch and pulled out a fistful of gray powder. "This is the powder of El'Him tree root," her voice became quiet as a falling leaf. "The El'Him is our most sacred tree, and only grows in the highest mountains. It takes centuries for a seedling to mature. It's then a delicate process to grind the root into a powder of sufficient purity to communicate across great distances. Your mother and I kept in touch over the years by using the alchemy I'm about to show you. With it, you'll be able to speak with her tonight."

R'Venin scooted forward, swallowing hard. "What do I have to do?"

"Please, do as I do," she nodded toward the bag. "And say as I say. But you should probably keep your eyes open for now." She winked, then closed both eyes.

R'Venin grabbed a handful of powder, mimicking Kar'Nevala's

extended arm, as she lifted her hand higher above the flames and took a deep, nasal breath. She sang in a throaty alto voice, followed by R'Venin's rough baritone.

"Ja'isa ki par'vat dird'hai,
Ja'isa ped lam'baho ja'ata hai,
Ja'isa hee var'sha ba'hatee hai,
Ja'isa hee a'ag jal'atee hai,
Ja'isa ha'va mein a'avaaj ho'tee hai,
A'ur ha'va pra'shan sa'kon j'vaala am'ukhee,
Pa'van pi'takee shak'ti ke sa'ath,
Main usa'ke na'am se bo'lata hoon."

"Now," Kar'Nevala whispered, pointing to the symbols around the bowls' edge. "These markings are written in an ancient language—the first tongue of Pirth'Vee Grah. You will need to spell the name of your mother's bowl. I will point them out, but you will have to touch them yourself. Then cast in your powder."

R'Venin obeyed. Following Kar'Nevala's finger around the rim and pressing his pad into each symbol she indicated. Once she pulled her hand away, he tossed his handful into the flames.

The powder exploded toward the ceiling, billowing plumes of slate-colored smoke and mist. Twisting and swirling like a maelstrom in a bottle, the foggy column turned on itself and coalesced into a misshapen head and shoulders. The misty currents slowed as the jawline, ears, Neb, and eyes of a female V'Jeeta resolved like dissipating ripples on a crystal lake. The woman's eyes squinted. "Kar'Nevala?" P'Vrit's soprano voice echoed from within the pot. "Is that you?"

R'Venin's eyes misted over. "Mother?" he croaked.

"R'Venin? R'Venin, my son!" Hands emerged out of nowhere, covering her mouth and nose. P'Vrit's head bobbed as her sobs echoed around the prayer room. R'Venin wiped at his face with both hands, swallowing hard.

"I can see I'm now intruding," Kar'Nevala grunted as she knelt forward to put her hand on the bowl. P'Vrit's head turned, her eyes widened, and a beaming smile opened on her face.

"Kar'Nevala," P'Vrit cried. "Thank you for restoring him. Thank you for saving my first son. I can never repay you."

"I'm pleased to be of service, your majesty," the Pra'Acheen chuckled. "Come visit and make me some of your Butternut broth. That will be payment enough."

"Agreed, Mistress," P'Vrit cried. "I'll even bake the sweetbread you like."

"A little too much," Kar'Nevala patted her belly. The women gazed at each other for a moment, the longing to embrace etched on each of their faces. "Now, my young prince, to be heard, you simply speak. To be seen, you must touch the bowl for it to resonate with your appearance."

Kar'Nevala took R'Venin's hands and placed them around the bowl. The metal pot felt cold despite the billowing smoke and flames.

"My son," P'Vrit cooed from the mist. "Oh, you look as handsome as ever. I've missed you so much."

R'Venin pulled the kettle closer to his face—puckering his lips to kiss her cheek—but Kar'Nevala pushed his arm back down. "You can't touch," she reached as if to place a hand on P'Vrit's shoulder, but it passed through. "It's just smoke. An image of your mother projected into the mist." He set the bowl on the tile and hunched, keeping his face close to the billows.

"Stoke the flames with more El'Him powder if the image starts to dissipate," she grunted as she got to her feet. "There's enough in that pouch to talk all night. Fair weather, your majesties."

"Fair weather, Kar'Nevala. Safe nesting," P'Vrit called as the old woman disappeared behind the curtain. Her eyes fixed on R'Venin. "We have a lot of catching up to do."

Chapter Six

Confessions

"That's everything I know from the moment the battle started until I woke up in that Pra'Acheen hospital." R'Venin wrung his hands, looking away from his mother's image floating in the haze.

Crackling flames penetrated the silence for several painful moments as P'Vrit's face dimmed in the mist. R'Venin threw his tenth handful of powder into the pot. Her face peered from the haze with narrow eyes and scrunched brow. "What aren't you telling me, my son?"

R'Venin shifted his weight, crossing and re-crossing his legs, leaning from one side to the other.

"I didn't want to return from battle," he blew out his breath. "I've spent the last four seasons training for war so Father could have his precious Silver Silk. I told him I'd been studying alchemy with you. I tried to convince him, with your help, I could find a cure for the White Claw, and we wouldn't need the silk as a treatment anymore. When he refused, I didn't see any alternative to endless fighting over a plant. So, I decided to fall. I spotted a Ch'Hota squadron—one I had no hope of defeating—and flew straight into them. I didn't care if I survived the battle. I didn't care if I survived the fall. I wanted no part of his lust for bloodshed. I didn't want to become like him. I just wanted out."

"Oh, R'Venin," P'Vrit's voice softened. "You embody everything your father does not. Intelligence. Kindness. Empathy. These are not weaknesses, as he believes. These are your greatest attributes. You could have been the leader who brought the V'Jeeta into a new era. The Windfather knows I tried to encourage your strengths, but I could only do so much, given what I am."

"The highest female shall be given voice only after the lowest male has spoken," R'Venin whispered.

P'Vrit nodded. "The words of P'Phet."

R'Venin gazed through the smoke, looking through his mother's eyes. "Why did you never tell me you apprenticed with the Pra'Acheen? Why did you never tell me there was a fifth element of alchemy?"

"First. Because your father—as the high king—forbade any knowledge not written by P'Phet," she sighed. "Also, I was very young at the time. I only remembered a few things I'd learned from Kar'Nevala. As for the fifth element," P'Vrit's head swiveled in all directions. "There's something I've wanted to tell you for many seasons. Something I think you're ready to hear."

Unconsciously, R'Venin straightened and gazed around the little prayer room.

We're all alone. What's she worried about?

P'Vrit leaned forward. "Before I learned about the fifth element," she whispered, "when I first entered as an initiate, I made an oath to adhere to certain principles. I joined the Order of the Wind."

"YOU WHAT?!" R'Venin roared, immediately covering his mouth and watching the drape for someone to come bursting in. He rolled onto his knees and leaned into the smoke.

My mother betrayed P'Phet's teachings. Apostatized and joined a damned Ch'Hota religion? No!

"Shhh!" P'Vrit hissed. "No one knows. Not even your sister, B'Luren. Especially not your father. It had happened before my father betrothed me to him. I was a child, but even then I believed in the Order's teachings, and I joined in secret. If it's ever discovered, he'll have me killed. Or worse. He may have you and the rest of my children plucked and ground-cast. You'd be little better than soil-diggers after he finished with me."

R'Venin groaned within himself, rocking on his knees. "How could you betray P'Phet like that? How could... why did you?" R'Venin stuttered.

P'Vrit bowed her head, enfolding herself in her wings. "Because the Windfather told me it was true," she sighed. "I felt his breath in my hearts, and I knew—without a doubt—the teachings of P'Phet were wrong, and the Order was right."

R'Venin's fists unclenched as he leaned back on his heels. All the air left his body in a single, deflating sigh. An eternity seemed to pass before he breathed again. "How can you burden me with this secret?"

P'Vrit's hand emerged from the smoke, disappearing on his cheek. "Because you and I are so alike. And because I know I can trust you," her whisper, barely audible. "You're a good man. One day you'll be a wonderful husband and father. I just wish I could be there to see that."

R'Venin's eyes flashed wide. "What do you mean?" His arm passed through her smoky hand, swiping it away.

"Your father returned from battle with heavy hearts. His heir, his first son, lost to the ravages of war." She didn't look up. "No one left alive knows what happened to you after you charged that squadron. The Ch'Hota decimated his armies. He says it'll take several seasons, and all the Silk we have in reserve, to replenish the flock. I think, if you want to disappear, now would be the time. You can follow a new wind and be happy."

"What about you? Why don't *you* disappear? You could probably get yourself to Copperleaf and hide among the Pra'Acheen. It seems like Kar'Nevala would be happy to take you back under her wing."

"No," P'Vrit shook her head. "My place is here. It would look suspicious if I—his first wife—vanished without a trace. Dishonor is not the least of your father's concerns."

It seems like a lot of things could dishonor Father. R'Venin thought, as he knew this to be true.

"Shall I ever see you again, Mother?" R'Venin's voice wavered and his face fell.

"When you've found a branch, send a message to Kar'Nevala," she soothed. "She'll contact me through the bowl. Perhaps, someday, you'll get one of your own, and we will be able to talk more than occasionally. Maybe I'll even teach B'Luren how to use it."

"I'd like that," he choked with welling eyes.

P'Vrit looked up past R'Venin's head. "Dawn is approaching." R'Venin looked up, realizing for the first time how bright the oculus shone above. "Your father will be awake soon, and in need of his morning meal and service. Pleasant breezes, my son. I love you."

"Pleasant breezes, Mother," R'Venin croaked. "I love you, too."

P'Vrit's head bowed low into the smoke and puffed her cheeks. Her image scattered as the embers floated from the bowl and swirled in lazy circles before R'Venin's face.

"I miss you!" he said aloud to the painfully empty room.

Chapter Seven
The Question

R'Venin pushed through the embroidered curtain and ducked into the darkened hallway. The fragrance of jitterleaf tea wafted through his nose as his eyes adjusted to the flickering light spilling from beyond. Following the scent through the corridors, R'Venin found Kar'Nevala sitting cross-legged on the balcony next to a simmering pot whistling over a bed of fire-crystals. He glanced at the trees as a shadow darted across the moon to see the dawning sun still a few songs away.

"Just in time," she said, taking the kettle off the glowing stones and setting it down next to a quartet of cups made from hollowed-out gourds. Each one etched with a different elemental symbol. "I hoped the tea would be ready by the time you finished speaking with your mother."

"Have you been waiting up all night?" R'Venin walked to stand next to the crystals, letting the heat spread across his legs and feet.

"Oh, no," Kar'Nevala laughed. "I'm not that gracious a host. I've only been up for half a song. I heard you talking in my prayer room as I passed to answer nature's call. I assumed you wouldn't be able to sleep after sitting up all night with P'Vrit. So I made some tea. You still have a long journey ahead, helping Ba'Jai and Ja'Naam home to the Bluewoods."

Kar'Nevala patted the floor next to her and then poured the sand-colored tea into two of the gourds.

R'Venin sat as she lifted the Mountain cup and handed it to him. He crossed his legs and took the drink, nodding. "Thank you."

"Would you petition for us?" she asked as R'Venin put the cup to his lips.

R'Venin looked down at his cup as he lowered it into his lap. "I don't know how to petition as you do," he mumbled.

"How does it differ?" She asked, smiling. "Show me."

R'Venin paused, letting the steam waft to his nose. He set the gourd on the floor with a sigh and stood, turning to face the dim sunrise. He cleared his throat, pausing several times as he raised his hands. He flattened his palms toward the sky as if pushing against an invisible ceiling, lifting his wings like a mother protecting her children from the rain.

I've never prayed in front of an outsider before.

"Holy Windfather," R'Venin cleared his throat again. "You have made us your chosen flock. You have given us the words of P'Phet to guide us. You have blessed us, above all others, to rule over Pirth'Vee Grah. In your wisdom, we will be blessed with victory because of our obedience to the Sacred Scrolls. In your wisdom, we will rid the world of falsehoods. May our enemies bow to the light and join our ranks, so they will not suffer to fall to our might. Let it be so."

R'Venin avoided Kar'Nevala's gaze as he sat back again in the crossed-legged position. Out the corner of his eye, he spied her staring into the pile of crystals and humming to herself. She lifted her cup and slurped.

"You disapprove of how I petition." R'Venin turned his head, peering out from below his brow.

She smiled, taking another loud sip of tea. "My opinion is

irrelevant," she said, tilting her head and closing her eyes. "And I also don't think it matters so much to the Windfather *how* we pray. I believe he only cares whether we pray with sincere hearts."

R'Venin looked back down into his untouched tea.

I don't think I've offered a sincere petition since I was a hatchling.

"I've pleaded all my life that my people would find a cure for White Claw," he whispered. "But, the Windfather has never answered."

Kar'Nevala took another slurp of tea. "Perhaps you've been asking the wrong question."

R'Venin looked over, his brow furrowed. "What do you mean?"

Kar'Nevala shrugged. "Sometimes when we don't get the answer we want, it's because we're asking the wrong question. If I wanted to know how many songs it took to fly around the sanctuary, would I land on the ground and start walking? Windfather's answers come from asking the right questions."

R'Venin put his gourd on the floor and leaned over on one arm. "Is there a cure for White Claw? Is there a way for the flocks to end the wars?"

Kar'Nevala refilled her cup and took a noisy sip. "Where does Silver Silk grow?" she asked, watching the tea swirl.

"Everyone knows this," R'Venin sighed. "In the valley of the central plains. Between the three flocks."

Kar'Nevala smiled as she breathed the fumes into her nose. "Does the Silk grow only in the central plains because the flocks surround it? Or do the flocks surround the central plains because the Silk grows there?"

"Legends of my people say the Silk was carried there by the Windfather to bless the V'Jeeta and lure our enemies closer."

Kar'Nevala nodded with hooded eyes. "Would it surprise you the Pra'Acheen stories say the Windfather led my people to the valley long ago to save us from the southern quakes? And that the Silk had nothing to do with our migration to the north?"

"That may be your legend," R'Venin bristled, scooting himself away from Kar'Nevala. "But, to us, the Silk is everything. It's the only known treatment for White Claw. Without the Silk, our warriors have poor seed. They either sire imperfect hatchlings or none at all. They destroy hatchlings that are born weak or deformed before their first sunrise. Without the Silk, my flock is slowly dying, wasting away to mongrels. So, tell me. Can White Claw be cured?"

Kar'Nevala set her cup on the floor and stood. Reaching out, she took R'Venin's hand. He stood at her tug, following her to the railing. "You're still asking the wrong question, my young prince."

"Then, what is the right question?" R'Venin pulled away, throwing his hands in the air as his wings flared. "If you know the answer, why won't you tell me?"

"If you're not ready to ask the right question," she said, shaking her head with a sad look. "You're not ready for the right answer."

R'Venin's arms and wings fell, his shoulders slumping. "Then how will I know what the right question is?"

Kar'Nevala stepped forward, taking R'Venin's hands in hers. "Kneel."

R'Venin's eyes narrowed as he turned his head slightly away, looking down at his healer with one eye. "Why?"

"To start learning how to ask the right questions." She smiled, tugging his hands downward.

R'Venin rolled his eyes. Sighing, he knelt on the floor. "Now what?" He cast a glance into the trees.

"Bow your head."

Bow my head? That will help me get answers?

"Bowing shows humility," Kar'Nevala said as if answering his thoughts. "We cannot learn if we aren't willing to be taught."

R'Venin rolled his head before letting it fall slightly forward.

Kar'Nevala lowered herself into a kneeling position, looking up. "Now, hold out your hands." She extended her arms, palms up. "Like this." She nodded her encouragement as R'Venin remained stiff.

Another sigh escaped as he held up his hands, his elbows were still drawn tight to his body as if carrying the sacred scrolls through the royal library.

"This shows your willingness to receive the answer you're seeking." Kar'Nevala's voice changed in timbre, becoming low and reverent. "Lastly, close your eyes."

"Close my eyes?" R'Venin grumbled. "And the reason for that is…?"

"Closing one's eyes when petitioning the Windfather demonstrates a willingness to accept whatever answer is given." Her voice broke. "With no expectations or preconceptions as to what we believe that answer should be. And to show the faith that an answer will come," she added.

"So," R'Venin smirked, "Do these answers come in the form of a sacred scroll? Written on holy parchment?"

Kar'Nevala looked up with a cross glare. "If you'd rather continue petitioning your way, and getting the same results, tell me now."

R'Venin's head bowed lower as he muttered an apology.

Kar'Nevala took a breath and closed her eyes. "The Windfather speaks to our hearts. That is where you'll find the right questions, as well as your answers."

"Okay," R'Venin fidgeted on his knees, shaking the tension from his wings and arms and closed his eyes. "I'm ready. Where should I start asking the right questions about White Claw?"

R'Venin's eyes opened as he heard Kar'Nevala using the handrail to get up off the floor. "Wait," he reached out, catching her hand. "I thought you were going to teach me how to petition the Windfather?"

Kar'Nevala put her hands around his face. "I just did," she chuckled.

"But you're not ready to ask the right questions. White Claw is a natural consequence of life. Only Windfather can change our nature."

R'Venin's body slumped again, his wings draping off the balcony's edge. "I need to find a cure and stop this pointless war. When will I be ready?"

"Go with Ba'Jai and Ja'Naam to the Bluewoods. Learn the ways of the Ch'Hota. Then, when you're ready to be taught, you may return here to study with the Pra'Acheen."

Chapter Eight
R'Venin's Shadow

R'Venin sniffed in the crisp morning air as he walked from the library into the surrounding forest. His new, calf-length, linen tunic swished in the breeze. Slung from his shoulders, between his wings, a rough-spun rucksack filled with his armor, pulled his back straight.

Streams of sunlight pierced through waving limbs overhead and danced on the cobblestone path like rippling waters. Ba'Jai's hand clung to his shoulder strap, forcing him to lean to one side. Twenty paces from the library walls, a screen of flowering shrubs encircled the sanctuary. The stone lane passed through a tall arbor of trees, and the limbs from either side joined in the middle to form a naturally covered porch.

A six-wheeled wagon, two wingspans long, pulled by a team of muzzled runnerhounds waited under the trellis. The hounds stomped, padded, and clawed their feet, pushing against their harnesses.

The driver, an adolescent Pra'Acheen sitting above the front wheels, scrutinized R'Venin with hooded eyes as he gripped the reins tighter in his hands. The boy jerked his head behind him, and then fixed his eyes on the restless hounds.

R'Venin nodded to the young man as he transferred Ba'Jai's weight to the wagon's step running along the side. The bed, filled with lidded baskets, reeked of grain and fertilizer.

"Guess you'll have to ride on top." R'Venin nodded to the wagon. "I'll follow above if your sister wants to go on ahead."

"Why don't we just chain you in razor-briar?" Ba'Jai winked. "We'll tie you to the back, and just drag you if you can't keep up."

The driver's wings perked up as his head turned slightly.

R'Venin leaned in. "Why are you doing this?" he whispered. "Why are you helping me? Do you believe the Windfather told you to save me?"

Grabbing the wagon's handrail and hefting himself up, Ba'Jai fell into the baskets on his uninjured shoulder with a grunt.

R'Venin rose onto the runner step, holding the handrail with both hands. "Well? Do you?"

Adjusting his position, Ba'Jai shifted his weight. Once settled, he stared R'Venin in the face. "Yes. Absolutely."

R'Venin dropped off the step, staring at the ground.

"Ja'Naam," Ba'Jai yelled over R'Venin's head. "The driver won't wait forever."

"My name's Chara'Vaha," the youth muttered.

Ba'Jai jerked his head around. "Sorry, Chara'Vaha," he said, patting the bench next to him before turning back around. "Chara'Vaha won't wait forever."

R'Venin twisted his neck to look back. Ja'Naam knelt in front of Kar'Nevala, her hemline fanned out across the entry stones. Her face lit with a radiant smile while affectionately Kar'Nevala stroked her folded wing. Their animated words fell to babbling by the time their sound reached R'Venin's ears. "You're sister is very...,"

"Intense?" Ba'Jai finished. "You think she's passionate now. Just wait until we hit on a subject she cares about."

"What *does* she care about?" R'Venin sloughed off his pack and tossed it into the wagon at Ba'Jai's feet.

Ba'Jai chortled. "When you figure out what she doesn't care about, you let me know." He leaned back, picked up a basket lid, and shielded his eyes.

The sound of backwinging and quick footsteps announced Ja'Naam's presence. "Let you know what?" she asked, waving back at Kar'Nevala. She hopped once to see over the wagon's edge, finding Ba'Jai's rumpled form. "Let you know what, Ba'Jai?" she yelled. She faced R'Venin, planting one hand on a jutted hip while pointing her extended talon at him. "Let him know what?"

R'Venin stared, mouth agape. *I'd rather be back in the crimson fields right now.*

"He's to let me know if your cooking has improved," Ba'Jai snickered. "Or if it'll still kill a wild rockskipper!"

Ja'Naam's jaw dropped, her eyes widening like full moons as her cheeks flushed. R'Venin covered his mouth, stifling the howl exploding from his belly. She pressed her lips into a thin line, pinching off her giggles and raised a clawed finger, opening her mouth to speak.

"I'm sure you're a fine cook," R'Venin chuckled. "As fine as you are an alchemist. Kar'Nevala spoke highly of you."

The old Pra'Acheen never said a thing about Ja'Naam's ability, but anything to avoid those claws.

"R'Venin has offered to fly behind the wagon," Ba'Jai said lazily. "In case you wanted to go ahead and get started on the evening meal. I know how long it takes you to forage the market."

Ja'Naam's shoulders relaxed. "That's a kind offer, R'Venin," she bowed her head. "But I should stay with my brother. Someone may have to slap him out of this delirium that makes him think he has a future as a jester." She hopped onto the handrail and slapped the lid covering his face before launching between the trunks. Ba'Jai sat up grunting, swatting for her foot as she disappeared above the arbor.

"Chara'Vaha," Ba'Jai said as he laid back, shading his eyes again with the lid. "I think we're ready to go. And please, don't feel like you need to spare the hounds for her sake."

Not looking back, Chara'Vaha raised his hands, whipped the reins, making the runnerhounds growl, diving into their yoke. The wagon creaked forward, bouncing on the cobbled path. Thirty wingspans above, Ja'Naam beat her wings in a steady rhythm, meandering through the limbs in lazy curves. R'Venin walked beside the wagon until it cleared the Bowery and then jumped toward the sky, but landed on the wagon's tail in a crouch.

Balancing himself with outstretched wings, he stared at Ba'Jai's reposed figure. His fingers interlocked across his chest, feet crossed atop another basket. His body rolled back and forth with each jostling rock and root on the trail. "What do you want to ask me?" he muttered, his eyes peeking from the lid.

R'Venin lowered his head, picking at a basket's frayed edges. "Why do you think the Windfather told you to help me?"

Ba'Jai sat up, letting the makeshift sunshade fall off his head. He remained silent until R'Venin looked into his eyes.

"Are you certain you want to know?"

* * *

Ka'Ala dashed from tree to tree—from one shadowed limb to the next—as she followed R'Venin, Ba'Jai, and Ja'Naam a hundred wingspans above the ground through Copperleaf Forest. Her hearts raced with each flight through the spotlights that rained down through the canopy like columns of fire. Flakes of bark stuck to her hands as each tree hop caused sap to fall and accumulate on her body, adding to her natural camouflage. The peaty odor filled her nasal slits, blocking out every other scent in the forest.

I spent so much time alone, and moving only at night, avoiding all contact. And I've never been much of a tracker. I hope I can keep up.

She kept one eye on Ja'Naam as her oil-black wings billowed at every warm updraft, keeping herself above and behind her unknowing guide. As she glided through a pillar of hot air, a geyser exploded below and launched her tumbling above the canopy. She shielded her eyes from the glaring sunlight as she righted herself above the trees, scanning the treetops. Her wings shimmered to a patchwork of greens and yellows as she dove into the nearest branch large enough to hold her weight.

Flying creatures of a thousand species flitted about the leafy barrier between ground and sky, creating a symphony of life. Each one seemingly intent on chasing its favorite insect while avoiding their natural predators. Ka'Ala's head spun, searching the branches to get her bearings.

Oh, no. I've lost them!

Her eyes widened as she dove into the foliage, darting in all directions for any hint of gold plumage. She flew in sweeping arcs between the branches, her head swiveling rapidly back and forth in search of Ja'Naam.

Windfather. You told me to follow. I need your help to find them again.

A weak growl pulled Ka'Ala's attention to a nest just below her feet. The dome of twigs and mud nestled between three branches had one large opening on the side from which two hatchling red-wing, branchclimber heads emerged, eyes closed and mouths agape, screeching for their supper. Their scarlet quills, just beginning to unsheathe, still contained flecks of eggshells.

A deep, rattling growl thundered above Ka'Ala's head as her perch suddenly swayed with a new weight. She froze in place. Swallowing hard and holding her breath, her hearts pounded, trying to escape her chest. Her skin tingled as shivers ran up her spine.

Oh no! I didn't catch her scent. Stay calm! No sudden movements.

She turned her head, wide-eyed, as she gazed into the eight milky eyes of an adult branchclimber. It's four clawed legs hugged the trunk as her four crimson and black-tipped wings spread open, blocking the light from above. The taste of blood, and spoiled meat, filled Ka'Ala's mouth as the beast snorted.

"Oh, no," Ka'Ala breathed. "Easy, girl. I'm not going to hurt your babies. But I'm not going to be a meal either."

The branchclimber moved around the trunk, grabbing onto a second branch with its left legs, retracting its wings. Ka'Ala backpedaled along the limb, feeling her way with her feet, while keeping her eyes locked on her pursuer. She peeked at the nest as the babies' cry for food intensified.

The mother's head snapped between Ka'Ala and the newborn branchclimber as the branch drooped further with each step toward the tip. The tree rumbled under Ka'Ala's feet as the giant predator transferred her weight to the limb, growling deep in her throat. With all four pincer-like claws wrapped around the branch, the mother spread her wings and crouched, coiling to strike.

Ka'Ala jumped just as the branchclimber lunged, catching her foot with one of its front claws. She twisted, pounding her wings to wrench her leg from its grip. She screamed as her knee almost dislocated in her effort to free herself until the branchclimber lost its grip and dragged its claws along her shin, leaving three deep gashes through her leggings. She pounded her wings, flying straight up while ignoring the throbbing pain drumming up her leg.

I have to beat her to the light. She won't follow me above the canopy.

The branchclimber roared, its legs clamoring along the branches like a spinner as its wings heaved its body upward. A hundred animals flew from the treetops like pollen as Ka'Ala burst through the foliage. She put twenty wingspans between herself and the huntress below, who howled at the lost morsel for her offspring.

Gaining her bearings, she banked north, beating her wings to regain her lost ground, then dove back into the canopy. Withering leaves tore away from branches as she punched through the foliage. Twigs clung to her feathers with each brush through the canopy layers as she raced to find Ja'Naam. A fresh draft rose to meet her when she passed over a thundering waterfall. She swooped, cutting through the billowing mist, and shook off the bits of detritus from her wings. While hovering over the wet cacophony, she spotted Ja'Naam perched a hundred wingspans away. Below Ja'Naam, the wagon carrying Ba'Jai and R'Venin lumbered along the rough path cutting through the forest.

Just as Ka'Ala banked in pursuit, a massive gust blew her into a lone Bluewood towering next to the falls. The crack of a tree limb masked the snapping in her body.

Ow! My ribs!

Falling to the ground, Ka'Ala clamored for a hold with one arm while wrapping her chest with the other. Tumbling from branch to branch, she thudded into a pile of leaves nestled between two exposed roots. Angry tears fell as she gritted her teeth then curled into a ball.

Why, Windfather? I know everything is a trial of faith, but how am I supposed to follow them if I'm hurt like this?

The bed of fallen leaves writhed and hissed, spreading out like fingers from the trunk.

"Oh, no," she breathed. "Not-." She looked down at her torn and blood-soaked flesh dripping onto the pile. Her mother's voice rang in her ears.

Never let your blood touch the ground.

Two dozen flying firesnakes slithered from under the pile. Their webbed quills vibrated, surrounding Ka'Ala in a rattling concert of fear. White venom dripped from the spikes, leaving tiny smoke trails as the acidic liquid burned the soil. The firesnakes encircled Ka'Ala, rearing up and fanning their quills.

Ka'Ala's eyes moved slowly between the fiery eyes of each serpent. Their crimson scales glinted like rubies in the sun, while exposing their sawtooth fangs with every menacing hiss. The roar of water caught her attention as a plan formed in her mind.

Let's play 'Seek the Hidden.' Have to get behind the falls.

Ka'Ala pushed herself from the ground, moving as fast as her burning chest and throbbing leg would allow. The firesnakes swarmed around her, slithering in a tightening circle as she raised herself into a crouch. She closed her eyes and breathed, willing her hearts to slow.

Without warning, the nearest firesnake lunged, striking Ka'Ala's arm with a fiery quill. She screamed, gripping the inflamed skin with her hand and hopped over the hissing circle, landing on her undamaged foot. The acrid scent of burnt flesh filled her nose as a burning sensation danced across her arm. The serpentine throng shrieked in unison and swarmed, flapping their webbed quills to rise off the ground. Venom pelted the surroundings like caustic spittle as they raced behind Ka'Ala toward the falls. Droplets hissed as they hit the water, steaming into green puffs of smoke.

Lumbering through the shallows beneath the falls, Ka'Ala hopped through the water. The firesnakes swarmed around her, pelting her skin and feathers with their searing venom. Ka'Ala's high pitched screams died under the turbulent falls. She dove headfirst into the watery curtain, intending to brace herself against the impact of solid rock on the other side. She fell instead into a small grotto.

The firesnakes shrieked as they dashed into the falls, only to scurry out again, never quite reaching their quarry. Ka'Ala washed the venom from her body under the dripping stalactites in her meager shelter.

She sat in the shallow water, wrapping her arms and wings around her legs. Her body convulsed. "Windfather," she sobbed, flinching away each time a firesnakes' quills pierced the thin veil. "I don't know what to do! Please, help me!"

Mask yourself as your quarry, Windfather spoke into her mind. *Relief is nigh.*

Ka'Ala concentrated against the fear and pain, shifting her colors again. Instead of inky feathers, pale skin, and pearly eyes, she took on the golden shades and aquamarine highlights of the woman she trailed and lost.

Chapter Nine
Sisters

Ja'Naam remained still, perched on the thick limb watching for predators in the branches ahead. Below, the wagon lazily made its way across the dirt path cutting between roots worming through the soil. She waved a hand as Ba'Jai made eye contact with her and returned the gesture. R'Venin turned his head and raised his hand, giving her a thin smile.

Ja'Naam's hand froze for a moment, and then she returned a courtesy wave. *He's got a handsome face, but I could never bond with a V'Jeeta.*

A shrill cry of terror in the distance pulled Ja'Naam's attention away from her brother and the wagon. She turned, searching for the source. Another scream—piercing and panicked—made its way to her ears, followed by muted, inaudible words from somewhere lower to the ground.

Ja'Naam stepped off the branch; her wings billowed as she caught the air and glided toward the cries. Another scream rose into the air, and Ja'Naam located it behind a nearby pool, dulled by the thunder of falling water.

"HELP ME!" the frightened woman's voice cried. "Please,

someone! HELP!"

Ja'Naam drew in a large breath to yell back, but the air caught in her throat as she spotted the tornado of firesnakes attacking the falls. Clouds of pale green smoke rose around the sheeting water as their venom fell like rain. A few drops from the quills flew into the air, bursting into flames.

The unseen woman's voice rose in pitch each time a firesnake darted through the waterfall's protective shield.

I can't say anything. It'll draw the firesnakes. What do I have?

Ja'Naam opened the leather pouch hanging from her hip, examining its contents. A small alchemy bowl, a sling, and a few vials of various powders. *Nothing. I have nothing. I can't think. Windfather, what do I do?*

Wide-eyed, her hearts raced as her hands went cold. She searched around the pool's edge as the firesnakes' hissing rose in volume and their assaults on the falls multiplied. Tracing up the falling water, she searched in vain for anything to chase away the fiery, flying serpents when she spotted it.

Three wingspans above the pool, an open geode of electhium clung to the cliff face. The white crystals glowed in the shaft of light that rained down onto the falls from the canopy above.

"That should do it," she mumbled under her breath.

Ja'Naam reached into the sack tied around her waist, pulling out the sling while keeping her eyes on the firesnake horde. She lowered herself to the ground and leaned toward the pool's edge, daring a glance for smooth, round stones. With one eye on the falls, she picked out a handful of rocks and then crept back to a thicket of bristleleaf shrubs.

The woman's voice faltered as she kept shouting for help. "Windfather. Anyone. Help me!"

Ja'Naam inched between the dense vegetation as she circled the pool until she was almost to the stone face. She knelt behind a boulder as mist billowed across the water's surface, dampening her skin and feathers like morning dew. She peeked around the rock, calculating the distance to the geode and the weight of her first projectile.

I wish Ba'Jai were here. He's a much better shot than I am.

Ja'Naam nestled the rock in the sling's thong and stood behind the boulder, exposing her head. She watched the firesnakes go into a frenzy as she began swinging the sling in a circle. The whistling over her head rose in pitch as her projectile picked up speed. Taking her eyes off the chaos for a split second, she found her target above and launched the rock. It smacked into the cliff face a hand span from the geode, ricocheted off the wall with a crack like lightning, and fell into the pool near the far edge. Two firesnakes fled from the splash, speeding away from the herd only to return seconds later.

The mass of swirling snakes sped up after the crack of stone against the rock face. Their hissing increased more intensely, and the quills began emitting active puffs of flame. The concealed woman's cries also grew in volume, sounding like a frightened child in a thunderstorm.

Ja'Naam reloaded, wound up, and released. This time, making contact with the geode, but only shifting its position. A shard of electhium fractured off the geode with her third shot, falling into the water. The chemical reaction caused wafts of gray smoke and tiny sparks of lightning to erupt from the spot. The firesnake horde raced to the foaming area, and three serpents were struck by the sparks, falling dead into the water.

The geode teetered close to falling after the fourth shot. The swarm's hissing intensified with each crack of stone. Ja'Naam loaded her fifth shot, stepping clear from the boulder as she spun the sling above her head. She launched the rock, nicking the geode on the back end. It tumbled down the rock face, landing with a giant splash in the water and sunk out of sight.

The pool bubbled and churned, emitting firebolts and puffs of smoke. Ja'Naam eased back behind the boulder as the firesnake swarm moved away from the waterfall and its hidden prey, crowding around the roiling spot of water. The predators' screeching unified in pitch as the flames bursting from their quills turned into a hellish pillar of fire. Ja'Naam covered her ears against the cacophony as the bubbling water rose higher.

Lightning shot in the air, striking the flying swarm as it circled the boiling spot. Flying serpents spiraled out from the flaming column like meteors, leaving smoky trails as they flew in random directions, falling dead in the water or flopping onto the wet ground, still sizzling. Ja'Naam flinched as a zapped firesnake struck the boulder near her head and fell, writhing at her feet.

An explosion under the water's surface plumed into the air, drenching the last remaining firesnakes in electrified mist. The air crackled as the lightning searched for anything on which to cling before dissipating. Ja'Naam heard the mystery woman scream in pain as a lingering bolt found its way across the boulder's damp surface, the discharge dying on her wing like a pinprick.

The waterfall seemed deathly quiet after the firesnakes' angry chorus died. "You can come out," Ja'Naam stepped from behind the boulder and into the shallows at the water's edge. "They're gone."

An injured woman emerged, holding her wings above her head and shielding herself from the watery curtain. She had Ch'Hota colors but facial features dissimilar from everyone else in the Bluewoods. She hugged her chest with one arm, slumping over, her face grimacing. Water flowed down her face in heavy rivulets.

"Blessed Windfather," Ja'Naam yelped. "You're hurt." Rushing into the pool, Ja'Naam put her arms around the injured woman's waist, taking as much of her weight as she could handle.

"Thank you," the woman whimpered as her wing collapsed across

Ja'Naam's golden shoulder. "And thank you for saving me from those damn firesnakes. I thought I was going to be trapped in there forever."

"Lucky for you, firesnakes hate getting wet," Ja'Naam panted as they sloshed toward shore. "I'm Ja'Naam, of the Coastal Bluewoods. What's your name?"

* * *

Ka'Ala's mind raced. *What do you say to the woman you've been stalking, and who just saved your life?*

"I'm Ka'Ala," she grunted through her teeth, "and I'm—."

The time has not come to reveal yourself, Windfather whispered.

"I'm not from around here," Ka'Ala muttered. "You could say I'm wind-blown. My home is far away."

"Let's set you down over there," Ja'Naam nodded her head toward a small boulder.

Ka'Ala groaned with each wrenching step as Ja'Naam hefted her away from the pool. She yelped, hugging her side, as she sat down on the flat stone.

"Where does it hurt?" Ja'Naam scanned Ka'Ala's wings, arms, and legs, counting the burn marks under her breath. "I can see you're favoring your side. Did you hurt your chest?"

"I think I cracked my ribs and Y-bone fleeing a branchclimber," she grimaced as Ja'Naam raised her arm out of the way. "I perched between a mother and her cubs without realizing it."

Ja'Naam blew out a breath. "You're lucky to be alive," she sighed as she felt along Ka'Ala's side. "How did you manage to get trapped by those flying firesnakes?"

Ka'Ala sucked air through her teeth as Ja'Naam found a rib splintering out of her chest. "I fell into their nest at the base of that tree," she pointed over Ja'Naam's shoulder. "I barely made it to the falls."

Ja'Naam untied a leather pouch from her waist, dropping it to the ground. Bits of leaf and dirt puffed out as she knelt between Ka'Ala and her sack. "I don't have many elements with me," Ja'Naam mumbled as she rummaged through the bag. "These were for my brother once we get home."

Ka'Ala craned her neck to peek at the cache. "Are you an alchemist?"

"No," Ja'Naam laughed, taking powder-filled vials from the sack and holding them up to the sunlight. "I don't know what I'll be. But at my parents' insistence, I've been studying alchemy with a Pra'Acheen master. Here we are."

Ja'Naam gave Ka'Ala a bright-eyed smile as she pulled a vial filled with a mauve powder from the sack, uncorked it, and drew in a deep breath through her nose.

"What is that?" Ka'Ala groaned, adjusting herself on the rock.

"It's needleleaf from the eastern sea," Ja'Naam held out the vial with an open palm. "It's the tree element to heal the burns. But I'm not skilled enough to fix your bones."

Ja'Naam reached into the pack, leaving the needleleaf and retrieving a small brass bowl. In three paces, she came to the water's edge, bent over, and filled the container to overflowing before returning to kneel at Ka'Ala's feet. "Drink half of this." She pushed the bowl into Ka'Ala's hands. "I'll use the rest for the draught."

Ka'Ala lifted the cup to her lips and hesitated. "Why are you doing this for me?" she asked, lowering the bowl to chest level. "You don't know me, yet you risked your life."

"Let's call it a family trait," Ja'Naam reached out, placing her hands over Ka'Ala's.

Music lilted on the wind as Ka'Ala stared into Ja'Naam's face. Two flittering melodies danced around each other like flutterbies on the breeze.

Your Sister, the Windfather whispered to her hearts.

Ka'Ala's lip trembled. "Thank you," she whispered. "You don't know what this means to me."

"We may be from different forests, but we're all created in the Windfather's image." Ja'Naam's eyes glistened. "Many feathers. One flock."

Ka'Ala smiled, revealing pearly teeth. "One flock," she choked.

"Now," Ja'Naam wiped the wetness from her cheeks. "Drink up, so we can get you ready for travel. Do you have companions nearby? Can we help you get somewhere?"

"I'm alone," Ka'Ala lifted the bowl, draining it in three gulps. *I've been alone for quite a long time.* "I've relied on the Windfather's graces for many seasons."

She handed the bowl to Ja'Naam, who stifled a laugh. "Thirsty?" she patted Ka'Ala's knee and returned to the pool for more.

"Oops," Ka'Ala covered her mouth, then winced at the sudden motion. "I forgot. You said only drink half. I guess I'm a little distracted."

Ja'Naam retrieved another full bowl of water. "Here," she chuckled, handing over the vessel. "*Half* this time."

Sipping from the bowl, keeping her eyes on the water level, Ka'Ala drained less than half and handed it back. "Half," she said, shrugging her shoulders with a slight head tilt.

Ja'Naam set the bowl on the ground with a smile and stood, walking around the water's edge to the canted wall of rough stone. The waterfall's mist billowed around her as she climbed up the craggy face. Ka'Ala's face screwed up as Ja'Naam grabbed random rocks lodged in the rough wall, examining them for a moment and tossing them over her shoulder. She shuddered as the rippling water made the floating firesnakes bob around the surface. Slicks of white ooze seeped outward from their dead quills, giving them the appearance of milky

Hopper pads.

"Ah, Ha!" Ja'Naam's gleeful outburst pulled Ka'Ala's eyes from the surface to find her leaping from the wall with something clutched in her fist. She opened her wings to glide above the dead serpents and landed next to the bowl. "The Windfather always provides," she beamed, holding out a luminous yellow stone.

"It's a rock." Ka'Ala's eyebrows raised.

"It's a sunstone," Ja'Naam laughed. "This will energize the water <u>and</u> provide the mountain element I need to complete the potion."

Ja'Naam dropped the sunstone into the bowl while she chanted "T'vacha ko'band ka'rane ke'lie" five times above the falls' roar, blowing across the brim with each chorus.

The water immediately bubbled. She pulled the vial of needleleaf back out and broke it on the bowls' edge, tipping the contents into the churning water.

Again, Ja'Naam chanted the same words over the surrounding noise. A flaxen swirl rose from the soup, rolling like a carpet. The frothing cup slowed to a simmer, then congealed into a berry-colored mud.

"I'm a little surprised that worked." Ja'Naam picked up the bowl with one hand and dipped in her index finger, retracting the talon. "Now, where are your burns?"

Ka'Ala sniffed the air, flaring her nasal slits. The scent of warm, loamy soil inspired a deep breath. "Smells like home," she sighed.

Ja'Naam stood and circled Ka'Ala, applying the paste to the exposed burns on her arms, neck, legs, and wings. Each dab cooled the points of fire like an icicle set to her skin. The pockmarks of raw flesh disappearing as Ja'Naam's hand massaged the ointment smoothly over Ka'Ala's surface wounds.

"Let's get your legs."

Ka'Ala turned as Ja'Naam knelt, smearing paste down her legs and around her calf-feathers. "Looks like they burned some holes in your outerwear. Especially across your back and legs," she commented as she swabbed Ka'Ala's feet. "Do you want me to heal those as well? If we don't, they can become infected."

Ka'Ala visibly stiffened as her throat tightened.

No one outside the order is supposed to see, Windfather.

All is well, child, he whispered in her hearts. *There is no sacrilege with a sister.*

Ka'Ala nodded and unhitched the fastenings of her cloak. Ja'Naam assisted in pulling off the pockmarked leggings. The mist flowing off the pool made Ka'Ala's skin tingle. She stood there, shivering in nothing but the white silk breechcloth with strips that rose up to her waist and looped around her neck. Ja'Naam dabbed more ointment up the backs of her legs and then froze.

She must see the markings.

Ka'Ala envisioned what Ja'Naam must have discovered. Delicate interweaving scars of curlicues, branching tendrils, and crosses wove up and down her back, legs, and arms like a living tapestry.

"You're Gir'Agit, aren't you?" Ja'Naam's voice barely a whisper. "I read about you at the sanctuary, in the ancient scrolls of The Consecrated Ones."

Ka'Ala turned as Ja'Naam stood. They stared into each other's eyes for several moments.

Do I tell her?

Ka'Ala's hearts burned, swelling with peace. She released her concentration on her colors. Her golden feathers, with blue and green highlights, faded to midnight black, her tan skin paled to the color of fresh winter's kisses, and her irises changed from high-sun yellow to pearl. "Yes," she breathed as a tear escaped. "I am a Gir'Agit. And... I'm the last one!"

Chapter Ten

A New Trust

"So," Ja'Naam beamed. "The legends are true."

"More than less," Ka'Ala fastened the last tog on her cloak, shifting her colors to match Ja'Naam, and sat back on the rock, wiping her misty forehead with the back of her hand. "Over the years, listening to the trappers and hunters I came across, I've heard pretty much every version. Most are mostly right. Some are hilariously naive."

"Let's get you to the wagon." Ja'Naam reached out for Ka'Ala's arm, pulling her up and wrapping the other around Ka'Ala's waist again. "You can ride with my brother."

Ka'Ala tested her weight on her right foot, cringing as the bandages squeezed against the torn wound running from calf to toe. Her eyes brimmed over with tears as she sucked air through her teeth. "I'm only going to slow you down," she winced. "You should fly ahead and get some help."

"I'm not leaving you," Ja'Naam said, shaking her head. "I may not be the most knowledgeable about living in the woods, but I know enough to know that no one should be out here alone. Especially when ground-cast. Now, let's go. I don't think Ba'Jai is far."

For two hundred steps, they trudged in silence along the forest floor, keeping a pace that caused Ka'Ala to wince as little as possible. A gentle breeze stirred the waist-high grass as they fell into a slow but steady rhythm.

"Can you tell me about the scars?" Ja'Naam asked with the innocence of a child.

Ka'Ala smiled as she breathed deeply, gazing into the sky with longing eyes.

May I?

It is permitted, Windfather whispered.

She blew out her breath. "Where to begin," she sighed. "The markings symbolize my holy oaths with Windfather. They remind me of oaths my people made at the sacred altars of the Emerald Island."

"*The Emerald Island*," Ja'Naam breathed. "So, it <u>is</u> real."

"Yes," Ka'Ala laughed. "Long ago, Windfather led my forebears from enslavement back to their ancestral home, a promised land, where we could worship him in peace."

"Where is it?" Ja'Naam's eyes widened.

Ka'Ala bowed her head, muttering. "I don't know."

Their footfalls and the chattering of scurrying animals broke the silence until Ja'Naam cleared her throat.

"Is it true you can read minds?"

Ka'Ala stopped and rolled her head back, laughing into the trees. She winced, hugging her ribs tighter. "I think that's my favorite fantasy," she cringed and laughed simultaneously. "No. We're not telepathic. But we are superb listeners."

"Listeners?" Ja'Naam giggled in harmony with Ka'Ala's painful chuckling.

"If you listen with your hearts," Ka'Ala resumed walking, "you can hear the truth within another. And, with practice, you can hear the Windfather's voice penetrate your very soul."

"Can you teach me how?" Ja'Naam whispered.

Ka'Ala squeezed her tight. "As long as you have faith, and the willingness to act, you are ready to learn."

Several quiet moments went by before Ka'Ala faltered. "I think I need to sit for a moment," she said with labored breath.

"There," Ja'Naam pointed at a fallen tree where they could rest in an adjacent clearing, long enough to lie down on, three wingspans off their path. They pushed through the tall yellow grass, checking every few steps for the sound of rattling quills before settling themselves onto the upended trunk.

"How much farther do we have to go?" Ka'Ala held her chest.

"We still have a half-day," Ja'Naam looked up into the sky. "It'd only take a quarter day in the wagon. But Ba'Jai and R'Venin probably don't know I'm no longer following. We scraped talons just before we left the sanctuary."

You don't know it, Ja'Naam, but I watched from afar.

"Always trust Windfather," Ka'Ala recited, forcing herself to slow her breathing.

"May I ask another question?" Ja'Naam sat next to Ka'Ala. She pulled a rosy bean pod from a vine spiraling around the logs' broken branches and opened it.

"Of course," Ka'Ala nodded. "But I'll let you know if I can't answer."

Ja'Naam popped a pale pink bean into her mouth and offered one to her new friend. "No, thank you," Ka'Ala scrunched her neb. "I've never cared for them. They give me bad vapors."

Ja'Naam giggled and ate another bean. "You said Windfather freed you from enslavement? From where?"

Ka'Ala's face turned down as she smoothed a wrinkle in her leggings. "It was once called Shak'Ti Sha'Alee V'Jeet," she sighed. "It's in the Granite Spires, in the high desert."

"You were enslaved by the V'Jeeta?" Ja'Naam's eyes widened as she leaned closer, moving her hand from the log between them to rest on Ka'Ala's lap.

Ka'Ala placed her hand on top. "Yes. At least my ancestors were." She gave Ja'Naam a sad smile. "Long ago, the V'Jeeta discovered the emerald island and learned how we could hear heartsongs. They carried away the young and killed everyone else. They were forced to serve in the King's court as soothsayers and advisers. Telling the King, who had ill or pure intent."

Ja'Naam wrapped her wing around Ka'Ala, pulling her in. "If your people returned to the emerald islands, how is it you're the last one?"

"If you don't mind," Ka'Ala's shoulders slumped as she breathed out. "I'd rather not talk about that right now."

"Of course," Ja'Naam whispered, pulling Ka'Ala tighter into her wings and rested her head on Ka'Ala's shoulder. The grass rustled in the breeze as a swarm of dovehawks bolted into the air.

* * *

R'Venin floated down, landing in the stream next to the wagon. The runnerhounds gulped noisily; their muzzles dipped past the nostrils in the rippling creek. Chara'Vaha stood beside one, scratching its shoulder while watching R'Venin with cagey eyes.

"I couldn't find Ja'Naam," R'Venin panted. "I found the perch where we last saw her before she disappeared, but there's no sign of her."

Ba'Jai put a hand on the wagon's sidewall, pushing himself into a sitting position on the baskets. "It's not like her just to wander off," he grunted. "I need you make a wider circle while I wait here with the wagon."

"Of course," R'Venin bowed.

"Will you stop that," Ba'Jai snapped. "You're not my slave. And you're not my servant. But I do need your help to find my sister."

"Sorry," R'Venin scowled. "Feathers don't change."

"I know," Ba'Jai sighed. "I'm sorry too. We're both new at this. I'm just worried about Ja'Naam. The forest is dangerous, and she's not exactly a guardsman."

"Alright," R'Venin nodded, shrugging the clunky pack from his shoulders and heaving it into the wagon beside Ba'Jai's feet. The bag clattered and clanked as he wrestled it between two baskets. "I'll go search again. If I don't find her in eight songs, I'll come back."

"Thank you, R'Venin. I'm in your debt."

"It's small in comparison." R'Venin jumped into the air, flapping hard to gain altitude. He soared through the trees, feeling the wind on his face. Every scent piqued his attention. Pine needles. Rotting leaves. Branchclimber dung. Firesnake venom. Wild runnerhound urine, and a thousand other plants and animals. His nasal slits flared with each new odor, following its trail for a moment until the next new stench crossed his path.

Once I find Ja'Naam and bring her back to Ba'Jai, then what? What kind of life will I have among the Ch'Hota? I've heard V'Jeeta dissenters and refugees find favor among the Bluewoods.

Five songs later, R'Venin continued his meandering search pattern as he passed over a glittering waterfall. His throat tightened against the dryness in his mouth. Circling down, he spotted faint blotches of gray ooze dissipating across the pool toward a small creek. Dozens of red serpents blocked the brooklet's mouth like a log jam.

Landing at the pool's edge, R'Venin gazed around, staring deep into the surrounding forest. Aside from leaves dancing on the wind, he spotted no movement. The roaring falls called to him. As he strode into the pool, the billowing mist collected on his body, wetting his skin and feathers. Using his hands like a slough, he let the sweet water fill his belly.

Panting, he dipped his body under the waterfall, washing off the sweat of the day before returning to the shoreline. Shaking from tips to talons, he rained on the rocks and grass, sitting at the water's edge. A glint of reflected sunlight drew his eyes to the ground. He stepped closer and bent over, finding a broken glass vial and a patch of grass stained with reddish mud. Leading away from the glass shards, he spotted a pair of footprints heading into the forest and away from Ba'Jai. He knelt to examine the prints, running his fingers along the edges.

One pair has a steady but loaded stride. The other favoring the right foot. But which ones were Ja'Naam's?

R'Venin ran forward, leaping from a stone at the water's edge and taking flight. Perching every twenty wingspans, he stopped to catch a glimpse of the trail. A few hundred spans from the pool, he spotted Ja'Naam sitting on a fallen tree with another woman—Ch'Hota by the look of her feathers—cradled under her wing. Ja'Naam had a handful of pinkish beans and was popping them one by one into her mouth.

"Ugh," R'Venin groaned. "Wild beans. Good for only one thing, and it isn't eating."

Suddenly, a crowd of dovehawks burst from the grass and flew right over the huddled women. R'Venin's eyes widened as he raised his head.

Away from danger, R'Venin thought. *What danger?*

His eyes followed their trail backward, scanning the swaying grass until he spotted it. Forty wingspans long. Its sleek body was zig-zagging through the brush on a thousand legs, each ending with a spear-like talon. Its flaxen and cedar colored hairs blended into the mustard blades of the meadow. Its head, with two pairs of mandible pincers and a circular array of obsidian eyes, bobbed back and forth as it continued on a switchback course toward its unsuspecting victims.

"A sleepbreather," R'Venin breathed. "No." He looked down at his simple tunic, patting himself down in the vain hope of finding a hidden pocket filled with a weapon. His shoulders fell as he searched the nearby limbs for anything to use against the monster. He spotted a shrub of bronze pitcherflowers growing from a nearby branch.

He darted down, ripping the pitcherflowers by the roots and spilling acid from their inner pots onto the branch below. The orange liquid sizzled, pluming an acrid billow of rusty smoke into his nose.

If I can get to the beans before that monster gets to Ja'Naam, we might survive. Can't alert the sleepbreather.

R'Venin took several deep breaths and soared down with the bouquet of pitcherflowers in his hand.

Chapter Eleven

The Deadly Sleep

R'Venin arced through the air, circling downward, and keeping one eye on the sleepbreather and the other on Ja'Naam and her friend.

The friend looks like a Ch'Hota—but not quite. A half-flock, perhaps.

The women were nestled close to each other, oblivious to the danger that crept toward them.

As the behemoth zigged away, R'Venin took the opportunity and dove straight down, aiming at the exposed end of the fallen tree jutting from the ground. He landed hard, his impact causing the log to teeter upward.

Startled, Ja'Naam leaped off the log, while the other woman yelped and dug her claws into the bark. Ja'Naam picked a stick off the ground, holding it like a club. The one who was a stranger to R'Venin cowered behind Ja'Naam's flared wings. "Back off, V'Jeeta," she growled. "You'll find more than your match here."

"Ja'Naam! It's me! R'Venin." R'Venin held up his free hand, balancing the cluster of pitcherflowers in the other. "I'm not here to hurt you."

Ja'Naam's eyes widened. "Oh, sorry," she lowered her club and squinted at the bouquet. "Those aren't for me, are they?"

R'Venin rolled his eyes and knelt at Ja'Naam's feet. He grabbed a handful of pods and tore them open one by one with his teeth. Holding the bouquet at arm's length, he poured the beans into the wide-mouthed pitcherflowers. Once filled, each flower closed its flap and inflated to a palm-sized balloon—swelling like an air bubble rising from deep underwater. The bloated flowers drooped, hanging from his grip like a day's catch at the river.

"Not exactly," R'Venin's eyes widened as he looked over Ja'Naam's head. "You need to get out of here. Fly!"

"We can't," Ja'Naam put her arm around the stranger. "This is Ka'Ala. She's injured. She can't fly."

R'Venin kept his eyes on the meadow, watching the sleepbreather snake back toward them.

"Then stay still to avoid being spotted," R'Venin snapped an engorged pitcherflower from its stem and drew back his arm, ready to throw. "And whatever you do, try to avoid breathing. I'm going to try and lure it away."

"Lure what away?" Ka'Ala followed R'Venin's eyes into the grass. "What's out there?"

"What is that?" Ja'Naam pointed at a patch of dividing grass as she shielded her eyes from the setting sun across the meadow.

"It's a sleepbreather," R'Venin whispered. "But I've never seen one this far West before. They usually stick to the Eastern Plains. I can't imagine what drove it away. Stay low but keep your noses off the ground. And stay perfectly still. If we're lucky, it won't sense us. Just keep moving."

Ja'Naam and Ka'Ala crouched, huddling closer to the fallen trunk. R'Venin shifted his feet to keep himself facing the monster as it began circling the log. Only the sound of grass waving in the breeze came to R'Venin's ears. Not a single creature within earshot disrupted the absolute silence.

At that moment, gray fog seeped between the blades of grass, parting around the log as if it were a rock in a stream. The faint aroma of Rossa blooms swirled in the air. "Mm," Ja'Naam sniffed in a deep lungful before her eyes rolled back. "That smells... so—."

"Ja'Naam," Ka'Ala hissed, catching Ja'Naam's head before it struck the log's side. Her body went limp, collapsing like a rope ladder cut from above. Her eyes rolled, unfocused.

The sleepbreather poked its head up from the grass, sniffing the air. A deep rumble erupted from its throat as its pincers tapped excitedly along the edges of its hooked beak. Spotting R'Venin on his perch, the sleepbreather roared, gray mist pouring from its mouth.

"Try to fan the mist away as best you can," R'Venin said, keeping his eyes on the beast as it reared its tubular body high into the air. Two dozen taloned legs flailed in the breeze as if looking for any surface on which to cling. "I'll draw it away."

R'Venin threw a pitcherflower at the monster's chest, exploding on contact with its scaly plating. Multiple legs flailed as the rosy foam splashed and sizzled within the dense bristles covering each appendage.

R'Venin leaped into the air, bulging cluster in hand, gaining altitude on the sleepbreather in a tight circle. Below, Ka'Ala cradled Ja'Naam's listless form as she blew away the fog with her uninjured wing.

The sleepbreather snapped the air, spitting puffs of gray smoke at R'Venin as he threw pitcherflower grenades at the beast. Fifteen wingspans above the ground, as the brute coiled in on itself, R'Venin threw a bomb directly at its face. The acid cloud burned off a pincer on one side, the other hanging limp like molten wax.

The monster roared, lunging at him in the air. R'Venin dodged, barely pulling his leg out of the way before the sleepbreather bit it off.

Hovering in mid-air, R'Venin looked down at his hand. "Three left," he mused. "Better make them count."

The sleepbreather's neck curved, its face dripping blood from the broken pincer dangling from one side. The feral growl, thundering from its throat, drowning out all other forest sounds.

R'Venin shot a glance over his shoulder to find himself lined up between two thick branches of a young Bluewood tree. An idea popped into his mind.

I hope this works.

R'Venin backflapped until his talons scraped the nook between the branches. Transferring the remaining pitcherflowers to his throwing hand, he opened his wings to their full span.

"Come on—you mindless dirt-licker," R'Venin yelled, waving his arms. "Come get a taste." His eyes widened as the beast lunged. R'Venin tossed the clump of pitcherflowers into the demon's gaping maw and arced backward. The sleepbreather's pincers brushed R'Venin's legs as the flowers exploded inside its mouth. R'Venin tumbled through the air for a moment before he opened his wings, flying upward to avoid pieces of the monster's head following after him.

R'Venin circled back to the log to find Ka'Ala struggling to fan the foggy remnants away.

"I'm pleased to see the gas didn't get you too," R'Venin landed on the trunk, fanning the mist away.

"Is she going to be alright?" Ka'Ala stroked Ja'Naam's face with the backside of her hand.

"She'll be fine." R'Venin hopped off the log, landing at the women's feet. "The sleepbreather's breath is meant to stun its victims long enough to make an easy meal out of them. She just needs some clean air and fresh water. Here, I'll take her."

R'Venin knelt beside Ja'Naam's limp form and took her face in his hands, softly blowing into her nasal slits while his wings gently fanned her body. Ja'Naam repeatedly blinked, each time her eyes came more into focus.

Ja'Naam coughed up a puff of gray smoke and gasped like she'd been underwater for too long. Her eyes widened as she focused on R'Venin's face and swung, catching his cheek with a clawed hand.

"Ow!" R'Venin dropped her head and pulled back, holding his smarting cheek. "What in the windless sky was that for?"

Ja'Naam clapped her hands over her mouth, eyes wide. "I'm sorry," she muttered behind her fingers. "I just reacted on instinct."

Just assumed I was a typical V'Jeeta here to conquer or kill, huh?

Ka'Ala stared from one of them to the other with wary eyes.

"You seem to do that a lot." R'Venin rubbed his burning cheek. He held up his fingers to find traces of blood. "Ba'Jai sent me to find you. He's worried."

R'Venin stood and offered a hand to each woman, grunting as he took their weight, Ka'Ala needing several seconds longer than Ja'Naam to get to her feet. "Can you fly?"

"I think so." Ja'Naam nodded, testing her wings. "But Ka'Ala can't. We'll have to walk."

"I don't think that's a good idea," R'Venin looked over Ka'Ala. "I think I can take your weight. At least, long enough to get you back to Ba'Jai. You can ride in the wagon with him."

Ka'Ala took a half step back, clutching her side. "I don't want to be a burden," she mumbled. "I'd rather walk."

Ja'Naam wrapped an arm around Ka'Ala's shoulder. "Give us a moment," she looked at R'Venin as she turned Ka'Ala and herself around to face away, raising her wings to make a wall. Their muttered conversation became lost in the forest cacophony until Ka'Ala's voice broke through.

"It's alright, Ja'Naam," Ka'Ala pushed Ja'Naam's wing down with her hands. "I've heard his song. He has pure hearts."

Ja'Naam folded her wings and turned her back to R'Venin. "Are you sure?" she hissed. "He's V'Jeeta. His people enslaved yours. How can you trust him?"

Ka'Ala put a hand on Ja'Naam's shoulder. "I trust Windfather," she whispered. "Besides, you might want to listen with your hearts. I think one day, you'll find something unexpected. Something you've been longing for."

The women turned in unison. "Very well. You may carry me to the wagon." Ka'Ala stared into R'Venin's face with fiery eyes and raised a taloned finger. "But not a handspan further."

R'Venin looked at Ja'Naam for help. She shrugged and gave her head a small tilt, pulling one corner of her mouth down. "Not a handspan further," he bowed his head and held his arms open.

Ka'Ala sighed, tucking in her wings as R'Venin moved toward her. She winced and hissed through her teeth as he wrapped one arm around her shoulders and lifted her from behind her knees. "I'll try to make this as quick and painless as possible," R'Venin murmured, looking down into her face.

"Thank you," Ka'Ala whispered, casting a quick glimpse at Ja'Naam.

R'Venin glanced over to see Ja'Naam staring intently at Ka'Ala. "I promise I won't let anything happen to her," he soothed. "Now, if you'll follow me, I'm sure your brother is anxious to know I've found you."

R'Venin bent his knees, grunting as he jumped into the air. Ka'Ala moaned at the sudden jostling to her ribs. Ja'Naam followed and rose higher above the ground, as R'Venin arced away from the dead sleepbreather hanging from the tree limb.

* * *

"By the way, it's fortunate I found you," R'Venin called to Ja'Naam over the rush of wind in his face as she banked closer to him. He kept his wing beats steady, like a war drum. "You were heading in the wrong direction."

"I have a perfect sense of direction; thank you." Ja'Naam drifted closer and scowled. "We would have made it to the outskirts of Azuralia by nightfall."

"Azuralia is three stars North from here." R'Venin laughed. "You would have ended up in the coastal swamplands if you'd kept going in that direction, and I can prove it."

R'Venin looked down to see Ka'Ala with her eyes closed and a tight-lipped grimace on her face as he caught an updraft and rose into the canopy. Ja'Naam followed until they burst through the topmost leaves. Wispy pink and orange clouds gathered in the distance as the sun drew closer to the horizon. He kept his wing beats steady as he flew westerly.

"The sun is east," he nodded over his shoulder, "The Granite Spires are behind us. The Bluewoods are ahead of us, there. Three stars north is Azuralia. But you were off course by two stars south."

Ja'Naam gazed between the sun and the towering teal and cerulean patches in the distance several times. "Fine!" she exploded. "So, I can't navigate as well as others. Who needs to navigate when they never leave home?"

Ka'Ala's eyes opened. "You've never left home before?"

"I never wanted to," Ja'Naam's voice barely carried over the breeze. "My parents wanted to expose me to Pra'Acheen alchemy. So, I left home for the first time three seasons ago. And I've been there until Ba'Jai brought you to the sanctuary. Oh, there's the wagon!" Ja'Naam suddenly shot downward through the canopy.

"I'll make this as soft as a wishflower," R'Venin smiled as he opened his wings to glide down in slow circles.

"Thank you," Ka'Ala's voice came out tight and strained. "You do have good hearts."

* * *

R'Venin's knees buckled as he landed in the stream next to the wagon. Ba'Jai and Ja'Naam's whispered conversation stopped abruptly as he tilted Ka'Ala out of his arms and onto her own unsteady feet. "There," he said, slightly out of breath. "Easy as molting."

Ja'Naam leaped from beside Ba'Jai in the wagon and floated down next to Ka'Ala. "I'll help her from here," her voice came out subdued.

"I think it'd be best if we both help," R'Venin lifted Ka'Ala's arm around his shoulder as Ja'Naam wrapped an arm around her waist and took her other hand. "I've carried her this far."

"You did carry her this far, and we're grateful." Ja'Naam's voice had a rough edge to it. "But you can rest for a moment, and I'll help Ka'Ala into the wagon."

R'Venin took a half step to the side. "Why don't you want my help?" He narrowed his brow. "I've sworn a life-debt to your brother for sparing me. And that extends to you, as his family. I'm just trying to settle a debt I can never repay. Why won't you let me help?"

"Because you pointed out her sense of misdirection!" Ba'Jai hollered, raising on his elbow, he peered over the wagon's sidewall.

Ja'Naam's mouth dropped. "BA'JAI!" She tried to move toward the wagon, but Ka'Ala wouldn't release her hand.

"It's not R'Venin's fault for what the V'Jeeta did generations ago." Ka'Ala squeezed Ja'Naam's hand, bringing her attention away from Ba'Jai. "Would you punish the earthquake for hurling a single grove into the sea?"

Ja'Naam lowered her eyes, patting Ka'Ala's trembling hand. "I'm sorry."

Ka'Ala lifted her face to look into R'Venin's eyes. "She's protective of me," she smiled. "I know it must seem odd. She and I have only just met."

R'Venin searched the faces of all those gathered at the watering spot. Even Chara'Vaha and his runnerhounds stared back at him with great interest.

"I don't understand." R'Venin's head swam in a fog.

Ka'Ala tilted her head and closed her eyes as if listening to the water quietly trickle under their feet. Several moments went by in near silence, broken only by the rippling current and a runnerhounds' low growl.

"Yes, Windfather," Ka'Ala whispered as she opened her eyes and clutched Ja'Naam's hand with both of hers. "All is well."

"Now, I don't understand," Ba'Jai mumbled.

Ja'Naam exhaled softly through her nose. "Ka'Ala," she asked, tilting her head, "what is it?"

"If both of you will help me to the wagon, I'll explain." Ka'Ala scrunched her nose and gritted her teeth. "I need to lie down. I hurt all over." She took one of R'Venin's outstretched hands and limped toward the wagon. Once there, R'Venin and Ja'Naam lifted her one step at a time until Ba'Jai helped her drop down to the baskets.

"Thank you," Ka'Ala breathed with a heavy sigh.

"Chara'Vaha," Ba'Jai called over his shoulder. "It's too close to nightfall. Let's get going."

The young Pra'Acheen snapped the reins, and the runnerhounds dove into their braces, pulling the wagon through the shallow water and back on to the well-worn path. "We should reach the Midland Bluewoods by dusk." His high tenor voice pierced the cacophony of squeaky wheels. "But we'll have to finish the trip to the Coast after dawn."

R'Venin and Ja'Naam grabbed onto the wagon, lifting themselves and sitting on opposite side rails, each studiously avoiding the other's gaze as the wagon swayed and rocked over the bumpy terrain.

"Very well," Ba'Jai adjusted himself back on his elbow. "We'll secure your lodging, and feed for the hounds, for your trouble."

Chara'Vaha nodded, keeping his eyes on the trail.

Glancing across the three silent passengers beginning to crowd into his makeshift ambulance, Ba'Jai slightly frowned and said, "I'm sorry, R'Venin. I guess there's still a few split feathers between our flocks."

R'Venin dared a peek at Ja'Naam but found her facing the woods with welling eyes. "It's understandable." He turned his gaze to Ba'Jai. "My people have waged war over the Silver Silk for as long as the scrolls have recorded. A thousand thousands have died at our hands, and as many have been killed by the Ch'Hota. It would take an act of the Windfather to end the feud. There's a lot of anger. On both sides."

Ba'Jai nodded as the wagon creaked through the dimming shafts of light. Evening songs whistled above the leaves for what seemed like ages.

"It's not the Silk," Ja'Naam whispered.

"What?" Ba'Jai asked as R'Venin sat taller on the sidewall.

"It's not the Silk," Ja'Naam repeated, clearing her throat. "And it's not the war."

"Then what is it?" R'Venin asked, his voice soft. "Why do you hate me? What can I do to prove myself?"

"I don't hate you," Ja'Naam croaked as a tear spilled over her cheek. "I..."

R'Venin leaped from the wagon, landing in the middle of the path, a wingspan from the trotting runnerhounds. Chara'Vaha cursed, pulling the reins with all his young strength. "I should have run you over!"

Ja'Naam fell into the wagon, landing on top of Ba'Jai. Ka'Ala rolled forward, grunting in pain as Ba'Jai propped himself up, shouting, "What, in Windfather's name, are you doing?"

R'Venin knelt in the dirt, opening his wings to expose the soft parts. "I can no longer fulfill my life-debt," he shouted at the ground. "I ask that you kill me now or let these animals do it for you."

The runnerhounds sniffed their muzzles toward R'Venin, pulling against the harnesses as if knowing their supper awaited them. Chara'Vaha eased his hold on the reins. "My hounds could use a good meal."

"Ja'Naam," R'Venin shouted over the stomping feet and snapping jaws in front of him. "If my death can help heal the pain in your hearts, I give it willingly. I wouldn't be alive now if it hadn't been for your brother. And if my continued existence only hurts someone he loves, then let me die if it'll end the suffering of so many."

Ja'Naam rose to a kneeling position, heat rising in her tear-stained face and clenched teeth. She drew in a breath as if to yell, then suddenly stopped as Ka'Ala reached out and put a hand under her chin. "That's not Windfather's will, Ja'Naam," Ka'Ala soothed. "He has a plan for R'Venin, but it's not to die today."

Ja'Naam hunched forward, burying her face into Ka'Ala's arms. Her body shook with muffled cries as Ka'Ala wrapped her wings around Ja'Naam like a cocoon and wept with her. Ba'Jai scooted across the baskets to sit next to Ka'Ala and created another layer around the sobbing women.

Ba'Jai looked over at a bewildered R'Venin still kneeling on the ground while the runnerhounds growled and sniffed the air around him. After making eye contact, Ba'Jai waved R'Venin over to the wagon on Ja'Naam's left side. While he neared, his footsteps slowed and Ja'Naam's wailing rose in volume. The triple layers of feathers opened like a spring flower at his approach. Like the central petal to be unveiled, Ja'Naam leaned away from Ka'Ala and straightened her back.

She wiped the trails of moisture from her cheeks, sniffling and taking several deep breaths. With her eyes still lowered, she cleared her throat like a frightened child sneaking into her parents' nest.

"He has good hearts." Ka'Ala again lifted Ja'Naam's chin, staring into her eyes with her piercing gaze. "Trust the Windfather with yours."

Ba'Jai knuckled a tear from his eye as Ja'Naam's lip quivered. "R'Venin." she breathed. "Please forgive me for the distrust and hatred I've shown you. I can do better." She opened her wing and turned it over while keeping her eyes closed as if in meditation.

R'Venin looked from face to face. Ba'Jai's seemed intent on watching his sister's every micro-expression as she kept her wing outstretched.

Can a people really change their hearts so quickly?

Ka'Ala's eyes burrowed into R'Venin's with a slight nod. "The Windfather has a plan and the means to carry it out."

R'Venin slowly unfolded his wing, letting it open toward Ja'Naam's, and gently brushed his tip along the trailing feathers of her wing before tucking it back behind him.

Ba'Jai smiled, massaging Ja'Naam's shoulder as the tiniest of smiles crossed her lips, and her head bowed slightly. "Thank you, R'Venin," she whispered, turning her head to look at his face, allowing her smile to expand.

"Thank you, Lady Ja'Naam, for..." R'Venin bowed his head then stepped back from the wagon, clearing his throat. "Well, for not letting those hounds eat me."

"Lady Ja'Naam," Ja'Naam mused. "I like that."

"I doubt you would have tasted good to them," Ba'Jai chuckled. "You're probably a little too tender, being a spoiled little prince and all. Too fatty for the hounds. They'd be sluggish for the rest of the trip, and then we'd never make it the Midlands before dark."

Ja'Naam laughed outright, while Ka'Ala clutched her side, trying not to giggle. "We'd better keep moving then." Ja'Naam stood, causing the wagon to tilt. "I think we've kept Chara'Vaha from his delivery long enough. R'Venin and I will fly ahead to secure food and lodgings for the night, and so we don't weigh down the wagon any further. We'll meet you along the trail once everything's in order. Agreed?"

"Agreed," Ba'Jai, Ka'Ala, and R'Venin said in unison.

"It's about damn time," Chara'Vaha muttered under his breath and snapped the reins hard. The hounds reared up slightly and then moved into a quick trot down the darkening path.

Ja'Naam opened her wings as the wagon pulled out from under her feet. She landed on the ground next to R'Venin, still looking dazed, and raised her arm toward the disappearing coach. "Will you lead the way?" She asked softly.

"Of course, Lady Ja'Naam," R'Venin's mouth opened into a grin as he bowed at the waist with a grandiose arm gesture. "If you'll follow me, please."

She nodded, then launched into the air before R'Venin could stand upright. "Try and keep up this time," she laughed as she flapped hard, rising between the branches.

R'Venin ran a few steps down the trail before jumping up, flapping hard to catch up with the wagon. Ba'Jai and Ka'Ala watched with curious eyes as he landed on the tail and began rummaging between the baskets.

"Did you forget something?" Ba'Jai asked as R'Venin opened up his pack, digging through the various pieces of black armor.

R'Venin withdrew a pair of jeweled gauntlets. "We'll need something to trade for lodging and food," he answered. The sun-warmed carbon-feather weave made his skin tingle as he slid his hands inside the gloves.

"We truly appreciate that," Ba'Jai nodded, pointing at the jewels. "But I think that's more than enough to pay for a few rooms and a stable."

"It's to pay for a healer as well," R'Venin tightened the gauntlets. "For both of you."

"Thank you, R'Venin," Ka'Ala said.

"Yes," Ba'Jai added. "Thank you. But Kar'Nevala was unable to repair my wing, and my sister says she's the best healer at the sanctuary. I doubt anyone else will have better luck."

"I just want to help," R'Venin locked eyes with Ba'Jai, "In any way I can. We'll be back soon. Now, I need to catch up with your sister." Without another word, R'Venin launched into the air in the direction Ja'Naam headed.

"You'd better hurry," Ba'Jai called after him. "She might already be lost again."

In the quiet above the canopy, as R'Venin raced to catch up with Ja'Naam, the waning sun caused the shadows of flora and fauna below to reach for each other, overlap, and hold hands as they inched toward twilight.

Chapter Twelve

Western Crossroads

R'Venin and Ja'Naam flew in silence above the canopy with the waning sunlight behind them. Remnants of warm updrafts filled their noses with scents of leaves, flowers, and the occasional fecal marker of a territorial carnivore. After several leagues of flight, the trail below them transitioned from a dirt path wide enough for a single cart to a cobblestone road big enough to allow three or four coaches to pass by.

Fire crystals glimmered in the distance, calling weary travelers to a haven from the forests' nocturnal hunters. Lanterns, varying in size from minuscule to immense, flickered their welcoming glow from the grove of Bluewood towering above the canopy. Even from far away, R'Venin spied the platforms, elevated walkways, and perches that signaled the extensive village's growth.

As they approached, the forest died at a timber wall just shorter than the canopy. R'Venin's eyes followed the barrier as it encircled the village, serpentine around the central grove. Ch'Hota guardsmen, positioned every fifty wingspans near a raised platform, peered into the forest or chatted in small groups with each other.

A guardsman manning a platform above a pair of massive wooden gates spotted R'Venin and Ja'Naam. He signaled them with his spear to a sign written in the common tongue above the giant doors.

Welcome to the Western Crossroads
ENTRY INSPECTION REQUIRED

Another gesture from the guardsman ordered them to descend to the ground where a mob of carts, wagons, and pedestrians gathered into a queue. Ja'Naam waved back, nodding her head.

"We have to go through the gates," She called over the wind. "They'll imprison us if we try to sneak past the wall."

"We treat travelers the same way in the Granite Spires," R'Venin shouted. "At worst, suspected spies are killed. Anyone who bypasses our borders without permission is exiled to the Northern Deserts and left to fend for themselves."

"The Ch'Hota aren't so harsh," Ja'Naam stared him down.

R'Venin held her gaze. "That's why most V'Jeeta see you as weak and deserving of extermination."

Ja'Naam looked at R'Venin with contemplative eyes. "I suppose that's one way to see it." She said, rolling onto her back and diving for the ground.

R'Venin followed her, circling downward as Ja'Naam billowed her wings to land. They touched down at the back of the queue to the anxious stares from the Ch'Hota and Pra'Acheen moving toward the entrance. A group of ten Ch'Hota dressed in red-stained tunics and carrying pitchforks huddled closer to a small caravan. Their wagons, weighed down by a thousand ears of Crimson Maize and hundreds of Silver Silk bundles, creaked as they jostled with every handspan forward.

Small Ch'Hota children stared as if their worst nightmare had materialized right in front of them. Vendors pulled the flaps of their carts closed. Wagon drivers sat taller in their seats. Pra'Acheen families huddled a little closer together while giving him pleasant smiles. A lone V'Jeeta woman, wearing a hooded robe and carrying a simple bag seemed to be the only member of the multitude that didn't cringe away from R'Venin's presence.

"It's no surprise they're all staring at me," R'Venin muttered as the line inched forward. "They're wondering if I'm going to draw a blade and kill them all."

Ja'Naam stepped forward, keeping pace with the creeping mass, and leaned in to whisper. "I suspect so. But maybe it's your gauntlets," she tapped a nail on his wrist. "It does make you look more like a warrior than the V'Jeeta merchants and workers who travel our lands. Some may even just wonder how much they're worth."

R'Venin blushed, trying in vain to pull his tunic's sleeves over the sparkling gloves. He glanced over his shoulder as the space between himself and the Ch'Hota behind him grew a talon's width with each step toward the gate.

"Take her, for example," Ja'Naam pointed to the V'Jeeta woman as she just reached the inspection gate. "No one stares at her, nor cowers. Why do *you* think that is?"

"It's commonly known that V'Jeeta women are more docile," R'Venin cringed inwardly as his father's words escaped his lips. "What I mean is, they're not known as warriors, or violent at all for that matter. No one fears what can't hurt you."

R'Venin watched the Ch'Hota guards' inspection of the V'Jeeta woman from five wingspans away. The woman's words never reached his ears, but even their unintelligible voices seemed to be approved by the crowd. The lead guardsman tore the bag off her shoulders with a rough jerk, tossing it to another who dumped the contents onto the ground. A female guardsman put her hands up and down the V'Jeeta's body then gave the leader a surly shake of her head.

Several people in the crowd craned their necks to get a better angle, muttering to each other and nodding their heads. Some covered their eyes or looked away. Some whispered into their children's ears, held up for a clear view.

"It would seem that some fear *any* reminder of an enemy," Ja'Naam whispered, the words catching in her throat. "No matter how innocent and harmless others might see them."

The V'Jeeta woman's head dropped after the lead guard waved her through, and the mob moved toward the gates.

Step by step, the crowd divided into three single files as a single guardsman, standing several paces in front of the entrance, directed the incoming traffic. Carts and wagons veered toward a large portal. People on foot sifted to one of four smaller entries. The guard smiled at Ja'Naam, waving her to the queue at his back, then halted R'Venin while he motioned a column of Pra'Acheen to his right. A moment later, the guard thumbed over his shoulder, letting R'Venin get in line three people behind Ja'Naam.

Soon enough, she reached the front and had a brief exchange with the lead guardsman. He waved her through with a sly grin and salute to his helmet. His eyes followed Ja'Naam past the inner gates, admiring the gentle sway of her wingtips, until she came upon the V'Jeeta woman kneeling on the ground. Ja'Naam stopped and appeared to talk to the woman, then knelt beside her and started reaching into a sewer grate.

When R'Venin reached the inspection point, all the guards' eyes narrowed. Several backs straightened as spears and sword handles became wrapped with whitening knuckles. "State your business," the lead guardsman snapped. He eyed R'Venin tips to talons, locking onto his gauntlets for a second too long.

"I'm here with the woman that just passed through." R'Venin pointed to Ja'Naam on the other side of the gates, "and her brother. He and another in our group are injured. We've flown ahead to secure lodging for the night."

The guard sneered. "You're with her, are you? Yes, she mentioned traveling with injured friends." He jerked his head over his shoulder. "The Windfather must favor you. You must be his favorite filth."

The surrounding guards all laughed as R'Venin glanced around, yet all the time keeping the leader in his line of vision.

I'd never survive if they attacked.

"Where did you get those fancy gauntlets?" His eyes locked onto R'Venin's wrists with hungry eyes.

"Family heirloom," R'Venin tugged at his sleeves. "I'm going to trade or sell them to get food and care for my friends."

The guard rubbed his chin and tapped an arrhythmic pattern on his helmet's strap. "I think you should donate one of your rubies. To support our protective detail, of course."

The crowd snickered and whispered behind their hands.

No one else had to 'donate' to the cause. But, if this is how it has to be.

R'Venin picked at a thumb-sized stone on his left gauntlet until it pried loose from the mounting. "In support of those who risk their lives," he murmured as he dropped the jewel into the lead guard's open palm. The other guards showed gleeful smiles, greedy eyes, and a couple even patted one another on the back. "Now, may I pass?"

"Any friend of the Guard is welcome at Crossroads," the lead guard said, stepping aside with a flourish. "Do enjoy your stay, and please... come again."

R'Venin passed through the raucous laughter of guards while the crowd of travelers snickered behind his back. When he reached Ja'Naam and the V'Jeeta woman, he got down on one knee.

"Finally made it past the gate, I see," Ja'Naam grunted as she squeezed her arm through the tiny openings in the grate. "This is Kod'Hee of the Seventh Plain."

R'Venin turned and found Kod'Hee with her head bowed and

arms across her chest. Her tattered wings open and upturned. "I know who you are, High Prince R'Venin," Kod'Hee said in barely a whisper.

R'Venin looked around but saw no one within earshot. "The High Prince died in battle," He reached out and gently pulled her wings in. "I'm just a simple V'Jeeta now. Do you understand?"

"I know what it is to fall from grace myself," Kod'Hee nodded. "Many seasons ago, long before you were born, I was one of your father's concubine's in the First Tower——at least until I could no longer pouch an egg. Then he beat me and cast me out like a moldy worm. Now, I'm unwelcome no matter where I go."

R'Venin's hearts ached.

Did Father ever beat Mother?

"What are you searching for?" he asked.

"The guards decided they needed to do a 'more rigorous inspection' of Kod'Hee's pack," Ja'Naam huffed. "And they dumped all her belongings, including her money purse, over the grate. Now, except for a few coppers that bounced onto the stones, the coins are all lost."

"It was all I had," Kod'Hee wept as she kept trying to push her spindly arms further through the grate. "And I have nothing else to trade, and I need to buy silk or I'll..."

R'Venin glanced at Kod'Hee's white-tipped talons. "You have White Claw." R'Venin caught sight of Ja'Naam's misty eyes.

"Rare among V'Jeeta women," Kod'Hee's voice cracked. "And..."

"And painful," R'Venin finished. "You can't fly because your wings are so brittle."

Kod'Hee sat back on her heels and nodded, fumbling with her empty coin purse as tears dropped from her eyes, splashing in the dirt.

R'Venin looked down at the empty bag.

It's the least I can do.

He lifted his left gauntlet, again clawing at the jewels until he pulled the twelve smallest gems away. "Open your purse," he said softly. Kod'Hee's eyes widened like the moons, blurred with the tears cascading down her shocked face. "For services rendered to the queen."

"Your majesty," she croaked as R'Venin dropped the stones into the dirty linen sack. She pulled his hand to her face, kissing each knuckle three times. "Oh, thank you. May P'Phet smile upon you. Forever."

R'Venin nodded, leaned over, and kissed her forehead. "Fair weather."

"Fair weather," Kod'Hee cried as R'Venin stood and helped Ja'Naam from the ground. "Thank you!"

* * *

R'Venin, sullen and lost in thought, followed Ja'Naam absentmindedly through the village streets. At some point, he found himself in front of a large stable at the base of a towering Bluewood. A hand-painted sign with an ivory background and fuchsia lettering by the barn doors read: Welcome to the Warbler's Roost.

"This should be big enough for Chara'Vaha's wagon and team." Ja'Naam's bright voice brought R'Venin out of his stupor.

"Should be. It looks like there are several empty stalls," R'Venin peered into the stable, then glanced into the branches above, judging the housing structure. "But I hope that's larger than it looks on the outside."

"Follow me," Ja'Naam jumped first, flapping hard and zig-zagging left and right as she built altitude. R'Venin followed until they reached the branches carrying the load of a wooden walkway. An opening tall enough for R'Venin to walk though with extra headroom stood between two boughs. A braided grass curtain of pinks and purples blocked their view of the interior, but the warm glow of fire crystals and sunstones poured between the cracks in the weave. A roar of laughter, the scent of strong liquors, the shuffling of furniture on wooden floors, and the lilt of a warbling soprano filtered through the intricately painted tapestry. Another sign, matching the colors below, hung above the lintel. "Are you sure you want to stay *here*?" R'Venin coughed at the fumes that filled his nose as Ja'Naam parted the curtain.

"Are you judging this place by its appearance?" Ja'Naam winked. "I thought we were getting past that." She crossed the threshold and disappeared behind the parted veil.

I'm not getting caught out here on my own.

R'Venin lunged in after her, dividing the curtains with his hands and stepping into a two-story atrium. Ja'Naam strolled between groups of customers sitting on the rough-sawn floorboards around two dozen low tables; each had a clay pitcher in the center and shared trays of fruits, nuts, and vegetables. The scent of strong liquors and musky perfume filled his nasal slits. A few glances darted his way, though most ignored the new arrivals.

Men and women, mostly Ch'Hota—with a smattering of Pra'Acheen and V'Jeeta—lined the tables. They clinked glasses, passed plates of food, and laughed. A stout Ch'Hota woman in flowing lavender silks sang to the crowd as a piper, a harpist, and a drummer accompanied her trilling melodies in an alcove to his left. Her face showed signs of age, but her voice rang out sweet and clear.

Across the room, standing in front of a chest-high countertop, Ja'Naam waved him over. R'Venin crossed the room, weaving between the raucous groups of guests. Ja'Naam absentmindedly drummed her claws on the wooden surface as her gaze seemed fixed on the singer. R'Venin leaned back against the partition and listened.

The singer's arms floated through the air as if dancing underwater. Her rippling silks followed her hands as if they were living swatches of air. The room bubbled with the cheerful melody as her voice raised and lowered, in volume and pitch, in harmony with the musicians. The singer made eye contact with Ja'Naam, and her smile brightened as she hit a high note and waved her hand with a slight nod. Ja'Naam waved back, bouncing on the balls of her feet with childlike adoration.

"You know her?" R'Venin had to raise his voice to hear himself as the singer finished her performance.

Ja'Naam joined the applause as the room erupted into clapping, shouts, and whistles. "That's Sher'Esh Ga'Ayak. She's my great-aunt!"

"That's Sher'Esh Ga'Ayak?" R'Venin's mouth dropped. "She's a legend! I heard her sing when I was a boy. I thought she died."

"Legend's never die!" Ja'Naam laughed. She whistled through her fingers as Sher'Esh took another bow and sauntered off the stage.

"So, we'll get the roosts for free, then?" R'Venin joined in the applause.

"HA!" Ja'Naam burst. "That'd be a first! Don't misunderstand. She's the sweetest woman I know, but she struggles to keep this place open just to have a private venue."

Sher'Esh moved through the crowd, stopping as various guests rose to take a moment to gush over her performance. Once the cheering died down, the last few customers sat back on the floor and returned to their meals.

"Ja'Naam, my sweet, sweet child," Sher'Esh gushed as she pulled Ja'Naam into a crushing hug. "I haven't seen you in five seasons. What brings you so far from home?"

Ja'Naam laughed, pulling away and letting Sher'Esh hold her hands. "I've been studying alchemy at the sanctuary of the Three Mothers with a Pra'Acheen master for the past three seasons. Ba'Jai wandered into the sanctuary, injured. We're on our way home to Bluewood Cove." She gestured to R'Venin. "This is R'Venin of the First Tower.

Sher'Esh's eyes lit up as her hands shot into the air. "Royalty!" she shouted.

"Shh!" Ja'Naam quickly pulled down her great-aunt's hands.

"What's the matter, child?" Sher'Esh seemed flustered. "I've performed for the last nine Quorums of Elders. I would have performed for the V'Jeeta royal court if they'd only asked me. But, as you know, their taste in music is a little less sophisticated than ours. No offense, your highness. But why shouldn't I advertise that a member of the V'Jeeta Royal family graced my little establishment?"

"Because my people believe I died in battle," R'Venin leaned in with pleading eyes. "And I don't want my father to think otherwise. He'd burn every village from here to Azuralia to find and bring me home. And I don't want to go home."

"R'Venin was mortally wounded in the battle over the central plains," Ja'Naam rested a hand on R'Venin's shoulder, pushing him away from Sher'Esh's face. "And Ba'Jai carried R'Venin to the sanctuary for treatment."

Sher'Esh reached out and pulled R'Venin into a crushing embrace. "Prince R'Venin," she whispered fiercely in his ear. "It's a pleasure to meet you." She pulled away, turning on the spot and casting her eyes around the room. "But where is Ba'Jai?"

"Ba'Jai lost a wing. It's a three-sun story," Ja'Naam waved her hands in Sher'Esh's face as her mouth gaped open. "He's on his way here in a wagon with a new friend. We need a few nests for the night, a stall for a pair of runnerhounds, and the best healer in the village."

"Of course, of course!" Sher'Esh said with a flourish as she gamboled behind the counter. "That'll be three silvers. How will you be paying?"

R'Venin removed the remaining jewels from his left gauntlet, the heft of the weight becoming noticeably lighter as each gem released its grip. He poured the glittering red stones into the dull clay bowl Sher'Esh had lifted from below the counter. They made a tinkling sound as each fell from his palm.

Sher'Esh's eyes misted, reflecting the fire crystal's glowing down on the treasure. "That's too much. These must be worth ten gold." She removed the largest stone from the bowl.

R'Venin stayed her hand and spoke quietly. "Your best roosts. A good meal for five. The best stall and feed for two weary hounds. Call for the best healer to come immediately. And..." he leaned in closer, "I was never here."

Sher'Esh nodded, picked up the bowl, and tipped the bowl's contents into the slot of a thick metal plate. Twisting back, she returned the bowl under the counter, pulling a scratchplate—a square wooden tray, two feathers thick around the edges, filled with soft clay—and clay bottle from below and set it on the counter.

Mother's was gilded. She taught me to write on it.

Sher'Esh scratched out a one-night boarding contract, then pushed the tray to R'Venin. "Your highness," she whispered, bouncing on her feet as her claws tapped on the counter like rain. "Will you scratch your name?"

R'Venin looked to Ja'Naam, then back, leaning forward. "Can't you give us the roosts without the contract?"

"I'm sorry," she breathed. She put a hand to her chest as her eyes darted around the room. "If the administrators ever found out, I'd be selected for examination. I'd lose my privilege. I can't let out the roosts without proper documentation."

"I can't leave a trail." He hissed across the counter. "Can't you help us? For the sake of your family?"

"When it comes to this place, I have no family." She said, shaking her head. "This isn't just a place for food, drink, and song. It's my home. I have only myself to keep me off the ground."

"Responsibility travels upwind," R'Venin sighed.

The strongest of the nest fend for the weakest.

"Very well." R'Venin's chin fell to his chest. "I'll—."

Ja'Naam reached out, putting a hand on R'Venin's shoulder and taking Sher'Esh's hand. "I'll sign the contract. It's no trouble." She said, squeezing tight and looking between them. "You won't leave a record, and you won't lose your home."

R'Venin nodded. "Thank you." He croaked. "I may owe you a spirit oath as well."

Ja'Naam pulled her hand away. "That won't be necessary," she said, reaching for the slate and scratching out her name. She then pulled a small tuft from her wing and pushed it into the clay.

Sher'Esh poured a tangy liquid from the bottle, using a rag to wipe it across the entire surface. Reaching under the counter, she retrieved a sheaf of parchment and set it on the counter. Then, overturning the scratchplate, Sher'Esh held it down on the page, counting to five under her breath. Once done, she peeled the sheet from the plate and held it over a nearby fire crystal. The blank page became mostly black as the heat turned the liquid to ink, revealing the inverted impressions.

She then slid the parchment into a stack, smoothed out the scratches in the clay, and put all the implements back under the counter. Turning back to the wall, she pulled three ornate silver keys from the top row of wooden pegs,

"I only have three nests left," she held the keys out to R'Venin. "But they're my best. Some of you may have to share." She gave Ja'Naam a wink.

"Aunt Sher'Esh," Ja'Naam hissed, her face glowing like the sunset. She took the keys from R'Venin's still open palm and pointed a taloned finger into his wide-eyed glance. "Not going to happen."

"Thank you for the rooms, Madam," R'Venin blinked his eyes back into focus.

"We'll be back soon," Ja'Naam said, reaching across the counter to embrace Sher'Esh again. "I promised Ba'Jai we'd meet him along the trail before he reached the village."

"Your meals will be waiting in your chambers," Sher'Esh gasped for breath as she leaned across the counter. "And I'll have my chambermaid, Na'Ukar, fetch the healer before your return. Show the guards your keys, and you won't have any trouble getting back through the gates. Dham'Akee's known to extort tribute from foreigners. But as my guests, he'll treat you right, or he won't get another song for ten moons."

Chapter Thirteen

The Whispering Woods

"Ugh!" Ka'Ala groaned as the wagon bounced over another exposed root along the trail. She sucked air through gritted teeth, clutching her side.

"Sorry," Chara'Vaha snapped the reins, pushing his hounds into a trot. "That's the last one. I see the road up ahead. The ride will be smoother now."

"Here," Ba'Jai handed Ka'Ala a leather water bladder. "Have a drink. There's not much left, but we'll get more once we reach the village."

Ka'Ala took the pouch and poured the remaining contents into her mouth. "Thank you," she groaned, setting the flattened bag on a basket as she stared at Ba'Jai's feet.

He shows me kindness I've not received in many seasons. Windfather has blessed me.

"So," Ba'Jai sat up, propped on one arm as he opened his remaining wing, balancing himself. "There's something between you and my sister. She's generous and friendly to all, but she's protective of you in a way she reserves for family. The way she treated R'Venin? I've never seen her behave like that before. Not even to the V'Jeeta in the

Bluewoods."

"She grieves for the loss of my flock," Ka'Ala interrupted. "She mourns the loss of a people that will soon be extinct."

"What flock?" Ba'Jai leaned forward. "I assumed, because of your coloring, that you are Ch'Hota."

"No," she replied after a moment, "I'm not Ch'Hota. My people were once enslaved by the V'Jeeta, but The Windfather freed us and carried us back home. Then a terrible plague swept through our lands and wiped us all out. All but me. As far as I know, I'm the last Gir'Agit."

"You're jesting," Ba'Jai laughed. "Those are fireside tales and twilight rumors."

Ka'Ala's eyes flitted up and back in the pause between her beating hearts. She swallowed hard, glancing back along the path, her face in full shadow. Dead leaves and dried blades of grass swirled in the eddies behind the wagon. The runnerhounds' steady canter beat a rhythm like a pair of massive door knockers.

She turned back toward Ba'Jai, her eyes looking like twin slivers of moonlight. She looked up to meet his piercing gaze.

"You're serious." He tilted his head slightly as his lips spread into a warm smile. "Can you tell me about your flock?"

I want to show him. They've been so kind to me.

A miniature whirlwind blew across the path and rested in the wagon for a moment, carrying Ba'Jai's scent to her. His heartsong rose in the breeze, and the smell of a thousand evening summer flights drifted from his feathers and taunted her senses.

The Windfather whispered. *You may share what you wish. But you are not to be his.*

The spinning air dissipated as quickly as it arrived, leaving Ka'Ala alone with the odor of dirt and runnerhound sweat.

"You've heard of shadowdancers and leafcoats?" Ka'Ala gave a sad smile and took a breath. "The Fire-Faces? The Walking Vines? The

Shadow Eaters?"

"Of course," Ba'Jai's face broke into a wide grin. "Those are stories for hatchlings to keep them off the ground until they can fly on their own. Why? Are you a leafcoat? Are you going to sneak into my roost at the high moon and pluck me while I sleep?"

"Only if the legends were true," Ka'Ala laughed, wincing as she clutched her side. "We're color changers. Camouflagers. We can blend in with our surroundings. Becoming virtually invisible."

"You can't hood me that easily," Ba'Jai's eyes narrowed, though his grin widened. "Prove it."

Ka'Ala nodded with a mischievous smile and laid down, keeping an arm between her rib cage and the baskets. She burrowed between the bushels and spread her wings like a blanket.

Ba'Jai's brow twisted with confusion. "This is your invisibility trick? Crouching into a ball like a frightened rockskipper?"

Ka'Ala held her breath, concentrating against the pain. Her feathers rippled and shimmered, then turned into splotchy shades of cedar, walnut, and umber, until she looked like someone dumped a misshapen pile of dirt and leaves into the wagon's bed.

"By the Sacred Tree," Ba'Jai whispered. "I don't believe what I'm seeing."

The mound opened up like a slow-moving eruption as Ka'Ala struggled to sit up again, changing color to her natural pale and ink. "This is what I really look like. It takes more effort when I'm weak," she huffed between labored breaths. "Normally, I can camouflage for many songs. It came in handy when I had to be among other travelers. I could pretend to be one of them, a nameless face blending in among the multitude."

"Yes," Ba'Jai sat with his chin against his chest. "Yes, I can see where that would be useful. But why hide? Why not just let others see you for who you are?"

Ka'Ala looked down as she folded her hands in her lap. "Because The Windfather forbade me from revealing myself," she sighed. "Until now." She looked up and locked eyes with Ba'Jai.

He simply nodded his head. "Windfather's decrees are always right."

Ka'Ala looked up over Ba'Jai's shoulder to see Chara'Vaha twisted in his seat with wide eyes staring back at them. "You mustn't tell anyone," her eyes widened like full moons. The youth just gawked into the wagon's bed; his eyes darted between Ka'Ala and Ba'Jai.

What would happen if someone with ill-intent discovered my secret?

Be still daughter, Windfather breathed, *And listen to his hearts.*

Chara'Vaha's face softened, returning to the dull rest of the disinterested. "Who would I tell?" he shrugged and gave the reins a firm snap. "At best, no one would believe me. At worst, I'd get plucked and banished to Cracked Shell Island."

"Thank you, Chara'Vaha," Ka'Ala smiled, turning her attention back to Ba'Jai and shifting her colors to match his. His lips pursed as he examined Ka'Ala's wings with narrowed eyes. She ruffled her wings, picking slivers of weave from the damaged one. "What is it?"

"That shape you turned into," Ba'Jai rested his arm on one raised knee, his pointing fingers swaying with the wagon's motion. "The coloring. I could swear I've seen something like that before. But I can't place it."

Confession restores the soul and cleanses the air.

"Ja'Naam didn't find me first," Ka'Ala stopped preening and folded her wings. "The Windfather led me to you, to all of you, before I needed her to rescue me."

Ba'Jai's head bobbed as the wagon jolted from the forest trail onto the rough-hewn stones. "Continue," he said softly, holding out his open palm. "Please."

The wagon's noise grew ten-fold as it lumbered across the

cobblestone road. Ba'Jai's last words seem to carry no further than Ka'Ala's ears. She glanced over Ba'Jai's shoulder to see the Pra'Acheen struggling to keep the runnerhounds from pulling into a full run.

I hope Chara'Vaha can't hear this part.

"I was in the tree where you lost your wing, saving R'Venin. I watched you fight off that wild runnerhound." Ka'Ala squirmed as she spoke. "Windfather told me to stay hidden from the world, and I was going to let the beast have you. But He told me to help you. He told me to hide R'Venin from the hound and leave my supplies for you."

Ba'Jai snapped his fingers. "That's where those packs came from? I thought they'd fallen off him, somehow hidden under his armor."

"No," she smiled. "I left all my belongings there and was told to follow you. You were easy to track since you were so distracted from carrying R'Venin. I was also outside the old Pra'Acheen's balcony when you told R'Venin the story of finding him in the Crimson Maize field. And I heard your heartsongs."

"Our heartsongs?" Ba'Jai's eyebrows scrunched.

Ka'Ala nodded. "Each heart has its own song, it's own melody. My people know how to listen to them. It helps us see the truth around us, and I heard your song harmonize with R'Venin's. Windfather whispered to me, and He desires you to be brothers. A bond deeper than his life-debt."

Ba'Jai sat back, staring deep into the forest. "I suppose I'm not entirely surprised."

The wagon creaked and groaned for many moments before Chara'Vaha pulled the team back into a slow walk. The sound of other carts and travelers grew as the sun winked its last rays beyond the mountains. "We're here," Chara'Vaha called over his shoulder. "I can see your friends coming out now."

Ba'Jai twisted around as Ka'Ala got on her knees, both waving toward the gates. R'Venin and Ja'Naam passed through the portal two hundred wingspans away and leaped into the air, flapping hard to close the distance.

"Are you going to tell them?" Ba'Jai turned back.

Ka'Ala's stomach lurched as if she'd eaten rotten fruit. *The time will come*, Windfather breathed in her ear.

"Not yet," she answered. "The Windfather will let me know when the time is right."

"Until then," Ba'Jai leaned closer and placed his hand on Ka'Ala's. "I'll keep your secret."

Ka'Ala removed one of her hands and sandwiched Ba'Jai's. A sweet melody, like musical honeyvine, wove through the air. As she looked into his face, she saw the glimmer of a romantic thought tugging at the corner of his mouth.

You are not to be his, The Windfather echoed.

"Thank you, Ba'Jai," she patted his hand, smiling sadly. "You have good hearts."

The flutter of backflapping brought their attention to the wagon's side where R'Venin and Ja'Naam landed. Ba'Jai released his grip on Ka'Ala's hands, turning to lean over the side. "Hello, sister. How's Aunt Sher'Esh?" he beamed down at Ja'Naam as the wagon lurched forward. "Still basking in the glow?"

Ja'Naam walked alongside, followed by R'Venin. "She's the same. How was your ride? Did you nap the whole way?"

"Yeah," Ba'Jai gave Ka'Ala a knowing glance. "I just woke up as the wagon bumped into the road. Were you able to get us some roosts?"

"Only three," R'Venin held up the silver keys in his left hand, his gauntlet glaringly emptied of its jewels. "Sher'Esh says we'll have to share."

Chara'Vaha's head swiveled around. "I'm not comfortable sleeping beside anyone who's not family," he said, glaring into each face. "I'd rather sleep in the barn."

"Ka'Ala and I will share. Ba'Jai and R'Venin will share," Ja'Naam answered, holding a key out to the youth. "And you can have the third all to yourself."

Chara'Vaha took the key, his face reddening like a sundown. "Thank you," he mumbled.

"You're welcome," Ja'Naam smiled. "But the first thing we need to do is get Ka'Ala to a healer. And then we'll feast and sleep. It's still a long way home."

Chapter Fourteen

Gha'Barahat

Ka'Ala gnashed her teeth as Chara'Vaha drove his wagon through the giant wooden doors of Sher'Esh's stable. R'Venin and Ja'Naam stood on either side. The cart shuddered as it bounced over the stone threshold and sloped down into a massive central corral. Ten wingspans across and five high, the heavy timber framing rose to a planked ceiling. Sprinklings of dust fell from overhead as the sound of muffled warbling penetrated the slats. Fire crystal sconces hung from each post around the keyhole-shaped space. Ten stalls opened into the center, with a washdown bay on one side of the ramp. Across from the washdown, a smaller opening led into a dark chamber with a sign reading "Bath House" over the lintel.

"Thank you, Windfather," Ka'Ala closed her eyes and exhaled heavily through her nose. "For bringing us to safety. But now, I'm ready to get out of this wagon."

"Aunt Sher'Esh must be doing well," Ba'Jai pointed to the business sign. "She's repainted the upper loft. Again. It had sundown colors last time."

R'Venin pulled his pack from the wagon bed and stepped away from the doors, looking up at the bright purples and pinks fading in the torchlight.

Ja'Naam moved around the wagon as it cleared the opening and walked along Ka'Ala's side. "Definitely more noticeable from the city gates, though," she said, stepping up on the side rail and offered Ka'Ala her hand.

"As much as it's going to hurt," Ka'Ala gripped tightly as the wagon lolled side to side over the uneven stone floor. "I'm looking forward to getting back on my feet and walking around."

Ka'Ala's head lifted as the sound of hushed voices slithered through the doors. The stream of pedestrians outside the stable skirted to the thoroughfare's other side as if R'Venin were a massive stone. A thousand eyes stared at his back as if he held a pair of flaming broadswords in his hands instead of the misshapen homespun sack. He dropped his pack to the side, letting the clatter echo across the cobblestone.

Ba'Jai grinned as the people scattered from the noise like ripples across a morning lake. "Give Ka'Ala a hand, R'Venin," he waved R'Venin into the stables, bracing himself on the wagon's side. "Perhaps people will be less afraid if they see you helping the helpless."

R'Venin nodded, leaving his pack on the ground, and flew above the short ramp to where the wagon came to a halt. Chara'Vaha set the brake lever and hopped off his seat, drifting to a bubbling fountain where he dipped his head into the shallow basin. "That should last me another few days," he mumbled to himself as he grabbed a yellow gourd from a nearby shelf, scooped up some water, and carried it to his team.

The hounds gulped and slurped the water, draining the gourd in seconds. Patting their heads, Chara'Vaha smiled and returned to the trough for more.

R'Venin came around to Ka'Ala's side of the wagon and got up on the rail, brushing wings with Ja'Naam. "Think you can trust me enough to get her out of the wagon?" A half-smile played on his lips as he scooped Ka'Ala under her legs and arms while she still gripped Ja'Naam's hand.

Ja'Naam's mouth turned up slightly at the corners. "I think I can trust you that far."

Ka'Ala's hearts burned as their symphony returned in her mind, even more tenderly than before. A tear escaped before she had a chance to stop it from falling.

Oh, to find eternal harmony for myself. Ja'Naam is so blessed.

"Ka'Ala," Ja'Naam gasped, letting go of her hand. "I'm so sorry. I didn't mean to hurt you."

Ka'Ala reached out for Ja'Naam's retreating hand, gripping it tight again. "It wasn't you."

"Then it was me," R'Venin froze. "I must have moved you too fast."

"It wasn't either of you," Ka'Ala looked into R'Venin's face. "It wasn't pain. It was something else."

R'Venin cocked his head and then stepped off the side rail and onto the stone. "What was it then?" he asked, setting Ka'Ala slowly on her feet.

Ka'Ala let her hand glide across R'Venin's shoulders as Ja'Naam led her other hand to the wagon's side. Her eyes darted for a moment to R'Venin as she leaned in. "I'll tell you later," she whispered to Ja'Naam. "When you're ready to hear."

The wagon rocked as Ba'Jai rolled over the side, grabbing the sidewall as his feet hit the ground. "Let's get Ka'Ala to the healer," he smirked. "Then you two can giggle to your hearts' content."

Ja'Naam spun on her heel and opened her mouth to speak.

"Does this belong to you?" a dainty voice called from the doorway.

The foursome turned in unison. An adolescent female stood in the steady lamplight, her shadow climbing the facade across the street.

She had gold and pine-colored plumage, similar to a Ch'Hota, but her emerald eyes glistened like a V'Jeeta. She wore a rough cloth lavender tunic with a dirty white apron tied at her waist.

"Is she a half-flock?" Ka'Ala whispered in Ja'Naam's ear. "I've never actually seen an offspring of two different races."

Ja'Naam smiled at Ka'Ala. "It's only uncommon because of how rarely the flocks mingle, let alone interbreed."

Ka'Ala heard the flutter in Ja'Naam's heartsong as her friend's eyes drifted over R'Venin before turning back to the doorway.

Next to the Half-flock stood a chubby, male Pra'Acheen with one purplish eye. The other glowed like a fireflier trapped in a nest of sooty feathers. He carried a lumpy pouch across his chest and a scowl. He wore a midnight blue robe decorated with a silvervine motif over a linen tunic. His stomach spilled over an oil-stained apron that had narrow pockets, each filled with a strange slender metal tool.

The girl tugged at the string holding R'Venin's pack closed, barely lifting one end off the ground. "Does this belong to one of you?" the girl asked more loudly. "Because if it does, it was almost stolen." The young Ch'Hota kicked the Pra'Acheen with the side of her foot. Her one-eyed companion looked away and shrugged, muttering something Ka'Ala couldn't hear.

"It's mine," R'Venin leaped forward and landed a dozen handspans in front of her on the ramp at eye level. "That's my pack. I'm R'Venin."

"I'm Na'Ukar," the girl said, holding out the rope to R'Venin. "Sher'Esh's chambermaid. She asked me to summon Gha'Barahat for you."

The scowling Pra'Acheen twisted his lips and cast his eye around the stable. His tight lips moved slightly, but still made no sound.

"Thank you for coming, Gha'Barahat," R'Venin took the line from Na'Ukar and dragged the pack up into his arms. "My friends are hurt. Please, come and see."

"Do you have my payment?" Gha'Barahat sneered, his nasal voice bounced around the room. "Na'Ukar promised I'd be well paid for my services."

"I didn't promise you anything, you old leaf-rot," Na'Ukar kicked him again. "I only told you what Sher'Esh told me."

Gha'Barahat blew his lips and stared, unblinking with his one eye, at R'Venin. "You have the bearing of an important fellow," he grinned. "Don't you?"

"Probably why you tried to steal his pack," Na'Ukar muttered. "I have to go prepare your roosts. Use the bathhouse. He's all yours."

Without another word, Na'Ukar leaped toward the ceiling and landed on a small perch just above the stable furthest from the doorway. The discordant reveling exploded into the chamber as she opened a hatch and disappeared.

Behind Ka'Ala, the runnerhounds's braces fell to the ground as Chara'Vaha removed the harnesses and led his team into an empty stall.

"I can pay whatever is fair." R'Venin stood taller and looked down at the little Pra'Acheen. "If that's what you mean." R'Venin bobbed his pack in one hand, seemingly to demonstrate the weight within.

"Let's get to it then," Gha'Barahat grumbled as he headed to the doorway to his left. "Who's first?"

"Ka'Ala first," Ba'Jai and Ja'Naam said in unison.

"She's hurt more than I am," Ba'Jai added. "You go." He put a hand on her shoulder. "I can wait."

"I'll take her," R'Venin said, pulling the pack tight to his chest and gliding to a spot between the bathhouse and the women. "I have to make the payment."

"Thank you, R'Venin," Ka'Ala exhaled as she limped away from the wagon. "But I'd like Ja'Naam to be with me."

"Of course. Here," R'Venin dropped his pack, letting the armor clang against the stone and echo through the stables. The runnerhounds growled and stamped claws, startled by the noise. He removed his right gauntlet and cuffed it around Ja'Naam's wrist. "Whatever the cost."

Ka'Ala smiled as she watched Ja'Naam lock eyes with R'Venin, letting herself get carried away in their harmony as the three of them moved slowly across the floor.

"I haven't got all night," Gha'Barahat's voice carried from the bathhouse.

"I'll take her from here," Ja'Naam pulled Ka'Ala's arm over her shoulder, taking the weight from R'Venin. "Thank you, R'Venin. We wouldn't be here without you."

Ka'Ala hobbled through the portal with Ja'Naam's help, walking into the moonlit bathhouse.

The sound of Ba'Jai's yell bouncing off the walls followed them into the darkness. "So, I'll just wait here then?"

Twenty steps through the snail shell entrance brought Ka'Ala and Ja'Naam into a lowered pool. Wafts of steam danced across the surface. Ka'Ala breathed in the mineral-laced air. "A natural hot spring," she moaned. "I haven't been in one in over seven moons."

"No dipping until after the incantation," Gha'Barahat growled as he poured out his satchel beside a stone bench. "Now remove everything but your breechcloth, and lie down."

Ka'Ala's wings fell as she let out a huge sigh.

"He's right," Ja'Naam laughed once through her nose. "If the minerals in the water remain on your skin, they could cause side effects with the Mountain element."

Gha'Barahat turned with a widened eye. "Where did you study alchemy, child?" A friendly smile was forming on his lips.

"The Sanctuary of The Three Mothers," Ja'Naam answered as she helped Ka'Ala remove her outer clothing. "Why?"

"Hmph. Pack of self-righteous, preening—" Gha'Barahat muttered and turned his back.

Ka'Ala exchanged a confused look with Ja'Naam and closed her eyes, listening. His heartsong came into her mind, sullen and low, laced with melancholy and pain. Behind the melody, a distant sound crept around the music, undefinable and fleeting.

Ja'Naam wrapped her arms around Ka'Ala, giving her a tight embrace. "Do you trust him?" she whispered in Ka'Ala's ear. "Are his hearts pure?"

"Perhaps not pure," Ka'Ala breathed back. "But I don't think he means us any harm. What I heard was mostly sorrow."

"Please lie down," Gha'Barahat grumbled. "I've got a game of bones to get back to."

* * *

R'Venin sat on the ramp next to Ba'Jai by the bathhouse entrance, fiddling with the straps to his pack.

"So, it's been nine songs," Ba'Jai sighed. "From what Ja'Naam told me last night, Kar'Nevala spent ten songs healing your wounds."

"Ten songs?" R'Venin jumped to his feet. "That's impossible. I was awake the whole time. It lasted only one song, maybe two at the most."

"I guess time doesn't mean much when you're limbs are being stitched together. Did it hurt at all?"

"No," R'Venin folded his arms, his voice quiet. "I felt no pain, just pressure like a bandage wrapped tight around your arm and then evaporating. Like smoke. Did it really take ten songs?"

Ba'Jai nodded. "That's what Ja'Naam said. And when she tried to heal my wing, she'd spent a three-quarter day in the incantation before Nar'Sahayak joined. And another song passed before Kar'Nevala said it was too late. For me, it seemed like three songs."

R'Venin started pacing the floor again. "I've got a lot to learn about alchemy if I'm going to cure the White Claw and help my people," he mumbled to himself.

"What was that?"

Before R'Venin could answer, muted voices erupted from the bathhouse entry. Muffled shouts and yelps carried from the dimly lit hallway and bounced around the stables. Suddenly, Ka'Ala emerged from the opening and leaped into the air, flapping her wings with wide, slow beats and hovered around the chamber.

Ba'Jai stood and joined Ka'Ala's gleeful laughter as Ja'Naam emerged with a wide smile. Watching Ka'Ala flit between the stables, Ba'Jai balanced himself with a hand on R'Venin's shoulder.

"He may be a grumbler, but he works miracles," Ja'Naam said, handing R'Venin's gauntlet to him, now four small gems lighter. "Again, thank you for your generosity."

Above their heads, Ka'Ala closed her wings like a shell, dropped like a stone, and opened her wings at the last moment. She landed in a dancer's pose, soft as a wishflower, and her face radiated a broad smile until she made eye contact with the others. She folded her wings and arms in on herself. "Sorry," she cleared her throat. "I didn't mean to have such an outburst. I'm just so happy that I'm not ground-cast."

Ja'Naam and R'Venin stole sidelong glances at Ba'Jai as Ka'Ala's hands flew to her mouth.

R'Venin's hearts sank. *I'd almost forgotten his lost wing.*

"Oh, Ba'Jai," Ka'Ala's eyes brimmed. "I'm so sorry."

Ba'Jai took the five paces to the room's center where Ka'Ala had frozen, her glistening eyes staring at him above her fingers. The street's noise sounded like a distant brook, blending with the random sounds of penned animals. Standing right in front of her, he put both hands on her shoulders. "Does the Windfather have a plan for all his creations?"

Ka'Ala bowed her head, letting a tear fall unimpeded to the floor. "Yes."

Ba'Jai took a deep breath. "Does his plan sometimes mean we will endure pain and discomfort?" his voice broke.

"Yes."

Ba'Jai lifted Ka'Ala's chin. "Why?"

"To strengthen us for the journey ahead."

"I accept being ground cast," Ba'Jai gave a sad smile. "Because I believe the Windfather has a purpose in denying me my flight."

"You don't have to be ground-cast," Gha'Barahat's gravelly voice resonated through the stables.

Ja'Naam startled, reached out, grabbing R'Venin by the arm. Ka'Ala cringed, taking a step backward and shaking her head, muttering inaudible words.

"Just because he lets you lose a wing," the old Pra'Acheen said, stepping out from the doorway with his satchel in one hand, "and one healer wasn't able to restore it, doesn't mean he means you to be flightless forever."

"What are you talking about?" R'Venin stepped around Ja'Naam to face Gha'Barahat. "The best healers in the Three Mothers couldn't save Ba'Jai's wing. I was there."

Gha'Barahat sneered and laughed. "Their best healers used only the alchemy condoned by the council. There is a magic that they're forbidden to teach."

"You mean The Unnatural," Ja'Naam spat. "I've heard of it. Alchemy is supposed to be a painless art. The Unnatural..."

"Can be uncomfortable, yes," Gha'Barahat nodded while he picked under his claws. "But you just said, sometimes the Windfather has us endure pain for a greater purpose."

"The Windfather never said it was acceptable to *cause* pain to his creations to force healing," Ka'Ala said in a quiet voice, stepping away from Ba'Jai. "Growth and learning come as we're able to accept the change. Attempting to bend His will to ours always has consequences."

"How does it work?" Chara'Vaha spoke from across the room, locking the wooden gate to his hounds' stall.

"It doesn't matter how it works," Ja'Naam turned her back to the old alchemist. "It's Unnatural, and Ba'Jai won't be doing it."

"Thank you for concern, sister," Ba'Jai closed the distance to his sister and pulled her into a tight embrace. "But I can speak for myself. I'm the one that lost a wing. Not you."

R'Venin put his hand on Ba'Jai's shoulder. "What are you doing? If Ja'Naam says The Unnatural is forbidden, you should listen to her."

"Forbidden to Pra'Acheen," Ba'Jai smiled, crossing arms to rest a hand on R'Venin's shoulder. "I'm also curious about how it works. I want to know all my options before I dismiss any of them."

"It's a Mirror spell. The incantation is quite simple," Gha'Barahat chuckled. "But I'll need your weight in Silk to provide the necessary amount of Mountain element to copy your remaining wing to your damaged joint."

"That would cost a fortune," Ja'Naam yelled. "It would take three lifetimes to acquire that much treasure. We just don't have it."

"She's right," Ba'Jai sighed. "Even if I chose to go through with the incantation, we can't afford the amount of Silk you require."

Ja'Naam wrapped her arms around Ba'Jai, running her fingers across the feathers of his remaining wing. The room fell silent. The crowds walking along the street outside thinned to a few stragglers— their drunken voices filled with laughter and raucous jokes.

Gha'Barahat shrugged and hopped onto the ramp, turning toward the door. He slung his bag over one shoulder and waved a hand without looking back.

"I can," R'Venin muttered.

Gha'Barahat froze in midstride.

"What did you say?" Ja'Naam pulled out of Ba'Jai's arms and turned her head.

"I can pay," R'Venin cleared his throat. "If Gha'Barahat can restore Ba'Jai's wing, and if he wants the incantation, I can pay for the Silk. It's the least I can do for risking his life to save mine."

"No," Ja'Naam clenched her teeth, turning to her brother. "No. You're not going through with this. You can't. It's unnatural."

Ba'Jai bowed his head. "How can I call myself a Guardsman if I can't fly? If I'm ground-cast, how will I protect Uth'Ala and our future children? How will I get up to the Hatchery to choose an egg and participate in the pouching ceremony? What if she returns the mating band I gave her? I'll have nowhere to go. As it is, I'll be blessed if I don't lose my ranking in the guard."

"I thought you didn't care about your rank," Ja'Naam choked.

"But Uth'Ala does," Ba'Jai whispered. "You know she comes from the upper branches. She was born to privilege. Only my status in the guard convinced her parents to allow my courtship. She'd never follow me to the ground. You know that. What will I do then?"

Ja'Naam and Ka'Ala both had wet eyes.

"Tell me, Ja'Naam," Ba'Jai's voice rose. "Are mother and father supposed to shelter me for the rest of their lives? And then what? Will it fall to you? You know I won't survive on the ground for long with one wing? Eventually, I'll die by one of a thousand creatures living below the trees. And when that happens, how will you place my remains into the pyre? My ashes won't rise to the Eternal Winds. My soul will fall into the Pit forever."

Ja'Naam shook her head. "I don't know. I don't know, but we can find a way. Maybe you can live with the Pra'Acheen? They live ground-sided. You could still be a guardsman."

"A guardsman of the Pra'Acheen?" Ba'Jai mocked. "They're scholars and artisans. No one bothers them because they have nothing of value except their knowledge and craftsmanship. Which they share freely with anyone who asks."

"Except for the forbidden knowledge," Ja'Naam murmured.

"That's not the point, and you know it!" Ba'Jai blew out his breath. "I want to fly again. And I need to know all my options before I give up."

"You never give up," Ja'Naam hit Ba'Jai's chest with a light punch. "You've always been the strong one."

"The truth is," he pulled her back into his arms. "I put on a good show. But you're the strong one. If I can't fly, I'm not a true guardsman. And if I'm not serving my flock, then my life has no purpose. I'm not done protecting my flock or my family."

Ka'Ala padded next to the embracing siblings while R'Venin watched. "You don't have to be a guardsman to serve your flock," she said, positioning herself in Ba'Jai's line of sight. "There are other ways to serve."

"My people may outwardly agree with you, Ka'Ala," Ba'Jai whispered. "But there's an unspoken code: A flightless Ch'Hota is just a meal."

Ja'Naam shuddered in Ba'Jai's arms.

"Well?" Gha'Barahat sneered. "Do you want to know more? Go through with the ceremony? Or are you ready to go out into the forest for supper?"

R'Venin lifted his pack off the ground. The armor within clanked and rattled as he hefted the bag onto his shoulder and looked at Ba'Jai with raised brows.

Ba'Jai closed his eyes for a moment and breathed deep. "Tell me everything about the incantation, and I'll give you my decision in the morning."

Chapter Fifteen

The Master Alchemist

R'Venin rubbed the morning dust from his eyes again as he aided Ba'Jai through the broad streets of Crossroads. Ba'Jai held onto R'Venin's shoulder for balance as they walked between dimming fire crystal torches on either side of the thoroughfare. Random Ch'Hota and Pra'Acheen merchants with open storefronts laid out their pottery, baskets, and jewelry. Wafts of candied fruits, sugared nuts, and confections from handcarts trundling toward the village center teased R'Venin's growling stomach.

Those smell good, though I'm still full from last night's feast. Maybe later.

The stone avenue pulled the heat from his legs as they turned right at a public fountain of red marble with sculptures carved into the central pillar. The artwork depicted a familiar historical conflict: The Third Crusade of D'Harma Yud'd. A fierce-eyed Ch'Hota guardsman at the carvings' apex, with gold-tipped wings, pointed his spear down toward a flock of V'Jeeta warriors. From behind the lead Ch'Hota, other guardsmen appeared to be swooping down from the sky like a meteor shower.

The V'Jeeta's hands angled up, shielding themselves while they exposed their wings' undersides. Water droplets ran down the V'Jeeta warriors' faces as if they were children frightened by a lightning storm. R'Venin adjusted the pack of armor hanging over his shoulder.

"I've heard the story of this battle all my life," R'Venin murmured, staring at the carvings as they navigated the edge. "As my Greatfather told it, the Ch'Hota invaded the Granite Spires to steal the entire Silk harvest for themselves. Though Mother always told it a little differently."

"Gha'Barahat said his place was less than twenty paces from the fountain," Ba'Jai pointed down the street.

"Yes," R'Venin shook the memory from his head. "I can see his slate hanging just down the way. Are you sure you want to do this? Remember what Ja'Naam said last night during the evening meal. She said this form of alchemy is unnatural."

"Yeah, I know," Ba'Jai nodded to an elderly Ch'Hota woman hanging mating bands on her shop wall. "But I fear losing Uth'Ala and having no offspring. I have to try. I am grateful to you, R'Venin. For your willingness to pay for the Silk. You're showing extraordinary generosity."

"I told you before," R'Venin glanced at an array of white-washed pottery with intricate black and red markings. "I've sworn a life-debt to you for sparing my life. The gems on this armor only serve as a reminder of my father's palatial prison. I'll finally be just an ordinary V'Jeeta. I'll be glad to be rid of them."

Besides, I have a crucial question to ask that old alchemist about White Claw, and this may be my only chance.

"I don't believe you'll ever be an *ordinary* V'Jeeta, my friend." Ba'Jai squeezed R'Venin's shoulder as they stepped up to a pair of wooden doors on sturdy metal hinges.

A cobalt banner of finespun silk hung from a pole jutting from the plastered wall over their heads, with silver spinners' thread, embroidered into the sheet, displaying the symbols for the five alchemy elements. The words "Gha'Barahat: Master Alchemist" rippled below the image as a gust blew down the street.

R'Venin knocked and stepped back. Unintelligible voices trickled from around the corner as they waited for someone to answer. A pair of Ch'Hota women, one carrying a new hatchling in her pouch and the other grey-feathered and hunched over, pushed a wobbly handcart down the street while Gha'Barahat's doors remained closed. The young mother nodded to Ba'Jai.

"You may have to knock louder," The elderly woman gave R'Venin a warm smile as they pushed the cart passed them. "Gha'Barahat is known to be a heavy sleeper."

"Thank you," R'Venin said and pounded his fist on the heavy door, the thuds scattering a handful of dovehawks perched on the window sill over their heads. After a minute, he beat again, banging his fist several times.

"Perhaps he's still out gambling," Ba'Jai smirked.

Above them, a window creaked open, and Gha'Barahat's nasally voice descended to the street. "I see you've found my humble little shop." Gha'Barahat leaned over the sill, wearing a shiny brown sleeping gown veined with gold embroidery. "I assume you've decided."

"Yes," Ba'Jai craned his neck. "I want the incantation. I want to get my wing back."

Half of Gha'Barahat's face pulled up into a smile. "Did you bring payment?"

R'Venin unshouldered his pack and opened the top flap, revealing the glittering carbon-feather armor inside. "I'm sure we can agree on a fair price."

Gha'Barahat's eyes widened. "I'll be right down," he said, closing the window.

R'Venin looked up and down the street as he closed the flap. He caught Ba'Jai's gaze out of the corner of his eye. He turned to find Ba'Jai's eyes wet. "What is it?"

Ba'Jai swallowed hard. "If this works," he said, choking on his words, "I may owe you a life-debt."

R'Venin reached across his chest to put his hand on top of Ba'Jai's, still resting on his shoulder. He opened his mouth to speak but just nodded instead.

If this works, our people may be one flight closer to peace.

Behind the door, the sounds of grunting and metal scraping on wood erupted into the street. One thick panel swung wide on its heavy hinges, squealing in protest. "Come in," Gha'Barahat huffed as he turned away from the entry. "And close the door behind you. I'm usually not open for business so early, but I make an exception for well-paying customers."

R'Venin let Ba'Jai enter first and pulled the door closed behind him. Gha'Barahat's shop looked like it belonged to a tinker instead of a healer. There were no shelves filled with jars of powdered plants or rare minerals. No yellowing or frayed parchment scrolls stacked into pyramids. No bowls covered with intricately carved lettering emitting floral-scented mists into the air.

Instead, low workbenches littered with complex objects made of brass, iron, and copper stood against the walls. Half-disassembled spindles. Skeletons of wire and clay. Shattered crystal spheres. A cracked pot of loosely-wound scrolls, indecipherable runes peeking through the rings of parchment. Flickering oil lamps hung from the ceiling, casting dancing shadows throughout the cramped space. The scent of needle-leaves, liquor, and rotting fruit filled the holes between all the gadgetry.

"Drop that crossbar, will you?" Gha'Barahat yawned as he navigated between the tables and workbenches littering the small, dimly-lit room. Tying the pocketed apron around his waist, he pointed toward a gadget on the far wall. "Get on the scale."

R'Venin followed his fingers to a pair of platforms hanging by ropes to a pulley system. The system of pulleys and chucks hung attached to a thick floor beam. One of the platforms contained a wooden barrel. Hanging above it, a chute protruded from the wall with a sliding gate set between its sidewalls.

Ba'Jai moved across the chamber and stood next to the empty platform. Dipping under the ropes, his foot pushed the platform to the floor as he squatted into a crouching position.

"It would be better if you sit," Gha'Barahat grumbled. "And don't let anything touch the floor. I need to get an accurate measurement."

"Sorry," Ba'Jai said, dropping onto his rear and crossing his legs.

R'Venin stepped closer to watch as Gha'Barahat lifted the gate by a lever. Sand spilled from a hidden silo, pouring down the slough and onto the platform. The barrel filled slowly and lowered to the ground.

Gha'Barahat eased the gate down as the platform was nearly level with the barrel of sand. The grains trickled until the platforms were even, and Gha'Barahat stopped the flow. The scales creaked as Ba'Jai's platform, and the cone-topped mound of sand swayed in mid-air.

The alchemist then grabbed a metal object from a workbench. It looked long and flat and curled up on the edges with a wooden handle at the center. He pushed the sand over until the top was flat and then dropped the metal bar back on the workbench. He then put his face up to the barrel's edge.

R'Venin inched closer, peering into the barrel following the Pra'Acheen's eyes. Thin brass nails had been hammered into the barrel's face at regular intervals, with painted markings next to every eighth one. "Ten thousand," Gha'Barahat grunted. "It'll take ten thousand feathers worth of Silk to mirror your wing properly."

"TEN THOUSAND?" R'Venin and Ba'Jai said in unison.

That's more than all my gems combined, including my crown. But I must pay the debt.

R'Venin set his pack on a table and opened the flap, laying out armor pieces one at a time. Gha'Barahat's eyes widened, and a greedy smile spread across his face as each array of gems came into view. Lastly, he withdrew his helmet from the sack and reached inside to remove the nested silvervine crown.

"A single wing isn't worth it, R'Venin," Ba'Jai's head drooped. "Not at that price."

R'Venin's hand froze, his fingertips brushing against the cluster of gems. "If it'll restore your flight, then yes, it is."

"I can't let you do it," Ba'Jai swung his feet over the platform's edge, causing it to swing forward. He planted his feet and stood. The barrel of sand thudded to the floor like a war drum as Ba'Jai stepped to the table and began refilling the pack. "I won't allow you to waste your entire fortune on me. Life-debt or not. I doubt you have ten thousand feathers anyway. I've seen your armor up close, remember?"

"Let me help you," R'Venin grabbed Ba'Jai's hands, glaring across the table. "As you helped me. I noticed how you don't have your armor anymore. Nor your spear. You already traded it at the Three Mothers, didn't you? Was it to pay for your incantation or mine?"

Ba'Jai matched R'Venin's stare. His eyes focused like a beam of light under a magnifying glass, and his jaw clenched.

"You said the Windfather told you to save me," R'Venin's voice softened. "Maybe he spared my life because I needed to save yours."

Ba'Jai gave a throaty laugh. "I can't imagine the Windfather telling me to save you, and then let me get my wing ripped off so that you could spend your entire fortune to get me my wing back. If He didn't want me flightless, he could have just let me ignore you in the field."

R'Venin backed away from the table, his jaw clenched, and dropped the helmet onto the pile.

Ba'Jai's eyes flew open as he upturned his wing. "I'm so sorry." He bowed his head. "I shouldn't have said that. That was unfair."

"But it's true," R'Venin whispered. "The Windfather should have let me die. Then you'd still have your wing."

"Or I may have died in battle." Ba'Jai's voice softened. "We'll never know what might have happened. We can only move forward based on what *has* happened."

Ba'Jai reached across the table. R'Venin stared at it for a moment before taking it, gripping around Ba'Jai's elbow.

"We'll figure something else out," Ba'Jai said, his forced smile keeping its distance from his eyes.

"There is another option," Gha'Barahat grunted as he reached into his food cabinet for another strip of jerky.

"What is it, and how much will it cost?" Ba'Jai cut off R'Venin before he could speak.

"Most of the cost of mirroring body parts is in the bones," Gha'Barahat grumbled as he walked across his shop to the table covered in spindly metal gadgets. "They're tricky, which is why it takes so much silk to force their growth. But if you're open to an alternative to bones, I think I can mirror your wing for a mere three-thousand."

"What alternative?" R'Venin asked, craning his head to see over Gha'Barahat's shoulders.

Turning around, Gha'Barahat lifted a framework of brass rods and hinges in the arrangement of a wings' skeleton. "With this. I can modify the incantation to mimic your natural bone structure with metal and then graft the tissue on top. You'll be able to tell the difference from your remaining wing, but you'll still be back in the air and at a much more purse-friendly price."

R'Venin turned back to the table and started counting the gems, adding up their value under his breath, and the armor into two unequal piles. After a few minutes of moving pieces back and forth between the stacks, he looked up at Ba'Jai. "This larger pile should be about three-thousand feathers. That'll leave me with enough to get settled in the Bluewoods. Do you want to fly home, or ride in a wagon?"

Chapter Sixteen

The Unnatural

Gha'Barahat jiggled the pouch full of precious stones as R'Venin reloaded his armor into the pack. "Follow me," he chuckled as he walked, almost dancing, away from the workbenches toward a doorway. A dust-covered tapestry matching the banner outside filled the opening. The beaming Pra'Acheen held the flap aside as R'Venin and Ba'Jai crossed the threshold and descended a short flight of stairs.

The steps narrowed as they entered an oval-shaped room with a domed ceiling. Faint wisps escaped R'Venin's mouth as he landed at the bottom and wrapped his wings tighter around his body. Ba'Jai covered as much of himself with his remaining wing but needed his arms to protect the parts that the tunic didn't hide.

"Damn," Ba'Jai mumbled looking up, the small opening in the ceiling allowed a small fraction of morning light into the tomb-like chamber. "Would it kill him to have a few torches down here?"

In the center of the room, directly below the oculus, stood a round table on six stone legs. The black marble, veined with silver and blue, had the five elements carved into its surface. The central marking, the symbol of the Windfather, appeared bowl-shaped with a hole in the center like a washbasin. At the outer images' apex, four thick leather straps with buckles extended up through the table's surface. Each metal buckle had three prongs that lined up with the rows of holes lining the belt.

Opposite the steps, a wide wooden cabinet stood against the wall. On top of which, a shallow copper basin sat next to a stack of leather-bound wooden rods.

This must be his prayer room

"Ba'Jai," Gha'Barahat said as he poured out the gems into a metal strongbox at the base of the stairs. "Remove all your clothing—except your breechcloth—and lie on the table, face down."

Ba'Jai stripped off his tunic, shivering slightly as the cold air pricked at his bare torso. He then climbed onto the table and propped his chin on interlocked fingers.

"R'Venin," the healer's voice took on a hint of menace. "Please bind your friend down to the table. He mustn't move during the incantation."

"What?" R'Venin's voice filled the chamber.

Ba'Jai rolled over onto his side, eyes wide. "Why do I have to be tied down? I promise I can hold still."

"They all say that," Gha'Barahat chuckled. "Now, please. If you want your wing back, you'll do as I say, or I can't guarantee my work."

R'Venin and Ba'Jai exchanged a look until Ba'Jai nodded and laid flat on the table, arms and legs spread wide. R'Venin moved around the table, starting at Ba'Jai's right arm and ending at his left.

"Are you okay?" R'Venin asked. Ba'Jai nodded but remained silent as he shivered.

"Now, R'Venin," Gha'Barahat opened a hidden door in the wall. "I'll need you to collect the bundles of Silk and feed them into the potion as I perform the incantation."

The door led into a deep antechamber, two wingspans wide, one wingspan tall, and four wingspans deep. All along the walls, wooden shelves four hands deep stood laden with fist-sized bales of Silver Silk.

"I've never seen this much Silk in my life. Not even after collecting the harvest. You have a Sovereign's envy in here!" R'Venin breathed, staring into a large storeroom. He shook his head and blinked several times. "How many bales will Ba'Jai need?"

Gha'Barahat shrugged and tilted his head. "Five should do it."

R'Venin stepped into the room just far enough to transfer the bundles into his arms' crook and backed out.

"Place them next to the Mountain symbol, and then put this under the table." Gha'Barahat knuckled the basin atop the cabinet as he bent over, opening and closing several drawers until he retrieved two glass jars. A head-sized one filled with a mossy colored powder, and a larger jar filled with a glowing purple liquid. He uncapped and sniffed each one, nodding as if to confirm their contents.

R'Venin lifted the basin and walked it around the table, setting it on the ground. Gha'Barahat followed, mumbling in words as Kar'Nevala had before.

The Pra'Acheen knelt and poured the amethyst fluid into the basin and chanted an inaudible phrase. Next, he scooped a handful of the mossy powder into the basin five times, repeating new indecipherable words with each toss. Grey smoke rose with each word but stopped just below the table as if an invisible canopy held it in place.

"Push the basin to the spot below the Windfather symbol," Gha'Barahat said, rising and returning up the steps. "I'll be right back. I forgot the bones."

R'Venin got down on his knees and slid the basin across the rough wooden planks. Smoke swirled above the basin like a ghostly orb, never expanding or touching anything around it.

"Are you sure you want to go through with this?" R'Venin whispered under the table. "I may just be a novice at alchemy, but I'm not sure I trust this Pra'Acheen. Forget the gems. It's not too late to stop."

"No." Ba'Jai's voice sounded hoarse through the stone. "I've been thinking about it. If I don't try, I'll just be a burden and cast down. This may be my only chance of a normal life."

"Very well," R'Venin crawled out from under the table and stood up as Gha'Barahat returned, holding the metal wing frame. The Pra'Acheen whistled as he made his way around the table and laid the artificial frame on Ba'Jai's back, flaring it out from his lost wing joint.

Ba'Jai sucked air between his teeth as Gha'Barahat ripped the bandages from his scarred back, revealing a protruding piece of bone. The wing nub rolled in its socket, mirroring the movements of its intact twin, as Ba'Jai's back tensed.

"You'll need to hold as still as possible," Gha'Barahat grumbled. "Otherwise, the fusion won't be straight, and you'll end up with a crooked wing. Once we begin, there's no turning back. If I'm interrupted, you risk losing your other wing."

"I understand," Ba'Jai relaxed his back and took several deep breaths. "No stopping. No turning back."

"Now we can start," the paunchy Pra'Acheen snickered, looking to R'Venin. "When I point to the basin, place the first bundle of Silk. And again, each time I give the signal. Otherwise, stay out of the way, or give your friend something to squeeze. Those grippers on the cabinet will do."

R'Venin reloaded his arms with the bales and took them to the table's head directly in front of Ba'Jai. Dropping the bundles on the floor, he reached over and grabbed two sticks wrapped in braided leather strips from the top of the cabinet.

"I wish I could do more," R'Venin said, placing a stick in each of Ba'Jai's hands.

Ba'Jai wrapped his fingers around the sticks several times as if molding them into his palms. "You've done more than I could have asked for," Ba'Jai said, craning his head off the table. "I'm grateful you're here. Ja'Naam would've already talked me out of it."

Gha'Barahat disappeared under the table and began chanting. R'Venin crouched, giving himself a view of the basin and Ba'Jai's back. The purple fluid swirled like an eddy in a river while the blob of gray smoke twisted. It tightened into a spinning column, yet remained trapped under an unseen barrier.

When Gha'Barahat pointed at the basin, R'Venin tossed the first bale of Silk into the whirlpool. The solution changed from purple to lavender, and then to a soft white glow, casting shadows onto the ceiling. The column of smoke spun faster as sparks of embers flew out and fizzled on the floor. Suddenly, the smoke burst into a pillar of fire and gyrated like a hooded serpent waiting to strike.

The heat from the flames warmed R'Venin's face like the morning sun as the fire snaked its way through the hole in the table, slinking around Ba'Jai's abdomen. The temperature rose until the flames wrapped themselves around his broken wing nub.

"Does it hurt?" R'Venin whispered, his eyes transfixed on the fire gathering on Ba'Jai's back.

"No, it feels good," Ba'Jai's body relaxed as he took a deep breath. "Like spreading your wings to the sun after flying through the rain."

The flames churned as Gha'Barahat's voice rose in volume and pitch. Tendrils of fire reached out and latched onto the metal bones, spreading across the rods until the entire framework glowed like molten ore.

Gha'Barahat pointed to the basin with two fingers, but R'Venin's gaze was fixed on the fiery display. The grouchy Pra'Acheen slapped R'Venin's knee with his wing and pointed again, never stopping his incantation.

"Sorry," R'Venin muttered as he threw the second bale into the pool. The liquid flashed, and the flaming column grew thicker, swirling faster and turning from warm reds and oranges to yellows.

"Okay," Ba'Jai grunted, squeezing the leathered sticks and fought against the arch in his back. "That's getting hot."

The swirling column of fire split and bent, molding its shape to the metal structure. The framework morphed, squealing like swords scraping along a Blackstone wall. The metal splintered, divided, and weaved itself into the shape of natural wing bones, becoming hollow and perforated. The frayed skin around Ba'Jai's wing joint bubbled and splayed like a morning flower.

Gha'Barahat jabbed his finger toward the basin a third time. R'Venin grabbed another bundle and cast it into the liquid as the alchemist's voice rose again.

"Ngh!" Ba'Jai grunted, driving his forehead into the table and pulling his arms and legs against the restraints, breathing heavily through his nose.

"Holy Windfather," R'Venin whispered as Ba'Jai's muscles grew along the framework as if being dragged by fishers' hooks.

Ligaments threaded themselves into the pitted metal surfaces. Muscle tissue ballooned into existence stretched taut by new tendons. Arteries grew like vines, weaving through muscle fibers, narrowing as they branched in fractal patterns. Veins emerged, collecting like streams to a river flowing toward Ba'Jai's back.

Gha'Barahat signaled R'Venin for another bale.

R'Venin hesitated, looking between the remaining two bundles in his hands. "Can't you see how much pain he's in?" he yelled.

"R'Venin," Ba'Jai growled through gnashed teeth. "No...stopping... no... ARGH!" Ba'Jai's back twisted. Droplets of blood sprayed against the wall as the arteries began delivering their life-giving fluid to tissue yet to form.

Gha'Barahat stood, never breaking the incantation, and tore a bundle of Silk from R'Venin's grasp. Casting the bale into the basin with a sidelong throw, he glowered up at R'Venin. The Pra'Acheen's single eye shone like a full moon.

Ba'Jai's writhing ebbed as the Silk burst into flame. The snaking fire across his artificial skeleton faded to a dull glow as it drew away from the bone tips, collecting at the joint. Tendrils reached across his back to the other wing joint, forming a loose circle around each, joined in between like a pair of manacles.

"Lift your wing to its full span, Ba'Jai," Gha'Barahat's voice resonated around the chamber. "Try to touch the ceiling."

Ba'Jai raised his wing in jerky movements. R'Venin reached out, about to put his hands on the wings leading edge.

"NO!" Gha'Barahat thundered. "He must do it himself unless you want your hand permanently mimicked onto his wing."

Ba'Jai grunted until his wingtip came to a few handspans shy of the ceiling. The tattered skin, still bubbling around the joint, rose along with the ephemeral manacles. Like twinned smoke rings, the glowing bands lifted from his back, pulling and stretching the skin like a death shroud across the frame.

R'Venin stood off to the side, holding the final bundle of Silk as Ba'Jai's face twisted in concentration.

Ba'Jai's breathing became steady as the new drapes of skin fused at the bone tips.

Looks like a hatchlings' wings. Featherless. Fragile. Like K'Marot when he birthed from Mother's pouch.

"Almost there," Gha'Barahat said to himself, catching R'Venin's eye while pointing at the basin.

R'Venin tossed the last bale of Silver Silk into the steaming bowl. The Silk burst into white-hot flames, rising on all sides of the stone table at once. They gathered around Ba'Jai's natural wing and swirled like a snow devil. The green and gold feathers ruffled as tiny white streams of mist grabbed and ripped them from their sheaths.

R'Venin's brow furrowed as the torn feathers turned shades of gray, drained of all color. He narrowed his eyes to see through the quill storm to see Ba'Jai's wing still rippling with the same tones as before they walked into the shop. The white plumage twirled in the spinning vortex until it seemed no longer joining the dance.

The feathery cyclone slowed and came to a halt, hovering over Ba'Jai, as if air and gravity no longer had an effect.

"Drop your wing and brace yourself," Gha'Barahat mumbled. "This is where it's going to hurt."

Ba'Jai barely took a single breath when the cloud of quills spun in reverse. He gripped the leather rods tighter and let his natural wing fall and drape over the table. Just as he took another breath, the flurry picked up speed and expanded until it collapsed in on itself. Ba'Jai screamed as thousands of needle-like quills pierced his hatchling skin and buried themselves deep into the muscle.

The room fell into near silence. The only sounds were Ba'Jai's labored breathing and Gha'Barahat's shuffling footsteps. "Pleasure doing business with you," he groaned as he made his way up the stairwell.

R'Venin unbound Ba'Jai's wrists and ankles, helping him roll over onto his side, panting.

"And I thought losing the wing was painful," Ba'Jai croaked, letting the leather-bound sticks fall to the floor. "I'll be alright. I just need to lie down for a moment. How long was the incantation?"

R'Venin looked up to the oculus. "About three songs," he tilted his head, peering deeper into the opening. "That whole incantation only lasted three songs? I still don't believe it."

"How is that possible?" Ba'Jai asked.

"I don't know." R'Venin spotted the Pra'Acheen as he made it to the top step and raced after him. "But I'm going to find out."

* * *

"Master Gha'Barahat, wait!" R'Venin tore up the stairs, bursting into the shop to find the Pra'Acheen lighting up a long-necked pipe.

The scent of dizzyroot filled his nasal slits as the one-eyed alchemist took a long pull and blew a cloud of green smoke into the air.

"I don't give refunds," Gha'Barahat sneered as he squatted down onto a short wooden stool. "Your friend hasn't even tried it out yet."

"No, I... I mean... I need to know..." R'Venin's words spilled out as he paced on the spot before the smoking alchemist. "How did you do that? How did you rebuild Ba'Jai's wing in three songs when Kar'Nevala spent more than that trying to save it, but couldn't?"

Gha'Barahat took another pull on his pipe and held it in until his eyes watered, and a grin spread on his face. He blew out the smoke, choking and giggling at the same time. "What you should be asking is why they call it *The Unnatural?*"

"Very well," R'Venin scrunched his face. "Why do they call it unnatural?"

"Time," Gha'Barahat winked with his false eye, nodding. "Time."

"Time?" R'Venin took a knee, putting himself at eye-level with the old Pra'Acheen. "What do you mean?"

Gha'Barahat studied R'Venin's eyes, sucking on his pipe rapidly and then pinched his mouth into a tight line. "Time heals. Time destroys. The body can heal from just about anything if it has enough time. But if time is against you, there's nothing you can do. Time can heal a tree even after it's been hacked up in battle. Time will cut you apart just as sure as a river tears through a canyon."

R'Venin glanced around the workshop, surveying the various instruments. "I'm not sure I understand."

Gha'Barahat pointed his pipe's stem toward R'Venin, swaying it like a conductor's baton in the air as he took a deep breath through the nose. "I like you, R'Venin," he leaned forward, returning the pipe to his lips for another tug. "You're not like the other V'Jeeta I've met, puffing up as soon as they walk in the room. And you're not quite like a Ch'Hota either. There's something unique about you. Not sure what. But different. So I'll tell you this much."

R'Venin leaned in closer.

"The body wants to be whole," Gha'Barahat blew a cloud of green smoke through his nasal slits. "To return to its natural state. But it also wants to conserve energy and take the path of least resistance. If the body has enough time, material, and energy, it can be restored to its natural state. Without those three things, it takes the shortest path it can to prevent further losses. Thus, letting the wing die to preserve the rest of the body. The other Pra'Acheen alchemists call it Unnatural because if you can provide the body with the right materials, you can force it to take a shortcut. I just speed the process along."

"Can 'The Unnatural' cure White Claw?" R'Venin breathed, leaning in.

Gha'Barahat sucked on his pipe, holding it in his lungs for a long moment. "I suppose anything's possible," he tilted his head back and blew rings into the air. "If you're willing to pay the price."

"Can you teach me?" R'Venin held out his hands, palms up, and exposed his wings' undersides.

Gha'Barahat chuckled and stood. "That just takes time." He winked his false eye again.

Chapter Seventeen

Homeward Flight

At high sun, Ka'Ala watched from a wingspan down the elevated walkway as Ja'Naam gave her goodbye's to Sher'Esh. Outside the curtained doorway, the older woman chattered non-stop about her performance the previous night, projecting her voice each time she mentioned her *secret guest* in the audience.

"Thank you for staying with me, Ja'Naam. And thank you for recommending me to *my illustrious patron*. I expect he'll be a regular visitor in the years to come," the older woman beamed, then leaned in to whisper. "Though I still wish he'd let me tell people I hosted royalty. It would give my reputation as a gracious innkeeper such a lift."

"Thank you for understanding," Ja'Naam wrapped her arms around Sher'Esh and squeezed. "I'm sure he appreciates your discretion."

"Oh," Sher'Esh swatted her hand through the air. "I'm anything if not discrete. You know I can keep a secret."

Ka'Ala turned her head to hide her rolling eyes.

I've heard your heartsong—anything to keep the attention on you.

"Now," Sher'Esh's voice softened. "Give my best to your parents. And tell my sister to visit me soon. I'll even let her share my room for free."

"Of course," Ja'Naam laughed. "Mother's been talking about flying out. Now's not a good time since Father's started losing his feathers."

"Well, I'm sure he'll be as fresh as spring and flying soon," Sher'Esh's eyes twinkled.

Ja'Naam's eyes moistened. "I hope so."

Above the rooftops, Ka'Ala spotted the dark-feathered R'Venin flying toward them. "Ja'Naam," she turned, waving her fingers toward the embracing women. "Here, they come."

R'Venin's tunic fluttered in the breeze as he glided through the air close to a pair of mismatched wings.

Ja'Naam and Sher'Esh joined Ka'Ala at the railing. Ja'Naam covered her mouth, staring wide-eyed. "What has he done?"

Narrowing her eyes, Ka'Ala focused on Ba'Jai's face, which twisted in a mixture of what looked like concentration and agony. His wings (one glittering with the greens and golds she'd grown familiar with while riding in the wagon) flapped naturally in smooth arcs. The new one, somehow colorless in dull grays like stones in the moonlight, seemed to move in a jerky rhythm. R'Venin's flight path kept bringing him closer to Ba'Jai as if readying to catch him.

"Hmm," Sher'Esh pursed her lips. "I see Gha'Barahat's skills are improving. Such a shame he doesn't care about aesthetics."

Ja'Naam took Sher'Esh by the hand. "We've got to go," she said quickly. "I'll write soon. Fair Weather."

Without another word, Ja'Naam side-rolled over the railing and glided to the ground, back-flapping as she fell.

"Thank you for the lodging and food." Ka'Ala nodded and jumped over the bar, opening her wings to glide down after Ja'Naam.

"Fair weather, children," Sher'Esh called over the edge. "Come again soon. Tell your friends about the Warbler's Roost: The jewel of Western Crossroads."

Ja'Naam landed on the cobbled street right in front of the open barn doors. Pedestrians and cart-pushers altered their paths as Ka'Ala joined her on the ground. They looked up, spotting R'Venin and Ba'Jai making their way above the village, apparently using the street as a guide.

"I can't believe he went through with it," Ja'Naam whispered, staring into the distance beyond her brother. "Though I suppose I understand. I told him not to mate with Uth'Ala. I warned him that she was a preening short-feather, only interested in how well he looked in his armor. But he wouldn't listen. He felt his future was with her and no one else. Our hearts don't choose who they bond with, do they?"

Now is the time, Windfather breathed in Ka'Ala's ear. *Be her second witness.*

"No," Ka'Ala sidled up to Ja'Naam. "Our hearts don't always choose. But sometimes, they're nudged in the right direction. I know we've only just met, and it's not my place to say anything..."

"What is it?" Ja'Naam muttered, keeping her eyes on Ba'Jai's fluttering flight path.

Ka'Ala took Ja'Naam's hand, drawing a smile and glance from her new friend. She squeezed it and took a breath. "R'Venin has... pure hearts. He's genuine... true," the words coming out rough and broken.

Ja'Naam turned to face Ka'Ala. "Yes," she sighed. "He's been very generous. And kind, and—" Ja'Naam swallowed hard.

"You've heard his heartsong," Ka'Ala whispered. "Haven't you?"

Ja'Naam wiped away the tears brimming in her eyes, nodding. "Last night. While he carried Ba'Jai up into our roost."

"And it scares you," Ka'Ala said, pulling Ja'Naam into a one-armed hug.

A tear spilled onto the ground as Ja'Naam turned away. "I've never thought of myself as prejudiced. I've met only a handful of V'Jeeta. At home, they keep to themselves in small enclaves. I never considered the possibility of becoming mated to one. But—."

Ka'Ala closed her eyes as Ja'Naam's melody grew, rising and falling with missing notes. Incomplete. She could almost hear Ja'Naam's hearts thundering in her chest. "But now your hearts soar at his approach, and you don't know what to do with it."

Ja'Naam nodded.

Ka'Ala opened her mouth to speak but couldn't utter a sound. "*Speak the words I put in your hearts,*" The Windfather's words caused Ka'Ala's hearts to burn. She pulled Ja'Naam into a full embrace and spoke quietly in her ear.

"The Windfather will bring your hearts peace," she whispered. "He has a plan for R'Venin. And, if you're willing to step forward, not seeing the path, you will be a key factor in him fulfilling his destiny. You will find joy and sorrow at his side. In the end, all will be well."

Ja'Naam relaxed, letting Ka'Ala carry her as she wept, shaking with tears. People on the streets cast sidelong glances and side-stepped the sobbing women clinging to each other. Several moments passed before Ja'Naam took a deep breath and pulled away, wiping the wetness from her face. "Thank you, Ka'Ala. I needed to hear that."

"Thank the Windfather," Ka'Ala said. "He gave me the words. I was just the voice. Are you alright?"

Ja'Naam nodded and smiled. "Yes," she took Ka'Ala's hands. "I'm fine."

Ka'Ala looked over Ja'Naam's shoulder, spotting R'Venin and Ba'Jai just reaching the rooftops across the square. "They're here." She cleared her throat. "When will you tell him?"

Ja'Naam blew out a breath. "One branch at a time, I guess."

"Ja'Naam," Ba'Jai's voice boomed from across the plaza. "I've got my wings back."

Ja'Naam spun around, catching sight of Ba'Jai, who seemed to be having trouble beating his wings in unison, as R'Venin backflapped to keep himself at level with him. "It looks like Gha'Barahat just slapped some parchment on your back with clay paint," she said, putting a smile on her face. "Oh, no."

Ba'Jai's new wing stalled in mid-flap. His arms flailed as he lost a few handspans of altitude before R'Venin grabbed onto his wrist and slowed his descent.

"What happened?" R'Venin grunted, flapping harder with the extra load of Ba'Jai and the armor-laden pack across his back. "You were doing so well."

R'Venin let go of Ba'Jai as his feet touched the ground. "I lost my focus," he pinched his face as he glanced at Ka'Ala. "I had to concentrate on making it work. I guess you take flying for granted until you have to re-learn how. I'll practice as we finish the journey. Gha'Barahat said not to use it for a while every two or three songs. I can just ride in the wagon with Chara'Vaha."

Ka'Ala and Ja'Naam shared a look. "He's already gone," Ka'Ala said, pointing toward the empty stable. "He left about two songs after you. He said he thought you'd have changed your mind and be right back, but he wasn't willing to wait."

"How far is it to the Bluewoods?" R'Venin asked.

"If we could fly without stopping, which I can't, it would only take three-quarters of a sun," Ba'Jai sighed. "But that's not the problem. The shortest path between here and Bluewood Cove takes us across the Canyon."

R'Venin and Ja'Naam's eyes both fell, matching Ba'Jai's mask of hopelessness. "Is it really as bad as it sounds?" Ka'Ala looked from face to face.

Ba'Jai and Ja'Naam both nodded with solemn eyes.

"I've only heard stories," R'Venin answered. "But my father once told me a story of his greatfather. An entire legion of warriors died in the briar, trying to sneak onto Ch'Hota lands instead of attacking by air. The deeper into the canyon they went, the more V'Jeeta got tangled up and poisoned by the thorns. The only warrior who made it back to the Spires was a young flag-bearer who refused to go in."

"No one comes back from Razorbriar Canyon," Ba'Jai said. "No one. And the trek around would take four suns, with no villages for refuge along the way. It's a perfect natural barrier unless you're airborne."

"What are our options?" Ka'Ala asked.

Ba'Jai and Ja'Naam discussed a few options, each one less likely to succeed than the last, their heartsongs becoming melancholy and dim. R'Venin's song seemed to rise, even and steady. Ka'Ala caught sight of his gaze and followed it up into the clouds. Her eyes widened as she caught sight of his focus. Ten Thousand wingspans above, a herd of skyswimmers played in the jet-stream. Their white ovoid-shaped bodies, mottled with tan spots, zipped around each other through the air. As they rolled over, they showed off their graphite backs, which tapered to dull points on both ends.

That might work.

"R'Venin has an idea," she said, cutting off Ba'Jai and Ja'Naam's rising debate.

"What is it?" Ja'Naam asked, nodding to her brother.

"We could ride a skyswimmer," R'Venin pointed to the sky. "Catching them is simple enough, but from what I've heard they're hard to control. Wild skyswimmers are playful but stubborn. Keeping them on course would take all of us working together. With a few wingspans of rope, we could make a bridle to steer, and harnesses to keep from falling off. And we'd get to Bluewood Cove in two suns. However, we wouldn't be able to rest for the entire journey."

"How do you know all this?" Ba'Jai asked, smiling. "I've never even heard of tamed skyswimmers."

"My battle training took me into the Northern Mountains," R'Venin averted his eyes for a moment. "I met some skyswimmer wranglers. And they shared some of their stories."

"Did you get to catch one?" Ja'Naam asked with eager eyes.

Ka'Ala swallowed the lump in her throat while R'Venin paused. "Not exactly," he said. "But I did watch them do it. From afar. When I should have been practicing aerial swordplay."

The foursome stared at each other while the crowd continued to pass by. "I'm not sure I'm comfortable with this," Ba'Jai crossed his arm. "I won't be able to help you catch one."

"I'll do it," Ja'Naam spoke up. "I'll help."

"Ja'Naam," Ba'Jai protested. "It sounds dangerous. No offense, R'Venin, but I'm not convinced your plan will work if you don't have any experience."

"After all he's done for us," Ja'Naam said forcefully. "For you. And yet, he's still willing to do more. He is risking himself again so we can get home. I believe in him, and I'm willing to help. Even if it's so that he doesn't do it alone."

Ba'Jai opened his mouth, but Ka'Ala cut him off.

"I believe in him too," she said, moving to stand next to R'Venin. "I'll help."

"I'm sorry, R'Venin," Ba'Jai's shoulders fell. "My sister's right. You've done more than anyone could ask, life-debt or not. What do you need us to do?"

R'Venin grinned. "We'll need about a hundred wingspans of rope, a fire crystal, something to reflect sunlight, and the biggest billowberry we can find. This is going to take all of us together."

* * *

R'Venin kept himself in the updraft as he climbed higher into the atmosphere, keeping a firm grip on the floating garnet-colored globe trying to pull away into the clouds. Deep inside, the fire crystal continued to heat the berry juice, making the fruit expand with each passing moment. The fruits' sweet scent dissipated quickly as the warm slipstream whisked by, ruffling his feathers. In one hand, he held onto a bristle sticking out of the bulbous surface, and in the other hand, he carried a reflecting glass borrowed from Sher'Esh. Between his wings, he had a pack filled with water bladders.

Ja'Naam and Ka'Ala, each laden with a pack of dried fruits, vegetables, and nuts, held onto ends of braided guidelines on opposite sides of the balloon. They let the updraft carry them effortlessly into the thinning air.

"Maybe we should rethink this plan," Ba'Jai shouted, tightening his grip on the rope as he dangled from the floating orb. The strands rose to the balloon's base and split into three. One strand stretching to each of his companions. His new wing flailed like a banner, while his natural wing kept the wind out of his face. Centered on his back, he carried a pack filled with R'Venin's armor and Ja'Naam's medicine bag.

"This is the only way," R'Venin yelled back. "As I said, you'd have been left behind if the three of us did this on our own. Besides, you're the ballast. I needed you to keep the billowberry steady so that I can lure in the skyswimmer. Are you ready?"

"If this works," Ba'Jai twisted the cord around his hand a few extra times. "I'm going to have an amazing story to tell Uth'Ala. She may swear a life-debt to *you*!"

R'Venin laughed, then waved his hand to Ja'Naam and Ka'Ala. They each signaled back with a nod.

Time to find out if I was paying attention.

R'Venin raised the glass and angled it to reflect the sun onto the billowberry. With the spot of light directly in front of him, he turned the mirror until it hit the side of a skyswimmer. The mammoth creature, the largest in the herd, seemed to ignore the flash. With its seven pairs of wings, it rolled over and suddenly dove. A group of smaller skyswimmers scattered at its approach and then regrouped to give chase.

R'Venin tried following the herd with his beacon but didn't get any response. "This is harder than it looked." He shouted to Ba'Jai.

Ka'Ala waved her free hand, getting his attention and pointed to a trio of medium-sized skyswimmers meandering among the herd. Intermittently, a dozen smaller ones would fly and touch their noses to their underbellies, latching on for a moment, before darting away. One of the skyswimmers seemed to get less attention than the others as it fell behind the group.

"Nursers," R'Venin shouted into the wind, looking down at Ba'Jai's frustrated expression. "I'd almost forgot. The nursers are the easiest to bait because they're always hungry."

"That's wonderful," Ba'Jai wrapped the rope around his other hand, and let go with the first. "Why don't we invite *Mother* over for a bite."

"I think one of them is out of milk," R'Venin replied. "Only a few younglings are approaching it." He realigned his glass, aiming it at the trailing nursers giant black eye.

R'Venin held the shaking light for several moments until the skyswimmer veered in their direction.

"Remember," R'Venin roared. "Hold onto that rope until you're near the mouth. Then get to Ka'Ala. I'll fly to Ja'Naam. Our weight on the rope should be enough to force the skyswimmer to take the harness, and we can steer it to Bluewood."

R'Venin signaled to Ja'Naam by twisting his wrist. She acknowledged by wrapping the rope around her hand and arm. He repeated the same gesture to Ka'Ala as the skyswimmer loomed closer.

The mammoth creature approached in slow, sweeping arcs. It's pointed snout seemed to pull back into its head, giving its nose a rounder shape until a split appeared. The line deepened like a chasm until the skyswimmer's jaws opened to form a circle the same diameter as its body.

"Try to keep the reins level," R'Venin shouted to the women. "We need them centered in her mouth."

Ka'Ala and Ja'Naam both nodded. R'Venin and the others angled their wings, using the slipstream to turn as one and keep themselves lined up with the skyswimmer's approach.

"I hope these hold," R'Venin muttered to himself as he checked the bundles of sharpened stakes tied to either side of the ballooning fruit. "I never got a good look at the bits the wranglers used."

The beast's giant toothless mouth reared closer, revealing an inner jaw with twin tongues that seemed to be reaching out for the flying treat. Just as its mouth was about to clamp down around the swollen berry, R'Venin shouted, "Now!"

Ba'Jai released all but one strand of rope as he opened his wings and angled to his side, carried by the draft toward Ka'Ala. R'Venin took the other two lengths and veered sideways to Ja'Naam. The reflecting glass slipped out of his hand as he tried to slide it into his tunic's pocket. It twinkled as it tumbled to the ground.

"Pull," he yelled. Ba'Jai clasped hands with Ka'Ala across the beast's massive head. Each team opened their wings, braking against the wind. The strands pulled taut, cutting into the inflated berry until it burst, squirting juice and billowberry gas into the skyswimmers' eager mouth. The opening clamped shut but remained split by the reins as it rolled over and jerked its head in all directions.

Ba'Jai and Ka'Ala held tight to each other's hands as their bodies beat mercilessly against the skyswimmer's body. R'Venin, with a line gripped in his hand, reached out and took Ja'Naam—still clutching her rope with both hands—by the waist.

The skyswimmer looped and swirled through the sky, dragging

the amateur wranglers along for the ride until it seemed too weary from fighting and returned to flying in lazy serpentine patterns back toward the herd.

"Take my hand. We need to get up on its back," R'Venin shouted into Ja'Naam's ear as he released her waist and stretched out his arm. She nodded and let go of the rope with one hand, grasping for his as he drifted away. Opening their wings, they arced themselves up and landed on the skyswimmer just above its primary wings. As they touched down, Ja'Naam turned her head and shouted. "Ba'Jai!"

R'Venin looked over to find Ba'Jai and Ka'Ala struggling to fly above the skyswimmer's secondary wing. They bounced off the massive sail-like appendage with each of the creatures upswings. Their reins had lodged under the primary wings, pulling them toward its body with each flap.

"Do you think you can handle the reins while I go help them?" R'Venin yelled above the din.

Ja'Naam leaned back on the rope, digging her feet into the animal's flesh. "I don't think I can hold on by myself," she shook her head. "Can you?"

R'Venin took Ja'Naam's strand and leaned into the wind, putting himself into a half-lunging position. "Yes, I think so," he jerked his head to the side. "Go help them."

Ja'Naam formed her wings into a wedge as she sidestepped across the skyswimmer's backside. Ba'Jai and Ka'Ala grunted with each slap of the skyswimmer's wing. Ka'Ala seemed to be losing her grip on the rope as Ba'Jai strained to carry their weight with one hand.

"Ba'Jai," Ja'Naam screamed. "Don't let her go. I'm coming."

Ja'Naam bobbed on her knees, putting herself in sync with their rise and fall. After being smacked up, Ja'Naam dove, plunging downward and catching her brother and friend in each arm and quickly twisted her hands into the whipping strands of twine. The rope slid free of the beast's primary wing and snapped tight, pulling the trio in a wide arc like a pendulum. "Steer toward R'Venin," she grunted as their weight stretched her arms, wrapping her wings around their legs. "My arms are going to break."

"Ja'Naam," Ba'Jai yelled. "Hold on. Ka'Ala, you've got to get us over."

Ka'Ala angled her wings, pulling their group above the skyswimmer.

R'Venin entwined one arm within several loops of rope and reached out with his other hand. "Ka'Ala," he shouted. "Grab hold."

Fighting to bring them down slowly upon the skyswimmer's back, Ka'Ala strained against the slipstream, She traded hands on the line and grabbed R'Venin's wrist with Ja'Naam clinging to her waist. Ba'Jai tucked his wings and dropped hard onto the creature's back, digging in his feet. The animal didn't seem to notice.

R'Venin sunk his talons into the skyswimmer's flesh and pulled Ka'Ala down. Ja'Naam let her legs fall, gripping with her feet and helping bring Ka'Ala to rest. Once all four had landed and plunged their talons into the fleshy hide, they huddled together, tucking their wings behind them. "We need to slow the skyswimmer down before we can tie off the lines," R'Venin yelled to the others. "Everyone, hold on to each other and pull back. Ba'Jai, take this end, and give me yours."

R'Venin held out the end of his rope, exchanging it for Ba'Jai's. All four mashed closer together to overlap the reins across all their backs.

"What now?" Ja'Naam leaned forward, shouting around Ka'Ala.

"We need to pull on the reins as one," R'Venin yelled back. "We can't pull to one side or the other; otherwise, she'll just spiral, and we may lose our footing."

"You take the lead," Ba'Jai hollered across the group.

All eyes focused on R'Venin's feet. He started bobbing at the knees, building a rhythm with one foot behind. The other's repositioned their feet to match, bouncing in sync.

"On three, take one step backward," R'Venin yelled. "One, two. Step!"

As one, they shifted their weight and back-stepped, using their wings to balance. The rope stretched, vibrating in the wind. The skyswimmer's head pulled against the reins as a rumble quaked from deep under their feet while the wind seemed to abate slightly.

"Is that normal?" Ja'Naam yelled, looking at R'Venin.

"I don't know," he answered, pulling the corner of his mouth down. "The wranglers never mentioned it."

"She's heading back for the herd," Ja'Naam pointed with her chin.

"Let's keep going," Ba'Jai shouted across the group, he resumed bobbing. "One, two. Step."

The beast's grumblings increased as its approach to the herd slowed. "It's working!" Ka'Ala whooped.

"Yes," R'Venin replied. "But we're still going too fast. Two more, and we should be safe to tie off the lines and settle in."

Stepping back as one, they pulled the reins tighter until the wind seemed to be no more than a stiff breeze. A sweeping whine emerged from the skyswimmer as the distance from the herd increased.

"Oh," Ja'Naam moaned, looking up to Ba'Jai at her side. "She's being left behind."

"She'll be able to find the herd after we get you home," R'Venin said. "They always return to their migration routes once released. Quick. Tie the ends together while Ba'Jai and I hold the reins."

R'Venin and Ba'Jai opened their wings, taking all the weight on the lines. Ka'Ala and Ja'Naam reached behind them and tied knots, weaving the ends into the opposite lengths as R'Venin and Ba'Jai kept an arm around their waists for support.

After the knots, Ja'Naam and Ka'Ala traded places, which put Ja'Naam next to R'Venin.

"Good," R'Venin tugged on the linked strands. "I think that'll hold. Now, for the hard part."

"That wasn't the hard part?" Ba'Jai chuckled.

"Not even close," R'Venin smiled and shook his head. "Unless you think staying awake for two days is easy."

"Whatever it takes for all of us to get home safely." Ja'Naam looked up to R'Venin. "Losing some sleep is a small price to pay."

"Agreed," Ka'Ala added.

"Insomnia it is, then." Ba'Jai rolled his neck. "Let's get started."

R'Venin, Ja'Naam, Ka'Ala, and Ba'Jai moved forward with arms interlocked, letting the reins slacken. The skyswimmer eased forward, picking up speed.

"Which way to the Bluewoods?" R'Venin focused his gaze on his footing.

Ja'Naam's head arched to find the sun, then gazed to the ground. "We need to turn six feathers West," she pointed with her forehead. "Home is that way."

"Alright. Everyone, pull to the right," R'Venin leaned away from the group. They all followed, keeping a firm grip around each other's waists and moving in unison. The skyswimmer pulled against the rope, but quickly relented to the bit and turned away from its herd.

"And so, the adventure begins," Ba'Jai laughed, squeezing Ja'Naam's arm around Ka'Ala's body. "Mother and Father will be amazed when they hear how we got home. And how we made our new friends."

"I think they'll be more shocked about your wing," Ja'Naam's eyes darted to the gray feathers ruffling in the breeze.

"Perhaps," he shrugged. "I'll just tell them it's R'Venin's fault." He leaned forward and gave R'Venin a wink.

R'Venin rolled his eyes. "I suppose in a way, that is true," he shouted as the wind picked up along with their speed. "Perhaps, once we arrive, you should point me in the direction of a V'Jeeta refugee camp."

"Not a chance, my friend," Ba'Jai yelled into the slipstream. "We've been through too much together to part ways now."

"My brother is right," Ja'Naam said, looking forward to the horizon. "That doesn't happen often, but he's right this time. After all you've done, you're family now. No matter what."

Ja'Naam tilted her head, resting it against Ka'Ala's. "As are you, sister."

"Being part of a family again—sounds good." Ka'Ala's words were barely audible.

"Then let's go home," Ba'Jai beamed, casting a glance across the group.

"Home," R'Venin said, leaning forward into the wind.

The skyswimmer picked up speed, blitzing through the scattered clouds.

Part Two

Chapter Eighteen

Secrets

"It's been nine cycles, R'Venin," the female V'Jeeta voice echoed from the bowl, her face and upper body floating in the swirl of smoke. "Father still believes you're either dead or a prisoner in Stonetree. Maybe it's time to let him know you're still alive."

R'Venin stared at the wisps that formed as he sat cross-legged in his prayer room. He reached out and took another handful of El'Him tree powder and flicked it into the low fire flickering within the bowl.

The powder flashed, filling the room with the scent of honeyroot petals. Her features sharpened in the fog as the smoke billowed upward above the flames. He could almost imagine her fern-colored eyes in the pewter-colored mist. "I'm not ready to come home, B'Luren," R'Venin sighed. "I'm so close to a cure for White Claw. I want to have something to offer Father when I come back. Something that'll help him realize that fighting over the Silver Silk isn't necessary anymore."

B'Luren's face radiated a soft smile. "Mother and I are so proud of you, little brother. How close are you?" Her figure seemed to reach beyond the mist and into an unseen container.

R'Venin took in a deep, slow breath. "I've managed to slow the White Claw in dozens of V'Jeeta prisoners, to varying degrees." He rubbed his temples. "But I'm still struggling with a persistent side effect."

B'Luren's ethereal form shifted as if she was adjusting her kneeling position. "What side effect?"

R'Venin looked away, staring at the wall hand-decorated with the four elements in clay paint.

Should I tell her? Can I trust this secret to anyone? Not even the Ch'Hota alchemists at Stonetree prison know yet. They might use it as a weapon against the V'Jeeta.

"I'm not even certain if it's a side effect of the treatment, or just another symptom of the White Claw," R'Venin waved away the question. "I've still got more testing to do before I can bring the results to my overseers and the Ch'Hota High Council."

B'Luren smiled in the mist. "I'm sure you'll solve the problem."

One solid and one gaseous, the two figures stared at their respective fires for several silent moments.

"I miss you and mother," R'Venin whispered. "I'm grateful to have a way to speak with you, but it's not the same. I wish I could have been there when you joined the Order of the Wind."

A misty arm protruded from the smoke, reaching out to touch R'Venin's face. Her hand dissipated against his cheek. "I wish you could have been there too," B'Luren smiled. "But you know if anyone in Mother's entourage had recognized you, it would have gotten back to Father you're still alive. It was risky enough asking for permission to go to The Three Mothers for a new crown. Mother has put herself in danger if Father ever learns about the true reason we went."

"You were always her favorite," R'Venin smiled. "Kept you within pouching distance."

"Only to keep me out of trouble," B'Luren laughed. "You know that."

"And you're still causing it," he chuckled, but his eyes turned serious.

"You know what Father would do to you. If he found out you were keeping me, and my life among the Ch'Hota, a secret."

B'Luren ruffled her neck feathers. "Well, Mother has kept secrets from him since her childhood." Her expression became hard. "And all the other wives and concubines keep their own secrets. So, I suppose it's just part of being a courtier."

R'Venin nodded with a rueful smile. "I just hope you don't get in trouble for me," he muttered while adding more El'Him powder to the fire. "Let's change the subject. Have you been espoused to a mate yet? Will you be a warrior's wife?"

B'Luren's face hardened. She tilted her head upward as she closed her eyes, taking in a slow breath. Her wings wrapped around her chest like a heavy blanket as she reached up to brush at her face. "Father announced it at the last full moon. During devotion," she growled through gritted teeth. "Just after we spoke last. We will bind our feathers at the Festival of Fertility. My husband-to-be is B'Ahz of the Fourth Tower. Father hopes this alliance will bolster his position among the clans. And he's a *fearless warrior of a mighty bloodline.*"

R'Venin winced. "You sounded just like Father. You're not pleased with the match?"

B'Luren's wings tightened around her shoulders. "I know I should be. They're a wealthy clan, and he's a strong flier. He's handsome and a lot more intelligent than he looks. He may even be as smart as you." She smirked and looked at the floor. "But his intelligence borders on devious. Father may see it as a strength, but I've seen hints of cruelty."

R'Venin reached out, hovering his hand over where B'Luren's shoulder would be if she were in the room. "Just like Father." Her face lifted to meet his gaze.

"I understand now why you let him believe you died in battle," she whispered. "It's why I keep your secret. There's no path but his. Is there?"

R'Venin dropped his hands into his lap, intertwining his fingers. "I'm still hopeful," he soothed. "If I can cure White Claw, maybe it'll lead him to pursue other peaceful solutions to our people's problems." R'Venin smiled then dropped his gaze to the bowl's rim, glancing unfocused at the glowing symbols.

B'Luren unwound her wings as she leaned forward to peer into R'Venin's face. "You don't believe that. Do you?" she asked with her wispy face just a hand's span away from his. "That he'll change? That he'll turn away from everything the sacred texts teach us about the V'Jeeta destiny? That he'll turn away from P'Phet himself and ignore the command to subjugate every other flock on Pirth'Vee Grah?"

"You know the teachings of the Order," R'Venin fidgeted, looking up from the bowl. "About having faith and loving one's enemy. Serving those who would enslave you. There's a better way to resolve our conflicts."

"I'm glad you've found peace," B'Luren bowed her head. "And can freely live what you believe. Mother and I have only each other. Every day, we have to pretend to believe P'Phet's teachings, unable to speak what we feel in our hearts openly."

R'Venin squared himself to B'Luren's ghostly form. "P'Phet was wrong," he snipped. "He taught that we must conquer the world and that our flock has a destiny to shadow over all others. That they must yield or perish. But there's a better way. Cooperation, not conquest, is the only lasting solution. That's why I'm working so hard to cure White Claw with no side effects. If we no longer need the Silver Silk as a treatment, we can put more effort into building up our flock instead of obsessing on destroying theirs."

B'Luren shook her head and straightened her back. "We mustn't discuss this anymore. Father would have me ground-cast if he even thought I was listening to Ch'Hota teachings."

R'Venin tossed another handful of powder into the flames. "How's

K'Marot? Is he still angry?"

B'Luren's arm reached outside the cloud of smoke again, then flicking her hand toward her bowl. "Yes," she whispered with widening eyes. "And it seems to get worse with each high Sun. He leaves the tower at daybreak and doesn't return until nightfall. I've asked him where he goes, but all he'll tell me is *I'm spending time in the Northern Mountains.*"

R'Venin's head popped up, a wry grin crossing his face. "The skyswimmer wranglers? What would he want to know about them? Is he planning on stepping down as Father's war chief?"

"I don't know what he has planned," she shook her head. "The last time I asked, he just smiled with that glint in his eye. The one he gets when he's planning a campaign. Whatever he's plotting, it's going to be bloody. Let's change the subject again. How's your little flock coming along? The last time we spoke, you mentioned Ja'Naam was Nesting again. Has she sleeved an egg yet?"

"Not yet." R'Venin's smile broadened as his chest expanded. "Her pouch hasn't quite opened. Ja'Naam's supposed to see the brood mothers in twelve suns to see if she's ready to receive the egg. If she is, we'll seed it on the following quarter moon."

B'Luren covered a face-splitting smile with her hands within the mist. "Have you chosen an egg?" Her eyes widened in anticipation.

R'Venin's nape ruffled. "Not yet, but we're choosing a female," he beamed. "Ja'Ven will be getting a little sister this season."

B'Luren clapped her hands and tilted her head back while she silently yelled toward the ceiling. "Have you talked about names yet?"

R'Venin sat in silence for a moment. "We'll present her to the Elders as P'Vrit," he beamed.

B'Luren's eyes glistened. "Mother will love that."

R'Venin gazed at the smoky image of his sister without speaking.

B'Luren stared back from the mist.

The low flame became the only sound filling the room for a moment. In unison, R'Venin and B'Luren both stoked their bowls. The infusion of El'Him powder brought B'Luren's image back to full resolution.

"How's that little hatchling of yours?" She asked, breaking the silence. "How big has he gotten? Is he flapping off the ground yet?"

R'Venin's chest puffed out as his crest tilted forward. "He's growing faster than you'd believe. He's already fourteen spans high, and his wing feathers are just beginning to lose their sheaths. He's not flying yet, but he'll be ready to branch in another moon. For now, he just hops around, flapping as hard as he can trying to catch the air. He has his mother's coloring, bright greens, and blues, all across his body. But he has my eyes, and I believe he'll have my wingtips. They're already coming in as dark as mine."

"I would love to meet him." B'Luren beamed. "Someday, perhaps, if the flocks are no longer warring. I would also like to meet your mate, Ja'Naam, and thank her for making my little brother happier than I'd ever seen him while living in the First Tower."

"I would like them to meet you too," R'Venin swallowed the lump in his throat. "I miss you, sister!"

"Now, don't get all swampy on me, R'Venin." B'Luren's lip trembled, dabbing at her eyes with a cloth.

A deafening crash erupted from outside the room. The clanking of metal on wood rang through the heavy cloth flap. B'Luren's shadow jumped and craned her neck to see behind R'Venin's hunched shoulders. "What was that?"

R'Venin sighed and chuckled simultaneously. "That would be my son getting into the closet again."

* * *

R'Venin burst out of the room, slinging the heavy flap over a metal hook embedded into the wall. The swishing material of deep indigo with gold embroidery blew away the smoky remnants behind him. He stretched his arms toward the carved-out ceiling and opened his wings to their full span, brushing against the sidewalls of his roost. "Ja'Ven!" he called out as his wing joints popped. "Are you nosing around again?"

Directly across the room, a niche in the wall led to an antechamber covered with a gilded tapestry embroidered with the five elements. R'Venin flapped his wings once, hopping over the nest of vines and leaves in which he and Ja'Naam slept. His bare feet touched down on the smooth parquet floor half a wingspan in front of the alcove as the sounds of another metallic avalanche clanged beyond the opening.

R'Venin's helmet peeked around the corner at the level of his waist and then withdrew as if yanked away by a hidden crook.

"Ja'Ven," R'Venin growled, suppressing a laugh. "Is that you under there?"

The black and red helmet returned around the corner, and R'Venin could see his son's emerald eyes through the single slit across the face. "No," said a muted voice trying to sound older. "I'm not Ja'Ven. I'm Dev'Adoot. The messenger of the South Wind. I've come to deliver a decree from the Great Windfather."

Ja'Ven, giggling under the helmet, retreated into the alcove.

"And what, oh mighty Dev'Adoot, is the message you have to bestow upon me? A lowly mortal?" R'Venin stifled a full-chested laugh.

Ja'Ven peeked out again, the helmet jostling around on his head. "The Great Windfather decrees that Ja'Ven needs a treat," he said, trying to make his voice boom behind the mask. "And as a reward for his bravery, he is to be given Auric Plums and Roasted Pine seeds with

Sweet Sap."

"I'm sorry, mighty Dev'Adoot," R'Venin guffawed. "Auric Plums are out of season and are very expensive. How do you expect me to pay for such a treat?"

"With this!" Ja'Ven's voice blurted out in its usual chirpy tone as he jumped out from behind the opening holding R'Venin's silver crown in his hand.

R'Venin's eyes widened as his stomach dropped. His wings tensed, pulling away from the symbol of his royal birth. "Ja'Ven, where did you find that?" he whispered.

"It was at the bottom of the closet," he said, matter-of-factly, as he hid the crown behind his back. "Under your armor."

R'Venin closed his eyes, taking two deep breaths. "How many times have I told you to stay out of there?"

"I don't know," Ja'Ven shuffled his feet.

R'Venin reached out with an open hand saying, "Give that to me," his voice barely above a whisper. "Now."

Ja'Ven put the jeweled ring into his father's palm, his eyes filled with worry.

R'Venin got down on one knee, enfolding his son with his wings as he took the over-sized helmet with his free hand off Ja'Ven's head. He tucked the crown inside the helmet before setting the pair down on the floor. R'Venin ignored the quiet thud as his headgear fell onto its side, exposing the glittering red jewels encrusted within the woven strands.

"What is that, Father?" Ja'Ven's eyes darted to the ground.

R'Venin stared into Ja'Ven's eyes for what seemed like eons.

How do I explain it? His father is the First Prince of those who seek his destruction.

"It's a relic from my past," R'Venin sighed. "From the place I left long ago. A place to which I hope to return someday. But for now, it must remain hidden."

Ja'Ven cocked his head. "But why?"

R'Venin smiled despite himself.

Here comes the endless stream of 'why.'

"I can't explain why," R'Venin chuckled, rubbing the green and gold tufts on Ja'Ven's head. "I just need you to trust and obey me. Will you do that?"

Ja'Ven's eyes narrowed as he smiled. "Only if we can play tickle-chase," he hunched his shoulders and wriggled his fingers.

R'Venin took Ja'Ven's head with both hands, planting a kiss on his child's forehead. "Let's put away my armor together," he said, nuzzling their heads together. "Then, we'll play tickle-chase until your mother comes home. Agreed?"

Without skipping a beat, Ja'Ven picked up the helmet. The crown spilled onto the floor as he flitted back into the antechamber. "I'll race you!" he shouted.

R'Venin picked up the crown with one hand while barely touching it with the fingertips of the other. Feeling along its surface, he subconsciously counted the rubies nestled into woven threads of silvervine.

Twenty-Seven. The largest for the First Tower. Eight smaller, one for each of the others. The rest for the sake of opulence. And I was set to inherit it all.

His fingertips reached the largest star-shaped ruby-the size of his thumb-raised away from the circle of lower gems in a nest of swirling tendrils.

My Father's house. Will I ever see the Granite Spires again?

Another crash of metal yanked R'Venin's attention away from his longing for home. "Oops!" Ja'Ven's tiny voice came from the armory.

R'Venin stepped around the corner. Ja'Ven stood inside the closet, holding the helmet to his fullest height, not quite reaching the peg sticking out of the back wall. Each attempt to return the headgear caused Ja'Ven to make another piece of black armor fall.

Ja'Ven turned with sad eyes. "I can't reach it," he whined, holding the helmet out to R'Venin.

R'Venin stepped to his son and turned him back toward the cabinet interior before lifting him at his waist. Ja'Ven leaned forward and set the helmet onto the peg. "I did it!" he shouted, raising his arms and wings into the air.

"You see?" R'Venin laughed, tossing Ja'Ven into the air. "We can do anything together!"

"Again, Father! Again!" Ja'Ven giggled, pointing to the ceiling.

"I thought you wanted to play tickle-chase?" R'Venin said, jiggling Ja'Ven up at arm's length.

"Oh, yeah," the boy answered, wriggling out of R'Venin's grip and landing on the floor with a light thud.

Piece by piece, the carbon-feather armor plating reformed the outline of a V'Jeeta warrior. A score of the smallest remaining rubies clung to each piece. "Now, you go hide," R'Venin said, concealing the crown with his wingtips, "And I'll come to find you."

Ja'Ven ran out of the armory, shouting. "One, two, three..."

R'Venin unveiled the circlet and pushed it to the back of the topmost shelf.

That should keep Ja'Ven from finding it until I can conjure a better hiding spot.

"Now, where's that son of mine!" R'Venin bound out of the armory through the roost and out into their home's main room. "He needs a tickle!"

Ja'Ven's shrill squawk echoed throughout the chamber. Hopping around and over their furnishings, Ja'Ven flapped his winglets, which did little to keep himself airborne while R'Venin pretended to lunge at him. Chasing around their home, Ja'Ven held a slight lead on R'Venin. Every few steps, R'Venin would swipe his arm and run his talons across Ja'Ven's back or wings, making sure he never got too close. The resulting squeals of delight bounced off the walls and spilled out onto the balcony.

The sunlight peeking through the exterior crystal plating swept halfway through the house by the time R'Venin saw two familiar shapes of green and blue float closer. Breathing heavy, R'Venin stopped the chase.

"Father," Ja'Ven whined through deep breaths. "I want more tickle-chase."

R'Venin pointed toward the figures at the doorway. Ja'Ven turned just as Ja'Naam and Ba'Jai landed on the platform.

Ja'Ven ran over to the pair, flapping his little wings with all his might. "Mother! You're home!"

Chapter Nineteen

Nesting

Knocking over a carved bench that sat next to the fire pit, Ja'Ven ran into Ja'Naam's waiting arms. The woven mating band of silvervine jingled as her knee hit the floor. R'Venin's hearts swelled as his eyes traced along the onyx feather that dangled from the circlet by a golden clip shaped like an intricate sunburst. The one he'd fastened on himself after braiding the vines in the ceremony. Beside it, another clip shaped like a star hung to the strands clinging onto a bundle of tawny fluff.

Ja'Ven's first molting. After seven seasons, I still can't believe she agreed to be my life mate. We have an exceptional son, and a daughter will be next.

Ja'Naam wrapped her wings around Ja'Ven as he nuzzled his face into her neck. "I missed you, Mother." He squeezed tightly. Her feathers rippled in the breeze flowing across the balcony as the gilded tips sparkled in the sunlight.

Ba'Jai waved to R'Venin, pulling his mismatched wings under a soiled linen cloak. R'Venin smiled and returned the gesture as he righted the bench on his way over.

"I missed you too, my son." Ja'Naam knelt down, keeping Ja'Ven bundled in her arms. "I have a surprise for you. From your greatmother."

Ja'Ven pushed away, his face lighting up with wide eyes and a broad smile. "What is it?"

Ja'Naam craned her head, looking at Ba'Jai behind her. Ja'Ven followed her gaze as he shrugged the pack off his shoulder and lowered it to the floor. The bundle squirmed as the fabric settled, undulating in circular patterns.

"Is that what I think it is?" R'Venin groaned, fixing his gaze on Ja'Naam. "I thought we agreed he wasn't old enough yet."

Ja'Naam swatted away his comment. "Open it," she said, unfolding her wings.

Ja'Ven peeled away from Ja'Naam's embrace and knelt before the writhing parcel. Ba'Jai squatted next to the bag, holding the bottom corners to the floor while Ja'Ven untied the flap. The boy gasped as a pair of bright yellow antennae poked from inside, sweeping through the air in random patterns. "It's a fuzzypede!"

The feelers extended further from the pack's opening, followed by a fluffy cerulean head with mustard stripes. The creature's onyx eyes gazed unblinkingly from either side of its head as it probed its new surroundings. Ja'Ven reached out an open palm, lowering it to the floor below the fuzzypede's head. The animal's antennae curled around his hand and arm.

As the delicate whips reached the crook of Ja'Ven's elbow, he giggled. "He likes me!" he beamed as the fuzzypede crawled up his arm on twelve legs, each one ending in a broad six-toed foot that adhered to his skin. The fuzzypede continued its march over Ja'Ven's shoulder, around his neck, and down the other arm, dangling its front legs off his hand in the air.

"Hold your hands out like this." Ba'Jai formed his arms into a ring.

Ja'Ven copied Ba'Jai's posture, putting his hand under the fuzzypede's head, its antennae feeling along his wrist and arm before resuming its journey. Ja'Ven squealed each time the animal brushed its fine hairs across the back of his neck.

"Thank you, uncle Ba'Jai," Ja'Ven beamed. "Thank you, Mother."

"You're welcome," Ja'Naam and Ba'Jai said in unison.

"We'll talk to your greatmother after the evening meal," Ja'Naam stroked the fuzzypede's hairs.

"With the speaking bowl?" Ja'Ven asked, taking the fuzzypede with both hands.

"Yes," she answered, her smile drooped slightly. "It's important to thank her as soon as possible."

R'Venin's mouth pinched to a flat line. "She's not doing well, is she?" he asked, looking between Ja'Naam and Ba'Jai.

Ba'Jai stood and met R'Venin's gaze, shaking his head. Ja'Naam's eyes glistened as she focused on Ja'Ven with a sad smile.

R'Venin took a deep breath, nodding.

They lost their father two seasons ago. Their mother will soon follow.

"I suppose now that it's here," R'Venin sighed, pointing at the fuzzypede. "He needs a name. What're you going to call him?"

Ja'Ven held up his new pet, its feet reaching out for anything on which to take hold. "I'll call him Pal'Atoo," he turned the fuzzypede around to face him. "Do you like that?"

The fuzzypede extended its feelers, probing around Ja'Ven's face, causing the hatchling to laugh and roll his head around.

"Pal'Atoo it is then," R'Venin patted Ja'Ven's back. "You'll be responsible for taking care of him."

"I will!" Ja'Ven laid Pal'Atoo across his shoulders, stroking his body.

"Why don't you gather some leaves and take him to your nest," R'Venin gave Ja'Ven a little push. "Let him get used to his new home. I want to talk to your mother and uncle."

"Yes, Father," Ja'Ven turned and walked away with his arms encircled in front of him.

Once Ja'Ven cleared the archway to his roost, R'Venin reached down, offering his hand to Ja'Naam. Her face fell as she stood.

"Your mother's not doing well, is she?" R'Venin pulled Ja'Naam into his arms.

She shook her head against his chest, tightening her grip around his waist.

"The healers say she has a few more moons," Ba'Jai said, casting a glance over R'Venin's shoulder. "She can't fly anymore and has trouble even walking around her home. Her village has done all they can to help, but it's only a matter of time now. At this point, it would be a mercy if the Windfather just took her into the Eternal Tree."

R'Venin's mouth pinched as he nodded, then looked down. "I'm sorry, my love. I know how close you two are," he breathed into Ja'Naam's ear.

Several moments passed before Ja'Naam took a deep breath and wiped her face. "How was Ja'Ven while I was away?"

Deep down in his throat, R'Venin laughed. "He got into my armor again," he said with a smile, then it quickly faded. "This time, he found the crown. He asked me what it was."

Ja'Naam stood back as her jaw dropped, her eyes widening. "What did you tell him?"

"I said it was a relic from my past, and it had to be kept secret," R'Venin shrugged. "I think it pacified him. For now. And maybe he'll be too distracted with his new fuzzypede to go sniffing for it again."

Ja'Naam put a hand on R'Venin's face. "You gave up so much."

R'Venin leaned in to give her a soft peck. "But I gained so much more."

Ja'Naam breathed in his scent and wrapped her wings around him, pulling him down to a soft kiss. "I have good news," she breathed, her smile widening. "My pouch is opening early." She opened the folds of her tunic, revealing the seam across her abdomen and tugged at the flap of skin.

A faint musky scent rose to R'Venin's nasal slits as he peered down into the dark pocket. His eyes glistened, widening like moons. Without warning, he bent down and scooped her up. Spinning her around, he opened his wings to full span, brushing the tips along the walls as laughter filled their little home.

"Let's get another dangler for your mating band," R'Venin beamed. "Tomorrow. We'll go down to Ka'Ala's shop and tell her the news." He dropped her to the floor, taking her face with both hands, pressing his lips to hers.

Ja'Naam broke free from R'Venin's embrace. "It's supposed to be bad luck for a mother-to-be to get a child's talisman before she's pouched," she grinned, playfully slapping his chest.

"Since when do you hold to ancient superstition," R'Venin laughed, looking down at the delicate jewelry dangling just above the floor. "It's a symbol of your legacy. You don't have to wear it yet. But let's celebrate. Our flock is growing again."

"Very well," Ja'Naam's smile split her face. She wrapped her arms around his neck as his hands lifted her by the waist. They giggled and kissed until Ba'Jai cleared his throat.

"Alright, you two," he mumbled. "Save it for the high moon."

"Sorry, Ba'Jai," Ja'Naam muttered, unwrapping herself from R'Venin's arms. "I forgot. You haven't... ever since—."

"I haven't enjoyed a physical bond with anyone ever since Uth'Ala flew to another man's wing?" Ba'Jai grimaced.

"I know it's been hard, my friend," R'Venin sighed as Ja'Naam stepped away to hug her brother. "But I have to say; I think you're better off. She became so cold to you after Ja'Naam and I sealed our bond. I think she hated the idea of being related to a V'Jeeta."

"I always said you were too good for her," Ja'Naam added, tightening her grip around Ba'Jai's waist.

Ba'Jai pulled himself out of her arms, gazing out toward the colossal Bluewood trees. Hundreds of people flying between the massive trunks, walking along platforms, and gathering among the branches. The cacophony of a million voices, like a rushing brook, filled the air. Two hundred wingspans down, the roofs of a thousand buildings covered the forest in all directions. The ground looked like a tile mosaic with streets like grout lines.

"It wasn't you, R'Venin. It was me," he finally said under his breath. "I've never told you this, Ja'Naam. But you were right. Uth'Ala only bonded with me because she believed I would advance in the guard. But after—." Ba'Jai rolled his shoulders, tucking his wings tighter under the cloak.

"After you lost your wing." Ja'Naam put her arms around Ba'Jai's waist.

He nodded. "After I came home with this," he thumbed over his shoulder, "and got reassigned to the cavalry because I couldn't fly in full armor, Uth'Ala grew distant. She once said she didn't like how I smelled of runnerhound when I came home from sentry duty. I pretended everything was fine. I didn't want to believe she'd turn me away because of an injury, but... Eventually, she moved back to her father's house and demanded a severance. You know the rest."

"Come with us tomorrow," Ja'Naam took Ba'Jai by the hand. "I know Ka'Ala would like to see you again. She often speaks of how much she's appreciated your friendship over the years."

"We'll see," Ba'Jai sighed, giving her a half-smile. "Maybe I'll take Ja'Ven to the stables and show him the new runnerhound pups while you two are shopping."

"I think he'd like that," R'Venin sidled up to Ja'Naam, putting an arm around her waist.

"And then, afterward, you could meet us at Willowlimb," Ja'Naam raised her eyebrows. "The five of us could have our evening meal together in the bazaar."

"Okay," Ba'Jai nodded, looking down. "It *would* be nice to see her again."

Chapter Twenty

The Seer of Willowlimb Bazaar

"Here it is," Ka'Ala lifted a folded linen bundle from the chest of drawers at the back wall of her mercantile. The three-sided canopy of sand-colored canvas glowed from the afternoon sun. Glimpses of pedestrians appeared through the slit in the center panel of fabric that swayed with the breeze. Shadows across the sloping roof changed shape like clouds, as the cacophony of bartering drifted into her ears. An occasional gust pushed the flaps of her shop open. The cooler air carried the smells of baked goods, roasted worms, raw nuts, and vegetables, as well as the stench of sewage into the stifling heat.

Next to the chest, a double-layered curtain of linen blocked the view through the arched doorway leading to the only other room. Her eyes glanced to the edges, catching just a sliver of light from beyond the veil.

She turned and gently laid the packet on one of two wooden planks she used as tables. She peeled back the top layer of cloth to reveal a glittering mountain symbol pendant of braided silvervine. "Just as you requested." She let the fabric drop into a pile next to the woven ornament and looked up.

Across the table, a middle-aged Ch'Hota couple stared down at the trinket with glistening eyes. The vibrant blue and green tips of their wings just beginning to lose their luster like a mural faded by the sun.

The man stood two heads above Ka'Ala; his mustard-colored eyes focused on his mate's face. The woman was just a half-head shorter than her companion. Her daffodil-colored eyes glistened as she stared down at the ornament. They each wore simple rough-spun tunics that fell to their knees with a leather apron hanging around their necks. The man's looked like it had fallen into the fire on more than one occasion, while the woman's apron had grain-dust trapped in every seam.

Ka'Ala shrugged her wings, turning her head as if glancing into the backroom of her shop. Her wings radiated in the golds, blues, and greens of an average Ch'Hota woman. She tilted her head slightly and closed her eyes for a quick moment before returning her gaze to her customers.

"It's perfect," the woman breathed, clasping her hands over her chest. Ka'Ala smelled fresh-baked bread as flecks erupted from her hands. Subtle burn scars across the backs of her hands danced in the light like a spinner's web.

"So beautiful," The man put his arm, etched with similar markings, around his companion's shoulders and squeezed. "Just like our little Ha'Rish."

"It was an honor to make this for your lost one," Ka'Ala whispered, glancing up at her shop's doorway as a young Ch'Hota couple walked in with arms entwined. She gave them a quick smile. "I'll be right with you. Please look around." She raised her hand, gesturing toward a shelf of painted pottery, woven baskets, and jewelry.

Turning her eyes back to the couple, she found the woman hugging herself around her waist. The man had pulled her in tighter, resting his head on hers. Their heartsongs swelled like a crashing wave. Low and mournful at first, then rising with intensity to a near-deafening climax before pulling away again.

So much love. So much pain. Windfather, favor them in their grief.

"I'm so sorry," Ka'Ala said, her worried eyes darting back and forth between them. "How old would she have been?"

"She..." the woman choked, covering her quivering mouth.

The man brushed the back of his hand on his mate's face. "She would have been three moons if the Windfather had given her breath."

Ka'Ala picked up the ornament from the table and held it out to the woman. "May this bring you some peace in your sorrow."

She bowed as Ka'Ala placed the delicate treasure into her hands. The woman then turned and presented it to her partner. The man took the pendant and got down on one knee, pulling back his tunic's hem to expose his thigh. With the trinket in one hand, he offered his other to the woman. She held it as she put her foot on his leg. The cuff around her knee jangled with six other ornaments: Three trees, two wind, and one rain.

He tied the mountain symbol to the band, in the descending line of other dangles, to rest against her sandy skin. Once finished, she removed her foot and helped him up, wrapping her arms around his waist. "How much?" the man asked, his voice breaking.

"Two gold or eighteen bronze," Ka'Ala brushed a silent tear from her face, her eyes shimmering like pearls.

The man's eyes fell as he pulled a leather sack from his waistband and poured the contents into his hand. One golden sphere, the size of his thumb, sat in the middle of silver ones. He touched each one, muttering under his breath. "I've only got one gold and five bronze," he sighed, looking up with sheepish eyes. "Can I give you this now, and come back with the rest after my next wages? We'll leave Ha'Rish's pendant with you until we can pay in full." He reached over and squeezed his mate's arm.

The woman nodded, tears spilling down her face, as she got down on one knee and began fiddling with the strap with trembling fingers. Her heartsong filling Ka'Ala's ears with a swell of mournful tones.

"That's not necessary," Ka'Ala held out her open palm. "I'll consider myself fully paid. May the Windfather strengthen your hearts."

The woman's eyes widened as she covered her gaping mouth. Standing, she rushed around the table and pulled Ka'Ala into an embrace. Ka'Ala felt hot tears run down her neck as the woman sobbed in her arms.

"Thank you," the muffled words barely reached Ka'Ala's ears though her mouth was a hand-span away. "Thank you. May the Windfather bless you."

Ka'Ala pulled herself out of the woman's tight grip. "He always does," she whispered, brushing the wetness from her face. "Now, if you'll excuse me, I have other customers waiting. Fair weather."

"Fair weather," the man said, reaching out for his mate, guiding her back around the table and toward the sunlit bazaar outside.

As they cleared the doorway, Ka'Ala poured the coins into the leather sack hanging from her waistband and turned her attention to the younger couple. They stood close, stroking each other's back feathers as they took turns pointing at the various mating bands displayed on a sheet of shimmering cloth. Ka'Ala gave them a sidelong glance as she returned the linen swatch to the chest.

The young woman looked closer to a maturing adolescent as Ka'Ala got a better view of her face. The hem of her rose and lilac-colored tunic kissed her feet while she swayed in his arms as if in a daze. Her young feathers glimmered like a waterfall, even in the diminished light of her shop. She rested her head against the young man's chest; her eyes twinkled as she gazed at the various circlets. Armbands and bracelets of silvervine jangled as she pointed at different jeweled items.

The young man glanced at Ka'Ala, raising his chin slightly and showing her a full smile that never reached his eyes. His azure cloak, a few sizes too big for his frame, appeared drab next to her gown. His feathers had the windswept appearance of a public messenger.

Ka'Ala nodded and smiled back then turned away, pretending to reorganize the colored spools of thread, folds of leather, and a potter's wheel. With her head down, she closed her eyes and listened. Two distinct melodies formed in her mind. The first, a steady processional like a harp heralding the arrival of a long-awaited king. The other, hard, powerful, and all-consuming.

Ka'Ala closed her mind to the discordant songs, the coins jingling as she walked over to stand next to them. "Which design do you like?" she asked, clearing the catch in her throat.

"This Mountain one," the boy tapped a dark umber strap of leather woven with gray stone beads.

"No," the girl pointed to a band of silvervine, woven with silky blue thread, dangling with clear pear-shaped gems. "This Rain one. Isn't it pretty?"

The boy leaned down to put his mouth to her ear. "I can't afford that," he pleaded. "We agreed we'd get something simple, and then get you a nicer one in our tenth season."

"Pssh," The girl pushed herself away, giving his chest a weak slap. "Father will buy it for me. You can work extra evenings to repay him."

The boy's eyes closed as his chin dropped to his chest.

"I'll let you have some privacy," Ka'Ala said, sidestepping away to the other side of the shop. She could hear the girl's side of their argument, apparently unwilling to lower her voice.

"You said you loved me... Am I not worth it... What do you mean by that... Of course, I do... I don't see why not... I think you're being selfish... Maybe you should be smarter with your earnings, then..."

Ka'Ala sang to herself, drowning out the girl's increasingly shrill objections. Half a song later, she jumped as she felt a tap on her shoulder. She spun around to find the boy standing there, his eyes pleading.

"We'll talk about this after the evening meal," the girl huffed as she bounded out the door. "When you're ready to appreciate what you have."

Ka'Ala put her hand to her chest. "You startled me," she blew out her breath. "What can I do for you? Did your betrothed not find something to her liking? Do you wish to request a custom design? Perhaps something with both Mountain and Rain symbols?"

"No," the boy sighed. "That's not it. She's angry that I came here to look for a mating band instead of a merchant closer to her trunk."

"Why did you come to my shop then?" Ka'Ala looked around. "As you can see, I'm not the most gifted artisan. There are others with far more variety and skill. I sell barely enough to keep my shelves stocked and keep my belly from grumbling."

The boy put both hands on the table and leaned forward. "Are you the seer?"

Ka'Ala stepped back; her wings raised a handspan as she swallowed hard. "The what?"

"The seer," the boy's voice seemed on the verge of breaking. "I've heard stories of an artisan who can predict a couple's future; she knows if it's a good match or not. My sister came here six seasons ago to buy her mating band. She said her artisan told her that she'd chosen well and would have a happy life; she's never been more at peace. And a friend of mine said his artisan warned him to reconsider his choice after I told him I'd seen his betrothed with another man just days before they mated. He went through with the ceremony, and now he's miserable. Each of them said the artisan lived in this quarter, and you're the fifth artisan we've visited today."

Ka'Ala breathed in slowly through her nose, focusing on her hands, as she swept nonexistent dust from the table.

Help me, Windfather. I don't want to draw attention to myself. What do I say?

Be Honest, but choose your words carefully, my child, Windfather whispered from the doorway at her back.

Ka'Ala raised her eyes to find the boy searching her face, the corners of his mouth pulled down, fighting a quivering lip. Her wings dropped as she stepped up to the table, leaning forward to cover his hands with hers.

"What's your name?" Ka'Ala peered into his face.

"D'Oot," he said with a quick bow and tucking his wings.

"I wouldn't describe myself as a seer, D'Oot," she said in a measured voice, loud enough to keep her words inside the shop. "I get certain feelings when I'm around people. I get a sense of their personality. Sometimes, when they're in a strong emotional state—like when two people are picking out mating bands—I can tell if their nature is compatible with each other. When it is, it's like I can hear music in harmony. When it isn't, the melodies clash, and it just becomes noise."

"What did you sense between Vy'Arth and I?" His voice cracked. "We're not a good match, are we? We're *just noise*, aren't we?"

Ka'Ala squeezed his hands. "What do your hearts tell you?"

"That I'm in love with her," D'Oot croaked. "Falling like a burnished leaf."

"And what do your hearts tell you about how she feels for you?" she probed.

D'Oot's shoulders fell. "She says she loves me, and I've never had reason to doubt her sincerity."

Ka'Ala nodded to herself. "Does she have the same hopes and dreams you have? Does she want the same life as you?"

D'Oot's head slumped to his chest. She then put a hand on his shoulder and he looked up to meet her gaze.

"Then what will love matter if you're flying in different directions?"

Ka'Ala searched D'Oot's face. In his watery eyes, she found resignation. She'd told him the truth. She knew it, and she knew that he knew it too.

Chapter Twenty-One

The Vision

Three songs later, Ka'Ala walked D'Oot to the archway and gave him an awkward pat on the back.

"Thank you, seer," he cleared his throat. "I have much to consider."

"It's just Ka'Ala," she gave him a quick bow. "Fair weather, D'Oot."

"Fair weather, Ka'Ala," he said as he looked skyward and launched into the air.

Ka'Ala stood outside her shop in the warm afternoon air, taking in the myriad aromas wafting by. Across the road, in the glazier's shop, she caught the distorted image of a Ch'Hota woman in a pane of reflecting glass. Ka'Ala raised her hand to wave, then she realized she was waving to her own reflection.

Disappointment crashed down as Ka'Ala felt her disguise fade across her scalp. She closed her eyes as her face tightened. When she reopened them, her reflection showed only gilded plumage on her head. She glanced around, wide-eyed, scanning the street for any signs that someone had seen her camouflage falter, even for a moment. But no one paid her any attention.

Ka'Ala darted into her shop, pulling the storefront hangings closed behind her, and bolted to the back room. With one arm, she swiped her privacy curtain aside and stepped into the unlit antechamber. Her muted shadow, diffused by the weak light penetrating the fabric, vanished as it got deeper into the room.

From tips to talons, her skin and feathers shimmered. The golds, blues, and greens drained down her body as if she stood beneath an invisible deluge of midnight ink. She closed her eyes and rolled her neck, then let her chin fall. She sighed, crossing the room and slumping down onto her bed like a cut marionette. Arms wrapped around herself, she huddled in the darkness with unfocused eyes toward the filtered light peeking under the doorway.

Windfather, how long must I hide? How long must I be alone?

Patience, daughter, she heard as a slight gust pushed against her curtain, brightening her room. *The time will come. See what you have gained.*

Ka'Ala nodded once. "Yes, Father," she whispered, her eyes falling to her feet. She sat motionless, listening to the slow rhythm of her shallow breaths for the length of a song. She reached to a low table beside her roost and picked up a hand-sized clay bowl revealing a fire crystal, the size of her thumb, set in a brass mount. The room brightened with a pale honey glow, casting soft shadows across the walls. Across from her, next to the doorway, a workbench stood littered with several unfinished pieces. She focused her gaze on the shelf above, letting the corners of her mouth turn up as she took in the menagerie.

Etchings on wood or plaster lined the shelves. Portraits containing groups and individuals gazed back at her with loving faces. Ja'Naam, her sister. The woman who saved her from the firesnakes. Ja'Ven, her joy. The boy who would become her son if tragedy struck. Ba'Jai, her friend. The man who has shown her unyielding kindness. Shil'Pakar, the Pra'Acheen who took her in as an apprentice. And R'Venin. The man she helped save and came to admire.

Ka'Ala stood and stepped to the workbench, reliving memories as her gaze drifted passed each image several times. She lifted a melon-sized wooden bowl off the surface, uncovering a fist-sized crystal, further brightening her room.

Thank you, Windfather, for the gentle reminder.

She refilled her lungs and stretched her neck, arms, and wings when a familiar voice called from outside her shop.

"Ka'Ala? Are you there?"

A smile spread across Ka'Ala's face as Ja'Naam's heartsong filled her ears. She turned toward the curtains, looking out through a tiny hole in the fabric. Standing in the doorway, with one panel held out to the side, Ja'Naam's eyes focused toward the backroom.

"Ja'Naam," her voice sang out, moving her head to peer into the corners of her shop. "Are you alone?"

Another hand appeared, holding up the sheet as Ja'Naam stepped in, followed by R'Venin's dark figure. "Not quite," he said, letting the curtain fall closed behind him.

Ka'Ala's smile widened as R'Venin's heartsong joined Ja'Naam's. "R'Venin," she swallowed to keep her voice from catching. "I'm so glad you've both come to visit. Would you mind setting the togs on the curtain?"

R'Venin turned and pulled the two drapes together, clasping the wooden pegs into corresponding leather eyelets, from top to bottom. Once secure, Ka'Ala shifted her colors back to Ch'Hotan and pushed through the curtains, meeting Ja'Naam between the tables with open arms.

"It's good to see you, sister," Ja'Naam squeezed Ka'Ala into a tight embrace. "It's been too many sunrises."

"It's only been a half-moon," Ka'Ala laughed. "But I've missed you too. Where's Ja'Ven?"

"Ba'Jai took him to see the runnerhounds," Ja'Naam sighed. "He still gets a little slack-feather around you after..."

"After I declined his offer of courtship last snowfall." Ka'Ala bowed her head. Her stomach flipped as if she'd just swallowed a fistful of beans. "And as I told him, he has good hearts, but Windfather forbade me from mating with him. I can only love him as a friend."

Ja'Naam's heartsong floated into her mind, bright and cheery, though the tempo waned as their eyes locked. Ja'Naam opened and closed her mouth, then took Ka'Ala by the hand. "One day," Ja'Naam said. "The Windfather will bless you with a mate. The right one, just for you."

Ka'Ala hugged herself with her other arm, unconsciously running a talon across her pouch slit, and nodded. Her smile never reached her eyes.

Only the Windfather knows the season.

"How is your shop faring?" R'Venin said, looking around. "I expect there are many seeking your wares, now that we're in the nesting season. Mostly betrothed couples looking for a mating band, I imagine."

Ka'Ala shook the stupor from her mind. "Yes, Windfather has blessed me." She cocked her head and listened. R'Venin's heartsong boomed in his chest. A triumphant march of horns. "But that's not why you came to see me, is it?"

She looked back to Ja'Naam who's smile was on full display.

"We've come to give you the good news," R'Venin stood tall, his chest puffed out with hands on his hips.

Ka'Ala's smile widened. "What news?"

Ja'Naam bounced on her toes.

"We're going to need another ornament for Ja'Naam's mating band," R'Venin stepped beside Ja'Naam, taking her hand. "Sooner than expected."

Ka'Ala's eyes widened as she covered her widening mouth.

"When?"

"Any sunrise." Ja'Naam laughed. "I'll go back to the hatchery when I'm ready to receive the egg. But she'll hatch among the new leaves."

"You've chosen a girl?" Ka'Ala grabbed Ja'Naam's hands. "I'm so happy for you. May Windfather favor you."

"He does," Ja'Naam replied, looking up to R'Venin. "Every sunrise."

"I'll make you another dangler right away." Ka'Ala pulled Ja'Naam into her arms. "What symbol will you choose."

"We haven't decided," Ja'Naam sighed. "I think it should be Tree, but—."

"And I think it should be rain," R'Venin interrupted.

"You got to name Ja'Ven, and choose mountain for him," Ja'Naam poked him in the chest. "As a son, that was your right."

"On the Granite Spires, the father chooses all his offspring's symbols," R'Venin said, turning to face his wife.

"But we're not on the Spires, are we?" Ja'Naam put her hand on his chest. "And you swore an oath to abide by our customs when you joined the Order of the Wind."

"I'll get my sketch plate from the back," Ka'Ala said, withdrawing through the curtains to her back room. The drape swished the floor as it closed, but the argument followed. She sat at her bench, fiddling with her slate and stylus, not wanting to listen.

"I know I did," R'Venin's voice rose. "But this is a tradition I don't want to give up. All my life, I imagined naming my children before the royal court and presenting their symbol to their mother, just as my father did. Just as my great-father did before *him*. It's our tradition."

"It's also V'Jeeta tradition to arrange marriages of their daughters as children," Ja'Naam's voice tensed. "Didn't you tell me your mother was betrothed to your father before she'd seen twelve seasons? Is that another tradition you want to honor? Will our daughter—who'll be named after your mother—be committed to a man three times her age for the sake of a political alliance?"

"No, of course not, but—."

"What about Ch'Hota traditions? It's our tradition for the mother to name—and choose the symbol—of the daughters. We're naming her after your mother; to honor her courage to live by the Order among the V'Jeeta. She and B'Luren risk their wings every day for their faith."

Ka'Ala heard a pair of feet shuffle toward the outer door. She moved to the curtain and peeked out the spy hole. R'Venin stood facing the closed flaps, his hands on his hips and head bowed. His hearts sang two distinct melodies. Booming drums clashed with palatial horns.

"Ever since we sanctified Ja'Ven in the holy pools," Ja'Naam's voice broke, "I've dreamed of standing beside you to present a daughter before the Elders; to cry her name and raise her toward the sky—just as you did with Ja'Ven—and then accept her dangler next to his on my leg. Are my dreams less valid than yours? Would you ask me to sacrifice my rights as a mother? As your mate?"

"I've sacrificed everything I once knew," he said. "I've given up so much."

"I know you have," Ja'Naam breathed. "And I don't have words to describe what that means to me."

"I try to be a good mate."

"You are. My hearts sing for you."

"I try to be a good father."

"You are. Ja'Ven loves you, dearly."

"I'm treated little better than the other V'Jeeta at Stonetree. I may as well be a prisoner myself."

"I know," she whispered. "I can't even begin to understand what that's like for you."

"Do I ask too much of you? Has mating with a V'Jeeta made you a low-brancher? Is this so you can be equal in the eyes of most Ch'Hota women?"

"Of course not!" she raised a hand to her chest. "How can you ask that of me? Do you believe most Ch'Hota would spurn someone for the shade of their feathers?"

"Yes. I see it in the way they avoid my eyes. I see it in the way they arc away from me in the air. I see it in the way they look at you when they don't think I'm watching."

"You think I don't see it too? Do you think I'd let anyone speak ill of you over the heritage to which you were born? You may have been born a prince, but that's not what makes you royal. It's the love in your hearts for what is right and true that makes you worthy of your crown. I would do anything to bring you the same honor you've brought to our family."

"Then why deny me this? Why deny me the honor of choosing the symbol of all our children? Is it for your pride?"

Ja'Naam moved behind R'Venin and put her hands on his back, gently stroking the feathers between his wing joints. "Would you circumvent the rituals of the Order, as decreed by the Windfather through his chosen seers? For your traditions? For your pride?"

R'Venin's wings fell, draping the dusty ground, as he buried his face with his hands. "Forgive me," his words barely penetrated Ka'Ala's curtain. "I've been a selfish fool."

Ja'Naam stepped around to face him, pushing his hands to the sides with hers. "There's nothing to forgive, my love."

Ja'Naam and R'Venin's heartsongs joined in a chorus that made Ka'Ala step away from the curtain. She collapsed next to her bed and stifled the sobs racking her body.

When, Windfather? When will I know this love for myself?

To know joy, you must know sorrow, Windfather whispered. *See.*

Ka'Ala's eyes glazed over as she stared with vacant eyes at the ceiling.

* * *

Ka'Ala found herself at the base of a colossal Bluewood. She couldn't see more than a wingspan in any direction. Black smoke, reeking of burnt feathers, gusted past. The sounds of clanging metal and battle cries, deafening in its proximity, erupted on all sides.

"Windfather," she shouted over the din, but her voice came out muffled, as if underwater. "What is this? Where am I?"

A rising scream came at her from behind. She turned just as a V'Jeeta warrior in black armor, wielding a two-sided ax, charged at her. She raised her arms to block his swing, but he passed through her like vapor. She spun to see him plunge his weapon into the shoulder of an unarmed Ch'Hota villager, cleaving his arm off.

A golden spear appeared from her chest, followed by a gilded Ch'Hota guardsman, running the V'Jeeta through and pinning him to the blood-soaked ground.

Ka'Ala spread her wings and pushed off the ground but gained no altitude. She looked down to see nothing holding her, yet she was unable to escape the fray.

Shapes of gold and black clashed, scattering feathers into the wind.

A half-sun passed before the cacophony of war faded to the plaintive cries of the damned. Voices of men, women, and children blared against her ears until one voice rose above the others. It was as if she was thrown into the eye of a hurricane, but then the smoke cleared.

Ka'Ala turned around, searching for the source of the single voice wailing in her ears. One moment, she stood alone within the stench of blood and roasting flesh; the next, a V'Jeeta appeared before her.

He knelt on the ground, facing away. His arms and wings stretched toward the heavens. He howled, draining his lungs to the soot-laden sky, took a breath, and continued.

"What happened here?" she shouted.

He ignored her as veridian blood dripped from his wingtips.

"Where are we?" Who are you?"

The warrior's heartsong rose over his screams, filling Ka'Ala's ears with a familiar timbre like an instrument learned in childhood, distinguishable from any of its look-a-likes.

"R'Venin?" She walked around until she stood before him. "R'Venin, what's going on? What happened?"

R'Venin, eyes closed, bared his teeth as if biting down on a stick. Tears streamed down his cheeks as his wailing continued.

Ka'Ala looked down at his outstretched hands. He had no visible wounds, though blood flowed from his palms, puddling at his knees. The pool grew in size until she could no longer see the edge.

She reached out to grab him but seized only smoke.

"R'Venin," Ka'Ala cried. "No. Windfather, help me. Help me save him."

R'Venin's figure morphed into a pillar of smoke and surrounded Ka'Ala until all she could see was blackness.

* * *

Ka'Ala found herself staring at the ceiling above her bed and heard a knock on her door frame.

"Ka'Ala," Ja'Naam called. "Are you alright? Why aren't you answering? Can I come in?"

"Yes," Ka'Ala cleared her throat, wiping her face. "Yes, Ja'Naam, I'm fine. Please come in."

"I heard you whimpering," Ja'Naam pushed through the curtains and sat down next to the bed, her eyes wide. "What's wrong?"

"I—."

It is not for her, Windfather whispered.

Her mate was in the vision. How could it not be for her to know? Ka'Ala insisted.

Windfather answered. *She will have her own sorrow to bear.*

"What is it?" Ja'Naam took Ka'Ala by the hand. "You can tell me anything."

"I wish I could." Ka'Ala sighed. "But not when the Windfather forbids it."

Ja'Naam squeezed tight. "As the Windfather decrees."

Ka'Ala nodded and stood, helping Ja'Naam off the floor. "Have you decided on a symbol?"

"Yes," Ja'Naam jerked her head toward the outer room. "We've come to an understanding."

"Tree it is then," Ka'Ala laughed through her nose, holding up her slate. "Let's go out and start sketching ideas."

Ka'Ala opened the curtain and stood off to the side, but Ja'Naam hadn't followed.

"Is it our news?" She said from beside the bed. "Is your sadness because you haven't found a mate yet?"

Ka'Ala let the drape fall. "Of course not," she said, moving back into the room. "I cherish your happiness with both hearts."

"Then why has your song fallen?" Ja'Naam closed the distance between them.

"You've been practicing," Ka'Ala smirked and hugged herself, turning toward her workbench. "How many hearts have you listened to?"

"I've tried listening to R'Venin, my family, a few neighbors, but I can only hear your hearts," Ja'Naam shrugged. "Although it was faint, I heard your grief from the other room. Why are you in anguish?"

Ka'Ala sat at her bench, setting her slate on the table, and scratched the rough outline of two hearts on the surface. "Because I've yet to find someone who makes my hearts sing as R'Venin does for you. No matter how much I petition the Windfather, he's yet to let me find a harmonious match. I sometimes worry I'll never meet a suitable mate, and my flock will truly die with me."

"I'm sure the Windfather has a plan for your happiness, sister." Ja'Naam nudged her way onto the seat next to Ka'Ala and put an arm around her waist. "All seeds in their season."

Ka'Ala put her head on Ja'Naam's shoulder and sighed.

Chapter Twenty-Two

Bargaining Favors

R'Venin approached Stonetree from above, with Ba'Jai drafting beside him. He pulled the fur-lined cloak tight around his neck against the pre-dawn air off the ocean. A gust over the water pushed him off course with a wet slap to his face. Coating the back of his throat, the brackish winds filled his nasal slits as the chill pierced through his neck and rippled down his back.

On mornings like this, I miss the desert heat.

Stonetree, a massive structure built by V'Jeeta prisoners in the early days of P'Phet, rose four hundred wingspans above the ground and stood one hundred wingspans in diameter. Nestled on a tidal island, waves licked at its giant foundation stones.

At the apex, a double-layered dome of iron latticed by the ancient ore-weavers, allowed sunlight to fill the central atrium. Ch'Hota Guardsmen lined the dome's circumference, keeping watch in all directions from behind the battlements.

At regular intervals below the ramparts, spear-laden patrols descended upon the tower, trading places with the pairs of gilded soldiers who manned the small ledges protruding from the walls.

Bands of metal hugged the column at every wingspan above the base like belts. Barred windows, sloping downward through the thick walls, dotted the circumference. Each portal allowed an occupant a view of the ground below, but never the sky. Trails of waste stained the walls like remnants of putrid streams heading for the seas below.

A covered bridge spanned the water to the mainland, meeting an open square fortress at the base. More guardsmen stood at the ready around the picketed walls overlooking the central yard. Dozens of caged wagons lined the inner court, pulled by three teams of runnerhounds each.

"How many prisoners are you transporting today?" R'Venin called over the wind.

"Nearly a full battalion." Ba'Jai swooped closer, just above R'Venin's wing. "They're being traded for an equal number of our guardsmen *and* their families. Why do the V'Jeeta take women and children as prisoners, anyway?"

"Leverage," R'Venin grimaced. "A despicable custom. It quells the guardsmen to see innocents under threat. It's one of the reasons I didn't want to become a warrior in the first place. I couldn't stomach shackling the women and children. The welts..."

"I can fathom," Ba'Jai's face twisted. "I've anointed many ankles with salve myself. The first time I saw it, one heart fell; the other wanted to lash out and slaughter the first V'Jeeta I saw."

"Where is the exchange taking place?"

"On the north rim of Razorbriar Canyon," Ba'Jai's eyes widened. "Two suns north of Western Crossroads."

"Will you be able to visit Sher'Esh?" R'Venin drifted closer. "Ja'Naam's looking forward to when Ja'Ven can fly on his own and she can take him to meet her."

"No. I won't have time. They'll need every guardsman to tend to the wounded and bring them home to safety."

"How long will you be gone?"

"It'll take three suns to drive. A full sun to perform the trade. But the return trip should take less than two suns. We won't be concerned with prisoners attempting to escape. We'll be back by the evening of Devotion."

"Stay your wings," a voice thundered from above.

A golden blur whipped past R'Venin, missing his head by a handspan. R'Venin and Ba'Jai opened their wings, braking to a hover and backflapped to stay aloft.

A giant of a Ch'Hota banked around and came to a stop in their previous flight path. A ring, laden with thick metal keys of varying sizes, jangled with each wing beat. Three guardsmen patrols, brandishing spears or nocked bows, closed in and formed a firing line behind him.

"Pleasant dawn, Vis'Haal," R'Venin's eyes narrowed. "Your aim's getting better. Last time you missed me by a full arm."

"Who is this, R'Venin? He smells like runnerhound dung." Vis'Haal growled and covered his nose. He turned to Ba'Jai. "And why are you not in full armor, guardsman?"

"This is Ba'Jai," R'Venin said. "He's my mate's brother."

"What's your business at Stonetree, mate's brother?"

"I'm a wrangler in the cavalry," Ba'Jai added, retrieving a scroll from his gauntlet and holding it out. "I've been assigned to drive a wagon for the prisoner exchange."

Vis'Haal snatched the scroll from Ba'Jai's hand, unrolling it and scanning the writing. His lip curled when he reached the bottom. He let the parchment roll in on itself and held it out.

"I've heard of you." Vis'Haal sneered as his eyes flitted between Ba'Jai's wings. "You used to have standing in the ranks until... It seems fitting an outcast would align with a castaway."

The guardsmen behind them laughed and murmured their approval.

"I serve the Ch'Hota as the council decides." Ba'Jai took the scroll and returned it inside his gauntlet, "And I align with hearts dedicated to the teachings of the Order, regardless of their plumage. Can you say the same?"

Vis'Haal's hand lowered to his belt, tightening around his swords' hilt.

"We'd like to get on with our duties, Vis'Haal," R'Venin inclined his head. "Will you allow us safe passage to the fort?"

Vis'Haal locked eyes with Ba'Jai for several moments before waving off the patrols.

"You've always shown proper respect for a person in your station, R'Venin." Vis'Haal flapped closer and jerked his head toward Ba'Jai. "I suggest you teach this low-branch some manners."

Vis'Haal closed his wings and dropped a few spans, nosed down, and swooped into the trees.

R'Venin and Ba'Jai opened their wings and glided toward the fort's main gate.

"He has no idea who you are, does he?" Ba'Jai asked.

"R'Venin is a fairly common V'Jeeta name." R'Venin shook his head. "Besides, who'd make the connection when both sides think I'm dead?"

Ba'Jai glanced over at R'Venin. "Only a genius or a fool."

* * *

Ba'Jai landed first in the courtyard. R'Venin dropped next to him amid other Ch'Hota in partial armor. The other runnerhound drivers, twig-limbed and underfed, stared with sunken eyes. Surrounding them, along the picketed walkway above, a cadre of guardsmen watched behind slitted helmets.

A wagon, laden with sixty blindfolded and bound V'Jeeta warriors, pulled away from the gated entrance to Stonetree.

"Ba'Jai!" A voice yelled from across the enclosure.

Ba'Jai smiled, raising his arm. "Master Vin'Eet."

R'Venin turned and watched an elderly Ch'Hota with autumn-fragile wings approach, leaning on a stick.

"Thank the Windfather you're here," Vin'Eet wheezed, though he smiled like a hatchling. "You're the last driver. Now we can finish loading and get underway."

"Vin'Eet," Ba'Jai put his arm on R'Venin's shoulder. "This is my sister's mate, R'Venin."

"Ba'Jai's told me about you, young one." Vin'Eet held out his hand, smiling.

R'Venin took Vin'Eet's hand but glanced at Ba'Jai.

"What has he said?" R'Venin asked as the older man pumped their hands.

"Not to fret, lad," Vin'Eet chuckled. "Only good tidings. Ba'Jai, please steer the remaining wagon into position at the gate. Once we've secured the prisoners, we'll be on our way."

"Yes, Master Vin'Eet," Ba'Jai inclined his head then opened his arms. "R'Venin, I'll see you soon. Give Ja'Naam my hearts for me."

"Of course," R'Venin stepped into the embrace, slapping Ba'Jai's back. "We'll wait 'till your return to have the sacred meal."

"Don't do that," Ba'Jai pulled away. "We'll have our own with the rescued prisoners after the exchange. Celebrate with your family. I'll come to visit after our return."

"Fair weather, brother," R'Venin said and walked toward the entry gates.

"Fair weather, R'Venin," Ba'Jai called to his back. "Give my best to the master alchemist."

R'Venin waved without looking, walking toward the entrance to Stonetree.

Two pairs of spiked portcullis, one wingspan square, formed the initial security break between the open air and prison interior. Four guardsmen on the ground level, with another four above, monitored the gates. Separated by three wingspans, the doorways angled toward the bridge to a Y-shaped intersection.

R'Venin fixed his eyes on the exit gate. A large wagon, with a barrel-vaulted cage, jostled as it filled. V'Jeeta warriors, stripped down to an amber prisoners' tunic with matching blindfold, trudged between wooden benches. A Ch'Hota guard guided them to a seat, while another slid their wings through slits in the cage.

Another guard attached a clamp from one prisoner's wing to that of his neighbor outside the wagon. Once secured, a third guard placed a hood of rough-spun cloth over their heads.

None of their feathers look familiar. I wonder if they would recognize mine if they had their sight.

R'Venin approached the guard at the entry gate and reached into his sleeve. The guard tensed, angling his spear toward R'Venin and then a wall with a hundred keyholes to his right. "What is your authorization song?"

R'Venin withdrew a small brass cylinder with tiny pins along the surface and inserted it into one of the holes and turned. Behind the wall, a tinkling melody played like a wind chime.

The guard pulled his spear back and stepped aside.

"Thank you, guardsman." R'Venin inclined his head as he passed. "Fair weather."

"Fair weather, alchemist," the guard said, staring at the glyph on R'Venin's amulet.

R'Venin walked into the vaulted corridor of timbers until he reached the next portcullis, closed per Vis'Haal's orders. The guard on the other side jerked his head to an identical wall of keyholes.

R'Venin retrieved a second key from under his clothing and turned it in its corresponding opening, causing another melody of chimes to play. The guard sneered and nodded his head to the gates' wheel-man who raised the portcullis until R'Venin could pass under with a slight bow of his head.

"Fair weather, guardsman," R'Venin nodded.

"You should be joining your clansmen in chains, soot-feather," the guard murmured.

R'Venin stepped out onto the covered bridge. A thick dividing wall separated him from the last dozen V'Jeeta marching in the opposite direction. Their rhythmic stride became lost in the thick floorboards, but their scent carried between the wall slats. Musky and rich. The scent of granite outcroppings still lingering in their quills jabbed at his mind. He inhaled deeply through his nasal slits before he picked up his pace.

One day, brothers. We'll all be free from my father's quarrel.

* * *

With a reverberating high-pitched sound, the spiked metal head of a heavy club slammed against the bars.

"It's time for your treatment," Nira'Ash, the Ch'Hota guard hollered, continuing to bang the mace against the bars. "Wake up, you old fool."

R'Venin scraped the small cart along the corridor, less than half a wingspan wide, up to the cell door. The single spiraling ramp ran along the interior wall like a serpent around a hollow trunk. Only a few empty cells offered room off the path to move the cart out of the way for guardsmen to pass. Along the wall, shoulder-width openings allowed only privileged prisoners to stretch their wings in the limited space below the double-layer latticed dome and armed guards.

What looked like a bundle of rags stirred on the stone bench recessed into the wall. A small opening just above the platform let in a dull patch of light. R'Venin could see the water, the forest, and even the fort from the cell windows, but never the sky, clouds, or stars.

I can't imagine a worse fate than dying in this awful place.

"Did you hear me, charlatan?" Nira'Ash pounded on the barricade. "Your favorite alchemist is here."

The pile of rags shrunk as a wrinkled hand reached around and pulled the fabric tighter.

"I can manage from here, Nira'Ash," R'Venin put his hand on the guard's shoulder. "You don't have to oversee his regimen. I'm sure you have better things to do. He's not going anywhere."

"I don't know why anyone would care to keep him alive," the guard growled, "when the council will most likely condemn him to death for what he's done."

"Martyr or miscreant," R'Venin grabbed his alchemy satchel, a copper bowl, a bundle of twigs, and a few vials from the cart, "isn't the first mandate of the Order to alleviate the suffering of all Windfather's creations?"

"This cretin was born of the flame, not the wind," Nira'Ash slammed his club once more, putting a slight bend in the rod. "I hope he dies in here, painfully, just like my father. You hear me, Gha'Barahat?"

Nira'Ash spat into the cell and stomped away, rapping his club on each cell door down the curving hall as he rounded out of sight.

"Is that oaf finally gone?" Gha'Barahat groaned.

"Yes," R'Venin unlocked the cell door, grabbing a stool off the cart as he stepped inside. "How're you feeling today?"

Gha'Barahat rolled over and stared through the bars to the opposite wall with his one eye. A filthy strip of cloth covered the other socket. His skin sagged like the meager blanket around his shoulders as he pushed himself up to sit. His wing joints cracked as he stretched—too many flightless seasons in a cage.

"I'm dying, my young prince," Gha'Barahat wheezed. "Nira'Ash will get his wish."

R'Venin froze, locking eyes for a moment with the old Pra'Acheen, and then put the stool on the cold floor. He placed the bowl between the seat and himself on the ground, shoving the wood underneath.

"When did you figure it out?" he breathed, unstopping a vial of blue liquid. He held it under his nose for a short whiff and poured the full measure into the pot. He stooped low and muttered the incantation into the pool five times. "K'shay dhe'ema ka'rane ke'lie." Once the last drop fell, the color paled in hue.

"Two snowfalls ago," Gha'Barahat slid off his stone bed and hobbled to the stool.

R'Venin set the wood ablaze with a fire crystal set within an iron handle and dumped a handful of needle leaves to the kettle. "What gave me away?"

"With little else to do, the V'Jeeta in here talk a lot," Gha'Barahat held out his hands to the small fire. "Especially at night when the guards make fewer inspections. Newer prisoners share what's happening on the Spires. Gossip. Rumors. I'm sure you've heard most of it."

R'Venin nodded, glancing over his shoulder. "The king led several campaigns against the Ch'Hota over the high prince's death. Unsuccessfully. Their armies are dwindling, thus their willingness to exchange prisoners. Something he never considered in the past. His younger son, K'Marot, is now the chief captain over their armies."

R'Venin poured a white powder into the bubbling mash and recited the weekly incantation. A seafoam-colored mist rose and swirled in the faint light.

"The future doesn't bode well for the V'Jeeta, I think," Gha'Barahat said, leaning over the bowl. He inhaled deeply until he'd snorted every last wisp. "Unless they can restore their numbers and former strength."

"But how did you figure out who I am?"

Gha'Barahat laughed in his throat, followed by a coughing fit. He wrapped his frail wings and thin blanket tight around his shoulders, hunched over in bone-rattling convulsions. A few moments passed before he could breathe without gasping for air. "It was your interest in curing the White Claw."

R'Venin looked down at the pot. Dying flames sputtered as embers escaped into the air.

"I recognized you immediately," Gha'Barahat continued, "when they arrested me for tipping the scales with my customers and threw me in here. I remembered what you did for your Ch'Hota friend, paying for his new wing. How's it working for him?"

"He's able to fly," R'Venin glanced up. "But he can't carry the full weight of his armor. He works with runnerhounds now."

"Better than being ground cast." Gha'Barahat shrugged and smacked his lips. "You wouldn't happen to have any dizzyroot, would you?"

R'Venin shook his head and snorted. "No."

"Perhaps down in your stores?" Gha'Barahat leaned forward. "I won't tell anyone where I got it. I swear."

"No," R'Venin said. "And I doubt the administrator will allow it. You were saying?"

"Right," Gha'Barahat's shoulders fell. "Two seasons ago, during the new leaf, another band of V'Jeeta prisoners arrived. An old general was among them."

"I remember him," R'Venin said. "Ath'Ak. General Ath'Ak. He was the king's most faithful warrior. He helped train me in the ways of combat. I had to avoid him. Knew he'd recognize me. He didn't last long. The White Claw had left him too weak to last more than two moons in here."

"Well, one night he was talking to the others. It seems he never believed you'd fallen in battle. He inspected every corpse and prisoner exchange looking for you, convinced you were still alive. One of the other V'Jeeta, a warrior who trained at the same camp as you, mentioned that the high prince spent more time with the alchemists than learning swordplay."

"Ath'Ak then said, *a wise and cunning king is more deadly than a legion of skilled warriors*," Gha'Barahat grumbled a passing impression of the general. "He told them, by studying tactics and alchemy, you would one day end the war over the silk."

"Is that why you've been helping me treat their White Claw," R'Venin hissed, sitting forward. "To end the war."

Gha'Barahat threw back his head and laughed. Immediately, he doubled over, hacking. He wiped blood from his chin with a corner from his flimsy covering.

R'Venin reached into his cart and retrieved a bladder of water, holding it out to the wracking mass of skin and feathers.

Gha'Barahat took it with a nod and tipped it back, pouring three mouthfuls down his gullet.

"Thank you," Gha'Barahat panted, passing it back. "No, nothing so noble as that. I made quite a profit off the war. Healing the desperate and broken."

"Not that's it's doing you any good," R'Venin mumbled.

"True," Gha'Barahat turned down his lip and shrugged. "But I had a comfortable life while it lasted."

"So, then," R'Venin sighed. "Why were you teaching me Alchemy? If not to end the war?"

"I want to see the sun one more time before I die, young prince." Gha'Barahat glanced at the barred window. The sill, stained with dried trails of waste, opened to a sloping shaft. Beyond the far end, behind another set of bars, the ocean stirred below. Sunlight rippled off the crests, teasing the Pra'Acheen with its inviting dance. "I couldn't convince anyone to include me in a prisoner exchange. Neither the

V'Jeeta nor the Ch'Hota, think I'm worth one of their own."

"I can't get you out," R'Venin hissed. "There's no way."

"Ah," Gha'Barahat pointed to the ceiling. "But you can get me up."

"What do you mean?"

"You could smuggle me up to the ramparts at the top," the old man's eyes brightened. "Into the dome. I'd be able to see the sun again. Feel the wind on my face. Smell free air one last time."

"I'd lose *my* freedom," R'Venin stood, picking up the bowl and squashing the last embers with his foot. "My *family*. My place in the Order. Your price is too high."

"I'll make you a deal, R'Venin," Gha'Barahat stood, handing the stool over. "Give me a slate and stylus. I'll give you the recipe and incantation to cure White Claw, save for the mountain ingredient. You'll never figure it out anyway. When you're ready to accept my proposal, you get me to the dome for one last taste of wind. And I'll tell you the name of the final key to curing your people. Agreed?"

"You ask too much." R'Venin grabbed the stool from Gha'Barahat's hands and dumped it into the cart, followed by the bowl and satchel. Stepping out of the cell, he closed the door and slid in the key.

Gha'Barahat coughed as he shuffled to the barrier, curling bony fingers around the bars. "Just lend me your slate. Then you can think about it."

R'Venin gazed over at the feeble prisoner. His eyes filled with desperation, mirroring the dread filling R'Venin's hearts. He glanced down both sides of the corridor.

"Hand me your slate, my prince," Gha'Barahat whispered. "Quickly before another guard comes by."

"If this is a trick," R'Venin wrapped his fingers around the bar just above Gha'Barahat's. "I swear by the Windfather, I will take you out of this cell and put you in with the Ch'Hota's you swindled."

Gha'Barahat swallowed, a flicker of a smile tugging at his sallow lips. "Agreed."

R'Venin turned and pulled a thin stone slate from his cart and a metal stylus from his belt, passing them between the bars.

Gha'Barahat turned away, but R'Venin grabbed his shirt front. "Right here," he growled. "Where I can watch you. And write down the quantities per person, so I know how much it will take to cure all my people."

"Of course," he nodded. "Of course."

Gha'Barahat scratched on the surface with a shaky hand, scribbling amounts and instructions between the list of ingredients.

R'Venin memorized the list as each item became legible.

For Rain: Eruption from a ground spout.

For Fire: Electhium crystals.

For Tree: Lisum'Wakatch stalks.

For Wind: Saph'ed pan'jon ko cha'anga.

Then Gha'Barahat wrote *For Mountain: I look forward to our next visit* and then handed R'Venin the slate.

R'Venin took it and held open his other hand. "The stylus?"

"Oh," Gha'Barahat removed it from his sleeve. "Silly me. Old habit."

"Fair weather, old man." R'Venin returned the stylus to his belt and buried the slate under his satchel. "Until your next treatment."

"Fair weather, young alchemist," Gha'Barahat coughed. "Let me know if the next full moons are as lovely as I remember."

R'Venin pushed his cart down the corridor until he reached his next patient, a female Ch'Hota who lost a talon trying to pick her cell's lock. She held out the stump, wrapped in a strip of blood-caked cloth. He redressed the wound, but his eyes kept flicking to the satchel.

What's your secret, old man?

Chapter Twenty-Three

Prepare and Purify

Ka'Ala finished taking her wares off their displays, tucking them into pockets sewn into a soft cloth, as Ja'Ven's heartsong rang like laughter in her ears. She looked as the boy ran into her shop with a fuzzypede draped around his neck like a scarf.

Ja'Naam came through the flaps a moment later. "Guess who wanted to show you something?"

"Aunt Ka'Ala," Ja'Ven squealed, careening around the table.

"My favorite little hatchling," Ka'Ala sang as she knelt just in time for Ja'Ven to jump into her open arms. She lifted him off the ground and spun in a circle, the boy spreading his wings.

"And who is this?" she asked, panting as she came to a stop.

"This is Pal'Atoo," Ja'Ven grabbed his animal by the neck and held it to Ka'Ala's face. The fuzzypede hung limp like wet twine. "Uncle Ba'Jai gave him to me."

"What a wonderful gift." Ka'Ala giggled, ducking her head from its feelers. "I'm so glad you brought him to see me."

Ka'Ala set Ja'Ven on his feet and took Pal'Atoo in her arms, cradling him and nuzzling her face into his wispy hairs. "He's so soft," she purred.

"And sheds half his coat every night," Ja'Naam sidled next to Ja'Ven. "Lucky for him, he eats the hairs that fall, so I don't have to clean up after him."

"Fuzzypedes make the perfect companions for a child," Ka'Ala whispered loudly into Ja'Ven's ear.

"Watch what he can do," Ja'Ven held his arms in a circle. "Put him on my shoulder."

Ka'Ala lowered Pal'Atoo onto Ja'Ven's outstretched arms tail-end first. The animal ran its feelers over Ja'Ven's head and neck for a brief moment before beginning its endless trek.

"Impressive," Ka'Ala winked over his head to Ja'Naam. "I think that's the smartest fuzzypede in the world. You've trained him well."

"Thanks," Ja'Ven beamed. "Do you have any leaves? I think he's hungry."

"There's some in a basket in the back," Ka'Ala smoothed the patchy feathers on his head. "Help yourself."

"Come on, Pal'Atoo," the boy said as he pushed through the curtain to Ka'Ala's back room.

"He's delightful," Ka'Ala laughed, turning to Ja'Naam.

"Yes," Ja'Naam sighed. "He dotes on that animal as much you dote on him."

"Well," Ka'Ala's smile widened. "If I ever find a suitable mate, I'll let you spoil my firstborn as much as you like."

"Agreed," Ja'Naam said, looking around the shop. "Your shelves are empty. Have you sold all your pieces?"

"May the Windfather bless me so," Ka'Ala spoke to the ceiling, moving behind the counter and rolled up the pocketed cloth. "But no. I need to take these to the treasury. I'm going on a pilgrimage."

"Oh?" Ja'Naam leaned on the counter. "Where to?"

"The Hiding Falls," Ka'Ala said like a petition. "For the convergence of the three mothers in the sky."

"It's real?" Ja'Naam put her hand over her chest. "I thought the falls were only a myth."

"So did I," Ka'Ala blew through her nose. "But Windfather has called me to go there, and I trust he'll show me the way."

"How long will you be gone?" Ja'Naam moved to stand on the opposite side of the table. "Will you be back for the sacred meal? We want you to be there."

"I'll be away for five suns," Ka'Ala lowered her voice and glanced out the door. "I'm not sure what to expect."

"I see," Ja'Naam nodded. "Can we walk with you to the treasury? Ja'Ven's never seen one of the city vaults."

"I would love the company." Ka'Ala hefted the bundle over her head, catching the straps as it landed between her wings. Then she tied the straps behind her back.

"Ja'Ven," Ja'Naam called through the curtain.

"Coming, Mother." His voice sounded muffled as if his mouth was full.

Ja'Ven peeked around the curtain with a dark brown paste ringing his lips.

Ja'Naam's mouth pinched, her hands balled into fists.

"Pal'Atoo found sweetsap," he mumbled. "Can I have some?"

Ka'Ala turned away, covering her mouth to stifle a giggle.

* * *

Guided by the Windfather, Ka'Ala reached the place she saw in a vision on the following high sun. It looked like a stream flowing into a small lake nestled in a pocket of dense trees with a thin ribbon of shoreline from the air.

The water looked like wet potter's clay, churned by an unseen hand.

She landed on the ivory shore, breathing heavily, and cocked her head to the dull roar of a nearby waterfall. Scanning the glade, she found only broadleaf trees dotted with blossoms of snowpetals. They fluttered in a breeze off the lake, filling the air with a fragrance that tugged at her memory.

Why do I know that scent?

"I'm here, Windfather," she panted. "What do I do now?"

Enter, he breathed.

Ka'Ala smiled as she closed her eyes and took a step into the water, anticipating cool relief on her skin. She immediately fell forward as there seemed to be nothing under the water's surface. She backflapped hard just before plunging face-first through the ripples, regaining her balance onshore.

"What was that?" she gasped, backing away.

"*Do not fear. Nothing within will harm you.*"

"Yes, Windfather," Ka'Ala crept to the water and knelt over the edge. The milky surface offered no reflection. She stretched out her hand to touch the ripples, but nothing broke against her fingertips.

She reached further—still nothing but air.

It's an eye trick.

She planted her other hand at the pool's edge. Her palm met the solid ground, but her fingers curled under, disappearing.

"A lip," she breathed, feeling further along the edge.

Ka'Ala wrapped both her palms along the illusionary barrier and flattened herself on the ground. Taking a deep breath, she lowered her head past the threshold.

In one instant, she stared at an opalescent pool. In the next, she saw another world, hidden within a vast lava dome five hundred wingspans across at the base.

Enter, my child, Windfather called from within as a gust of air pushed at her back.

She raised her wing, catching another flurry, and lifted off the ground enough to slide over the rim. She dropped a wingspan before opening her wings, gliding in a downward arc.

Wide-eyed, she circled the waterfall centered at the gigantic vault's apex. The arching walls had a silver sheen, distorting everything below. Lush fruit trees, shrubbery—and other flowering plants she didn't recognize—carpeted the floor from the walls to a basin of liquid alabaster.

The waterfall crashed onto a small island in the lake, spewing mist in all directions and sending gentle waves to its shores. In her peripheral vision, a strip of dark stone jutting from the flora caught her attention. The speckled outcropping sloped from the underbrush, disappearing into the milky waters.

There, Windfather said.

Ka'Ala banked and flew over, landing on a path made of ash-colored stones and mortar. Her breath caught in her throat as she turned back toward the falls. The walls reflected the sky as if she were on a lone island. Her eyes glistened as she fell to her knees.

"Memories of a dream," Ka'Ala choked. "It's just how Abhi'Bhaavak described the Emerald Island. Thank you, Windfather."

A gentle breeze gusted off the water, kissing the tears on her face.

Feast, then rest, daughter, Windfather breathed. *At sundown, you cleanse. At sunrise, you receive.*

* * *

The Three Mothers, the three moons of Pirth'Vee Grah, shone down through the dome's apex. Their glow cast a circle of light on the porcelain waters a few wingspans from the stone path. With a full belly, Ka'Ala lay on the shore letting the chilly fluid tickle her feet. It was thicker than water, like a hearty soup.

Behind her, corralled by black stones, a fire crackled on the sand.

She closed her eyes and sighed, listening to the chorus between the falls and insect life.

It is time. Windfather said. *Disrobe.*

Ka'Ala took a deep breath and rolled over, pushing herself up, and then walked toward her campfire. She removed her belt and tunic and dropped them next to the cloak she'd fanned out as a bed. Then her leggings, breechcloth, and bodice.

She hugged herself as she moved to the water, the misty air prickling at her bare skin. But it wasn't water. It was an opaque liquid, like a nurser's milk, and rippled like water when she dipped in a foot. The fluid stuck to her talons like paste.

Walk the path. Enter the falls.

Ka'Ala's hearts burned as she glanced at the stone trail a few paces away and headed over, taking a position at the pool's edge. In the distance, the falls rained on the island.

She stepped into the lake, submerging further into the chilly liquid with each step and gasping as she descended to her calves, then thighs, keeping her wings out of the white slurry.

I didn't realize it would be this cold.

She flapped, lifting herself out and forward, but a fierce gust blew her back to shore.

Walk the path. Enter the falls, Windfather advised.

Ka'Ala grit her teeth, holding her legs together, now painted as if wearing thigh-high stockings from the creamy liquid. She hugged herself and stepped back into the lake. The chill climbed her legs faster than before, causing her teeth to chatter when the fluid reached her waist. She flapped out again, but the wind returned her to the path.

"But it's so cold," Ka'Ala's voice broke. "I can't do this."

A warm breeze wafted across her two-toned skin as paste dripped off her calf feathers.

If you cannot endure the discomfort, you may not enjoy the reward. Trust, daughter, she heard.

Ka'Ala wiped her face. "Yes, Windfather. I will."

She braced herself and strode into the pool, jaw clenched. The slurry crawled up her body faster than she marched through it. Her wings trailed behind, skimming the surface when the water reached her chin. With less than a quarter of the distance left, the path's grout lines disappeared into the muck.

I have no choice but to swim, she thought.

Filling her lungs and ducking, she dragged her wings beneath. She crouched and kicked off the ledge with her toes, breaching the surface with her eyes shut by the plaster-like soup. She reached out with her hearing for the waterfall, each stroke and kick inching her closer. A full song passed between each desperate breath, and she paddled forward until her arm slapped down on a hard, polished surface.

Water blew across her face. It felt warm on her skin as the slurry melted away. With one arm clinging to the stone, she wiped at her face until she could open her eyes. Grunting between labored breaths, she dragged herself out of the lake and spat a mouthful of slurry.

She rested a moment, catching her breath, and crawled into the deluge. Her body soaked in the warmth as she steadied herself from the crushing torrent. With each passing moment, the weight on her body decreased as the falls washed away the alabaster coating. Bits of leaves, bark, and soil flowed across the island and vanished under the lake's surface.

Ka'Ala stood at the falls' periphery, turning in a circle and shaking the water from her feathers.

Return to the fire, she heard.

I don't know if I can, Windfather. I feel so weak.

I will keep you aloft, daughter, he soothed. *Return to the fire.*

Ka'Ala stepped to the water's edge, shaking and flapping the water off her body. She closed her eyes, facing the sky, and breathed for the space of two songs. She kept her wings moving, keeping the water from weighing them down again.

Jumping with feeble legs, she flapped with all her strength, her body weakly responding to her mind's commands. Yet halfway across, in her exhaustion, her wings failed.

She braced herself to hit the water, but a hot column of air caught her, billowing her wings open. She glided to her campsite, collapsing where she landed.

Rest, Windfather whispered. *Eat. I will call when the time comes to cleanse again.*

"How many times?" Ka'Ala whimpered. "How many more times must I cleanse before I'm ready to receive?"

"Thrice," He said. *"And thrice again."*

Ka'Ala broke down, her tears soaking into the white sand, as she pounded it with weak fists.

"Yes, Windfather," she sobbed. "I will obey."

* * *

On the third sundown, Ka'Ala knelt under a starlit sky next to the fire. Only ash remained of the clothing she wore on her journey to the falls.

Her new attire hugged her body like a second skin, having materialized beside her campsite during the night. Her breechcloth and bodice, silky like snowflower petals, and twinkled like the stars. The leggings, black as night, kept her skin at a perfect temperature. The cloak, tunic, and belt, weightless as a fog, matched any coloring she chose.

Ka'Ala drained herself of all color, becoming an ivory statue to match her pearly eyes.

I hope the Windfather never bids me leave this place.

She couldn't remove the contented smile from her lips, even if she wanted to, amid the tranquility of Hiding Falls.

Looking up beyond the dome's oculus, the three mothers lined up over the falls. Be'Tee, the smallest and youngest, kissed the ground where the falls began. Behind her, Ma'An, Be'Tee's mother, crowned over her child like a halo. And lastly, Da'Adeema, the first mother of the sky family, trailed behind her radiant daughters.

Da'Adeema flew between the stars.

Ka'Ala breathlessly sang her mother's lullaby to herself. Memories of her childhood made her eyes glisten.

She heard the Windfather's call and flew to Pirth'Vee Grah.
She sang and danced for five thousand seasons.
In time, she wanted a child.

Windfather spoke, louder than she'd ever heard his voice before. *The fulfillment of prophecy is near.*

"What prophecy?" Ka'Ala straightened, casting her eyes around.

The time is short for Be'Tee to give birth to the Fifth Mother of Pirth'Vee Grah.

Ka'Ala stood, her feathers regained their ink as she squinted at the moons. "The convergence," she breathed. "But the moons aren't aligned yet. So, what does this mean?"

She turned in a circle as though she'd spy the Windfather standing along the dome's perimeter.

"Windfather!" Her voice almost drowned out the rumbling waterfall. "What does this mean?"

The sound of insects, breezes, and even the waterfall died.

His one word sang in her ears. *See.*

* * *

Ka'Ala found herself flying over Razorbriar Canyon. It tapered and thinned to a small ravine in the distance. A pillar of smoke ahead caught her attention, pluming at the base where a half dozen wagons had been upturned and set ablaze.

She flew closer and spied hundreds of V'Jeeta warriors in full armor swarming the bonfire. They were tossing raggedy bundles into the inferno, cheering, and screeching war chants. Though they raised their weapons to the sky, they ignored her as if she weren't there.

A smaller group of warriors, three rows deep, formed a circle. In the middle, they tortured a Ch'Hota guardsman, kicking and stabbing at him with their spears and swords. His wings were limp, one dripping with blood, the other pale and riddled with holes.

Ba'Jai!

She flew close and landed next to Ba'Jai. A V'Jeeta boot kicked him in the head, knocking him to the ground, unconscious but breathing. She reached out to touch his shoulder, but her hands went through.

"Shall we add another body to the pyre, Prince K'Marot?" A swarthy V'Jeeta said. The crowd cheered their approval, tossing strips of cloth into the ring over Ba'Jai's body. "Our skyswimmer-borne brothers might need a stronger signal to begin the attack."

The uproar died down.

Ka'Ala stood and turned until she saw a young V'Jeeta holding up his hand. He wore a silvervine crown dotted with rubies on his head. Three scars ran down his face from brow to chin.

"No," K'Marot sneered, his nose twitched as he glared at Ba'Jai's body.

He squinted, crouching to examine Ba'Jai's artificial wing. He put his dagger into a hole and sliced the skin, exposing muscles, tendons, and brass bones.

"Give me an ax," he said. The nearest warrior handed over his weapon, while the rest gathered close.

A gust blew Ka'Ala outside their circle, blocking her view. Though her hand passed through Ba'Jai's unconscious form, she couldn't penetrate the wall of warriors. She saw the ax raised high and then disappeared out of view, followed by the clang of metal. Another swing and another clang. Again and again, to the triumphant cheers of V'Jeeta warriors.

"Take the pieces back to my father," she heard over the applause. "I'm sure the king will be eager to learn the Ch'Hota have been using strange alchemy to strengthen their guardsmen."

No. Don't desecrate him. I'll return him to his flock.

Ka'Ala struggled in vain as the circle closed tighter, each warrior then taking flight with a hint of gold in their hands.

She took off after them, but a fierce updraft blew her further above the ground. She fought the current to no avail. It carried her into the jet-stream where she found a herd of adult skyswimmers making lazy figure eights directly over the smoke signal.

Each had platforms between their fins, suspended by thick ropes across their backs. Every deck had two or three warriors and several barrels loaded with spears, pitcherflowers, and bean pods.

"Didn't R'Venin use something similar when he fought off that sleepbreather?" she said to herself, her voice muffled again.

Suddenly, K'Marot passed in front of her and landed on the nearest skyswimmers back.

"Warriors of the Granite Spires," he howled over the wind. "Your greatchildren's greatchildren will remember this day long after we've flown to the Eternal Tree.

"We take our battle to the hearts of our enemy, where they feel safe. After today, they will never feel safe again.

"They won't be able to share their lies with their children, about their noble fight for freedom. We decide what privileges they enjoy.

"Their heresy comes to an end before sundown. Today the Ch'Hota will know our resolve to rid Pirth'Vee Grah of their stench. Today, we cut out their hearts."

"TO BATTLE!" K'Marot raised his fist above his head.

Every V'Jeeta in the company returned his cry, holding swords, spears, and bows over their heads. As one, they formed into chevrons of darkness, heading westward toward the waning sun. Far in the distance, she glimpsed the Bluewoods towering from the coast.

"No," her scream came out muffled as her head swiveled toward home.

* * *

Ka'Ala's cry echoed through the dome as she fell to the ground, dampened by the waterfall's mist pluming off the lake.

"Why would you show me this?" She clutched her sides, rocking.

For this vision, have I prepared and purified you to receive.

"Can it be stopped, Windfather?" she choked. "Is there time to warn the Ch'Hota? When will this happen?"

It is already underway.

"NO!"

Ka'Ala leaped into the air, ignoring her campsite and everything she'd brought with her, flapping hard and piercing the oculus as fast as her wings could carry her.

Windfather, please help me get there in time to warn them. Please.

A tailwind slammed her forward. She tumbled for a moment, then found a new rhythm.

You will not arrive in time, daughter, Windfather breathed. *Yet, you will provide strength and counsel in the suns ahead.*

Chapter Twenty-Four

The Hearts of Ch'Hotee

"Ja'Ven," Ja'Naam cooed. "Feel the air. Let it guide your wings. Dance with it. Move with the breeze."

Mother and son soared between colossal Bluewood trunks; up and over massive limbs laden with homes, elevated walkways, and balconies. The mid-morning sun at their backs peeked through the branches as the turquoise leaves rustled in the breeze. Ocean air, laced with smoke and dried wood, wafted past Ja'Naam's nose. Her stomach grumbled as they flew over a fruit merchant, tantalizing her with promises of sweet nectar.

"Will Father be there?" Ja'Ven squirmed under the straps holding him between her wings and fell into her rhythm. "Will he be at the laying place?"

"No," she gained altitude to clear a massive limb in her path. "He's at Stonetree. The brood mother is just inspecting my pouch. We're not choosing an egg today."

"Aww," Ja'Ven buried his head behind Ja'Naam's neck and tried to wrap his wings around himself.

"JA'VEN," Ja'Naam slapped the feathers out of her face, fighting to keep aloft. "You must keep still while riding on my back. I can't fly straight when you move around like that."

Ja'Ven's wings bumped into hers with each upstroke.

"Yes, Mother," Ja'Ven mumbled into her back.

"It's alright," Ja'Naam looked over her shoulder. "I need you to practice. You'll need to fly by yourself soon. What if I sing you a story? My mother taught me to keep rhythm with her songs."

"Can I pick?" Ja'Ven said, pulling forward on her back.

"I'll pick," she laughed. "You keep the tempo with me."

Ja'Naam started singing.

In the center of Bluewood
Where the trees touch the sky
Came to live a new mother
Who had just learned to fly

Her dear mother, the third moon
Queen Be'Tee is her name
Gave her daughter a haven
Free from sorrow and flame

There beside the great ocean
And amid towering trees
Be'Tee planted a garden
The Hearts of Ch'Hotee

Be'Tee seeded her garden
With her own wand'ring stars
And the Windfather blessed them
With a gust from afar

There the brave little mother
Gave her hearts to be seeds
Into Pirth'Vee Grah nestled
By the ne'er-ending sea

Then the garden soon sprouted
Trees with trunk split in twain
Twisting into each other
The Hearts of Ch'Hotee

Ja'Naam swerved through thickening layers of Bluewood, each trunk becoming thinner and shorter than the last until they flew into a meadow bustling with life. Flowers of every color stretched for the sunlight dawdling across the pasture. Twinecoats and rockskippers, bellowing and bleating for their young, grazed through lush fields of grass.

The meadow opened like a bowl, cutting fifty wingspans into the forest at the base. In the center stood an ironwood tree with gold-tipped leaves and bark with a dozen yellow hues. Its trunk twisted and coiled as it rose from the ground, giving it the appearance of two trees entwined together. Even at forty wingspans in height, the tree seemed like a sapling within its enclosure of immense Bluewoods. A pool of spring water bubbled at the base, reflecting the clouds passing overhead.

"I see them," Ja'Ven squealed, pointing his little finger past Ja'Naam's head. "I see the hearts."

"There they are," Ja'Naam said.

"That's where I was hatched?"

"You hatched at our roost." Ja'Naam chuckled. "That's where you were laid."

"By Mother Anda'Daata." Ja'Ven fell silent for a moment. "I still don't understand," he rested his chin on her neck. "How was I laid here, but hatched at home?"

"Why don't you ask Anda'Daata?" Ja'Naam craned her head around. "Perhaps if she explains it, it'll make more sense."

Suspended between the Ironwood's thickest limbs, a bubble of woven boughs filled the gaps. Dozens of Ch'Hota, in various group sizes, flew in and out of the openings, dotting the surface. Some females came out with distended pouches, having received their eggs. Others came out as flat-bellied as Ja'Naam with downcast faces.

Banking around to the south face, she aimed for an arcade that belted the sphere. Ja'Naam lit on the balcony just outside the arch and stepped through, kneeling to release Ja'Ven from his straps. He pulled her tunic's collar into her neck as he slid off her back.

Spanning the corridor's length, plump women took residence on roosts of varying sizes padded with feathers and braided cloth. Each knelt under a loose velvet gown that spilled over their legs and onto the floor. Some dozed with their heads bowed. Others engaged in animated conversations with couples. A few had drapes closed around them.

Ja'Ven ran across the platform to a spot occupied by a fleshy woman with a genteel face. Over her gown, she wore a leather apron that covered a slit in the fabric.

"Mother Anda'Daata," Ja'Ven cheered, leaping into her arms.

"Hello, little one," Anda'Daata buried her face in the boys' neck. "How is my precious Ja'Ven?"

Ja'Ven gave the woman a quick summary of his new pet, learning to fly, and the delights of Auric plums. "Pal'Atoo loves sweetsap," he prattled. "He found some at Aunt Ka'Ala's shop and shared it with me."

"Oh?" Anda'Daata chuckled. "Well, be sure neither of you overeats. Sweetsap can make fuzzypede's sick and hatchlings too heavy to get off the ground."

"He's missed you since our last visit." Ja'Naam knelt beside the nest. "Can you tell?"

Anda'Daata pulled Ja'Ven onto her lap. "As I've missed him," she said, nuzzling her forehead to his. "Are you flying on your own yet?"

"I've been practicing," Ja'Ven beamed. "I can flap from the balcony to my roost at home."

Anda'Daata's face widened. "I can still remember when I laid you. And now, you're practically ready to soar across the western sea," she gasped, tickling him behind his wings. "Do tell me what you find on the other side when you get back."

"I will," Ja'Ven squealed, squirming out of her lap into Ja'Naam's arms. "Mother said I could ask you a question."

"Of course, my little one?" Anda'Daata beamed. "Anything."

Ja'Ven shifted on his feet. "Mother says she is my mother. She also says you are my mother. How do I have two mothers?"

Anda'Daata's eyes brightened. "That's our nature, little one. It's how the Windfather created us. You see, mature women like me lay eggs." She pulled aside her apron, showing her seated on a stool over a small clutch of blue-green eggs nestled in a basket between her feet.

She draped the cloth back over her lap. "But I can no longer carry the egg until it's ready to hatch. Nor can I produce milk for the hatchling until it can survive outside my pouch.

She held out her hand to Ja'Naam and pulled her to sit beside her, "Your mother hasn't started laying eggs yet, but her pouch can incubate one after your father seeds it, and then produce milk for the hatchling."

Anda'Daata's voice became quiet and misty like a morning fog. "Long ago, the Windfather shared his gift of creation with the first four mothers, who then shared the gift with their daughters. Be'Tee gave her stars to our mother, Ch'Hotee. Ch'Hotee had daughters, who carried her stars until their daughters were grown and then passed down their stars to their daughters. From mother to daughter, we've passed along the children of Ch'Hotee for generations."

"So," Anda'Daata nudged Ja'Naam, who knelt between the older woman and the boy. "I am your mother because the egg from which you hatched came from me." She gestured to her apron.

"And this is your mother," she took Ja'Naam by the hand, "because she carried that egg. She protected you in her pouch until you hatched, provided you with milk until you emerged, and loved you as only a mother can. Do you see how blessed we all are to have two mothers? A birth mother and a life mother? Do you understand now?"

Ja'Ven shook his head and stared with blank eyes. "Not really."

Ja'Naam and Anda'Daata shared a knowing look and chuckled.

"Perhaps once your mother has received another egg," Anda'Daata reached out and held his face, "and you see the process unfold, it will make more sense to you."

Ja'Ven pursed his lips and shrugged.

"And how are you, child?" Anda'Daata turned her attention to Ja'Naam.

"I am well," Ja'Naam said, wrapping her arms around Ja'Ven's waist. "Will you check my pouch? I need to know how many suns until I'm ready to receive. R'Venin and I want to start planning the seeding night."

"Of course," the buxom woman replied, smoothing out her apron. "Let's have a look. Ja'Ven, I have some scratch tiles in the cupboard behind me. Would you like to practice your lettering while I examine your mother?"

Ja'Ven nodded and crawled around to Anda'Daata's backside, opening a small cabinet and pulling out a basket of tiles and slotted board.

Anda'Daata raised her wings, forming a blind between Ja'Ven and

Ja'Naam. She then pulled a rope lying at her side, closing the privacy curtains, as Ja'Naam raised her tunic. The slit of her pouch reached from hip to hip. "Is this still tender?" She asked, pressing her fingers along the puffy edge.

"No," Ja'Naam said, watching the woman's hands move from one side of her abdomen to the other. "Not for two suns."

Anda'Daata nodded, pursing her lips. She slid her talons into the flap and pulled, opening the pouch and sniffing. "When was your last expulsion?"

"Three suns."

The older woman took a feather from her nest and dipped it deep into Ja'Naam's pouch, drawing it back covered in a pale yellow mucus. Anda'Daata dabbed it on parchment from her apron. The spot turned cerulean then turquoise.

"Hmm," she dabbed the paper again. "You're very close. Best to give it two more suns. Just to ensure a healthy hatchling."

"Two suns," Ja'Naam repeated, beaming. "R'Venin will be thrilled."

The crack of strange thunder erupted from above, followed by a dozen more, each rising in volume from the last.

"Aaugh," Ja'Ven yelped.

"What was that?" Ja'Naam gasped.

"I don't know," Anda'Daata gazed toward the ceiling. "I've never heard that sound in the hearts before."

Suddenly, gongs clanged from all around, followed by screaming.

"Oh, no," Anda'Daata covered her mouth. "The eggs."

* * *

R'Venin stood on the ramparts of Stonetree, taking the ocean air into his nose and feathers. He pulled his cloak tighter around his neck against the chilled breeze off the water.

He grabbed the bucket of empty vials from his cart and dumped it over the wall. The ooze fell past the masonry like globs of mud before dissolving into the waters below. Waves crashed on the prison's base, beating against the stones.

Then, from deep in the forest, drums rumbled. Numerous gongs, getting closer and louder, joined the line until the clarions at the fort took up the alarm.

What's happening? R'Venin thought.

R'Venin dropped his bucket as he saw Vis'Haal lead the entire regiment of guardsmen from the citadel into the trees, heading toward the center of the Bluewoods.

Within the prison, a chant rose from the cells. A war cry he'd not heard since choosing to fall.

To battle! To battle! To battle!

R'Venin looked into the sky. Far in the distance, a herd of skyswimmers swarmed over a single spot. Over...

The Hearts.

"JA'NAAM," He cried, launching off the battlements and racing to catch up with Vis'Haal, his cloak whipping around his legs. "JA'VEN."

* * *

"We're under attack," a guardsman yelled, dividing the curtains with his spear, keeping his eyes focused down the corridor. "Everyone must evacuate. Hurry."

Another blast shook the floor, rattling the dividers and causing parts of the ceiling to snap and splinter. The light peeking through the boughs rose and waned with each new roar.

Ja'Naam bent her knees to keep her balance. "Ja'Ven." She screamed, reaching out.

"Mother!" Ja'Ven cried, spilling the tiles as he scrambled around

Anda'Daata, jumping into his mother's arms.

Another flash of red lightning, followed immediately by angry drums, rang through the tree. Ja'Ven covered his ears and buried his face in Ja'Naam's chest. A nearby primary branch snapped, falling through the covered walkway and pulling a pair of matrons into a gaping hole. Desperate screams clawed at the curtains and died as quickly as they began.

"But the eggs," Anda'Daata cried, her eyes widening. "We need the escorts."

"There's no time," the soldier disappeared, leaving the drapes to swish with each new explosion.

"Ja'Ven, get on my back. Hurry." Ja'Naam yelled over the noise.

Ja'Naam knelt as Ja'Ven scurried under her arm and climbed between her wings. Her tunic became tied up in the knots, revealing her pouch.

"Anda'Daata," Ja'Naam held out her hands. "Let me help you out."

"There's no time for me, child," the woman croaked. "But you can save some of the children."

Anda'Daata reached under her apron and retrieved an egg from a pile underneath her and held it out. She fumbled the precious object as the floorboards rippled like the tide from Windfather's breath across the sea. She rose off her stool as the branches around her lurched to one side. Flecks of bark exploded off the surface like wishflower petals in a hurricane. Deep voices shouted frantic orders; their words lost in the cacophony of a thousand screams.

"But you said I wasn't quite ready," Ja'Naam shouted as she fell sideways and braced herself against the floor.

"You're going to have to be," the woman's eyes grew fierce. "Save as many as you can carry."

Ja'Naam nodded as Ja'Ven cried into her neck.

She slid forward and steadied herself on Anda'Daata's knees. The woman pulled open Ja'Naam's pouch. She winced as another explosion rocked her away, making a tear along one side of her flap.

Anda'Daata tenderly lowered the egg and pushed it to the bottom.

Ja'Naam's breath caught in her throat. She took a long sniff and blew out. "Another."

Anda'Daata retrieved another egg and slid it next to the first, adjusting the two to rest side by side. Ja'Naam was pinching her lips and clenching the gown's folds. "Another," she said through her teeth.

Anda'Daata placed the third egg above the others. The tear in her pouch widened. Ja'Naam buckled at the waist.

Anda'Daata sucked air through her teeth. "You can't take another, child. Go. Hurry. Save Ja'Ven and these two."

"No," Ja'Naam grunted. "I can do it."

She loosened the straps of Ja'Ven's harness and retied them over her pouch. The triplet bulges stretched her skin to near transparency. "Now, let's get you out of here too."

"There's no time," she lifted Ja'Naam off the floor. "You go. I'll get myself and the rest of my children out."

A fireball blew through the curtains, launching Ja'Naam into Anda'Daata. The women shrieked, followed by the crackle of eggshells. A branch fell through the wall, landing on the older woman's wing, snapping the joint.

Anda'Daata screamed. Ja'Ven howled into Ja'Naam's back, digging his claws into her neck.

"NO!" Ja'Naam cried.

"GO!" Anda'Daata yelled. "NOW!"

A barrage of thunder erupted from all around like a million drums. Ja'Naam stood on shaky feet, pushing through the blazing curtain, cradling her belly with both arms.

"Ja'Ven," she called over her shoulder. "I need you to flap with me. As hard as you can. Ja'Ven? Are you listening?"

Ja'Ven was crying, calling out to his mother and father.

"Oh Holy Windfather," Ja'Naam wept, laboring under her load. "Please help me save my son and these children. Please, I beg you. Save us."

She lost her step several times on her way to the balcony. Bracing herself against a column, she took several deep breaths before flapping hard and launching into the air.

Chapter Twenty-Five

High Road to Ruin

Unburdened with any armor or weaponry, R'Venin shot past Vis'Haal's battalion, ignoring his repeated orders to halt. On all sides, gongs, bells, and drums blared as he raced through the trees. Once he penetrated the canopy, he spied the source of alarm.

In the distance, figures in gold and black swarmed over the Hearts of Ch'Hotee like a gilded pillar of smoke. At the column's head, a small herd of massive skyswimmers swam in lazy circles.

Father committed nearly his entire army to this one campaign. But why engage so deep in Ch'Hota territory. He must know they'd never all make it out alive.

V'Jeeta warriors cast engorged pitcherflower blossoms into the tree from scaffolds and platforms strapped along the skyswimmers' sides. They exploded on impact, spewing fiery acid across the upper branches. A dozen guardsmen platoons fell aflame under the explosive projectiles as they rose to defend the sacred tree.

Hundreds of Ch'Hota fled the smoldering hatchery, escaping into the Bluewoods. Men and women carried armfuls of eggs. Some aided portly brood mothers in their flight.

A lone female V'Jeeta swooped from the fray, hurtling herself towards one of the mothers with a spear. She impaled the Ch'Hota and rode her like a runnerhound as they plummeted to the ground. The warrior billowed her wings before impact, letting the body crash to the meadow in a cloud of feathers. More warriors rained down, weapons drawn, slaughtering anyone rushing for the tree line.

R'Venin spotted Ja'Naam, struggling toward the forest. One arm cradled her misshapen belly, while she reached over her shoulder with the other clinging to Ja'Ven's wrist. He flapped his winglets frantically as she labored to keep airborne.

"Ja'Naam!" he screamed. "Hold on! I'm coming!"

R'Venin dove, flapping hard through clouds of smoke laced with burning flesh and feathers. He lost sight of her several times as he weaved between aerial combatants. He risked a glance up as he dodged a pair of warriors diving for the tree wearing pitcherflower-laden bandoliers.

From the platforms, V'Jeeta warriors tipped large barrels, dumping swollen orbs onto the gilded timber. As if throwing stones at a tunneler colony, the blossoms fell, swarming through the rising currents. The impact of a hundred thousand stings filled the valley with fire.

R'Venin fought to stay ahead of the blistering wall licking at his calf-feathers as he sprinted to Ja'Naam's aid. Ja'Ven fell off her back as she rolled to catch an egg slipping from her pouch. She spun to grab him by the ankle and hunched over, golden blood staining her tunic.

"JA'NAAM!" R'Venin shouted, only to have his voice drowned by the fireball gaining on his family.

Ja'Ven flapped erratically, pulling Ja'Naam away from the trees.

"NO!" He howled as a second blast overtook the first, swallowing them whole.

The shock wave blew him, tumbling, into the forest's edge, topping saplings until his head hit a Bluewood trunk. He fell, limp-winged, and landed in a wishflower bush. Blackness gathered around his vision as the branches enveloped him like a cocoon.

* * *

Clanging metal roused R'Venin to consciousness. He spat wishflower petals as he raised his head to find the sun peeking just above the distant tree line. Ember-filled smoke billowed through the forest as wailing filled his ears. Smoldering feathers of black and gold drifted away from the meadow, running from the din.

He heaved himself to his feet, using the trees for balance. Burnt flesh and fresh blood filled his nasal slits as he staggered toward the glade. Tripping on a root, he fell against a tree. Smoke tendrils fumed from his cloak and into the bark. The ground crunched underfoot. He looked down to see shards of eggshells in a pool of yolk.

Freshly laid. No germinal disc. Still a tragedy.

He walked faster, shaking the clouds from his eyes until he reached the clearing's edge. The once golden tree, now ablaze, looked like a dying spinner. It's fallen branches, snapped and fractured, laid open on the soil. The roosts and balconies hung like fiery serpents down the twisted trunk. Bonfires of splintered vats pockmarked the field.

Fallen? Or pushed from above?

R'Venin scanned the field, searching for Ja'Naam or Ja'Ven, but every unmoving body looked as charred as the next. He found a warrior, gasping for breath, a spear pierced through the chest. Kneeling at his head, R'Venin pulled off the helmet to see the face of an adolescent V'Jeeta.

"You're barely a hatchling," R'Venin gasped, lifting the boy's head onto his leg. "What are you doing here?"

"I answered the call of P'Phet and the king." He gagged, blood bubbling from his mouth. "My brother and I."

He pointed to a pile of feathers with a Ch'Hota mace sticking out from his chest. The handle pointed skyward, while the spiked head barely peeked above the caved-in armor.

"Our ancestors will welcome us to the Eternal Tree as heroes," he spat through gnashed teeth.

"You need a healer," R'Venin began lifting the boy. He screamed as his chest pushed against the spear, still pinning him to the ground.

"You would have me beg my enemy for help?" the boy groaned. "Like a coward? Never. Leave me. P'Phet will come for me and carry me to the Windfather."

"I'll not just leave you to die, little one." R'Venin pleaded. "You need help. The Ch'Hota do not seek your destruction. You've been lied to."

"It's you who've accepted the Ch'Hota lies, traitor." The boy swatted R'Venin's hands away to no effect. He convulsed, and tears poured into his ears.

"The only traitor here is the one who sends a child to die for _his_ glory," R'Venin whispered as the boy's breathing slowed. He reached up and grabbed R'Venin by the hand, his grip weakening.

"I want to go home," he whimpered with unfocused eyes. "Will you please take me home? To the spires? To my mother? I want to hear her song." His hand went limp and dropped to the dirt as his eyes gazed unblinking toward the clouds.

"I'm sorry," R'Venin breathed, closing the boy's lids. "But, I have my own little one to rescue."

Setting the boy's head on the soggy grass, R'Venin pulled himself to his feet and resumed his slow march through the flame-scarred meadow.

A moment later, his eyes came upon an older V'Jeeta warrior, with slate-tipped feathers, laying next to a Ch'Hota woman. She huddled on her side, wrapping her swollen belly with one arm and held a spear tip at his throat.

"Why?" she seethed. "Why would you do this?"

"You're Ch'Hota," he gurgled, coughing up blood. "My king commands it. That's reason enough."

She raised her hand high over his head. R'Venin's eyes widened as he spied the markings on his armor.

My personal guard.

"Nir'Dayee?" R'Venin yelled, lunging forward with arm outstretched. "Please, sister. Stay your hand."

The old warrior's head lolled to the side. "Prince R'Venin?" he croaked. "We thought you were dead, my lord. Or a prisoner in Stonetree. Have more escaped with you?"

The Ch'Hota woman scuttled backward, holding the spearhead at arm's length.

"I'm a friend," R'Venin held out his palms. "As Windfather breathes, no harm will come to you at my hand. I swear by the order."

She dropped the blade and fell on her face, sobbing.

R'Venin pulled his soiled cloak out from the sash and laid it on the Ch'Hota woman. Her fingers trembled as she wrapped it around her waist, muttering a frantic petition to the Windfather.

"Why have the V'Jeeta attacked so far into Ch'Hota lands?" R'Venin reached down, patting her shoulder. She cringed, balling herself tighter. "Why have you destroyed the hearts of Ch'Hotee?"

"Your father's command, my lord," Nir'Dayee gurgled, gazing up to face R'Venin with unfocused eyes. "How are you still alive? I watched you fall nine seasons ago in the central plains. Your father tortured and killed every other member of your guard for failing to protect you in battle and then not returning your body to the spires. I, alone, was spared to live in dishonor."

"My brother rescued me," R'Venin droned as he stared across the field. Patrols of blood-stained guardsmen led groups of warriors, bound in ropes, toward the setting sun.

"My lord, R'Venin," Nir'Dayee stammered. "Prince K'Marot searched for three suns looking for you. Why would he not mention rescuing you sooner?"

R'Venin ripped a swatch from his sleeve and pushed it into the trickling wound at Nir'Dayee's neck and scanned the meadow.

"Orders, my lord." Nir'Dayee slurred. "Destroy the Ch'Hota. Our orders are to kill every enemy in our path, sparing none. Not even women and children. If you show your enemy mercy, you give them the false hope of surviving."

R'Venin put his weight into the rag as a sick heat rose like a bed of coals from his stomach, hotter than the flames he dodged racing to save his family. Hotter than the desert sand during the longest days of sun. Years of training came howling through his mind like wildfire.

Nir'Dayee seemed to grow younger before his eyes. Memories from his childhood erupted into R'Venin's mind.

* * *

R'Venin ducked his father's swing, spinning on one leg as Nir'Dayee— his personal guard—taught him.

"If you show your enemy mercy," K'Rawin smirked, swatting at R'Venin's legs with his wooden staff.

R'Venin jumped, holding his stick up as a shield, as he hovered at eye level with his Father. His feet, dangling at K'Rawin's waist level. "You give them false hope of surviving."

The midday sun pelted down on them as they stood atop the tallest spire in the canyons. Striated rock of whites, reds, and browns surrounded them below. A ring of V'Jeeta, adult warriors, and hatchlings stood along the tower's edge watching as father and son sparred in the heat.

Sweat dripped from wingtips as the full summer heat rained down. Drums echoed off the canyon walls from the shadows below, beating in R'Venin's young ears. The circle of onlookers pounded their staffs into the granite plateau, kicking up dust in time with the beat.

"Strike First. Strike hardest." K'Rawin chanted, lunging his staff toward R'Venin's head.

"Never relent until they are docile or dead." R'Venin parried the blow, rolling away with a backflip in midair.

"If your enemy will not yield," K'Rawin flapped into the air and spun close with a roundhouse kick.

"We will make them yield," R'Venin dropped to the ground, flattening himself as K'Rawin's wing brushed along his back.

The spectators cheered, speeding up their percussive applause.

Father and son circled the ring, eyes glinting as each held his rod out at shoulder level. K'Rawin winked. R'Venin smiled and lunged, running at his father as if his stick were a spear.

K'Rawin swung his staff down like a two-handed broadsword, knocking R'Venin's weapon to the ground. The pole caught R'Venin in the stomach, launching him head over heels to land flat on his back. K'Rawin looked down at his son with the stick high over his head, then began his downward swing.

R'Venin held up his hand. "I yield!" He yelled. "Peace, father. I yield."

K'Rawin stopped his staff a handspan from R'Venin's face. "Peace?" He growled, swatting the rod from R'Venin's hand. It broke in half, splintering as it flew over the warrior's heads. The king picked up his son by his tunic and yanked him off the ground.

The warriors' drumming stopped the moment K'Rawin dropped R'Venin onto his feet. The hatchlings looked around the circle, scanning each face, young and old. The adults lifted their poles to their chests, standing taller and narrowing their eyes on R'Venin. The children followed, their gaze drifting between the two royals.

R'Venin brushed the dirt off his legs, then stood at attention with his broken rod at his chest.

"You ask for peace?" K'Rawin roared. "Your enemy defeats you in combat, and you ask for peace? Warrior of the Granite Spires; what do we say when a defeated enemy sues for peace?"

The adults raised their sticks into the air. "Peace is the bleating cry of those unwilling to pay the price for victory!" They howled in unison. The children just lifted their rods as they cast unsure glances around the group.

K'Rawin walked stiffly in a slow circle around R'Venin, each step bringing him closer until he almost stood on R'Venin's toes. He opened his dark wings and created a shadowy cocoon. "Never let me hear you beg for peace again, R'Venin," K'Rawin whispered into the crown of his head. "It shows weakness. And a V'Jeeta warrior never shows weakness. If you show weakness, you may as well be dead."

R'Venin looked up to find K'Rawin smiling down at him.

"Yes, father." He returned it with a twitch in his lip and then looked down.

"Now," K'Rawin lifted R'Venin's chin. "Give me your best punch and battle cry. And make it look good."

R'Venin's face broke into a wide grin. He cocked his hand back and jabbed forward with a scream.

"Oof." K'Rawin fell backward, blowing all his air out and rubbing his stomach. "Now that's how you punch your enemy."

The crowd raised their staffs and chanted R'Venin's name until K'Rawin pointed to another warrior to bring his hatchling into the circle.

R'Venin followed K'Rawin to the emptied spot and stood in front. His shoulder hunched slightly when K'Rawin rested the full weight of his arm on R'Venin's shoulder and took up the drumming with his pole.

R'Venin watched the sparring match, but his mind replayed his defeat.

* * *

R'Venin shook the memory away as Nir'Dayee coughed blood into the air.

"Help me, my prince." Nir'Dayee gurgled, lifting a shaking hand above his chest. "Help me take flight to the eternal tree. Recite the words of P'Phet with me."

R'Venin took his grasp, tugging the blood-soaked rag from the warrior's neck. His father's voice filled his ears instead of the dying guard. He said the words, but his mind spoke something else.

"If you show your enemy mercy, you give them the false hope of surviving."

Father raised me to be a weapon when I wanted to be a healer.

"Strike first. Strike hardest. Never relent until they are docile or dead."

I never wanted the life of a warrior.

"Peace is the bleating cry of those unwilling to pay the price for victory."

Father never let the seeds of peace take root in his hearts.

"If your enemy will not yield, you make them yield."

I'll never be free of his enmity.

Nir'Dayee's eyes closed as his last breath escaped. R'Venin draped the rag across the old man's eyes and stood, searching the field.

Where are Ja'Naam and my little Ja'Ven?

R'Venin moved frantically through the trodden grass. "Ja'Naam," he yelled. "Ja'Ven. Ja'Naam, where are you?"

He searched for five songs until he spotted Ja'Naam's profile peeking out of a pile of charred feathers.

He knelt and peeled back the burnt wings. A rising wave of heartache crested like a winter tsunami when he found Ja'Ven wrapped in her wings. His smudged face looked as if he'd fallen asleep after rooting for ground-tunnelers.

She held his head to her chest, like when she sang him stories before dreaming. Her ripped tunic revealed the frayed pouch. Yolk seeped out, collecting on the ground next to her.

Then he noticed the matching bloodstains, Ja'Naam's yellow mixed with Ja'Ven's green, on their chests and peered closer.

"They didn't die in the fire," he said to himself, "And they didn't die on impact. They bled out on each other. How did this happen?"

R'Venin knelt in the dirt, pulling them into his lap. He then bent over, covered them with his wings, and wailed.

Chapter Twenty-Six
Wind and Ash

Ka'Ala reached the Bluewoods near sunset. Clouds the colors of an autumn forest drifted across the sky, turning to sickly ash as they passed over a column of black smoke. Rising from the forest's center, it drifted north as it cleared the treetops. She dropped onto a high branch, catching her breath. A million sorrows joined in the chorus as moaning and wailing reached her ears from all around. The stench of death permeated the woodland like an early morning fog, filling every crag and crevice.

I'm too late.

Taking a breath of sour air, she shifted her colors to blue-tipped golds and set off. The air grew noxious and thick with embers as she pushed toward the smoky fountainhead. Off in the distance, thousands of Ch'Hota carried baskets and barrels from the sea, dousing fires.

As Ka'Ala reached the meadow, she grabbed her tunic's folds at her chest. "Oh, no," she whispered. "The Hearts."

Below, the meadow looked like the remnants of a fire pit. Piles of wood gushed soot into the air as water drowned the petering flames. Stacks of black and gold bodies dotted the field. People hauled wood from the forest, building pyre's around the mounds.

The gaping absence of the golden tree seemed like a massive crater in an otherwise flat landscape. She flew low, gliding over the charred pastoral remains, and heard a song in her mind. The once triumphant horn lowed like a live tuskhead roasting on a spit.

"No," she choked.

Only one thing would make his song groan like that.

She followed the sound across the decimated pasture until she found the source and quietly landed next to R'Venin, kneeling as he looked up. Ash caked his face, though salty rivers carved valleys down his cheeks. His emerald eyes took an eternity to focus as he withdrew his wings.

Ka'Ala covered her mouth and closed her eyes. "Why, Windfather?" she wailed into her hands. "Why would you allow this to happen?"

You are not ready for the answer, daughter, Windfather breathed in her ear.

She uncovered her face and reached out, taking Ja'Naam's and Ja'Ven's limp hands in hers.

"She loved you like a sister," R'Venin said, barely audible. "She wanted you to come live with us so you wouldn't have to sleep behind your shop."

"She asked me many times," Ka'Ala sniffled, looking up to catch R'Venin watching her. "But I couldn't."

"I told her I thought you preferred being alone..." he droned as she nodded. "After so many years by yourself."

"I had my reasons," Ka'Ala whispered as she covered R'Venin's wings with her own, completing a protective circle. She bowed her head and hummed Ja'Ven's favorite dream-time song, thinking of the words.

Wandering stars fill up the night.
The new leaf breezes cross the sky,

And sway the boughs from left to right
To lift me where the dreamers fly.

The Windfather watches me play and glide
Betwixt his breath and swaying tree.
For 'tween the limbs I'll dance and hide,
Until he comes to branch with me.

My little one, He'll softly say,
I have a dream for you alone.
I'll take you from your troublesome day,
The Eternal Tree, from ne'er you'll roam.

Ka'Ala repeated the song five times before the flicker of an approaching light caught her attention. A trio of Ch'Hota elders came out of the forest and made their way into the field, kicking up ash with each step. They held staffs topped with fire crystals above their heads like beacons. Behind them, men carried women's bodies, and women bore children's bodies through the forest. The procession trudged toward the meadow, heading for the pyres built around the remains of Ch'Hotee's Hearts.

One of the Elders, a wizened Ch'Hota named Sha'Anti, stooped over R'Venin and put his hand on Ka'Ala's shoulder.

"Brother and sister," his eyes glimmered in the soft glow. "Whom do you mourn?"

Ka'Ala opened her mouth to answer but closed it to swallow as she wiped her eyes.

"My mate," R'Venin muttered. "And only-born."

Ka'Ala reached out, resting her hand on R'Venin's. "My sister," her voice cracked. "And her only-born."

"Do you wish assistance carrying them to the pyres?" Sha'Anti said. "That they may be raised to the Eternal Tree with the others?"

"No." R'Venin shook himself out of his stupor and locked eyes with Ka'Ala. "I'll carry Ja'Naam. Ka'Ala, since Ba'Jai's not here, will you bear my son?"

Tears spilled down her cheeks. "Of course," she said, pulling her wings back.

Sha'Anti moved on, returning his staff above his head.

R'Venin opened his wings and crawled from under his family, resting their heads gently on the ground. He then scooped up Ja'Ven, pulling him out of Ja'Naam's embrace, and laid him in Ka'Ala's waiting arms. R'Venin then wrapped Ja'Ven's drooping wings across his body like a blanket and touched foreheads.

R'Venin stood, helping Ka'Ala to her feet. She nuzzled her face to Ja'Ven's as R'Venin knelt to pick up Ja'Naam's body. The Elder helped fold Ja'Naam's wings across her body as R'Venin stood. He lifted her until her face rested on his neck and fell into step with the crowd of mourners.

Ka'Ala did the same with Ja'Ven and marched beside R'Venin and the others. "There's something I need to tell you," she said. "About Ba'Jai."

"Do you know where he is?" R'Venin said, his eyes focused ahead but unseeing. "I haven't seen anyone else from the convoy, either."

"I think he's dead," her voice cracked.

"What makes you say that?" R'Venin turned his gaze to meet hers.

"Call it," Ka'Ala looked into his brimming eyes, "a feeling."

All around her, Ch'Hota, not carrying the deceased, moaned a grief-stricken song, but Ka'Ala paid no attention to the words. R'Venin's lament filled her hearts and mind like crashing waves. He trudged with head bowed, not even watching the ground ahead of him. He glanced over, staring at the broken body of his son. His jaw clenched; his chin quivered.

R'Venin pulled Ja'Naam's body tight to his chest. "She always told me how much she trusted your feelings. I pray they find each other in the Eternal Tree, along with Ja'Ven, and forgive me."

Ka'Ala moved closer. "Forgive you for what?" she whispered.

A second song raged from his chest.

A swelling fury.

A call for death.

A herald for vengeance.

He's planning something.

R'Venin and Ka'Ala trudged in line until it was their turn to place his family on a pile of branches. He put Ja'Naam beside one of the dead brood mothers, took Ja'Ven, laid him on top, and then wrapped her wings over his body. Once he shrouded their faces, he moved to Ja'Naam's feet. His movements became frantic as he spun in a circle, searching the grass.

"It's gone." He croaked.

"What's gone?" Ka'Ala stepped forward, casting her eyes along the ground.

"From Ja'Naam's mating band." R'Venin pushed through the crowd, ducking low to put his face closer to the soil. "Ja'Ven's talisman. The Fire Symbol. The Sunburst you crafted for us. It's gone."

Ka'Ala clutched her hand to her chest. "Oh, no." She gasped.

R'Venin scoured the immediate area for a moment and suddenly dropped to his knees, his heartsong wailing like a lost child.

"R'Venin," Ka'Ala said, kneeling beside him as the crowd formed a small circle. "I'm so sorry. Perhaps, I could make a new one. To honor them."

"Thank you, but..." R'Venin shook his head. "It won't be theirs. Their skin did not warm it, fill its etches with their scent. It would just be a piece of jewelry."

Ka'Ala nodded.

R'Venin stood and helped Ka'Ala to her feet.

As he walked back to join the other mourners, he shouldered his way to the front, ignoring the glares of people still carrying their dead to the pyre. Moving between two guardsmen laying a fallen comrade in blood-soaked armor, he reached out and pulled a feather from Ja'Naam's wingtip. Then another from Ja'Ven. Moving back to the crowd's edge, he poked them into his tunic and stood next to Ka'Ala.

She moved close and leaned against him. He stiffened his back like a statue as his hearts battled inside his chest.

* * *

The fifteen Ch'Hota elders each took a position by the pyres closest to what remained of Ch'Hotee's Hearts. Standing at the circle's inner edge, R'Venin shivered in the breeze swirling through the field. All around him, grievers embraced one another. Tears fell like rain as their cries howled through the air.

R'Venin, Ka'Ala, and every other mourner backed a wingspan away as Sha'Anti marched around the pile, stopping to ignite the wood at every third step. He stopped his procession near R'Venin, jabbed his staff into the ground, and raised his wings to the sky.

The encircling crowd followed his example, raising their wings and then gently fanning the flames. Sha'Anti lifted his gaze toward the stars. They flickered and disappeared, chased away by the growing blaze.

R'Venin reached for Ka'Ala's hand as the man next to him took his. This action continued until a single chain made by hundreds of people spiraled into the darkness.

R'Venin bowed his head and closed his eyes. Petitions from other funeral pyres, led by the Elders, faded to murmurs as their words reached his ears.

"Great Windfather," Sha'Anti's voice carried over the assembly. The first row of people repeated his petition, followed by the second and moving outward like a ripple on still waters.

"We come before you under the three mothers to mourn a terrible loss."

How can you watch and do nothing?

"We have lost our hearts. The sacred tree of Ch'Hotee."

The V'Jeeta rage across the world.

"We have lost mothers and fathers."

They destroy anything they can't control.

"Most importantly, we have lost nearly an entire generation of children."

How can you let one flock prosper while another roasts in their fire?

"We turn our hearts to you, beloved Windfather."

I don't know if I believe peace is the answer anymore.

"Comfort us in this tragedy."

The only comfort will be the end of their terror.

"Speak peace to the hearts of those who have suffered most."

Their suffering is yet to begin.

"Whisper to us your wisdom."

I will use the unnatural wisdom.

"Help us to understand."

They will understand sorrow beyond anything they've ever known.

"Help us to accept your will."

They will never suspect my plan.

"Help us to forgive."

They deserve no mercy.

"Gather us under your mighty wings."

They will fade like water in the desert.

"Protect us from the raging storm."

I will deliver a deluge in which they will drown.

"Carry our dear ones to the Eternal Tree."

Cast my enemies to the frozen wasteland.

"Let them feast in the never-ending forest."

Let them starve and thirst forever.

"Let their hearts become the wandering stars in the sky."

Let their hearts turn to stone—useless pebbles on the expanse.

"Guide us always. As the wind blows."

"As the wind blows," Ka'Ala repeated along with the entire meadow.

R'Venin kept silent as he opened his eyes and found Ka'Ala watching him with knitted brow.

"What is it?" he said.

She shook her head. "I'm not sure."

Sha'Anti started flapping but didn't leave the ground. The crowd around him all started beating their wings, turning the rising smoke into a swirling column. One by one, they launched off the ground, circling the fire and wailing into the sky. Crying the names of their lost ones as they gained altitude.

"Ja'Naam, daughter of Marda'Ana and Sang'Ya," R'Venin shouted, leaping into the air with Ka'Ala trailing after. "Mate of R'Venin, son of K'Rawin and P'Vrit. Ja'Ven, son of R'Venin and Ja'Naam. Rise on wings of wind and ash. Take your flight to the eternal tree."

The rising smoke twisted as the mourners encompassed the column, flying higher and faster until it dissipated in the wind blowing above the trees.

R'Venin repeated the observance until he reached the northbound breeze and peeled off, heading toward his home deep in the Bluewoods. Ka'Ala followed, moving to his side. They flew in silence until they passed the market district.

R'Venin glanced over as they passed above Willowlimb Bazaar. "You're not going home?"

"I don't think Ja'Naam would want you to be alone tonight?"

Ka'Ala drifted closer.

"You can take our roost." R'Venin glided a handspan away. "I'll take the balcony. I doubt I'll sleep anyway."

He flapped hard and pulled away, leaving Ka'Ala to trail behind.

* * *

Ka'Ala glanced across the bed as moonlight peeked under the drapes. With dimly lit sconces, the room seemed like a cave deep underground. She rubbed puffy eyes, drained of all moisture.

Swallowing against the desert sand coating her tongue, she rose off the bed, draping a blanket over her shoulders like a shawl to cover herself; her wings and legs exposed to the night air. The hanging pots of water on the balcony beckoned to her like an oasis.

When she parted the curtain to leave the bedchamber, she spotted R'Venin sitting in his prayer room, with the veil still hung on its peg, staring into the bowl. He'd stripped off his tunic and laid it across his legs. In only a breechcloth, the marigold glow of fire crystals cast shadows from the bowl on his bare face and chest. His wings draped off his back, spreading across the floor like a dirty river of tar.

She retreated behind the veil and bumped into a sconce, wincing as it shattered on the floorboards.

"Sorry," she hissed to herself, picking up the crystal and dropped it in a bowl next to the bed.

"It's alright, Ka'Ala," R'Venin cleared his throat. "I've done that many times myself."

Ka'Ala poked her head through the curtain. "Have you slept?"

R'Venin's shoulders sagged, and he shook his head. "I've spent most of the night debating on whether to tell my mother and B'Luren. I don't know if I dare to speak the words at all. If I say it aloud, it'll be too real, and I don't want it to be real. I want it to be a night-terror, and wake up beside her."

"Sorry I disturbed you," Ka'Ala shrunk back. "I'll leave you alone."

"I've never felt so alone in my life," R'Venin mumbled.

Sit with him, Windfather whispered.

Ka'Ala stepped across the narrow hall, sitting down opposite R'Venin, letting her bare legs spill out from under the blanket. She sighed as the warm spot created by the crystals radiated into her skin.

"You're never alone, R'Venin," Ka'Ala met his eyes, then glanced down. "The Windfather is always with us."

R'Venin's heartsong trumpeted like a charging tuskhead, though he remained motionless.

"Where was he when my people attacked innocent mothers, women, and children?" R'Venin muttered. "Where was he when my mate and son were flying for their lives? And where was I? Trying to pry the secret to cure the V'Jeeta of White Claw from that Pra'Acheen parasite. I should have joined the guard instead of wasting my time healing stomach tremors and prisoners' bowel issues. Then maybe I could have done more to protect my family and the Ch'Hota."

"You did what you thought would help the most," she reached over the bowl, exposing the scars on her legs. She caught R'Venin looking down, his brows knitting together. Ka'Ala yanked her hand back and cleared her throat, pulling her legs under the blanket. "Ja'Naam told me it's one of the things she loved most about you. Your desire to heal. Not just wounds but the flocks."

R'Venin gave half a smile. "What else did she tell you?"

"She told me," Ka'Ala's mouth twitched at the upbeat to his heartsong, "That you made her feel more precious than any Ch'Hota suitor she'd ever known. You treated her like a queen."

"I supposed when you're born a prince, it comes naturally to treat your mate like a princess."

"Given what we know about the V'Jeeta royal court," Ka'Ala

looked into the empty bowl, "you learned to respect women from your mother, not your father."

R'Venin's head drooped. "I can't even tell her that Ja'Naam is... Ja'Naam..." They stared into the glowing crystals below the bowl for two songs as the wind whipped through the branches outside.

Reveal yourself, Windfather breathed.

Ka'Ala sneaked a peek at R'Venin.

"I don't know if Ja'Naam ever told you this," she cleared her throat, "but I'm not Ch'Hota."

"I knew you weren't full Ch'Hota." R'Venin looked up. "I assumed you were a half-flock because you have darker feathers and paler eyes."

She took a quick breath. "I'm Gir'Agit."

"The Gir'Agit are a myth," R'Venin snorted, looking up. "Shape-shifters and soothsayers. Fables to scare children into obedience."

Ka'Ala stood and lifted the blanket over her head, holding it over her torso and exposing her shoulders and arms.

R'Venin scooted away as her eyes and feathers shifted colors to look like a V'Jeeta, then an elongated Pra'Acheen, and then relaxed into her natural state.

R'Venin sat back, staring for several moments, as he eyed her tips to talons several times. "Who else knows what you are?"

"Ja'Naam and Ba'Jai both knew." She knelt, her head tipped down. "Windfather commanded me to reveal myself to them when we first met in Copperleaf. I wanted to tell others, but He told me to conceal my true nature from anyone else. Especially you." Ka'Ala looked up, locking her gaze on him.

R'Venin's brow furrowed. "What do you mean, especially me?"

How much do I tell him?

"Do you remember Ba'Jai's story? About fighting the wild runnerhound, and then losing sight of you?"

"Yeah," R'Venin smirked, nodding. "He's told that one so often.

The hatchlings love it."

Ka'Ala took a slow breath. "I'm the reason he lost sight of you in the forest. I was the one who hid you from Ba'Jai and the runnerhound. I left the medicine on the ground for him to find to save you. The Windfather sent me to help you, but I never expected…"

"Never expected what?" R'Venin leaned forward.

Ka'Ala looked up, swallowing a lump in her throat. "I'm ashamed to admit it, but when I first saw Ba'Jai carrying you through the woods, I was hoping you'd die of your injuries. I hated you. All because of what your ancestors did to mine. But then, the Windfather told me you and Ba'Jai were meant to become family. I just never expected to become part of it. My hate and mistrust kept me alone for so many seasons. Ja'Naam and Ba'Jai welcomed me into their family as a sister. Because of them, I've learned to forgive the Ch'Hota for not coming to our aid when the V'Jeeta invaded our skies and took us as slaves. And, because of your hearts, I've learned to forgive the V'Jeeta for their sins against my flock."

"I never believed the legends." R'Venin sighed. "About the Gir'Agit. If I hadn't just witnessed it with my own eyes…"

"The legends are true," she raised an arm from under the cloak of bedding, twisting her arm to show off her intricate scars. "Changing colors is only one of our gifts. We can also listen to the heartsongs of the people around us. I even tried teaching Ja'Naam how to do it."

"I always wondered how she seemed to see inside my chest." R'Venin curled his legs underneath him and scooted back to the bowl.

"It's a gift from the Windfather," Ka'Ala sighed. "She learned how to listen to your hearts. She loved you more than the wind. The ones to whom we're closest always have the clearest songs."

"I'd give anything to hear her sing right now." R'Venin locked his eyes on the crystals, his mouth pinching into a tight line. "But my father has made that impossible. He took them away from me."

Turn his hearts from anger, Windfather breathed. *Listen.*

Ka'Ala closed her eyes and cocked her head, listening over the rustle of leaves beyond the room.

"You're planning something," Ka'Ala whispered. "Something savage. I can hear it in your hearts. It's growing stronger than your grief for Ja'Naam and Ja'Ven."

"And what if I am?" R'Venin glared up without moving his head, his face like stone. "Do you believe we should just forget what happened today? Brush the dead off of our feathers and absolve the V'Jeeta? Do you think that will bring an end to their bloodlust? Because it won't. You don't know them as I do. This attack will encourage them. They won't stop, and it'll only get worse. We have to fight back, strike at them, in the same manner that they attacked us."

"And then what?" Ka'Ala said softly, opening her eyes. "What happens if the Ch'Hota attack and kill their brood mothers and children? How will they respond? Who will be left to rebuild if everyone is dead? There must be an alternative to more killing."

"Appeasement has never dissuaded my people!" R'Venin threw his hands up. "We've always had higher numbers. The only thing keeping us in the Spires until now was our fear of the Ch'Hota's superior weaponry. Now that they can barrage an enemy from the sky, another wave will be coming once the king replenishes his army. And next time, they won't stop until they engulf the entire Bluewood forest in flames. Then they'll hunt the Ch'Hota down one by one until they're all dead or enslaved. Just like the Gir'Agit." He pointed at Ka'Ala.

"How are you going to do it?"

R'Venin picked up a sprig off the floor and poked it into the crystals, setting the tip on fire. "I've been picking up bits of alchemy from a Pra'Acheen," he blew a puff on the twig, making it glow. "The one who healed you and Ba'Jai in the Western Crossroads. He's told me almost all the ingredients to cure White Claw. There must also be a way to speed up the disease. Make it more potent. When I get back to the prison, I'm going to get the information. I'll beat it out of him if I have to."

"You would inflict pain on another?" Ka'Ala shook her head. "To get revenge? You're better than that. It would break Ja'Naam's hearts to know what you're planning."

"If my father hadn't already slaughtered them," R'Venin snapped. "We wouldn't be having this conversation."

"And what if it was your neighbor that held the secret?" Ka'Ala leaned forward slightly. "Or Ja'Naam's mother? Or me? Would you torture me? Where do you scratch the line?"

Chapter Twenty-Seven
Ka'Ala's Vow

"Cruelty is the only language my father understands," R'Venin shouted, swatting the speaking bowl into the wall. The brass bowl clattered and rang as it rolled to a stop. "He just slaughtered an entire generation of the unhatched. The Ch'Hota have lost most of their brood mothers. He's bent the branch in his favor, and unless something evens the weights, the Ch'Hota will soon be extinct. Just like the Gir'Agit. Do you want to see that happen?"

"Of course not." Ka'Ala shivered, pulling the blanket tight around her neck. "But making one person suffer to get revenge on another will only stain your feathers. Ja'Naam wouldn't want to see that happen to you. And neither do I. The Windfather wants me to warn you against the course you're contemplating."

"The Windfather," R'Venin scoffed. "Where was he when my family and a thousand Ch'Hota died? Why didn't he warn the V'Jeeta against their course? How could he allow my father to kill so many, and then dissuade me from seeking revenge?"

Ka'Ala tilted her head, listening to an unseen voice.

Because their ears stopped listening, many seasons ago. They were the first flock to turn their hearts from me. If R'Venin presses forward on this trail, the Ch'Hota will follow, and the air will be purged of the Ch'Hota and V'Jeeta by each other's hate.

R'Venin buried his face in his hands, sliding his wings off the floor and shaking the dust off before tucking them in. "What am I supposed to do? Just let their deaths go unanswered? Be the warrior my father always wanted and let the V'Jeeta conquer? I have to do something."

"But you don't have to answer hate with more hate." Ka'Ala slid her arm out from the blanket and reached over the fire crystals. Her fingers almost touched his head when she jerked her hand back. "If you do, you'll condemn every Ch'Hota prisoner in the Spires. Just before the attack, Windfather showed me a vision while I was away at the Hiding Falls."

R'Venin's eyes narrowed. "What happened?"

"I didn't see much," Ka'Ala leaned forward. "But I did see the convoy. It was attacked. They loaded the wagons with V'Jeeta warriors in disguise, not guardsmen. They overpowered the Ch'Hota and killed them all. Even Ba'Jai. Their leader seemed interested in his artificial wing."

"He had three long scars," Ka'Ala raked her hand down her face. "And he looked like you, but younger."

"That must've been K'Marot." R'Venin cocked his head and mumbled to himself. "I wonder how he got those."

"Yes," Ka'Ala said. "That's what they called him, Prince K'Marot. His warriors blocked my view, but it looked like he killed Ba'Jai with an ax, and he told his warriors to take the pieces back to the king. After that, he flew up to the skyswimmers and led the attack on the Hearts of Ch'Hotee. That's when the vision ended. I tried to get back in time to warn the guard, but I was too far away. When I got back, I found you with..."

"Why didn't the Windfather give you the vision sooner?" R'Venin held out his arms. "Why not show you when they started planning the attack? We could've prepared. Sent the guardsman to fight them before they reached the Bluewoods."

"Who would've believed me?"

"I would have," R'Venin stiffened. "Ba'Jai and Ja'Naam would've believed you too."

"And if you had," Ka'Ala gave a slight shake to her head, her eyes pleading, "who would've believed you? Or Ba'Jai? Or Ja'Naam? None of us have connections to the Quorum of Elders. I'm a simple artisan. You're a prison alchemist. Ba'Jai was a demoted guardsman. Ja'Naam spent her days tending Ja'Ven. Would they have taken the threat seriously if it came from any one of us?"

"No." R'Venin's shoulders fell. "Then why not give the vision to the quorum? Why you?"

Ka'Ala shrugged.

"I wish I knew what to do."

Ka'Ala bowed her head for a moment, then looked up at him. "You have a choice. Complete the cure and heal your people or abandon your vows to the Order and Windfather."

"How can I cure my people," R'Venin growled, "knowing they may just use it as justification for their crusade?"

"How can you condemn the world to never-ending bloodshed," Ka'Ala sighed, "knowing you had the power to end their suffering and offer a peaceful end to the war?"

"It's what they deserve."

"Is it your place to decide that?"

R'Venin raked his nails across his head. "No."

"If you still want to honor your vows," Ka'Ala reached out and put her hand on R'Venin's knee. "I'll help you."

"And if I decide otherwise?"

"Then you're not the man..." Ka'Ala pulled her hand away, held it over the bed of crystals, and cleared her throat. "...Ja'Naam fell in love with, and I'll let the Windfather decide your fate alone."

R'Venin crossed his legs and arms and wrapped his wings around himself.

"I need some time to think. You'll have my decision at sunrise," he said, staring into the crystals. "I'd like to be alone now."

Ka'Ala nodded and rose to her feet. She picked up the fallen bowl and placed it on the floor next to R'Venin.

"As you wish," Ka'Ala whispered as she pulled the curtain off its peg and went back into the bedchamber.

* * *

Ka'Ala folded the blanket before sitting down and getting back in her leggings and tunic. Once fully dressed, she padded to the gathering room and sat on the balcony's edge, letting her legs dangle.

"Windfather," she breathed. "What will he do? What am I to do?"

I know his hearts, Windfather answered. *He will do what is right.*

"What is your will for me?" she glanced at the sky. A wandering star streaked across the night as the highest branches swayed in the coastal breeze.

To remain at his side.

"For how long?"

Until the end.

"The end of what? *As* what? For nine seasons, I've heard his hearts sing for Ja'Naam. My sister. They cry for her even now. I've never forgotten the first time I heard it in Copperleaf Forest. I've kept myself away despite Ja'Naam's pleas to have me stay with them because I couldn't be so close to him and not feel guilty for having an affection for him. Why did you let me hear his song at all if you intended him for her?"

A pair of chittering creatures scrambled between the branches over Ka'Ala's head.

At least you two have each other, she thought.

The time is not far distant, Windfather breathed, *that you will find peace in the arms of a good mate.*

"Who?" Ka'Ala hissed, her voice cracking. "The only men I know well are R'Venin and Ba'Jai. Or will it be someone else that you'll have me draft for several seasons?"

"And about Ba'Jai. After his mate sought severance, he made several attempts to dance for me, inviting me to the bonding festivals, singing for me. And you always told me to reject his offers. He's a good man that didn't deserve how I rejected him with no explanation. We might have been happy together. I'm just so weary of being alone. No one to sing for me or dance with me. Preen with me, and create a family with me. I want what Ja'Naam had. I want to feel like I'm home."

Be patient, daughter, Windfather whispered. *The time will come when hearts will sing for you, and you will remember your sorrow no more.*

"Yes, Windfather." Ka'Ala pulled her legs up and wrapped her arms and wings around them. Resting her head on her knees, she sighed. "I will obey."

* * *

R'Venin backed out from his prayer room before the sun peeked over the horizon. He wore his tunic open, tied at the waist, but loose around his chest. Hanging the drape on its peg, he turned to find his roost empty and bedding folded.

"Ka'Ala?" he poked his head through the opening. "Are you in here?"

"I'm on the balcony." Her muffled voice, barely audible over the pre-dawn symphony of early-rising creatures, floated down the hall.

He rubbed his eyes and yawned. Holding a hand to his growling stomach, he walked over. As he stepped into the gathering room, he spied her kneeling on the ledge with hands and wings outstretched.

"Get any sleep?"

"Enough," she said.

Ka'Ala remained statuesque as R'Venin approached at her side. Her eyes were closed, and her lips moved.

"I didn't mean to interrupt your morning petition," He took a half-step back.

"I'm beseeching the Windfather to comfort the many who have lost their loved ones." Ka'Ala looked up with tired eyes. "You can join me if you like."

"I would." He said, dropping to his knees. "But I'll just petition in my hearts."

Ka'Ala nodded and closed her eyes with a slight smile on her lips.

R'Venin opened his arms and wings, flinching when his feathers brushed against hers and repositioned himself to put a hand span between them.

Windfather, my hearts are filled with stones. Ja'Naam and Ja'Ven have flown to your tree. I feel like a rotted branch. Hollow and weak. I've vowed to fulfill my quest to heal my people. Help me. Please. Help me get the knowledge from Gha'Barahat. Help me cure the White Claw. Help me honor Ja'Naam and Ja'Ven so I may fly to them someday.

"As the wind blows," he mumbled, dropping his arms and wings. He opened his eyes and found Ka'Ala staring at him, her eyes brimming.

"As the wind blows," Ka'Ala breathed.

R'Venin gazed out into the trees. The sun emerged above the skyline, casting shadows through the woods. The symphony of night creatures faded, replaced by the echoes of pain. The usually vibrant morning songs, now subdued and mournful, barely rose into the canopy. They knelt side by side, motionless on the wooden planks, each looking out over the rising dawn.

"I've made my decision," he said, drawing the laces at his neck.

"I know." Ka'Ala fiddled with the hem of her tunic, stretched tight across her lap. "I can hear it in your hearts. I heard it the moment you came out."

R'Venin glanced at her sideways.

"I suppose I should expect more of that. Picking up on my thoughts. The way Ja'Naam did."

"I suppose you should." Ka'Ala straightened her back as she looked down at her hands. "I can promise I'll only use my gift to help you."

R'Venin pursed his lips and nodded.

"I have a plan," he said, looking around. "It won't be easy. We're going to need the Windfather's favor to pull it off. If the guardsmen catch us, we'll spend the rest of our seasons in Stonetree. Never to see the sun or feel the wind again."

"I understand," Ka'Ala leaned toward him.

"Do you?" R'Venin whispered. "Because I don't know if I do. I've lost everything but my freedom. I'm risking it, and yours, that Gha'Barahat knows the cure to White Claw and that I'll be able to get it from him. I'm also betting every life in two flocks that I'll be able to get the ingredients, in sufficient quantity, and perform the incantation, so they don't have to war over the Silver Silk anymore. If this doesn't work, I may be condemning millions of lives to die in endless war."

Chapter Twenty-Eight

No Turning Back

Ka'Ala flew with the crowd of Ch'Hota, heading for the sea in the early morning light. A few V'Jeeta and Pra'Acheen dotted the golden mass like inkblots. The crisp breeze off the water cut through the thin fabric of her borrowed cloak.

Surely Ja'Naam wouldn't begrudge me wearing the clothes I gave her.

She looked left and right, smiling at other women heading for Stonetree. They all had fewer feathers tipped with blues and greens. Ka'Ala subtly adjusted her camouflage to blend in as just another low-branch. The tunic and leggings Windfather had given her shifted to match the mustard seed hues all around.

Craning her neck, she caught a glimpse of R'Venin trailing fifty wingspans behind. He avoided her gaze but tucked a thumb in his belt.

Ka'Ala nodded and slid her hand to her sash, fingering the small roll of parchment held tight to her waist. She swallowed back the bile threatening to erupt as her stomach knotted.

If this ploy doesn't work, I may be able to escape. But what about R'Venin? Oh, Windfather. Protect him.

The stream of fliers nosed down as they pierced the timberline surrounding Stonetree, heading for the fort and main gate. She followed, gliding down on billowed wings until she reached the fort and backwinged into the queue. She shuffled forward as the line moved closer to the musical threshold.

The stench of runnerhound scat filled her nose as she glanced around the square. The beasts stared out from their stalls or stretched their necks, sloshing their muzzles in watering troughs. Wagons sat empty, their riggings hanging from wall pegs.

One by one, the people approached the gate to place their keys in their respective holes, emitting their duties' songs.

Ka'Ala moved toward the guardsman. She looked to the ground as his eyes caught hers.

"*Show meekness,*" R'Venin said as they set off from his balcony. "*Give the guard a reason to show pity, and he won't look too closely.*"

"Would you help me?" She asked without looking up, holding out the scroll. "I'm here to fill the open position of alchemist's assistant."

"I wasn't aware they needed more help," the guardsman unrolled and scanned the writing.

Ka'Ala fidgeted in place.

"One moment, please." The guardsman waved his hand to someone behind her. "Alchemist, come forward."

Ka'Ala could hear R'Venin's heartsong approach, quickening in its pace. She pulled the cloak tight around her neck as the veins throbbed in rhythm.

"Yes, guardsman," R'Venin said, sounding confused. "What can I do for you?"

Ka'Ala looked up as the soldier pointed the scroll at her. "This woman says there's an opening in your ranks. I've heard nothing about it. What do you know?"

"First I've heard of it." R'Venin looked over at Ka'Ala. "I suppose Vis'Haal's finally casting me down because I'm V'Jeeta."

"I'm not an alchemist." Ka'Ala dropped her head and averted her eyes, revealing the undersides of her wings. "I'm just a poor artisan who lost my shop in the attack. I need to find work, any work, to support myself."

The guardsman met R'Venin's gaze, pursed his lips, and nodded. "Maybe Vis'Haal doesn't care and just wants to keep a closer eye on you." His mouth twisted as he pulled his spear tight to his chest.

"Any closer," R'Venin shrugged, "and he'd be here to answer for himself."

"Will you sponsor this woman?" The guardsman tilted his head toward Ka'Ala. "Guide her to the administrator's chambers?"

R'Venin sighed. "Of course."

The guardsman pointed his spear, maneuvering R'Venin toward the wall of holes.

R'Venin inserted his key and twisted it, playing the alchemists' song.

"You may enter." He gently pushed the scroll back into Ka'Ala's hand. "This man will show you the way. You'll need a song key of your own to get through the gates next time."

"Thank you." Ka'Ala tucked the scroll back into her sash.

"Fair weather, guardsman." R'Venin inclined his head.

"Fair weather." The guardsman touched the brim of his helmet. "Smooth breezes, artisan."

Ka'Ala gave a quick bow. "Clear skies, guardsman."

R'Venin walked quickly under the portcullis. Ka'Ala followed, catching up to him at the second, but staying a pace behind him across the bridge.

* * *

R'Venin led the way through the lower prison complex, a quarry stone labyrinth of corridors and stairs, always keeping his right hand on the wall. He brushed it along sconces of fire crystals, counting them under his breath between turns.

"One. Eight. Nine."

They passed by armor-clad guardsmen in various states of alertness in front of wooden doors on thick iron hinges with each turn.

"These are the food stores," R'Venin said, waving his hand. "If you're ever asked to help cook or serve food, this is where you'll need to go. Don't bother going to the armory without an armed escort and scroll marked by Vis'Haal himself."

Steam seeped around the door's edges, bringing with it the stench of roasted branchclimber.

"Stay clear of the armory." Ka'Ala passed a guardsman leaning on his spear with closed eyes. "I'll remember that."

"One. Six. Five."

"I got lost every morning until I realized my overseer used this trick," R'Venin breathed, turning a corner after counting five. "To get out, use the opposite hand and count it backward. Five. Six. One. Nine. Eight. One. The alchemy stores are just down here."

He stopped at the fifth door along an empty corridor and inserted his key into the lock, though it didn't sing like outside the gates. He shouldered the door open; its rusty hinges screeching in protest as the bottom stile scraped across the stone floor. Once R'Venin finished pushing the door wide open, the sound of trickling water replaced the wood grinding on rock.

"Grab that cart," he hissed, pointing to the corner. "Collect the brass bowls on the third shelf and five bladders of water. There. At the bottom. While I collect the prisoner's treatment list and ingredients."

Ka'Ala grabbed a leather pouch from the pile and hooked a strap over a bent pipe jutting out from the wall. They worked in silence, letting the echoes of gurgling water mask their movements down the corridors. R'Venin piled sacks and vials of a hundred different elements into the cart's upper deck while Ka'Ala filled and loaded the bladders of water onto the lower section between the wheels.

"Why do we need all that water?" Ka'Ala grunted as she heaved the last sack in place.

"As a diversion," R'Venin whispered, throwing a dirty cloth across the bulging sacks. "I'll need a reason for having the cart weighed down if we get stopped by one of the guards. I'll tell them it's to flood a nettlewing nest in the ramparts. I have to do it once a moon anyway."

"That's not an alchemists' responsibility, is it?" Ka'Ala's face scrunched up. "That should be the custodian's task."

"It has been as long as I've worked here." R'Venin shrugged, checking his scrolls and taking stock of the overladen cart. He looked up and locked eyes with Ka'Ala. "From this moment forward, we're committed to success or treason."

Ka'Ala took a deep breath, grabbed two leather aprons off the peg, and handed one to R'Venin.

* * *

A half-sun later, Ka'Ala pushed the cart from behind while R'Venin pulled, trudging up the shallow slope from one cell to the next. The corridor thundered with trilling songs and full-throated shouts from the prisoners. Nira'Ash, again, escorted R'Venin through the corridors. He slammed his mace and tried to shout down each inmate, but as they passed each cell, the din grew with lewd taunts, requests for personal servicing, and threats of intimate violence.

Nira'Ash swung at more than one arm grappling for Ka'Ala, causing delays in R'Venin's plan as additional alchemists trailed behind mending broken bones.

"Shut your mouths and show some respect for this woman."

Nira'Ash hollered down the corridor. "Or I'll break more than your hands."

R'Venin gathered the spent ingredients from the cell of a young warrior who looked more scared than excited in Ka'Ala's presence.

"How far is *his* cell?" She yelled between breaths across the cart, flinching away from a V'Jeeta reaching for her from behind.

"Why'd you want this job anyway," Nira'Ash grumbled as he squeezed past Ka'Ala and the cart, swinging his weapon and smashing it into the outstretched arm. The crunch of a dozen bones was more like stepping on sand with all the noise around them.

The warrior screamed and pulled his bleeding sack of a hand back through the bars.

"Quit your squawkin'." Nira'Ash pounded the cell. "The healers will be along shortly. Probably tomorrow, given the ruckus you sacks of filth are making."

"He's next." R'Venin had to shout over the chaos.

R'Venin pulled, Ka'Ala pushed, and Nira'Ash lumbered up the corridor until they reached Gha'Barahat's cell.

Nira'Ash retreated down the hall, slamming his mace on cells and any protruding body part he found in his path.

"Gha'Barahat," R'Venin hissed over the din, hurriedly fumbling with the key as he kept his eyes on Nira'Ash. "I've come with that refreshment you asked for."

Gha'Barahat rolled over, peeking out from his filthy blanket. His mouth widened into a broad smile just before a racking cough caused him to buckle over and fall off his paltry bed. The chaos throughout the entire prison masked his hacking cough.

Ka'Ala held the cart steady as R'Venin pulled two flagons of water from the lower tray along with the dirty cloth. He pushed the door open and moved quickly into the cell. Kneeling, he set the sacks on the floor next to the withered Pra'Acheen. The older man was roughly the size of both sacks together.

Ka'Ala used her wings to partially block the lower corridor's view while R'Venin shielded himself from the upper vista. He lifted the bladders onto the stone ledge, replaced the filthy prisoner's blanket on top, and tucked it all around, making it look like Gha'Barahat was still asleep.

R'Venin then wrapped the old alchemist in the carts' drape and tucked the edges all around.

"WHAT IN THE WINDFATHER'S NAME IS CAUSING ALL THIS NOISE?" Vis'Haal's voice exploded from the upper corridor.

The taunts and jeers turned from Ka'Ala to the prison's chief guardsman. The large Ch'Hota ignored every word. His shoulders nearly filled the corridor's width as he strode into view. His eyes narrowed as they fell on R'Venin, still inside Gha'Barahat's cage. His brow furrowed deeper when he caught sight of Ka'Ala standing behind the cart. She kept her face down, revealing as much of her wings' undersides as the space allowed.

"What's the meaning of this, Nira'Ash?" Vis'Haal boomed.

"New alchemist's assistant," Nira'Ash said, slamming his fist against the cell door. "She's helping R'Venin with his duties by order of the administrator."

"There have been no such orders," Vis'Haal growled.

Ka'Ala glanced up to see R'Venin, picking Gha'Barahat off the ground. She bowed her head and flattened herself to the outer wall as Nira'Ash put a gentle hand on her shoulder.

Windfather. What do we do?

"I have the scroll right here." Nira'Ash slipped past the cart, holding it out.

Vis'Haal snatched it from Nira'Ash's hand and unrolled the parchment. His lips moved as he scanned the writing until he reached the bottom. His mouth twisted into an evil smile as he let it fall to the floor and roll down the ramp, coiling up as it went.

Ka'Ala's eyes popped open as the call of war drums pounded from Vis'Haal's hearts.

"That's not the administrator's mark, you filthy V'Jeeta," Vis'Haal leered at R'Venin's back. "It's a forgery. I finally have a legitimate excuse to kill you."

The heckling faded to silence as R'Venin's grip of Gha'Barahat slipped. One of the bladders tipped and splatted to the floor, the stopper bursting and spitting out its contents. The only sound other than Ka'Ala's hearts beating in her ears was the water as it trickled through the bars and down the hall.

Windfather. Guide us. Guide me.

Be ready, daughter, Windfather whispered in her ear. *Darkness cannot abide the light.*

R'Venin made eye contact with Ka'Ala as he turned slowly, holding Gha'Barahat like a sleeping hatchling in the crook of his arm. When he faced Vis'Haal, the chief guardsman folded his arms and nodded in triumph.

"I knew it was only a matter of time before your true feathers plumed," Vis'Haal smirked.

"You don't understand," R'Venin took a step toward the door.

"You should stay in that cell. I'll let you rot in there with him; then, I'll let you rot in there alone for a few seasons before I kill you."

R'Venin took another step toward the corridor. "I need his help to cure White Claw."

Nira'Ash gawked at the scene, standing between R'Venin and Vis'Haal, his neck swiveling as he watched the exchange.

"Of course, you want to cure it," Vis'Haal growled. "The more V'Jeeta there are, the faster you can wipe out my people."

"If I can cure White Claw, I believe I can convince the V'Jeeta to end the war over the Silk. We won't need it anymore."

"There's another option." Vis'Haal stepped forward, drawing his dagger from its sheath. "You can fulfill your oath to the Order of the Wind and let the Windfather decide which flock lives or dies."

In the cell next to him, a young V'Jeeta warrior stood, hunched slightly with his eyes fixed on the giant Ch'Hota.

R'Venin stepped up to the door and looked down at the floor.

"If you put one talon over that threshold, I'll kill you where you stand as a traitor. And I'll run through that Pra'Acheen coward in the process."

Vis'Haal pulled his second dagger from its sheath and rolled his shoulders, putting one leg behind the other.

Behind him, Nira'Ash squared himself, creeping his hand up the mace's shaft.

The warrior took one barely perceptible step toward the bars.

R'Venin locked eyes with Vis'Haal. "I have no choice."

"Then you choose death," Vis'Haal grinned.

R'Venin took a deep breath and raised his foot.

Become the terror of Vis'Haal's childhood, Windfather breathed as Vis'Haal raised his daggers to either side, his wings pulling up behind him.

A ghastly image erupted in Ka'Ala's mind. She released the cart, sidestepping to let it pass. Every eye in the corridor watched as it rattled down the slope and crashed into an empty cell. Standing in the middle of the hall, she ripped the thin overtunic off her body, letting it fall to the stones at her feet.

She stretched her arms and wings as far as they could reach and shifted. The dull gold feathers fluttered in an invisible breeze, changing to reds, oranges, and yellows. Her eyes and talons glowed white, brighter than the crystal torches lining the hall. The skin on her face, neck, arms, and legs rippled like embers in a fire pit.

"No! It's... it's a..." Vis'Haal whimpered, lowering his daggers as he backed into the cell. "It's a fireface."

Instantly, the young imprisoned V'Jeeta reached through the bars of the cell, interlocking his claws around Vis'Haal's throat, and began to choke him. The chief dropped his weapons and raked at the hands at his neck.

"NO!" R'Venin yelled as he came out of the corridor. "Don't kill him."

"Release him!" Nira'Ash barked at the prisoner, raising his mace as Vis'Haal struggled for breath. "Now!"

R'Venin ran up to the cell door into the warrior's view. "Warrior of the Granite Spires," he said, clasping his hand over the prisoner's forearm, "I command you to let him go."

The V'Jeeta's eyes narrowed as he retained his grip around Vis'Haal's larynx. "You have no right to command me, you traitorous valley-licker."

"As the king's firstborn," R'Venin whispered. "I have every right."

"Prince R'Venin?" He gasped. "You're alive?"

"Release this man, or his death will only bring more trouble."

"Trouble is all he's brought since they threw me in here. Better to face it with one less Ch'Hota scouring our noses."

"Spilling his blood will only bring death to you, and retribution to your brothers and sisters."

The warrior squeezed tighter. "P'Phet taught us to crush our enemies from within."

"The killing must stop." R'Venin tried prying his fingers between the V'Jeeta's hands and Vis'Haal's throat.

The guard's eyes bulged from their sockets. He stared at Ka'Ala with a combination of terror and agony. "I'll kill you all," Vis'Haal grunted through gnashed teeth, failing to wrestle himself free.

"Can you do it?" Nira'Ash grabbed R'Venin by the neck and held the mace over his head. "Can you cure White Claw? End the war?"

"R'Venin!" Ka'Ala shouted. In a moment, her coloring shifted from the bright reds and oranges to onyx and coal wearing the snowy tunic and leggings. None of the quarreling quartet took notice.

R'Venin made no effort to free himself from Nira'Ash's grip. "Not without his help." He held up Gha'Barahat's limp form, his arm swinging from under the blanket. "I made a bargain. To help him see the sun one last time in exchange for the final ingredient."

"And then what?"

"Then he returns to his cell and dies in prison."

Nira'Ash locked eyes with R'Venin for a torturous moment and then swung his club down on Vis'Haal's helmet. Vis'Haal went limp, as the warrior holding him to the cage retracted his claws and let go. The chief guardsman's head thudded against the opposite wall and collapsed across the corridor.

The young warrior spat into the corridor and sneered, backing away.

"I've always respected you," Nira'Ash said, releasing R'Venin's throat. "It hasn't been easy for you to live among the Ch'Hota. But if this is a ruse..."

Nira'Ash hung the baton from his belt and grabbed Vis'Haal by the legs, dragging him out of the way, then pulled a keyring off the unconscious man's girdle. "I'll give you one song to get to the dome, and then I'll have to sound the alarm. Vis'Haal's personal lookout should conceal you from the other guards for a short time. It'll be on your left as you reach the top."

"Thank you, my friend." R'Venin reached out his free hand.

Nira'Ash took it, squeezing the keys between their palms. "You can thank me by fulfilling your word. End the bloodshed."

R'Venin gripped hard. "Or I'll die trying."

Nira'Ash let go and waved his hand toward the upper corridor. "Go."

R'Venin took off at a run, the keys jingling as he shifted Gha'Barahat into his other arm.

Ka'Ala hugged the wall to get around Nira'Ash. He turned sideways as he felt her brush against his wings.

"What are you?" He whispered.

"It's a three-sun story." Ka'Ala gave him a weak smile and bolted after R'Venin. As she ran, the V'Jeeta's voice echoed off the stone walls.

"The Heir of the First Tower has returned!"

* * *

R'Venin ran past the cells, keeping one step ahead of the growing rally cry, with Ka'Ala close on his wing. They reached the final landing where the high sun cast a square of light on the ground, illuminating the stone floor at the base of an iron door. A smaller shaft of light penetrated through the keyhole halfway up the metal stile. He peeked through the barred window, finding no one within sight.

R'Venin held up the keyring to the lock's mouth, just large enough for his smallest finger.

"Which one is it?" Ka'Ala said over his shoulder.

"No idea," R'Venin whispered, fumbling with the keys one-handed.

"Let me do it for you." She took the ring from his hand, stepping between him and the door. She held the metal rods in a bundle as she fished them out one by one, sliding each into the hole. The fourth key fit and turned with a loud clang.

"Hide!" R'Venin hissed, pushing Ka'Ala away from the door frame and flattening himself against the wall. Ka'Ala crouched and shifted her colors, blending in with the reddish-brown stones around her.

The keys tinkled like chimes in a slight breeze as the square of sunlight vanished and the shape of a helmet drifted by like an eclipse.

R'Venin leaned his head out, searching for the patrolling guardsman.

"I can't see anyone else." He put his nose to the grill. "How about you?"

Ka'Ala stood and cocked her head. "Their songs are faint. Calm. I don't think they're close or suspicious. Can you see the lookout?" She stood on her toes, craning her neck to see just over the window's sill.

R'Venin leaned to the right, his chin gracing the top of her head, and peered out. Above and to the left, a wooden ramp with a short wall of pickets led to a covered stage overlooking the stone battlements. The platform's wooden walls had a large opening on each side, but they couldn't see the interior. "Yes, right there," R'Venin pointed with his chin.

To his right and from below, a resonant gong sounded, echoing through the domed courtyard.

The alarm!

Then a chant grew, echoing in the corridor.

The Heir.

The Heir.

The Heir.

R'Venin pictured Nira'Ash pounding his fist on a column of brass spheres. One globe sliding down a chute and colliding with a steel plate before falling through a funnel and landing on an identical stack, forcing the bottom sphere to eject from the bottom and repeat the action a level below. The process continued until the last gong, the count indicating on which level the alarm began.

Guardsmen along the parapets rushed to the latticed dome, inserting their spears into hooks and pushing clockwise. The outer layer of ironwork rotated to create openings large enough for more than half of them to dive into the atrium. Once through, the remaining guards pulled their spears free and focused on the space below.

"We need to hurry," R'Venin pulled the gate open, letting the keys clatter as he crossed the threshold. Keeping his eyes on the nearest guard, he signaled Ka'Ala to move behind him and then backed his way to the ramp until he couldn't see any gilded armor.

Ka'Ala crouched at the ramp's base and signaled him over. R'Venin hunched over as he carried Gha'Barahat, bent at the waist, up to the platform, and ducked around the corner. He laid the Pra'Acheen across a trapdoor on the floor, cradling his head as the cloth fell away from the old alchemist's head. His eyes pinched, squinting against the sun shining down on him.

Ka'Ala squatted between Gha'Barahat and the window, making a canopy of shade with her wings over his body.

"No," Gha'Barahat croaked, reaching toward the light. "Let me feel its warmth."

Ka'Ala dropped her wings as R'Venin helped Gha'Barahat sit up and face the ocean. The Pra'Acheen breathed deeply through his nose as the coastal air wafted into the small area. Along the walls, spears and swords hung from pegs and hooks. A shield in the corner wobbled with each gust, making its reflection dance across the thatched ceiling.

"Gha'Barahat," R'Venin said. "What's the mountain ingredient to cure White Claw? I fulfilled my end. Time to fulfill yours."

"Mountain," Gha'Barahat slurred, never opening his eyes or turning his head from the breeze. "White Claw. Yes."

"Tell me," R'Venin shook his shoulder. "Before they discover us. I still have to get you back to your cell."

Gha'Barahat turned his head slowly and opened his lids. Hollow sockets stared back at R'Venin.

"What happened?" R'Venin gasped.

"The great captain of the guard happened." Gha'Barahat snorted. "Vis'Haal. He heard me talking about seeing the sun before I died. Took my eyes. Might have had something to do with a pheromone-enhancing salve I taught him. I said he didn't follow the instructions properly. But I could've made a mistake. The mind wanders in prison." Gha'Barahat tapped his temple.

"What about the final ingredient for White Claw?" R'Venin growled. "Is your mind going to wander on that too?"

"No, no, of course not." Gha'Barahat felt through the air until he found R'Venin's face and gave it a tender pat. "It's all right here."

The man pulled his wizened hand away and held up his palm.

R'Venin stared at the criss-cross of lines and wrinkles, midnight purple scabs and scrapes across his skin. The filthy hands of a prisoner clawing his way through a wall. Then, he saw it—a symbol, hidden behind layers of dried blood and creases.

"Amycite," R'Venin whispered, slapping the top of his head. "Of course. The mountain ingredient is Amycite."

"Yes, my young friend. Amycite."

"But it's so rare. How will I gather enough to heal my whole flock?"

"Ah," Gha'Barahat waggled his finger blindly. "That's the simple part. You'll only need a barrel or so. My apprentice can help you with that. You'll find her at my workshop in the Western Crossroads. The trick will be to keep the incantation going long enough for all those suffering. All they have to do is fly through the column, breath in a few chestfuls, and nature will handle the rest."

"Thank you, Master Alchemist." R'Venin rested his hand on the Pra'Acheen's shoulder. "This could save our flocks."

"I don't know about that," he wheezed, bending over to lay on the floor. "Seems to me the Ch'Hota and V'Jeeta are perfectly content to kill one another over a plant. I'm sure they'll find something else to fight over. Maybe a rock this time. Or a stream. Maybe they'll simply continue the war because they like killing more than living."

"If I return to my father with the cure, I'm sure I can convince him and the general to cease wasting time and warriors in battle. I can help them see a better way."

"Hmph," Gha'Barahat snorted, stretching out and resting his head. "One more thing, my young prince. Don't get Amycite confused with Amycythium. They're nearly identical, but Amycythium will have a side effect you don't want to deal with."

The Pra'Acheen bent in half, coughing up lavender phlegm onto the trapdoor. Ka'Ala massaged his back as R'Venin leaned forward.

"What's the side effect."

Gha'Barahat coughed and wheezed, his face tightened into a grimace. He tried to speak, hissing. Each time he barely said, "St—" when another chest-rattling cough took over his voice. He struggled for breath several times, clutching at his own throat until he collapsed on the floor. His tongue fell out, dripping with blood and saliva.

"He's gone." R'Venin looked away from Gha'Barahat's face. "I hope the Windfather shows him mercy."

Those eyes may haunt me forever.

"What do you think he was trying to say?" Ka'Ala reached over and closed his mouth, wiping the blood off his chin with the cloth. "There at the end."

"I don't know. He took his final secret with him." R'Venin sat up, peeking through the lookout's openings. "It sounds like the riot is settling down. It's not as noisy."

Ka'Ala sat on her heels, sneaking a glance. "How do we get out of here?"

R'Venin shuffled to the oceanside wall and glanced around. "I say we jump over the ramparts from here. Dive along the side of the prison and make for the forest on the cove's north side. Hopefully, the guards will still be distracted before anyone spots us."

Ka'Ala shifted her colors to brilliant golds, matching the shield beside her, and grabbed a sword off the wall. "I'll go second. In case anyone spots us, they might assume I'm a guardsman chasing after an escaping prisoner."

R'Venin nodded. "Ready?"

Ka'Ala shifted her stance into a low crouch, flexing her wings. "Ready."

R'Venin scuttled back to the rear wall next to Ka'Ala and took several deep breaths. "Three. Two. One." He took one step and launched himself through the window, tucking his wings around him like a shell until he crossed over the ramparts and pitched for the breaking waters below.

Ka'Ala grunted as she followed a half-step after.

Salt air whipped through R'Venin's feathers, causing his eyes to water as he picked up speed. Passing row after row of barred windows, the V'Jeeta chant rose and fell like the waves.

The Heir.

The Heir.

The Heir.

R'Venin pushed the image of Gha'Barahat's eyeless sockets out of his mind.

It's time for me to go home.

Chapter Twenty-Nine

The Night Raid

A thick layer of ground clouds crept between the towering Bluewood trunks as if the Windfather's realm permeated the entire coastal grove. Ka'Ala flew from branch to branch under the muted light from the three mothers. Fire crystal torches on each balcony dotted the forest, chasing away the gloom, but only for a handful of wingspans. She fixed her eyes on each light as she passed, searching for recognizable markers. Like a dull gray wisp of smoke, she flapped softly in the damp air, hiding within pockets of mist. She hugged herself, clutching the leather tote to her chest as a meager covering. Her arms pimpled with each surge through the frosty haze, and the tools within poked at her breast.

I hope I can gather the rest tonight. I don't think we can risk another sunrise in hiding.

She imagined the fugitive banners hanging throughout the Bluewoods. A sketch of R'Venin and a listing of accusations:

Assaulting the chief guardsman at Stonetree.

Assisting in the escape and death of a Pra'Acheen prisoner.

Evading the pursuit, and possible murder of an unknown female Guardsman.

Her hearts quickened by the rattle of metal from her right, along with a few faint murmurings.

Hide, Windfather breathed as an updraft lifted her.

Ka'Ala banked, alighting on the first branch she found and flattened her body in the notch. The bag slipped, jangling down the side of the bough as she dug her nails into the bark. Splinters poked through her tunic and leggings as she shifted to match the slate and peacock bark. She held her breath as a Ch'Hota patrol drifted by like a pair of leaves caught on the breeze. She shifted the colors of her face and closed her eyes as a gilded wing appeared through the haze and dragged along her body.

"Look out!" A woman's voice rang, followed by a clash of metal.

"Hey," A man's voice yelled. "Watch your spacing, recruit."

"Sorry, sir." Her voice faded. "I almost ran into that trunk. Can't see anything out here."

"Doesn't mean we stop looking." His voice barely made its way back to Ka'Ala. "Sharpen your ears."

Steam billowed from her mouth as she let out her breath, her hearts pounding against the wood. Pushing herself up, she rolled off the side, catching the air as she fell and headed further into the trees.

After a thousand moons on my own, and I get lost in ground clouds. Windfather, please guide my path.

She followed a tug in her hearts between, around, and over trunks and branches, keeping her distance from glowing balconies and elevated walkways. A song later, a dark patch below called to her like a cave in a storm. She swooped up and stretched her wings to their full span, slowing her momentum without a sound, repeating the process until she touched down on the darkened balcony.

She padded across the boards, sliding into the shadows like a firesnake through fallen leaves. Her feathers shifted to oily slate as she let out a drawn-out sigh and moved deeper into the quiet residence.

Closing her eyes, she stretched out her mind for any sounds within. Only the heartsongs of sleeping Ch'Hota like dulcet lullabies played in her ears.

She crept down the hallway, brushing her fingertips along the plastered wall, toward the roost in the back. Ten paces in, she found the open doorway and thick tapestry she expected. In the faint light coming from a neighboring balcony, she spied the gilded alchemy icons embroidered on a field of deep indigo.

R'Venin's prayer room.

Pushing through, she let the heavy sheet settle back into place, tucking the sides to ensure her return to absolute darkness. Reaching into her tote, she felt around, taking out a palm-sized object. Her fingers brushed the fired-clay surface, rounded in the middle with a seam around its circumference, and flattened on both ends. Each end had a metal loop, chilled from its trip through the foggy night, that grew from a hole in the surface.

Ka'Ala pulled on the rings, twisting slightly, and the seam expanded with the hollow sound of pottery bowls scraping against each other.

A faint light erupted from within as the container split in two, holding a small fire crystal mounted on brass grips inside each bell. The room filled with a warm, honey-colored glow, highlighting the elemental symbols painted across the surface, which stood out like constellations.

Under her feet, a circular mat of woven grass nearly filled the space, a recent addition to the home's decor. At the center, R'Venin's speaking bowl sat on the Windfather's symbol dyed into the strands. Mountain, Tree, Fire, and Rain surrounded the bowl at four quadrants.

Ka'Ala hung her lights from pegs embedded into plaster above the drape. She walked around the rugs' edge until she stood opposite the drape and knelt at the bowl. Quiet as snowfall, she moved it to the walls' base and folded up the carpet. She continued rolling until the bundle stopped at the threshold, holding the curtain in place.

Spinning on her knees, she counted floorboards from the doorway until she came to the seventh panel on the left.

Over two, and up three.

She pulled a flat plate from her back, inserting it into a narrow slot, and eased the plank away from its brothers. Under the board, the faint light disappeared into a shallow compartment deep enough for a grown Ch'Hota to lay flat with a handspan leftover.

Moving toward the door, she pulled up additional planks exposing the entire cubbyhole. With the boards shoved against the wall, Ka'Ala lowered her feet up to her knees in the one-arm wide by two-arms long space. A lumpy sack of homespun cloth filled most of the enclosure.

Ka'Ala reached down and pulled open the flap facing her, revealing R'Venin's black and red carbon-fiber armor. She removed pieces from the bag and silently placed them around her. Gauntlets, leg and thigh shields, flexible armbands, wing talon covers, a girdle and chest plate, and a strip of segmented spinal guards. Finally, the helmet, the last piece still glittering in the dim light.

Her hearts fluttered as she held it up to her face, imagining R'Venin's green eyes penetrating from the shadows within, imagining hearing the timbre his voice.

* * *

"Once we get back here, we'll remove the gems from everything," R'Venin said, stuffing his armor in the homespun bag. "We'll need to travel light after sneaking Gha'Barahat out of his cell. And I won't be needing this armor to get to the Granite Spires. The only thing I'll need intact is this."

R'Venin reached into the helmet and pulled out his silvervine crown.

Ka'Ala's eyes widened as she drew a slow breath. "It's so beautiful." She said, reaching out but not daring to touch.

R'Venin offered it to her. "A beauty that comes with a cost I wasn't willing to pay. Go ahead, you can touch it," he said, thrusting it closer to Ka'Ala.

She studied the circlet, gliding her fingers along each braided strand as they culminated into delicate settings of rubies.

"Such amazing craftsmanship," she breathed. "I could study at the hands of a master artisan for a hundred seasons and still be unable to produce a piece to match this."

"It once belonged to my greatfather's greatfather," R'Venin scoffed. "And I'm sure it cost the livelihood of a hundred artisans until it was just right. That's why I'll need it unmarred for my return. It's an heirloom and a symbol of my heritage. I can't go home without it. We can strip everything else."

"I understand," she said, handing the headband back.

R'Venin nestled the crown back inside his helmet and lowered it into the sack.

* * *

Ka'Ala reached inside and tugged the crown from its padded setting. Once free, she set the helmet aside and stared at the handiwork, running her claws along the twisting strands.

Branches of life twist and turn, carrying us to and fro between each other's lives.

Ka'Ala touched a strand ending in a delicate leaf.

Some branches end before they have a chance to bud.

She followed a thread that disappeared behind a thicker bundle.

Some branches get lost among the others. Who knows when or where they will emerge again.

She traced a thicker fiber that had several others braided around it, culminating into one of the larger gems.

Others seem destined to carry a heavy load and stand prominently among the rest.

"May I be a branch that will always guide others to the Eternal Tree," she whispered. "As the wind blows."

Ka'Ala shook her head and wrapped the crown in several layers of fine cloth. Tucking it into a pocket deep within her tote, she pulled out some of her artisan tools and retrieved the helmet. In the dim light of two petite fire crystal sconces, she resumed prying the remaining gemstones from R'Venin's armor.

Ka'Ala's fingers shook as she pulled the last gem from the helmet. With the ruby secured in a pouch with the rest, she stretched her fingers, her knuckles popping with each movement. Standing in the secret compartment, she extended her back, twisting her neck and rolling her stiff shoulders.

Sighing, she climbed out of the hole onto her knees, replacing the boards in reverse order until the lock-plate remained. She set it in place then put all her weight on its tilted edge. With a soft pop, it pushed against the others to make a tight abutment with its neighbors.

Ka'Ala cocked her head, concentrating with eyes closed.

What time is it? How long until people start waking up for the dawn?

Nothing but a peaceful symphony answered as she crawled across the floor, dragging the rug back into place. Once she returned the speaking bowl to the room's center, she slung her bag around her neck and pulled the clay sconces off the wall pegs. The room resumed its cave-like darkness as she pieced the two halves together.

Ka'Ala reached for the curtain, curling a finger around the edge, and peeking out to the trees beyond. The fresh air felt like a winter blast on her nose after the stifling heat of the prayer room. Traces of moonlight gave the balcony a subtle sheen. Distant fire crystals glowed dully through the mist. A handful of heartsongs played drowsy arias from various directions.

Ka'Ala stepped out from the prayer room and slung the bag over her shoulder. She glanced into the empty roost and stepped in, kneeling beside a bundle of shredded blankets and clothes. She took a strip of cerulean cloth from the pile.

Ja'Ven's comforter. My gift to Ja'Naam on his naming day.

She picked up a swatch of runnerhound fur, the lining of a thick cloak.

Ja'Naam received this from her mother. An inheritance from her father at his ascension.

A strip of leather poked out from under a tan blanket of thickly braided homespun fabric. A pouch followed, the same size as her tote, clinking as it dragged across the shreds. She opened it to find crushed vials, a wooden stylus snapped in two, and a hand-sized copper bowl.

R'Venin's medicine bundle. Not even this was sacred from their search.

Ka'Ala laid the bag on top of the rag pile and stood, scanning the room for anything still intact. Every decoration. Every personal item, destroyed or missing.

The guardsmen didn't spare anything.

In the distance, starsingers whistled their high-moon melodies. Ka'Ala crept out to the balcony and stepped off the edge with open wings, gliding away from R'Venin's home. She looked back over her shoulder as the darkened platform blurred from sight and stopped a lump rising in her throat.

She kept her wingbeats steady, quiet, as she followed the coastal breeze away from the ocean. She smelled the musk of a laboring guardsmen patrol and flew a meandering path through the forest until it was no longer at her back. Another patrols' scent piqued her nose, followed by the rattle of armor closing fast.

"I think there's someone ahead," a male voice said.

"Let's check it out," another man said.

Windfather, What do I do?

Heed their words as if a stone, he breathed. *Mask yourself with meekness.*

Ka'Ala shifted her feathers to the dull colors of a low-branch Ch'Hota, slid her pack around to the front, and nosed down. The clanking sounds faded slightly, but she continued toward the forest floor, searching for the faintest trace of the putrid odor.

"Identify yourself," the second voice yelled, getting closer.

Ka'Ala ignored the command, drifting to her right as she caught the scent she needed. She banked around the base of a cloister of smaller bluewoods, backflapping hard. The fog near the ground clung to bark and shrubs as it retreated into the waist-high grass.

She quickly searched between the roots and found a fresh pile of branchclimber dung, glowing white against the trees gnarled base. Kneeling, she scooped a handful and plunged it into her tote, then squished the remnants into her other hand, coating the outside of her bag before smudging her face with the paste.

"You there," the voice called from above.

Ka'Ala made herself busy foraging around the roots for more droppings.

Armor jangled through the mist, circling her spot, and then two guardsmen landed behind her. "Stand and identify yourself, woman," he barked.

Not turning around, Ka'Ala crawled over an exposed root, moving around the trunk to her left.

"I said, identify yourself!" he yelled, grabbing her by the shoulder and spinning her around.

Ka'Ala fell backward, hands out, and widened her eyes as she stared at the guardsmen.

"Why don't you answer?" he growled.

Ka'Ala pointed to her ears as she shook her head, making gestures with her hands and fingers.

The second guardsman took a half-step forward. "She's earless," he whispered. "That's why she didn't answer. Look, she's digging through branchclimber dung. Must be gathering it to trade in the markets."

Ka'Ala's gaze shifted between the two soldiers.

The lead guardsman got on one knee, cupped his hands at his chest plate, and then held them together as one toward Ka'Ala.

Is that supposed to be a hand-word?

Ka'Ala reached out, scooping a nonexistent object from his hands, and ran two fingers down her throat.

The guardsman stood, holding out his hand. Ka'Ala took it, letting him lift her to her feet.

"Let's get back to patrol," he said out the side of his mouth, then looked back at Ka'Ala. "Fair Weather, lowly sister."

They jumped away, flapping hard. Ka'Ala watched them fade into the fog before taking off in the opposite direction.

"Thank you, Windfather..." she mumbled, shifting back to her natural coloring, "...for sending guardsmen who *don't* know how to talk with their hands."

* * *

Ka'Ala reached the grotto at daybreak. Wisps of ground clouds danced across the glassy pond's surface as she landed at the water's edge. Trudging into the shallows, she bent and splashed her hands and face in the frigid pool.

Branchclimber stench drained from her nose with each handful of water to the face. She knelt and skimmed the pouch across the surface, brushing at it, wiping away as much of her subterfuge as possible.

"You're back," R'Venin said, coming out from behind a drape of vines cascading down a rocky escarpment and into the water. "I was worried you'd been caught."

"I almost was," she said, dipping her satchel in the water for the third time. "A patrol spotted me on my way back. But, as you can see, I improvised."

"I'm glad you're safe." He said, coming closer to help wipe away the remaining flecks of dung. "I can't tell you how much I regret not being able to go back home. I'll never forget what you've done for me."

Ka'Ala couldn't help hearing the truth in his hearts match the softness in his eyes. She suppressed the lump in her throat and nodded, turning her face away. "Of course."

Anything.

He followed her as she stood and pushed aside the vines, revealing a stone niche, longer than it was wide. She bent down and started gathering up the scant belongings they'd brought with them—a blanket, a few pouches of seeds, and the sword she'd borrowed from Stonetree.

"You should rest," R'Venin said behind her. "We have a long flight to the crossroads. I'll stand watch."

"You'll be exposed," Ka'Ala spun around. "No. I can rest out here. You should remain concealed until we're out of the Bluewoods."

"Then, *you'll* be exposed."

"But I can camouflage," Ka'Ala spread out her wings and fluttered her coloring.

"Not if you're asleep," R'Venin countered.

"Well, we both need rest," Ka'Ala crossed her arms and jutted out a hip. "And neither of us can be out in the open. There's only one solution, then."

"What?" R'Venin looked up and the lightening sky. "Leave now? Forgo sleep and hope we don't get spotted by a patrol?"

"No." Ka'Ala stood straight. "We share the alcove."

R'Venin swallowed hard. "There's not enough room for both of us."

"I know this flies over propriety," Ka'Ala shifted on her feet. "And I know how much you miss Ja'Naam. But I believe, in my hearts, she would agree if it meant we were both safe and rested for the days ahead."

R'Venin crossed his arms, bowing his head and tugging at his lips for half a song. "Agreed," he murmured. "But I'll take the outside spot so you'll be behind me."

"Agreed," Ka'Ala let out her breath. "Thank you. You're a decent man. It's one of the reasons Ja'Naam's hearts thrummed for you."

"Dawn is coming," R'Venin looked up into the sky. "It's going to be warmer today. This fog will burn off by high sun, and we'll be easier to spot if we stay out here. I'll wait till you're asleep."

Ka'Ala nodded and moved toward the alcove, pushing aside the vines. She spread the blanket out and rested her head on a pouch of seeds. Drowsiness pulled at her lids almost immediately as she pressed herself against the stone wall. She flattened her wings as best she could, making R'Venin's spot as far from the curtain of vines.

Windfather. Ja'Naam, my sister. I know it's too soon for him to share his sleep. Forgive me. I just want to keep him safe.

* * *

"K*a'Ala. Arise.*"

Sunlight beamed between the tendrils of their floral curtain, shining into Ka'Ala's eyes. She squinted against the intrusion. She buried her face further into a body-length mass of feathers, with an arm and wing draping over the plumage.

The solid mass of down rumbled like a storm on the horizon as it rose and fell, like a calm ocean. She leaned into the unfamiliar warmth until R'Venin's heartsong played on the wind. A pensive ballad rose in her ears as she opened her eyes to see him cradled under her wing. She froze.

Ka'Ala. Arise. Hide.

She peered through the vines, spotting a pair of Ch'Hota guardsmen descending right at their oasis. She draped her wing over them both, having to pull herself closer to him, and used her feet to pull R'Venin's legs into the alcove. She shifted her colors to spotted gray, matching the stone at her back.

R'Venin stirred as the guardsmen, both male, landed on the far side of the pool. The wind picked up, rustling the leaves. Ka'Ala couldn't hear what they were saying as they stripped off their armor and began washing in the shallows.

R'Venin's eyes fluttered and opened. Ka'Ala put her hand over his mouth as he tried to sit up and stared through the blind to the bathing soldiers.

R'Venin looked down at his body to see Ka'Ala covering most of him. He moved her hand and whispered. "When did this happen?"

"I woke up just as they arrived," she breathed.

"No." R'Venin jutted his chin toward his feet. "When did *this* happen?"

"I'm sorry," Ka'Ala looked away. "I found myself like this when the Windfather woke me up. I didn't have time to peel away because the guardsmen showed up, and I had to hide us."

"I understand." R'Venin swallowed. "It's just... unexpected."

Ka'Ala looked into his eyes. "For me too, since I've never... Since I've slept alone for so many seasons. I'm sorry."

R'Venin turned to watch the guardsmen splashing water on each other. "Nothing to be sorry for."

He laid his head down on his arm, seemingly watching the Ch'Hota at play.

"We'll wait until they're gone," he whispered, his voice barely audible over the wind and water-play, "And then I think we should get moving toward the Crossroads. It may be too soon, but I think we should risk it."

I know he doesn't mean it the way I wish he does.

Ka'Ala's throat felt dry as a desert when she met his gaze. "I think so too."

Part Three

Chapter Thirty

Gha'Barahat's Apprentice

R'Venin watched from the upper branches of a Copperleaf tree as Ka'Ala spoke with a pair of Ch'Hota balancing a two-wheeled handcart laden with fresh branchclimber dung. He ignored the stench rising to his nasal slits, keeping one eye on the transaction and the other on the path for anyone who might see the exchange.

Ka'Ala's golden plumage gleamed like a sunrise compared to the low-branch couple in cloaks soiled with the ash-colored droppings. She dropped a ruby into the woman's open palm as the man let his handcart tip onto its back edge. Shadows lengthened across the road as the Ch'Hota bowed, shaking Ka'Ala's hands vigorously, their joyful trills reaching R'Venin's ears.

As the Ch'Hota couple turned to leave, Ka'Ala reached out and pointed at them both. They nodded and removed their cloaks, draping them on the cart's handle that spanned across the front, leaving them in smudged and frayed tunics in the cooling evening air. The man wrapped his arm around his partner, hugging her tight as they walked a short distance into a small copse of shrubs.

Ka'Ala pulled the cart's handle down to waist-height and pushed away down the path as the couple knelt between the bushes and raised their hands to the sky.

A pittance compared to what may come if this plan works.

* * *

R'Venin faked a limp as he pushed the cart closer to the gate. Glancing over his shoulder, he spied Ka'Ala—colored as a V'Jeeta—adjusting the filthy blindfold under her hood. Waving at their noses, the guardsmen gave R'Venin and Ka'Ala—smudged tips to talons in branchclimber dung—a wide berth as they crossed under the western gates. Fire crystal torches overhead did little to illuminate their faces in the moonless night. Their cart rattled across the cobblestones beside a caravan of wagons. Runnerhounds snorted, pulling against their harnesses away from the fresh scent of their natural predator.

Eight bells of different timbre sang from a distance like a massive wind chime in a storm, coming from the center of Western Crossroads.

"Close the gates," a raspy voice bellowed from above. "Lower the portcullis. Those desiring entrance, fly to the platform and yield to a search of your person and property. If you're unwilling to comply, may the Windfather protect you in the forest until dawn."

R'Venin gave Ka'Ala a sidelong glance. The gray smears along her face, neck, and hands mottled the tawny skin underneath.

She should have stayed behind and mated with a good man to live in peace among the Ch'Hota. Why is she so willing to risk her life for my people? They'd probably enslave her if they knew what she was.

Ka'Ala removed the blindfold from her face. Her eyes drifted from fern to pearl as a smile teased at the corners of her mouth.

"Your eyes," R'Venin hissed, looking around. "They changed. Are you okay?"

Ka'Ala dropped her gaze to the ground, letting her filthy cloak's hood drape her head. When she looked up a moment later, her pupils returned to the pale green.

So much like Mother's. And B'Luren's.

"I'm okay," Ka'Ala mumbled between labored breaths. "Just a little tired. This cart's heavy. How much farther?"

"I'm not sure," R'Venin leaned into the handle. "We came in from the south last time I was here. That's the gate closest to Sher'Esh's tavern if you remember. I'm not exactly sure how to get to Gha'Barahat's workshop from here. I do know it's northeast of the southern gate. I'm sure I'll recognize a few landmarks the closer we get."

"I've never been there," Ka'Ala huffed, her elbows locked against the crossbar. "I'll follow your lead."

"Maybe you can ask Windfather to guide our steps."

"As long as we move our feet..." Ka'Ala smiled at him, "he always will."

* * *

Ten songs past the gates' closing, R'Venin and Ka'Ala trundled past the fountain of D'Harma Yud'd. A group of Ch'Hota, Pra'Acheen, and V'Jeeta in clerical garb led unkempt men, women, and children in ragged clothes and outstretched hands away from the bubbling fountain.

"There's a soft roost and a few handfuls for all," a Pra'Acheen girl said as she wiped soot off a scrawny Ch'Hota boys face. "It may not be much, but it's better than sleeping out here in the cold."

"The last time we were here, that fountain was empty of wanderers," R'Venin muttered. "I've seen nothing like this in Bluewood cove."

"I have," Ka'Ala whispered. "On the outskirts of Willowlimb Bazaar. The wars created more hardship than most of the upper-branches have realized."

R'Venin blew out his breath, catching the eye of a Ch'Hota cleric wearing a tunic with the order of the wind embroidered into her lapel. She smiled, nodding her head, then turned to help an elderly V'Jeeta woman off the fountains' stone bench.

"It's just down here," R'Venin said, unable to peel his eyes away from the refugee until they turned the corner. A few paces further, he cast his eyes above the street, scanning for the banner of cobalt and silver.

They passed several sets of doors; many resembled the ones from R'Venin's memory until they reached the next avenue. Lined with women wearing painted faces and their soliciting men, the intersection smelled of dizzyroot and despair.

"I don't recognize this place," R'Venin's gaze shot from one side street to the next. "I could've sworn his workshop was a short walk from the fountain."

R'Venin's calf feathers bristled as a V'Jeeta woman stepped away from under a torch post, swaying her wings in time with her hips, as she moved closer. She wore a sheer poncho, the loose sides held together by threads of silvervine. Each step teased to reveal more underneath.

I know her. But from where? Oh, no.

R'Venin turned his head, pulling the hood further down his brow.

"What's wrong?" Ka'Ala whispered.

"The one coming this way," R'Venin hissed, raising a hand and scratching his head. "I know her. She was one of my brother's courtesans. What's she doing out of the towers? If she gets too close. If she recognizes me..."

"Hello, fair stranger. Don't be shy." The sultry lady cooed. "I'm Vesh'Ya. Three coppers for a song. Two bronze if you'd like your mate to watch. One gold for her to join."

* * *

"Excuse us," Ka'Ala said, tugging the cart into a U-turn. R'Venin kept his face in the shadows of his cloak as he lifted the crossbar and pushed into an arc.

"Aw," Vesh'Ya giggled, stepping close enough to touch R'Venin's sleeve. "For an extra bronze, I'll even bathe you first."

The nearest evening hostesses and patrons burst into roars of laughter, followed by the clink of bottles.

"Fair weather, Vesh'Ya." Ka'Ala didn't turn to look back as they walked away. "May the Windfather favor you."

"You're the one who needs His favor, sister," she hollered. "And a good rain."

"Maybe we just missed his shingle," Ka'Ala said over the ruckus. "We'll go back and look deeper."

"Who are you looking for?" Vesh'Ya landed in the street, blocking their path, her thin veil billowing around her legs.

R'Venin stared at the stonework along the building facade.

"Please move from our path," Ka'Ala's face softened. "We're not looking for companionship."

"Perhaps not," Vesh'Ya rested her hands on her hips. "But I can also provide information. I know everyone in Crossroads. Some very well. And for a copper, I can tell you where to find anyone in the city."

R'Venin watched Ka'Ala's shadow as she turned her head to look toward him. He nodded without looking up.

"We're looking for the apprentice of a Master Alchemist that has a workshop around here," Ka'Ala looked up toward the buildings. "Gha'Barahat. Do you know where it is?"

"Gha'Barahat?" the woman howled into the air. "Oh, yes. I know Gha'Barahat. We're *well* acquainted."

"Can you tell us where to find his workshop?"

Vesh'Ya held out her palm, nodding, and gave Ka'Ala a wink.

Ka'Ala dug into her satchel and pulled out a copper coin, dropping it into the woman's eager hand.

"The governor condemned Gha'Barahat's shop for delving in the unnatural." She smirked as she dropped the coin in a pouch hanging from her hip. "He exiled the apprentice for carrying on the practice."

"Where is the apprentice now?"

Vesh'Ya held out her hand, her fingers dancing in the soft light spilling from the crossway.

Ka'Ala fished another coin from her bag and held it over the lady's hand. "I want specific directions, agreed?"

"Agreed."

Ka'Ala slapped the money into her palm and crossed her arms.

"She's in the eastern woods," Vesh'Ya jutted her hip, making her purse jangle. "Along the V'Jeeta borderlands. Head toward the moonrise, and you'll be there in a three-quarter sun. It's unmistakable."

"Thank you." Ka'Ala snipped, steering the cart around the woman as she backed into a wall. "Fair weather."

"You could still use a bath," Vesh'Ya fell into step next to R'Venin as the cart moved away from the laughing crowd. R'Venin turned his head toward Ka'Ala, pushing harder against the cart's crossbar. "Five coppers. And I'll even keep my eyes closed."

Vesh'Ya moved into the cart's path, playfully tugging at R'Venin's sleeve.

"Come," she crooned. "I don't mind getting a little dirty. There's no need to hide from me. Let me see your handsome face."

R'Venin's heartsong raced in Ka'Ala's mind.

"NO!" She shouted as Vesh'Ya yanked R'Venin's hood.

R'Venin stopped short, letting the cart handle fall from his grip, and backed away.

Vesh'Ya smirked, then her eyes narrowed as she stared hard, leaning forward. "R'Venin?" she breathed, backing away. "Is that you?"

"Hello, Vesh'Ya," R'Venin said over his shoulder. Ka'Ala glanced at the revelers watching from the intersection.

R'Venin stepped away from the cart, taking Vesh'Ya by the arm and guiding her into the shadows between buildings. "I was hoping you wouldn't recognize me."

"I thought you were dead." She jerked her arm away. "That's what your brother said, anyway. Nine seasons ago. He was never the same after that harvest. Does he know you're alive? Did he send you to find me? I'm not going back. I'll match your face with his if you try to send me back."

The memory of K'Marot bending over Ba'Jai passed through Ka'Ala's vision.

That must be how he got those scars.

"Only a few people know I'm alive." R'Venin raised his hands. "K'Marot and my father. Most of the kingdom; they have no idea. I'm on my way home right now. It's a three-sun story."

"If you're not here to take me back to K'Marot," Vesh'Ya's shoulders relaxed. "Then, why are you here?"

"It's as she said," he pointed to Ka'Ala. "We're looking for Gha'Barahat's apprentice. That was the truth."

"After that, you're going home to the spires?"

"Yes. I've found the cure for White Claw. I'm going to present it to my Father and try to bring an end to the war."

Vesh'Ya looked from R'Venin to Ka'Ala and back, shifting on her feet. "Are you going to tell K'Marot where I am?"

"If you keep my secret," R'Venin put his arm on her shoulder. "That I'm alive. At least until I announce myself before the king. I promise never to share your whereabouts with anyone."

Vesh'Ya hugged herself. "Will you... will you tell my mother where I am?"

"Do you want me to?" R'Venin cocked his head, moving his

shadow off her face.

Vesh'Ya nodded.

"I'll try." He sighed and stepped back to the cart, picking the push bar from the cobblestones. "Fair weather."

"Pleasant breezes, Prince R'Venin," Vesh'Ya mumbled as she wiped her face and headed toward the rowdy onlookers.

Ka'Ala took her place beside R'Venin. Together they hurried away from the din. Passing by several shops and deserted streets, R'Venin was silent.

Ka'Ala leaned her head toward him, listening. His heartsong lowing like an injured animal. "Are you alright?"

R'Venin chewed on his lip for a moment. "She was K'Marot's first love. I thought he was going to mate with her, but then she vanished."

"She's terrified of him," Ka'Ala said. "Like a hatchling fears the thunder."

R'Venin nodded. The cart squeaked as the winding alley rose on a steep incline. "I didn't know she gave him the scars, or why. I guess it sort of makes sense now."

"It was kind of you to guard her secret." Ka'Ala huffed as she leaned into the cart.

R'Venin shrugged. "Not my secret to tell."

Who else's secrets do you protect? Would you safeguard mine if you knew it?

"Now that we know Gha'Barahat's apprentice is outside the city," R'Venin muttered, "there's no reason to keep up this guise. I say we abandon the cart, clean up in the fountain, and fly over the walls tonight. We could be in the borderlands by mid-morning."

"What about the guards?"

R'Venin shrugged. "They don't stop anyone from leaving. Just those coming in."

* * *

"That must be it," R'Venin pointed to a column of rosy smoke rising from a tent-like structure below. Thin fog clung to the ground like ghostly fingers as a breeze spilled through the small clearing. Sun-bleached boughs sat atop a mud-brick wall, forming a dome, holding up a patchwork canopy of cloth and leather. An arched opening faced the morning sun, mirrored by a twin entry on the opposite side. Above each doorway hung a drab and frayed cobalt and silver banner bearing the master alchemists' emblem.

Steam rose from stone pools filled by natural hot springs to the north—small bungalows offered shade for those lounging in the communal font. Curtains surrounded basins large enough for two or three people, providing privacy for smaller parties.

Legs, arms, and wingtips poked out from rickety lean-to shelters around the primary structure's perimeter in a pinwheel of dull golds, faded grays, and muted blacks.

Further east, beyond the edge of Copperleaf forest and the crimson field of the central plains, the white cliffs rose from the horizon like a beacon. Sunlight played on the peaks as clouds floated over the steppes. Dark splotches of shadow flitted around the cliffs like bits of dried leaf in a whirlwind. R'Venin reached behind his back, sliding a hand under the pack between his wings, and fingered the circular bulge pressing into his skin.

Once we have the ingredients, will this be enough to convince the sentries I'm the heir?

"You should shift your colors while no one's watching," R'Venin said, scanning the ground. "I think it'd be best to remain disguised as a V'Jeeta when we're in my home skies."

"Windfather has already whispered so," Ka'Ala cupped a hand around her ear. "Down there. Beyond the tree line."

R'Venin nodded and nosed down. Ka'Ala followed, keeping close to his wing as they circled down, exchanging wary glances. Their dung-stained tunics flapped in the air until they landed on the loamy earth, shielded from the structure by a thicket.

Shrugging the pack from his shoulders, R'Venin glanced over as Ka'Ala shifted. Her skin darkened to a shade just lighter than R'Venin's bronze complexion, and her feathers shifted to match his. He couldn't help but stare at her jade eyes.

"What?" She asked, looking down at her soiled clothing. "What is it?"

R'Venin's mouth twitched on one side. "For a moment… For a moment, your eyes looked just like my mother's. I didn't realize how much I'd missed them."

Ka'Ala's cheeks darkened as she turned away, smoothing her tunic. When she looked back, they were a few shades lighter. "Well, by sunfall, you will see them again."

R'Venin took a deep breath and led the way through the trunks, heading for the west-facing entrance. He gave sidelong glances into the lean-to structures as they walked, peering into the shadows. Duos and trios of V'Jeeta, Ch'Hota, and Pra'Acheen stared back with vacant eyes, their heads lolling slightly.

The females, dressed like the painted woman in the Western Crossroads, sat or knelt beside their male companions, massaging shoulders, stroking feathers, or kissing necks.

"What kind of alchemist shop is this?" Ka'Ala hissed, moving to R'Venin's side opposite the courtesans and their clients.

"The kind run by a trafficker, I'd wager," R'Venin said as a Ch'Hota woman pulled the flap of her tent, hiding herself and her customer from view.

Soft music drifted from the interior as they came to the entrance. Pushing through a thin curtain of homespun cloth, R'Venin stepped into the dark interior. All eyes turned, squinting at the influx of light, and gazed at their arrival with vacant expressions.

At his left, a group of patrons sat or lay on pillows, sucking on tubes and filling the room with scarlet fog. Against the wall, a Pra'Acheen trio played a stringed instrument that resembled a three-sided pyramid with chords that ran from a flat bar on the floor to a point at the apex. A musician on each side plucked at the strands, using a foot press to adjust the tension.

On his right, thin slabs of stone formed a low, semi-circular bar that followed the wall from one doorway to the other. Patrons, mostly V'Jeeta, sat on log stools drinking from glazed mugs or inhaling sickly-green fumes from tin bowls.

The musicians never broke their performance as R'Venin took a step into the room. Ka'Ala arrived at his side and let the curtain fall into place, returning the interior to relative darkness. A single hole at the dome's apex allowed a column of light to pierce through the billows of mist like a spear. The vacant gaze of every V'Jeeta man in the room focused on Ka'Ala, their eyes shifting from murky ambivalence to that of a starving runnerhound that came upon cagey prey.

"I'm looking for the apprentice of Gha'Barahat," R'Venin raised his voice above the plunking tune. "Master alchemist of the Western Crossroads. Can you tell me where to find him?"

Laughter burst from the crowd as patrons clinked glasses and pipes, mimicking R'Venin's words.

A shadow rose along the wall behind the bar, moving slowly behind the drinking patrons until the gray feathers and lilac eyes of a youngish Pra'Acheen woman came into view. Her tight-fitting ruby tunic allowed her legs to slip in and out as she walked.

I've seen her before.

"Gha'Barahat doesn't have an apprentice." The woman sneered. "Not anymore. Just an inheritor of his mad schemes. I'm his daughter,

Nar'Sahayak. You look familiar, but I haven't seen you in here before." She squinted her eyes, leaning forward.

"Nar'Sahayak?" R'Venin's brow bunched over his nose. "I thought you were Kar'Nevala's apprentice. At the sanctuary of The Three Mothers."

She took a half-step back and took him in, tips to talons.

"My nose followed a different wind." She scowled, pursing her lips to the side. Her jaw moved as if she were chewing on a seed stuffed in her cheek. "What did my fool of a father send you here for?"

R'Venin reached into his pack, withdrawing a scrap of parchment, and held it out. "He said you'd help me procure a few rare ingredients."

"For what?" she huffed as she tore the page from his hand. Her posture shifted as she scanned the list. "This... It can't be," she breathed as she ran her finger down the page several times. Her lips moved without sound as she closed her eyes, tapping her claws together in odd rhythms. "That damn cleric told me it was forbidden. But father swore to me he knew the secret. This is the cure for..."

"White Claw," R'Venin whispered, leaning in and cupping her hands with his.

The nearest V'Jeeta, an old male in scuffed armor, stiffened as he set down his drink and cocked his head.

Ka'Ala sidled closer. "We should talk somewhere else," she hissed in R'Venin's ear. "I sense black music coming. It scares me, and I don't know why."

"Is there somewhere else we can go?" R'Venin whispered.

Nar'Sahayak half-turned, giving Ka'Ala a narrow sidelong glance, then faced R'Venin. The musicians played through half a song, while her lilac eyes locked with his before she answered. "This way," she wrinkled the page as she curled her hand into a fist. "Follow me."

She led them behind the bar and kicked a floor runner into the wall, revealing a hatch. V'Jeeta eyes followed Ka'Ala as she walked between R'Venin and the Pra'Acheen.

Nar'Sahayak pulled the door by a rope handle, letting it thud against the stone bar, spilling more than one drink. "Go pluck your feathers," she yelled at grumbling customers. She gestured for R'Venin to follow her down the steps.

R'Venin nudged Ka'Ala between her wings and held out his other arm.

"Thank you," she said, her eyes darting to the leering drinkers.

R'Venin took the steps, his brow knotting as the patrons followed Ka'Ala's descending form.

You'd think they've never seen a V'Jeeta woman before.

As soon as Ka'Ala cleared the sill, they all went back to their drinking and murmured conversations.

R'Venin followed Ka'Ala and Nar'Sahayak down the narrow staircase of hewn stone and crumbling mortar. At the bottom, the landing turned to face an arched opening. A dull orange glow peeked up the stairwell from the lower room.

Nar'Sahayak disappeared around the corner, Ka'Ala shortly thereafter. As R'Venin cleared the doorway, he stared into the dull light, finding a tight array of floor-to-ceiling poles holding up a network of dilapidated beams. Dust rained on their heads as footsteps marched across the floor. Hammocks tied between the columns were strained under the weight of homespun sacks, varying in size and degree of decay.

Ka'Ala put her wings to the wall as the Pra'Acheen moved around a square counter and through the narrow aisles, spilling corked bladders and laced sacks onto the floor. R'Venin moved to the table as Nar'Sahayak dragged the bags across the ground, pushed the handles into R'Venin's hands, and slapped the countertop.

He raised them off the ground, laying them flat as he built the pile. Next came the bladder.

"That must be the pitcherflower juice." He sniffed the air.

"Nasty stuff," she huffed as R'Venin took it from her arms.

Her wing bumped a shelf, knocking over a clay jar from the top. It smashed on the floor, spilling white crystals in the aisle.

"That's electhium," R'Venin said, moving forward. "I need that."

"Yes, it is," Nar'Sahayak mumbled. "Kar'Nevala said you showed an interest in alchemy. If my father gave you the recipe, he must've owed you your weight in silk."

"Nothing so grand." R'Venin walked around the table, knelt beside Nar'Sahayak, and picked shards from the dirt. "I administered his treatments in Stonetree. The only alchemist's position I could get."

Nar'Sahayak's hands slowed but never stopped gathering the spilled crystals. "Can't imagine that'd be enough for him to give up one of his secrets. Did you beat it out of him? Wouldn't blame you if you did."

"I helped him see the sky again." R'Venin blew the dust off a handful and poured them into the container. "He gave me most of it after his last treatment. But once we got him to the ramparts, he told me Amycite was the mountain ingredient before he died."

"He died?" Nar'Sahayak met his eyes as she stood, closing the lid and adding the jar to the pile. "Did he say anything about me?"

"Not by name," R'Venin said softly as he got to his feet. "I'm sorry. He only talked about his apprentice and how I'd be able to get his help; I guess I mean your help, with the cure."

"I shouldn't have hoped." She rested her hands on the table. "Did he give you any instructions on how to prepare the Amycite? Crystalized? Powdered?"

"No," he shook his head. "He only said not to get it confused with Amycythium."

Nar'Sahayak spun around. "You're sure he said Amycythium?"

R'Venin took a halting step forward. "Yes, why? Does that mean something to you?"

"The trick to curing a plague is denying it the ability to spread," she mumbled to herself.

"What does that mean?"

Nar'Sahayak locked on his eyes for a moment and then turned her back on him, swatting her hand in the air. "Nothing. Just something that old croan at Three Mothers used to say. So, how are you going to pay?"

R'Venin started to shrug off his pack when the music above halted, and a dozen voices shouted. The chorus, unintelligible through layers of dirt and wood, rose as feet pounded on the floor overhead, showering them with debris.

"The dark heartsong," Ka'Ala hissed from the doorway. "It's here."

"Curse the Windfather," Nar'Sahayak groaned. "He's back. That's the fifth time this moon."

"Who?" R'Venin asked.

"The almighty protector of the borderlands," Nar'Sahayak muttered as she raked her nails down her cheek, then grabbed a piece of cloth from under the table and draped it over the pile. "I need to get upstairs before he starts drinking."

Ka'Ala darted from the doorway, spinning R'Venin around to face the stairwell, and gripped the folds of his tunic.

"Who's up there?" R'Venin asked, following Nar'Sahayak to the stairs with Ka'Ala in tow.

"Old slash-face." Nar'Sahayak gave a flourished bow. "The heir apparent of the Granite Spires."

Chapter Thirty-One

Shadowed Hearts

"Don't go up there." Ka'Ala held R'Venin back while Nar'Sahayak disappeared up the stairs, her hands trembling as she clung to fistfuls of his tunic.

"The heir apparent." R'Venin turned his head halfway around. "It's my brother, K'Marot. It's time to let the rest of my family know I'm still alive."

"It's too dangerous." Ka'Ala's voice shook. "He's too dangerous."

R'Venin turned around, pulling his tunic from her grip. His eyes met hers. "Your coloring," he said, a flash of surprise appearing on his face as he took her in from tips to talons.

Ka'Ala gasped, seeing her natural cream-colored skin in the glow of fire crystals. She put her hands to her face.

How did I not feel myself shift? Windfather, what's happening to me?

"Are you alright?" He said, blocking her view of the stairs with his wings. "Why did you drop your camouflage? Did the Windfather tell you to?"

He will desire you, Windfather breathed. *His base compulsions will overpower his rational mind.*

"No." She said, her lip trembling as she backed between the shelves with her hands out in front. "I didn't realize I had."

"Ka'Ala, what's wrong?" R'Venin followed her into the aisle. "You look terrified."

"I am." She choked. "More scared than I've ever been in my life, and I can't explain why. This feeling came over me; the moment I heard his heartsong approaching."

"Everything will be alright." R'Venin moved closer, reaching out and taking Ka'Ala's hands in his. "K'Marot will never harm you as long as you're with me."

"I'm not afraid he'll hurt me." Ka'Ala backed against the farthest wall. "He's going to try and take me for himself."

"I don't understand."

Ka'Ala cast her eyes at the ceiling.

How do I make him see?

"You know how the Gir'Agit were once slaves to the V'Jeeta?" Ka'Ala pulled her hands from R'Venin's grip, folding her arms. "And we were led back to our homeland?"

"Yes?" R'Venin mirrored her posture.

"Do you also know the legends of how V'Jeeta men couldn't resist the charms of Gir'Agit women?"

"Yes," R'Venin nodded. "You've mentioned how they were prized as mystics and soothsayers used by the ancient kings to perceive the hearts of their enemies. Women of such beauty that many clan leaders would go to war just to have one by their side. Legends. Myths."

"The myths are true," Ka'Ala groaned. "At least, the part about men fighting just for the chance to have one under their control. I don't understand how, or why, but I know it's real. And the Windfather told me your brother *will* try to take me under his wing. You can't let that happen. Please."

"How can I possibly prevent him from desiring you?" R'Venin held out his hands. "Even if what you say is true, I can't control his hearts. No more than I could change my father's."

"Has your brother ever wanted the same woman as you before?" Ka'Ala fiddled with the tassels of a bag on the nearest shelf. "Each desiring to make her your mate?"

"There was another clan leader's daughter once." R'Venin crossed his arms. "She was closer to K'Marot's age, and she caught his eye. But Father wanted me to mate with her to ensure a stronger alliance. But that was before I decided to fake my death. As I understand it, that warrior died in another battle, so they dissolved the arrangement. My hearts never beat for her, so I would have been happy to see K'Marot mated with her."

"Has he ever tried to take someone that was yours?" Ka'Ala bit her lip, locking eyes on him. "Someone you did love? Would he have tried to sway Ja'Naam's hearts if he wanted her for himself?"

R'Venin's head snapped back. "What? Never!" he said, backing away. "Father would have him plucked to bring such dishonor to his flock. K'Marot would never do such a thing."

"I'm sorry," Ka'Ala bowed, exposing her wings' undersides as she cleared the stacks. "I don't mean to insult your family."

The sounds of armor scraping against stone grew from the stairwell as Nar'Sahayak's voice yelled over the musicians. "You can't go down there. That's not part of our arrangement."

R'Venin turned his head, cocking his ears toward the commotion.

"I need more visiondust, and I know you're keeping your best down here." K'Marot bellowed, followed by a sickening crunch and a woman's yelp.

Embrace R'Venin as a lover, Windfather breathed softly into Ka'Ala's ear.

Nar'Sahayak stumbled into view, careening across the archway. She fell against the wall with her shoulder, cradling the side of her face with both hands. Her chin quivered behind tightly pinched lips.

Ka'Ala reached up, turning R'Venin's face toward her and jumped, falling on his neck with her lips as K'Marot reached the landing. "Pretend we're arranged," she whispered in his ear as she raked her claws through his feathers. "Please. For my sake."

R'Venin stiffened, his wings pinching together in the tight space and blocking Ka'Ala's view of the onlookers. Slowly, his shoulders relaxed, and he wrapped his arms around her waist, holding her off the ground. His hearts groaned in discordant melodies of major and minor keys, each rising louder as she kissed his skin.

"Don't move your wings," Ka'Ala whispered, pulling away, her eyes unmoving from R'Venin's. Her breath came fast and shallow as she slid down his chest to the floor. Closing her eyes, she shifted her colors until she felt the V'Jeeta camouflage return.

"Forgive the intrusion, son of the spires," K'Marot chuckled. "But I was under the impression this low-brancher didn't allow anyone but her down here. Who are you to receive such coveted privacy?"

"Be surprised," Ka'Ala breathed, gazing up at R'Venin with soft juniper eyes and tawny complexion. "You've been distracted."

* * *

"Who are you to divert me from my love-play, warrior?" R'Venin said, dropping his wings. Light spilled between the shelves, casting a honeyed glow on Ka'Ala's face.

"I am Prince K'Marot, next in line to the throne of the Granite Spires, you filthy dung trader," K'Marot growled. "And who are you?"

"I *am* the Heir of the First Tower, my young prince." R'Venin turned and stepped forward, opening his arms and wings as he moved past the sack-laden table.

"R'Venin?" K'Marot's face softened, then broke into a wide smile as he lunged forward and took R'Venin in a tight embrace. "R'Venin!

You *are* alive. I knew it!"

"I've missed you, little brother." R'Venin folded his wings around K'Marot. "And the rest of the family."

K'Marot lifted R'Venin off the floor and shouted to the ceiling. "Father will be beyond pleased. Where have you been?"

"Among the Ch'Hota..." R'Venin started, but Ka'Ala cut him off.

"In Stonetree," she said from the between the shelves. "As a prisoner."

"What is this, brother?" K'Marot released R'Venin, leering over his shoulder at Ka'Ala. "You've finally taken a consort? Even under all that muck, I can see how she appeals to you."

"I helped him escape." Ka'Ala shied away, her wings moving forward between K'Marot and herself. "Anything for the high prince. I love him."

R'Venin spun around, locking eyes with Ka'Ala. She cast a glance at him, her eyes pleading.

"As you should," K'Marot said, slapping R'Venin's shoulder with one hand and rubbing his chin with the other. He licked his lips as he looked her over, taking in her every curve. "What is your intention towards this woman, brother?"

R'Venin kept his eyes on Ka'Ala. She looked away, toying with her fingers.

"I'm bringing her back to the spires with me," he said, moving forward and taking her hands. They trembled in his until he reached up and lifted her chin. "With Father's permission, I'll take her as a courtesan as a reward for her service to the king."

Ka'Ala swallowed hard, licking her lips.

K'Marot chuckled in his throat. "Perhaps I should let you finish taking her while I renegotiate my arrangement with this one." He thumbed at Nar'Sahayak without looking.

"I've told you before, *your highness*," Nar'Sahayak winced, massaging her shoulder and casting spears with her eyes, "I'll sell you anything you want as long as my stores remain private to you and your *associates*. Otherwise, I'll have to keep my supplies where your lackeys won't loot them. If that happens, my costs go up. And so do yours."

"And I've told you before, you filthy Pra'Acheen," K'Marot turned toward Nar'Sahayak, "That <u>I</u> set the terms. I can't protect you from the dangers in the borderlands if you continue to flout my generosity. But for now, be silent while I speak with my brother."

Nar'Sahayak's mouth pinched into a line. "Yes, *your highness*."

"Now, before the air shifts," K'Marot turned back, "I'm sure you'd enjoy finishing your loveplay in a bath outside. Get cleaned and fluffed. Perhaps your soon-to-be courtesan would enjoy performing the duties expected of her."

"I'll keep to the old ways, K'Marot," R'Venin turned around, "and wait for Father to approve my decision before we mate. It will also please my mother."

"Psha!" K'Marot smirked. "A woman's pleasure is not a man's concern."

"You sound just like Father," R'Venin said. "Do you not care at all about Ban'Jar? What she wants for you? She's your mother."

"Like P'Vrit, Ban'Jar does as Father tells her." K'Marot crossed his arms. "Just as a woman should. At least she did."

"Did?" R'Venin stepped forward. "What happened?"

K'Marot's lips pinched, and his jaw clenched as if he were gnashing on raw meat. "Ban'Jar was not favored by our father like P'Vrit. Her pouch would no longer take Father's seed. For three seasons, she failed to produce a hatchling for him. When she claimed it wasn't her fault, he had her plucked and cast off the spires."

"Monster," Ka'Ala hissed under her breath.

K'Marot craned his neck and sidestepped past R'Venin. "What did you say, woman?" He yelled. "Why do you speak so disrespectfully to a sovereign? Since when do our long-held traditions offend a V'Jeeta woman?"

Turning his head, he glanced at R'Venin. "What's wrong with this one, brother?"

"Nothing." R'Venin moved around K'Marot as Ka'Ala shrank toward the shelves. "Perhaps she's been among the Ch'Hota so long she's forgotten the customs of the spires. But she's under my wing now, and no one lays a feather on her without my retribution. I'll take responsibility for her re-education."

"Make sure she learns her place again," K'Marot sneered, growling in R'Venin's ear. "The stench of pride fills my nostrils."

R'Venin bobbed his head. "Yes, nothing smells so foul as pride." He said, then led Ka'Ala around K'Marot toward the table loaded with his supplies. "However, I need to finish my own business with Nar'Sahayak. Can you finish collecting the supplies I asked for?"

Nar'Sahayak nodded and shuffled among the shelves.

"What supplies?" K'Marot came up to the table and slapped the bags. "This is all for you? What's it for?"

R'Venin smiled and grabbed K'Marot by the arms. "I've learned the cure for White Claw, brother. From an old Pra'Acheen alchemist in Stonetree. I know how to heal our people, so we won't have to fight over the Silver Silk anymore."

"Impossible," K'Marot broke from R'Venin's grip. "Our healers have been trying to cure it since our greatfathers' time. They've come up with nothing. The silk is the only thing that keeps our flocks from withering away like a vine in a drought."

"It *is* possible. We've been missing the key. It's part of the Pra'Acheen and Ch'Hota religions. I've learned some in my time among them, and I know how to perform the ritual. I can stop the war."

"You would go against the teachings of P'Phet?" K'Marot paced the floor. "Against the laws of our people? You would condemn your soul by toying with blasphemous mysticism?"

"If it would heal our people, and end the suffering, yes. I would gladly cast myself down."

K'Marot moved around the table, keeping wary eyes on R'Venin, and located Nar'Sahayak among the stacks. She had a sack in one hand and filled it with rosy crystals from a jar. "Does my brother speak the truth?" He scowled down at her. "Is there a cure for White Claw?"

R'Venin left Ka'Ala at the table and came up behind and knelt, peering at her around K'Marot's wing.

Nar'Sahayak's gaze shifted between the two V'Jeeta, her eyes narrowing each time she looked up. "Yes," she said, dropping the sack as she stood. Crystals rattled across the floor as the bag spilled over. "Yes, there is a cure. My father knew it. I didn't believe him, but I've seen the incantation and elements he wrote down for your brother. It makes sense. It *will* cure the White Claw."

"Then finish gathering my brother's ingredients, and we'll be on our way." K'Marot turned around, beaming. "I'll lead you home to Father. He'll proclaim a celebration for your return, and for bringing the cure under the noses of that Ch'Hota filth. We'll leave at once."

"I need to prepare the Amycite, the mountain element." Nar'Sahayak grunted as she knelt to gather the crystals. "It needs to be crushed to a fine powder. I'll need at least five songs."

"We don't need to wait for the powder," K'Marot laughed. "I'll have my warriors carry it to the spires once it's finished. Agreed?"

"Agreed." Nar'Sahayak mumbled. "How will you be paying?"

K'Marot tipped his head back and roared at the ceiling. "After all I've done to protect you, you want payment?"

Nar'Sahayak's jaw clenched as she breathed through her nose.

"I'll pay," R'Venin shouted, moving out of the stacks and opened his pack. K'Marot followed, his eyes widening as R'Venin retrieved the crown.

"R'Venin," K'Marot gasped. "You can't. You know what Father will do if you trade away your royal signet."

"I do," R'Venin's face turned hard. "And do you know what I'll do, as the heir of the first tower, if you blemish my honor with pilfered supplies?"

"My apologies, brother." K'Marot raised his hands. "Of course. I'll pay the Pra'Acheen."

K'Marot untied a purse from his belt and dropped it on the floor next to the table. "Here's for your troubles." He yelled. "Make sure my brother's supplies are in perfect condition. If I discover you've cheated him in any way, I know where to find you."

"I swear," Nar'Sahayak appeared from behind a stack, "that you'll get exactly what you've paid for. Your highness."

"Now," K'Marot slapped R'Venin on the back and pushed him toward Ka'Ala. "You take your playmate and bathe in the springs while I get you some decent clothes. You can't appear before Father looking and smelling like a dung-trader. Let's get you home."

Chapter Thirty-Two
The Heir Returns

Ka'Ala's stomach lurched with each beat of her wings. Every span forward drew her closer to the Granite Spires looming ahead. Like columns from a distance, their jagged profiles became more distinct with each passing song. Deep oranges, reds, tans, and grays became ever more distinct as their shadows rippled across the knolls and craggy terrain. Patchwork clouds drifted overhead, letting her shadow hide from the others if only momentarily.

Her silk robe, red like the darkest rubies, clung to her every curve and offered little protection from the leering eyes of each male V'Jeeta warrior in their traveling party.

K'Marot's emerald gaze lingered upon her more often than the others. As he and R'Venin talked throughout the journey, he adjusted his flight to keep her in view.

The hot desert air gusted into her robe, causing the thin straps to dig into her shoulders, as if begging to return to the weavers in the small village they flew over a half-sun ago. Flecks of bark and soil, carried by sandspouts, stuck to the veil draped across her face. Her eyes, weary from holding onto their juniper hue, squinted to block out the sun reflecting off the dunes.

Towering above the barren soil, red cliffs in the distance looked more like a serrated blade and the circling escort of V'Jeeta warriors like a ring of prison guards leading them to her execution.

Oh, Windfather. What am I doing? Why have you led me here? I'm sure to be enslaved once they discover what I am. It's taking all I have to blend in.

Fear not, my child, Windfather whispered. *I will hide you from their eyes.*

But how? There are thousands down there. How will you keep them all from sensing my heritage? I can hear their hearts all around me. They can feel it. I know they can.

I will cloud their minds, so they do not see.

I am having trouble believing, Windfather.

Doubt not, little one. I am stronger than your fear.

I know, Windfather, but...

I have gathered the world under my wings, and each creature is an instrument of my hands.

Ka'Ala looked over at R'Venin, flying close behind his brother, K'Marot.

* * *

R'Venin winced with each flap, laboring under the weight of ill-fitted armor. Drafting behind K'Marot, each forward thrust brought a twinge of guilt. With only a tunic as padding, the breastplate and pauldrons rattled with the tiniest movement. The spinal plates, spiked with serrated edges, jabbed into his shoulder joints with each upward stroke.

Will Father understand? His heir in borrowed armor? The only royal possession I have left is my crown.

He tugged on his over-sized helmet's chinstrap, cinching it tighter against the wind trying to carry it away.

R'Venin glanced at Ka'Ala, flying close at his side in robes of scarlet and ebony that whipped behind her like pennants. Her eyes, anxious behind the slit of a courtesan's veil, darted from one warrior to the next when she wasn't scanning the ground below. The rocky terrain of tans, pale reds, and grays spread out to the horizon and dry riverbeds cutting through the arid soil amid scrubby vegetation. Here and there, sparse clusters of desiccated succulents dotted the flat landscape where the remnants of annual rainfalls collected in murky ponds. Desert fauna scattered from their passing shadows, darting under stone outcroppings. Fine powdered dust and wood tar filled his nasal slits with each pass through an updraft.

As their eyes met, Ka'Ala gave R'Venin an almost imperceptible head shake as her eyes widened, and her mouth turned down at the corners. He drifted close and settled in directly below her.

"What's wrong?" he said, slightly louder than the wind.

"I'm afraid," she put her hands at his waist, matching his wing beats. "I kept myself hidden from the world to stay safe. Once my nature is discovered, I fear someone will enslave me, just as my people were enslaved before."

"I'll never let that happen." R'Venin patted one of her hands. "Stay close to me, and when we're in my father's presence, behave like the other courtesans. My mother and sister should be at the reception. If they are, I'll introduce you and ask them to take you under their wing."

"And if they're not?"

"Well..." R'Venin paused, craning his head to look Ka'Ala in the eye. "I suppose we'll just put our faith in the Windfather."

"I trust in Windfather," Ka'Ala dug her fingers into the fabric of R'Venin's sash. "I trust in you too."

R'Venin squeezed Ka'Ala's fingers and began drifting toward the ground as horns of a dozen timbres filled the air. Still five hundred wingspans away, the king's processional came into view as they approached the Granite Spires. Indecipherable cries echoed off the cliffs from a thousand warriors perched on every available ledge; their wings furled wide with weapons winking in the sun.

The cursed blessing of home.

* * *

Intricately carved openings dotted every rock face. Pointed, rounded, and elliptical arches led to deep recesses in the stone. Half-round columns jutted from the surface like vines along a trunk, pointing skyward and branching each time they reached a new balcony. Screens of delicate stonework, interspersed between columns and openings, provided shaded access to the interior spaces.

Larger-than-life-sized statues lined the peaked domes, each sculpted to honor a long-forgotten warrior, wielding spears or swords in an aggressive stance. Banners waved in the breeze between each effigy.

Canopies of fine-twined cloth shaded balconies cantilevering over the main gate; an entrance two wingspans wide and six tall protected by a gilded portcullis.

A crowd gathered in the entrance, mostly palace slaves. Each wore a rusty-brown tunic, wings shackled together at the mid-joint. The gentry flanked the monumental staircase, feeding into the exterior courtyard like a waterfall in front of them.

The king's wives and concubines, a stream of berry and scarlet, flowed down the steps and pooled at the base. Their tunics brushed the rough-hewn pavers as a gust rushed up the cliff face.

While still a hundred wingspans away, R'Venin spotted the familiar outlines of P'Vrit and B'Luren standing at the front of K'Rawin's harem under a portable canopy emblazoned with the king's crest.

Above-average height for V'Jeeta women, they were the tallest figures among a sea of garnet and crimson robes. He stifled a cry in his throat as his hearts fluttered.

Mother! Have your eyes searched for me, as I've watched for you since we first appeared on the horizon?

Surrounding the courtesans, female warriors in gleaming black armor stood at attention with their spears tilted to the side as if forming a corral.

A half-circle of male warriors, five rows deep, filled the space between the harem and the cliff's edge in the courtyard. Centered among them, K'Rawin gleamed like obsidian in his court robes. Ornate scales of polished slate cascaded from his shoulders over a tunic of coal-colored silk, rubies glittering from every intersection. His wings were bare except for the talon sheaths tipped in the same armored fabric.

Along the perches below the king's entourage, the leaders of every V'Jeeta clan stood among their personal guard in robes of onyx and sable, accented by silvervine and polished stones from the cliffs.

I only recognize a handful of them. None of the prisoners ever let on there was so much chaos among the clans. It is no transgression to mislead one's enemy.

"You'll need to stay aloft with the escort," R'Venin said just loud enough to rise above the cheering below. "Until I signal for you to join me on the plateau."

"Why?" Ka'Ala said, pulling behind R'Venin's wings to hide from the V'Jeeta-laden cliffs.

"It's forbidden for a woman to approach the king without permission." R'Venin fanned his wings to slow their descent. "Even his wives and concubines. His guard will kill you without hesitation if you alight with me before gaining his consent to introduce you formally. I'll follow K'Marot down; then I'll beckon you to join me.

When you do, bow as low to the ground as you can and expose the underside of your wings."

When Ka'Ala didn't respond, R'Venin craned his head to find her biting her lip. She swallowed hard and gave him a nod when their eyes met.

"It's going to be alright," he said, patting her hand again. "I won't let anything happen to you."

At that moment, K'Marot swooped closer. "Brother," he shouted over the celebratory din, "it's time."

R'Venin pulled Ka'Ala's hands out of his tunic and dropped a wingspan, tugging the sash back into place. He fell away, not looking back but keeping his eyes focused on the triumphant face of his father.

The chant of his name echoed off the cliffs, pounding into his chest.

Who am I to receive a hero's welcome? If they knew who I became in their absence, they'd probably call for my execution.

K'Rawin raised his arms, fists balled in the air, as the brothers closed the final wingspans to the plateau. His smile widened with each flap closer. A cheer rent the air like thunder as K'Marot pulled ahead, landing first, and immediately dropped to one knee with his head bowed. K'Rawin then fixed his eyes on R'Venin and lowered his hands with palms open.

R'Venin's smile never met his eyes as he closed the distance and fell to his knees, opening up his wings to reveal the undersides and focused his eyes on the ground.

The celebration faded. R'Venin shot a glance up to find K'Rawin pacing in a small circle, waving down the applause.

"This will be a day, long remembered," K'Rawin shouted as he strolled across the small courtyard made by his guards. "Many V'Jeeta have never returned from battle, and none have ever returned from the cold soil. But today, my first son—my true heir—has gained the favor of P'Phet and the Windfather and accomplished both."

Beside R'Venin, K'Marot's fists balled as he twisted his knuckles into the dust at his feet. His eyes narrowed as his jaw clenched behind tight lips.

"You all know, after all the battles we've fought against the Ch'Hota in their defiance to P'Phet's decrees, I had one inheritor left. K'Marot has successfully led our dwindling armies and brought honor to the clans. We will carve his name into the sacred tablets beside my greatfathers."

Thunderous applause erupted as K'Rawin's feet came into view, and K'Marot rose from his kneeling position. "Young K'Marot," K'Rawin shouted over the din. "You're inheritance is secure. You have done well in bringing the first heir home to me."

"Thank you, father," K'Marot's words almost died in the renewed chant of R'Venin's name. "My only desire is to bring honor to you and your flock."

K'Marot joined the circle of guards as K'Rawin stepped in front of R'Venin. "My son," K'Rawin's voice trembled. "My true successor. Arise."

R'Venin looked into his father's eyes and stood, keeping his wings behind him fully exposed. "Father," he swallowed as he held out his hands, palms up. "I..."

K'Rawin stepped into the open arms, wrapping his arms around R'Venin's neck, and shouting with laughter across the desert below. R'Venin returned the embrace as the guards and entourage took up the chant again.

K'Rawin spun out and held R'Venin's hand aloft. "My son, the Heir of the First Tower, has returned!"

R'Venin looked over the guards' heads and locked onto P'Vrit. Rivers poured from her eyes, soaking the thin cloth covering her mouth. Beside her, B'Luren's face also ran with tears as she bobbed on her feet, waving frantically in the air.

"Father," R'Venin choked. "With your permission, may my mother and sister approach?"

K'Rawin nodded and slapped R'Venin on the shoulder as he cut his hand down through the air, then laid his palm up and balled his fist. An aisle formed between warriors, like a river cutting through stone, revealing a direct path to the women gathered under the palace entrance.

"P'Vrit," K'Rawin bellowed. "B'Luren. There's someone here who requests your immediate presence."

The female warrior next to them pulled her spear out of the way. R'Venin's hearts pounded as fast as his mother's feet across the stone plateau. She called his name, her wings trailing behind her next to B'Luren.

R'Venin looked to K'Rawin, his brows raised. K'Rawin nodded and held out his arm.

"Mother!" R'Venin shouted as he dashed toward the gap, falling at P'Vrit's feet as they met. "Oh, Mother."

B'Luren and P'Vrit dropped into the embrace. All three blanketed each other in their wings as the gathering cheered the reunion.

"My son," P'Vrit wailed. "I've petitioned the Windfather every new sun for this moment."

"There's no time, Mother." R'Venin's voice broke. "I need your help. I've brought a friend back with me. I need you to take her under your wing and keep her safe in the palace."

P'Vrit nodded, putting her hand on R'Venin's face. "Of course."

"B'Luren, will you help?"

"Why must it be a secret?" B'Luren's brow pinched over her nose.

"What of Ja'Naam?" P'Vrit's brows widened. "And Ja'Ven? Why have you not brought them with you?"

R'Venin's lip quivered as his head dropped. "I'll explain later," he croaked.

He wiped the moisture from his eyes and pulled away. "Father, again, with your permission, there is someone else I'd like to come forward."

K'Rawin looked over the gathering with arms outstretched, the dust kicking up in a small whirlwind as he spun around. "Who would you present to me that isn't already here?"

R'Venin moved toward the cliff, facing his father. "The woman who helped me get through Ch'Hota territory. I intend to take her as my mate."

"The first of your courtesans?" K'Rawin slapped R'Venin's shoulder.

R'Venin bowed his head. "If that is the will of the Windfather."

K'Rawin turned toward the escort, still flapping fifty wingspans from the plateau, his eyes narrowing on the figure in scarlet surrounded by K'Marot's personal guard. He gazed at them for several moments until he finally nodded and turned away from the edge.

R'Venin locked eyes with Ka'Ala and held out his hand, gesturing for her to come to him. K'Rawin moved to his position at the center of his guard. They closed the gap, blocking P'Vrit and B'Luren from withdrawing to the other women, and angled their spears toward the oncoming visitor.

R'Venin kept his hand outstretched as Ka'Ala backflapped in front of him. She took his hand as she made the final drop. Pulling her in, he pressed his forehead to hers. Her whole body trembled. "It's alright," he breathed. "My mother knows to take you in. You'll be safe with her."

"I trust you," Ka'Ala nodded, her voice shaky.

"Keep your eyes down until he speaks to you by name."

The slightest nod rubbed against his forehead, and he peeled away, reaching down to escort her by the hand. They took a few steps forward, and then Ka'Ala prostrated herself on the ground, her wings pointing to the sky.

"Father," R'Venin spoke loudly for the sake of the crowd. "King K'Rawin, sovereign of the Granite Spires, may I present Ka'Ala, my savior, my friend, and my intended."

R'Venin bowed low as he stepped back, stopping at Ka'Ala's side.

"Ka'Ala," K'Rawin grumbled. "That's not a V'Jeeta name. To which clan does she belong?"

"She doesn't remember, Father." R'Venin bowed his head, speaking lower. "She grew up as a wanderer, keeping away from others. The rest of her family had flown to the Eternal Tree long before we met. She's been alone many seasons."

"She must be a descendant of the Tenth Tower," K'Rawin said low, looking at R'Venin. "A clan banished long ago for reasons long forgotten. Is that your clan, Ka'Ala? The Tenth Tower?"

Ka'Ala raised her chin enough to look up and find K'Rawin studying her with a furrowed brow. "I do not know to which V'Jeeta clan I should belong. I've been alone for most of my life. All I know is I desire to serve your son until the Windfather sings me home."

K'Rawin bent down and lifted Ka'Ala by the chin until she sat straight up and looked him in the eye. "And why would you do that?" He asked. "It's obvious why he would take an interest in you. You're exceedingly lovely. Is it his title? His wealth?"

"I didn't know who he was when I first laid eyes on him," Ka'Ala's eyes misted over, her lip trembled. "I do know that the Windfather led me to him. To help him, in any way, asked of me."

"I knew right away; he was an honorable man." Ka'Ala looked away from K'Rawin, locking her gaze on R'Venin. "I love him... for no other reason than he has noble hearts."

K'Rawin pulled her face back to him, studying her eyes, watching her mouth. The gathering rumbled with murmurs and hissing behind their hands as he looked her over. Then, he stepped a pace away without another word and spread out his wings, facing the gathering.

"R'Venin, my son," K'Rawin cried over the whisperings in the crowd. "I pronounce this woman worthy as your intended. We will prepare a great feast to honor your return, and she will be permitted to remain by your side so long as you desire her."

"Thank you, Father." R'Venin exposed the undersides of his wings, then helped Ka'Ala up. "I have a gift for you. Something that will benefit not only you but all V'Jeeta."

K'Rawin turned back. "The Windfather returned you to me," he shook his head, smiling. "What greater gift could I receive?"

"I found it, Father." R'Venin lowered his voice and took a half-step closer. "I learned how to cure White Claw. You can save our people from a slow extinction and end the war over the Silk."

K'Rawin's face darkened, his eyes narrowed as he took a step backward, crossing his arms. Guards stood motionless as the surrounding entourage whispered to each other while father and son locked eyes across the plateau.

K'Rawin loomed closer. "I will hear your proposal before the council," he growled and then turned to face his entourage. "In three songs, I call on all clan leaders to assemble. The women will return to their chambers. The rest of you, to your labors."

Without a glance to any member of his family, K'Rawin marched toward the central archway, his guard forming a double circle around him. The courtesans hurried through the entrance as if fleeing a storm. Warriors along the ledges took to the air, scattering in all directions, while the clan leaders flew higher toward the upper spires and the king's inner court.

R'Venin took Ka'Ala by the hand and led her to where P'Vrit and B'Luren remained still in the wake of a hundred pairs of marching feet.

"Mother. B'Luren," he said, looking around for any watchful eyes. A few stragglers nodded in his direction as they hurried off. "This is Ka'Ala, my friend."

"Welcome, Ka'Ala." P'Vrit stepped forward and smiled, putting her hands around Ka'Ala's shoulders. "My daughter and I will take good care of you."

"Thank you, your highness." Ka'Ala bowed her head to both women. "R'Venin has spoken highly of you as long as I've known him."

"Come," P'Vrit took Ka'Ala by the arm and pulled her toward the women who were regrouping in the entrance. "We can become acquainted while R'Venin joins the king."

R'Venin nodded as Ka'Ala looked back. "I'll join you shortly," he said, and then jumped into the air, following the clan leaders into the sky.

Chapter Thirty-Three
Scattered Leaves

Ka'Ala followed P'Vrit, led arm-in-arm by B'Luren, through the sunlit corridors. Silken banners fluttered as they strode across the parquet pattern carved into the rock floor. The steady rattle of armor echoed through the halls as their guards kept in-step on either side. Dusty air laced with floral oils filled her nasal slits with each step along the path.

Along the hallway, V'Jeeta women and children dressed in clean crimson tunics lined with silver piping stood with their backs to the walls; their overlapping wings matched the curve of the vaulted ceiling.

"Nau'Ka Ra'Anee. This is Lady Ka'Ala," P'Vrit said as she approached the first attendant, a V'Jeeta woman with ashen feathers, and rested a hand on her bony shoulder. "She is our guest. I ask you to treat her with the same respect you show me."

Ka'Ala covered her knotting stomach with her free hand.

Ja'Naam should be here. She was the elegant one. Who am I, but a scattered leaf?

"Of course, my queen." Nau'Ka Ra'Anee knelt, holding out her arms to the sides, palms forward. The guards formed a semicircle around P'Vrit. One on each side facing the kneeling woman, their knuckles whitened around their spears' shafts. The shields in their opposite hand raised to chest height. Three other guards faced outward with their wings touching the queen's, standing elbow to elbow like the wooden tips of a picket fence.

P'Vrit reached out and brushed the attendant's forehead with the back of her fingers. As they grazed her cheek, the matron took P'Vrit's hand in hers, as if holding a new hatchling, and pressed her lips on the knuckles. "Your roost is prepared."

At her words, every attendant knelt, holding out their arms, palms forward.

"Is it true?" The older woman whispered, clinging to P'Vrit's hand as she stepped away. "Has Prince R'Venin returned?"

P'Vrit squeezed and nodded, crinkles forming beside her eyes as her lips curled up at the corners.

The servant clapped her hands together and held them to her chest. "Praise to the Windfather."

Ka'Ala's hearts thrummed in her chest.

Yes. Praise Windfather for protecting R'Venin.

A symphony of strings played in Ka'Ala's ears as she watched P'Vrit move down the hall, pausing at each servant, brushing her knuckles across their foreheads before allowing them to kiss her hand. Occasionally, B'Luren did the same.

Where do I know that melody?

The servants' eyes shined as they murmured during each exchange.

"Peace be unto you, my queen. And you, Ladies."

"May P'Phet smile upon you."

"Praise P'Phet for returning your son."

"Blessings, high mother. Blessings high daughter."

Once every few people, Ka'Ala would catch P'Vrit looking at her with a tilted head and scrunched brow. On it went until P'Vrit came to a wooden door—twice as tall as it was wide—at the corridor's end, staffed by an elderly Ch'Hota wearing a pallid threadbare tunic and shackles around his ankles. His feathers looked faded, mangy, and ill-tended like he hadn't preened in many moons. He had the appearance of one wasting away from starvation with a small chest and sunken shoulders, though his eyes seemed clear as he focused his attention on the escort. The guards moved between him and the women, aiming their spears at the sallow-faced man.

"Your highness." He wheezed, bending at the waist. Twin stumps protruded off his back, waggling like blind hatchlings searching for a meal, linked together with a length of braided razorbriar. Ka'Ala stifled a gasp with her hand as he struggled to right himself.

Clipped. How awful.

Once upright, he lifted a thick iron crossbar and pulled the door open, revealing veils in a dozen shades of red just past a vestibule.

"Thank you, Gula'Amee." B'Luren nodded as she tugged Ka'Ala to the side, allowing P'Vrit to enter first.

"Your highness." Gula'Amee inched closer to the spear tips, keeping eye contact with P'Vrit over the guards' heads.

The warriors pushed him back against the wall, one raising her weapon as if to strike.

"Don't hurt him," P'Vrit said as she reappeared in the corridor, her voice barely carrying above the breeze flowing from inside the chamber. She stepped forward and put a hand on the warriors' shoulders, parting them like curtains. "He's not threatening me. What is it, Gula'Amee?"

"May I offer my humble thanks?" His voice shook.

P'Vrit's face pinched in a smile. "For what are you grateful today, doorman?"

"That I can see the suns, your highness." The Ch'Hota coughed into his elbow for a moment. "Thank you for letting me end my days in the light. May the Windfather bless you." He bowed his head, holding his arms out with palms forward.

P'Vrit reached out to the sound of murmurs behind her. "Thank you, Gula'Amee," she said as she pulled her hand away. "Enjoy the rays while they last. We all have a final sundown awaiting us."

"Thank you, your highness," Gula'Amee said, keeping his eyes down. P'Vrit's guards closed the gap as she moved away. "Fair weather."

Ka'Ala heard P'Vrit's melody grow sorrowful as she raised her head to her attendants. "Now, I wish to be alone with my daughter and guest. You will all please remain out here."

P'Vrit turned on her heel and crossed the threshold, high-headed, into the chambers. B'Luren followed suit, keeping her head erect and eyes focused forward as she marched inside. Ka'Ala glanced over her shoulder as the warriors formed a semicircle, facing outward. The door closed to the tune of metal scraping against wood.

* * *

Once locked inside, B'Luren released Ka'Ala's arm and parted the curtains with her wing, letting P'Vrit step through first.

At B'Luren's nudge to the small of her back, Ka'Ala followed the queen into the chamber. Sunlight pierced the egg-shaped ceiling from an oculus set halfway down from the apex. Ka'Ala took in her opulent surroundings. Groups of low gilded tables, embroidered pillows, and glazed bowls of fruits and nuts arranged in different sizes filled the room.

Protruding stone columns lined the perimeter, cut from the rock. Between four of them, intricately sculpted screens blocked the sun as sheer curtains rippled between the screens and the walls on either side. Beyond, a balcony three wingspans across reached out from the rock face with a squad of warriors watching the skies.

A series of clay cups lashed to a woven conveyor scooped water from a basin and dumped their contents on a stack of multi-colored rocks held at chest height between two screens. The stack rested in a bowl atop a spindle-legged tripod. The drive wheel, lashed to a series of weights, hung from the ceiling. As the water seeped past the brim, it dripped into the basin on the floor, where the scoops carried it up again.

On the opposite wall stood an array of bronze and wood pipes in sizes varying between her finger and leg. Clumped together in groups of threes, sixes, and twelves, they reached for the ceiling like grass to the sky. The bundles protruded from a sizeable, gilded box, inlaid with metals and precious gems, with gears and knobs on one side.

Folds of finespun ivory cloth peeked from behind the pipes, flattened by a finger-thick slab of reddish sandstone. Ropes on either end snaked through iron rings set in the ceiling, spliced into a thicker twine and looped around a wooden capstan set in the wall.

On the front—below the pipes—there was a horizontal slot above a shelf which held scrolls the size of her arm. A brass rod extended from either side of the slot ending in different shapes, a ring on one side, a hook on the other. From each scroll, a metal rod with markings too small to make out hung from a string.

I'd love to meet the artisan who fabricated these.

P'Vrit led Ka'Ala into the spacious chambers' center as B'Luren moved to each window, closing pairs of shutters or releasing heavy drapes. With half the light gone, P'Vrit turned and locked her gaze on Ka'Ala; her eyes narrowed, but a smile tugged at her mouth.

"There's something familiar about you." P'Vrit breathed, leaning in. "Where do you really come from?"

"What do you mean?" Ka'Ala's voice bounced off the ceiling as she pulled back. The queen pressed a finger to her lips with the other, her eyes darting toward the oculus.

"B'Luren," P'Vrit said, sitting down on a pillow next to the center table. She opened her wings and draped them on the floor. Keeping her gaze fixed on Ka'Ala, she then patted the cushion next to her. "It's quite dry in here. Would you please hydrate the air by a few scoops?"

"Of course, Mother." B'Luren moved to the fountain and tugged on ropes hanging from the ceiling, lifting the counterweights to their apex. She then turned a dial next to the drive wheel, increasing the conveyor's speed. For a moment, Ka'Ala could hear the Hiding Falls bouncing off the walls.

"Do you like the Ba'Ansuree's organ, Ka'Ala?" P'Vrit said, gesturing to the seat.

Ka'Ala moved closer and sat facing the queen, her wings high off her shoulders, exposing the undersides. "I don't know," she said, her eyes darting to B'Luren as the younger woman made her way around the room's perimeter. "I can't say I know what that is."

"It's a musical instrument." P'Vrit's smile widened, nodding toward the contraption of pipes and scrolls. "A personal favorite of mine. Would you like to hear a piece? I find it soothing." The queen then stared over Ka'Ala's head.

Ka'Ala cleared her throat, shifting in her seat, and letting her wings fall to shoulder level but still off the floor.

"B'Luren, Would you mind?"

"Of course, Mother," B'Luren said halfway between the screens and the instrument on the opposite wall. "What piece would you like to hear?"

"Hmm." P'Vrit raised her voice over the sound of trickling water. "Something by Suk'Hada A'yak."

B'Luren reached the organ and crouched, pulling one of the scrolls from the shelf by its knob-shaped end. Instead of papyrus, the sheaf appeared metallic, with holes punched in a regular pattern along each edge and irregular slots across the surface.

B'Luren loaded one end into the ring, setting the other onto the hook, and lifted the sheet. The slots were staggered along the surface, in lengths that ranged from a feather-width to several hand spans. After inserting the page into the slot and lowering a bar, holding it in place, she moved to the capstan and cranked the wheel.

The sandstone slab lifted away, raising the fabric until it reached the ceiling. Only then did she see telescoping rods at the slabs' four corners like table legs.

"Oh." Ka'Ala breathed. "It's a bellows."

"That's right!" P'Vrit clapped her hands together. "It makes the pipes sing."

B'Luren flipped a lever, and the bellows dropped from the ceiling slower than its shadow. Air wheezed until she turned a wheel, and the machine pulled the metal sheet into the slot. Then a harmony of multiple pitches filled the room, balanced against the gurgling fountain.

Ka'Ala closed her eyes as the heartsongs of both women lilted with the music, her hearts joining the chorus. Six melodies wove through the air like a tapestry, filling her mind with images created by her mothers' stories.

Ka'Ala opened her eyes as one of the melodies drifted, changing keys, to find B'Luren seated in a triad position between her and P'Vrit. The queen's gaze bored into Ka'Ala, though the corners of her mouth tugged upward.

"You and I," P'Vrit said, barely louder than the water. "We share a secret, I think."

B'Luren leaned forward and raised her wings over both women. P'Vrit did the same, overlapping one of B'Luren's wings with her own, and then gestured to Ka'Ala.

Follow their example, daughter. Windfather breathed. *You are safe here.*

Ka'Ala followed suit, placing her wings over and under the others, forming a feathery roof. Ka'Ala swallowed hard. "What secret could I possibly share with the queen of the Granite Spires?"

P'Vrit shook her head, though her eyes widened over a tight smile. "You are not of the Spires," she said. "You are Gir'Agit. As am I."

Ka'Ala's hearts drummed hard.

Can it be true, Windfather?

"At least," P'Vrit shrugged, "the egg from which I hatched had Gir'Agit lineage. I sensed a kinship in you from our first glimpse. Hearing your heartsong just now confirmed it."

Ka'Ala looked at B'Luren, who just nodded.

"How did you learn you were a half-flock?" Ka'Ala whispered behind her hand.

P'Vrit laughed through her nose. "I'm not even half," she said, shaking her head.

"R'Venin told me stories of you studying alchemy with the Pra'Acheen," Ka'Ala said, reaching out to place her hand on P'Vrit's knee and jerking it back. "Sorry. I didn't mean to breach protocol."

"Think nothing of it." P'Vrit reached across the circle and took Ka'Ala's hand in both of hers. "I've never met another soul with whom I've shared this connection. Except for my children." Her eyes drifted over to B'Luren.

"You can hear heartsongs too?" Ka'Ala exclaimed in joy and disbelief, her eyes following the queen's gaze.

B'Luren looked down. "No." She mumbled. "That gift passed over me."

"What about R'Venin?" Ka'Ala reached for B'Luren with her other hand. "Does he have it?"

P'Vrit and B'Luren shared a knowing glance.

"If he does," B'Luren sighed, "he's never shared it with either of us."

"But I do believe it's what makes him more sensitive to others,"

P'Vrit added. "And... I think it's why you're genuinely in love with him."

Ka'Ala pulled her hands away. "You can sense that?"

P'Vrit smiled with a tilt of her head. "Yes. And I can also sense he has no idea your affections are more than a masquerade for the king's sake. Your hearts beat for him, don't they?"

Ka'Ala's lips quivered. She took several breaths as P'Vrit and B'Luren squeezed her hands. "As much as I dared to allow. Perhaps even as much as Ja'Naam's and Ja'Ven's did."

Ka'Ala pulled her hands away, burying her face.

"And you feel guilty about that."

Ka'Ala's shoulders shook. "I was alone," she sniffled, looking down at her hands folded in her lap. "Hiding from the world, season after season, when Windfather blew us together. She realized what I was almost instantly and kept my secret from R'Venin and Ba'Jai. They took me in as their sister. And even though Windfather decreed they become one, my hearts still beat for him. I felt like a betrayer in their presence, even though he never knew. They became my only family. I did my best to remain faithful to Windfather's commands. After they had Ja'Ven and saw the kind of protector and provider he was, I loved him all the more. I'll be forever grateful they took me into their flock."

Reveal yourself. Windfather breathed.

Ka'Ala considered the two women—biting her lip—then her shoulders relaxed. Her eyes shifted from emerald to tourmaline, the color washing away like an oil painting under a waterfall revealing the blank canvas underneath.

B'Luren's eyes widened as her hand crept up to cover her dropping jaw.

Starting at her head, Ka'Ala's feathers darkened from brown to onyx as her skin paled from tan to chalk causing even greater contrast with her scarlet robes. She froze in place, her pearly eyes darting from mother to daughter.

"As the Windfather blows across the land," P'Vrit's eyes brimmed as she reached out, gripping Ka'Ala's hands with hers, "you can be yourself around us. We are also your flock now."

Chapter Thirty-Four

The Council of Nine Towers

"Heresy!"

"Blasphemy!"

"You're suggesting we hide our eyes from P'Phet himself."

"I don't believe they have that kind of power."

"The Windfather would never allow it."

R'Venin took a deep breath and glanced around the council chambers as the eight clan leaders shouted, each louder than the last. Their voices bounced off the stone walls and domed ceilings as they postured. Murmurs filled the spaces between raised voices from the bowl-shaped gallery surrounding the council pillars. Lining the gallery in full armor, the king's guard blocked spectators from the council.

The central space, three wingspans wide and ten tall, rose to the primary oculus. Overlapping sunshades of spinners silk, arrayed like flower petals, covered the opening. Diffused light bathed the chamber from the twin suns racing toward the horizon. Other portals ringed the dome, leading to corridors, rooms, and the outdoors.

Slender columns rose around the chambers' periphery, separating the central atria from a belt of ten alcoves along the circumference. Nine of the cavities, two wingspans wide and five tall, featured a different statue dedicated to a Granite Spires' clan leader. K'Marot leaned against a column demarking the First Tower alcove, arms crossed. He nodded as R'Venin's eyes met his, the scars across his face distorted by shadows. Behind him, K'Marot's guard surrounded the monument featuring a warrior with wings spread wide, carrying a spiked mace in each hand. K'Marot bore a striking resemblance to the statue.

How many generations of my father's line have ruled the Spires?

In every other alcove, seated around each effigy, an entourage wearing the clan's markings talked behind their hands as they watched and listened to the leaders. Frescoes and bas-relief sculptures covered every surface detailing each faction's history back to the rise of P'Phet as the first seer of Pirth'Vee Grah.

One lie after another, if you believe the Ch'Hota and Pra'Acheen.

The tenth chamber lacked any embellishments, every surface pockmarked, with only the fractured base of a long-forgotten statue remained.

Much like the spot on which I stand.

R'Venin looked down at his feet while the shouting continued. Polished marble spread to the walls from the worn-down remnants of a pillar, the girth of his chest, on which he stood a feather's width off the floor.

On either side of him, a circle of elevated perches, each varying in height and topped with a padded throne, rose above his head. K'Rawin, directly across the ring, sat atop the tallest pillar at ten wings above the floor, a gilded mace resting across his lap. On K'Rawin's right, the patriarch of the second tower sat one wing depth lower. On the king's left, the third tower's leader sat two wings below. The pattern continued back and forth until R'Venin's position.

The commotion grew like towering waterfalls after a monsoon until the king raised his mace. Hisses filled the room then quickly died, leaving only the sound of fluttering sunshades overhead.

"Continue," K'Rawin said, pointing his scepter at R'Venin.

"Thank you, Father." R'Venin cleared his throat. "Every season, we fight over the Crimson Maize. Why?"

Nervous laughter erupted as V'Jeeta glared at each other, some shrugging or shaking their heads.

Yes, it's an obvious question, but one that needs scrutiny.

Gu'Usa, the leader of the Second Tower, leaned forward. "For the silk."

R'Venin pointed at him, locking eyes. "Right. We fight to get the most silk. But why the silk? Why not the grain from which the silk grows?"

Gu'Usa held out his arms, looking around. "Everyone in the Spires knows this. This is pointless."

"It has medicinal properties." Sha'Atir of the Eighth Tower broke in. "Why do you ask such an obvious question?"

R'Venin ignored Sha'Atir's inquiry. "How do we use the silk in our alchemy?" he pressed.

Murmurs grew from all around. Various answers rose above the din.

"Closing scars faster."

"Strengthening feeble wings."

"Alleviating pain."

"Increasing pleasure."

"Opening our minds to dreams."

"Yes, yes." R'Venin waved his hands for quiet. "But what is the primary use for the silk in the spires?"

"To increase our numbers," K'Rawin said. "To replenish our ranks season after season, to rebuild our armies after each harvest from the devastation brought upon us by Ch'Hota filth. To overcome the effects of the White Claw, reducing our seed."

Angry roars erupted, filling the room with threats of battle and vows of victory. Warriors pounded fists and swords on their chest plates, spears against shields. R'Venin scanned the crowd, waiting for the sentiment to dissipate.

K'Rawin raised his royal mace again, hushing the rally.

"Do you know how the Ch'Hota and Pra'Acheen use the silk?"

"We don't care how those mongrels use it!" An unseen warrior shouted from the gallery. The war cries built up to a roar until K'Rawin stood, his eyes scanning the crowd.

"Do not interrupt my son again." He growled. Sitting down, he laid the scepter across his lap and nodded to R'Venin.

R'Venin gave a quick nod in return. "They use the silk for all the same purposes as we do, with one exception. They don't use it to increase their seed. They're not affected by White Claw like we are, not nearly to the same degree. And it doesn't affect them until further into their late seasons."

Low grumbling churned like a rock slide.

"What are you proposing?" Pra'Kop of the Fifth Tower said, standing and gesturing around the room. "That we live like the Ch'Hota? That we embrace their traditions? That we give up on the only means we have to ensure our survival?"

"No. No." R'Venin took a breath. "And, yes."

The erupting cacophony shook the walls. R'Venin held out his hands, unable to hear himself plead for them to allow him to continue. His eyes met K'Rawin's, who hadn't budged from his throne. Threats of treason, plucking, and clipping found their way to his ears.

"Please, listen to me," R'Venin shouted against the hurricane level uproar. "Hear me out."

K'Rawin stood again, holding his scepter high and spread his wings until the yelling faded to whispers.

"I'm still listening." He said, seating himself. "But I've yet to hear anything that I'm willing to entertain or decree among the spires."

"I'm not asking anyone to embrace Ch'Hota traditions or religion." R'Venin's voice raised in pitch and volume. "I am asking you to give what I've learned of their alchemy a chance to heal our people."

"And what is that?" Kro'Or of the Third Tower spat. "How is their alchemy any different from ours?"

R'Venin took a breath. "There is a fifth symbol of alchemy. Another component. One that we've been missing or ignored."

"Nonsense." Kro'Or sneered, leaning toward K'Rawin. "My lord, if I may suggest. Have the royal alchemist come forward to educate us."

K'Rawin nodded. "Chit'Itsak. Come forward."

An elderly V'Jeeta emerged from the alcove behind K'Marot wearing a floor-length cobalt tunic embroidered with silvervine.

He's new.

"He's been away for a long time, and Alchemy was never one of his primary responsibilities," Kro'Or said, opening his arms wide to the council. "Perhaps the high prince just needs a refresher on the elements."

"Of course." Chit'Itsak bent at the waist, and then stood erect and moved to R'Venin, holding out his hands. "There are four elements used in alchemy. Mountain, Tree, Fire, and Rain. These elements are found in the natural world, and when combined, they create potions for various purposes."

"Of course." R'Venin nodded. "That's what I learned in my youth. Tell me, master alchemist, what elements would I use to heal broken bones? Let's say to heal the left half of someone's body."

"My young prince," Chit'Itsak chuckled in his throat. "That is advanced alchemy. It would be more merciful to end their suffering with the draught of permanent sleep."

"Humor me." R'Venin smiled and gestured to K'Rawin. "And

educate us."

Chit'Itsak toyed with his robes for a moment. "Very well," he said, folding his arms. "Give me a moment."

He pulled at his lip, pacing in a circle as the crowd murmured and whispered to one another.

"Yes," he swirled his hand in the air. "Of course. You will need the following ingredients, but I won't be giving you the proportions. I wouldn't want you to try to perform alchemy beyond your skill level." He waggled his finger to the laughter of the crowd. "For mountain and fire, you can use molten lead. For tree, desert grass. And for rain, seawater."

A smug look crossed his face as he bowed his head and rested a hand on his chest. Kro'Or clapped, followed by a few clan leaders and a smattering of the gallery.

"Even if you had the proper proportions," Chit'Itsak said, standing upright, "I wouldn't recommend it."

"Why is that?" R'Venin asked.

"The process would be slow and excruciating. Better to let the patient fly to the Tree of Eternal Stars as a warrior, and not as an ailing and feeble pet."

"So, there's no way to heal a body so broken without pain?"

"None."

"Hmm." R'Venin nodded, taking a half-step forward. "What if I were to tell you that I witnessed a Pra'Acheen alchemist heal a man who had fallen from the sky, breaking every bone on the left side of his body, and he never experienced a moment of pain during the entire process?"

"Psh." Chit'Itsak scoffed. "I'd say you were the mark of a clever hoax. A brilliant performance. Must have been in your hatchling seasons. A wandering troupe, perhaps." A few chuckles echoed off the walls. "Don't be disappointed with yourself, my Prince. But not everyone can spot falsehoods. Especially the young. Perhaps a master such as myself..."

R'Venin let the laughter die as he walked off his dais, glancing around the room. His eyes came to rest on K'Rawin and locked his gaze.

"I was the man."

Gasps burst from every corner as K'Rawin leaned forward, his fist tightening around his scepter, though no other reaction showed on his stern face.

"I-I-I... I don't believe you." Chit'Itsak flustered. "That's impossible... that's..."

Over Chit'Itsak's shoulder, K'Marot leaned away from the column, planting his feet and resting a hand on the hilt of his dagger. R'Venin made the slightest gesture with his hand, shaking his head.

Suddenly, K'Rawin landed on the floor, his face a feather's depth from Chit'Itsak's face. "Are you accusing my son of bearing false witness?"

Chit'Itsak fell to the tiles, exposing his wings' undersides. "My king, of course not," He simpered. "I'm merely stating how he may have been deceived. You know how devious our enemies can be."

"The Ch'Hota, perhaps." K'Rawin dropped the mace. It bounced against his leg as it reached the end of a leather strap on his wrist. "The Pra'Acheen? They're not allies, nor are they our enemy. I've never known them to lie. And I've never believed my son would lie to me either."

R'Venin took a half-step away, his gut squirming under his conscience.

Lies of omission.

"Your Highness," Chit'Itsak whined, burying his face in the tiles. "I beg your pardon. Please, forgive me. I meant no disrespect."

The entire room stood and craned their necks as K'Rawin studied the alchemist for a moment, dragging the mace up by the strap until he had the handle nestled firmly in his grip. He tapped the hammer on his thigh shield in rhythm with his steps as he circled the prostrated alchemist. Clang. Clang. Clang.

"Only for your skills at making the remedy for White Claw, will I show you mercy." K'Rawin tucked the scepter in his sash.

"Thank you, my king." Chit'Itsak pressed himself further into the floor. "I am ever your loyal servant."

"Return to your place," K'Rawin grumbled.

Chit'Itsak picked himself up and scurried to the alcove, glancing over his shoulder. His eyes bespoke anger while his wing hid the rest of his face.

"Does anyone else wish to question my son's account?"

The gaping onlookers returned to their seats or retreated into the shadows.

K'Rawin turned, putting his hands on R'Venin's shoulders. "Is this true?" He whispered. "Were you truly healed by the Pra'Acheen?"

"Yes, father," R'Venin said, loud enough for the whole room to hear. "My wing, shoulder, hip, and leg were all broken. And a Pra'Acheen master alchemist restored me to full health with no pain. The whole process lasted only a few songs."

Murmurs broke out again.

"When did this happen?" K'Marot's question echoed above the din as he stepped away from the alcove, moving between the throne pillars. "Was it when you were a prisoner at Stonetree? Were you beaten for being a V'Jeeta? Did they discover who you were? Was it the prison alchemist who healed you? When, brother? When did this happen?"

R'Venin glanced at K'Rawin and swallowed. "It was nine seasons ago, at the battle over the crimson maize. A squadron of guardsmen overpowered me, and I broke from the fall. I awoke in the sanctuary of

The Three Mothers. They healed me, every broken bone, without any pain. Just... pressure. As if invisible hands molded me back together like clay."

"Then how did you get from Copperleaf to the Bluewoods?" K'Marot moved closer. "If the Pra'Acheen healed you, how did you end up in Stonetree? They don't take prisoners."

If I tell the truth, will that cut off all chances of them accepting the cure?

A voice whispered into his ear. *Always speak the truth, my son.* R'Venin turned his head, looking for the source, but saw no one. He licked his lips and swallowed.

"I swore a spirit-oath." R'Venin bowed his head.

"You what?" K'Marot shouted.

"To a Pra'Acheen?" K'Rawin yelled at the same time.

"To a Ch'Hota." R'Venin swallowed. "He saved my life. Twice. Once from a wild runnerhound, and by carrying me to the sanctuary. He lost his wing defending me from that beast and spent the rest of his life using a fabricated wing just to avoid being ground-cast."

K'Marot looked down to the side, his brows furrowed as he mumbled to himself. The rumble in the gallery grew, but K'Rawin ignored it.

"I knew I'd dishonored you," R'Venin said so only the king and K'Marot could hear. "I thought it would be better if I were dead. But then I thought if I could learn how to cure White Claw, I could come home with a gift worthy of your forgiveness. And I did it. I learned the cure from a prisoner before he died, a Pra'Acheen master. I can do this. We can cure our people and end the war."

K'Rawin stepped back, then leaped into the air, rising until reseating himself on his throne. Holding his mace aloft, he silenced the ever-growing chatter. "Tell me more about Pra'Acheen alchemy; this missing element." With a glance down, he motioned K'Marot back to the alcove.

"The missing element is Voice." R'Venin turned on the spot, his eyes searching the crowd. "It's Air. The Voice of the Windfather. He gave us the elements with which to build, and the knowledge to use them. But speaking in His name lends power to the potion, making it more effective. I've learned a few incantations other than the one for White Claw. I can show you. Is there anyone willing to let me demonstrate?"

Silence filled the chamber. Even the banners seemed frozen in place.

"Can you heal scars?"

R'Venin spun around to the familiar voice. K'Marot stepped out of the alcove, his eyes hard as he turned his head slightly to present the disfigured side of his face.

"Yes," R'Venin said, moving to close the distance between them. "It's common among the Ch'Hota and Pra'Acheen to heal cuts immediately, so they don't become scars. That's one of the reasons we think they look untested in battle. Along with the potion, it's a simple incantation."

"When can you do it?" K'Marot asked with narrowed eyes. His eyes flitted to a man standing in the nearest alcove wearing a blue and silver tunic. "Do you need time to prepare like some of the alchemists around here?"

"Prince K'Marot, you can't." One of his guards hissed from the shadows. "You can't use heathen alchemy. P'Phet would…"

"He'd what?" He barked over his shoulder. "P'Phet decreed the V'Jeeta would rule over every flock on Pirth'Vee Grah. We take what is rightfully ours. Their lands. Their possessions. Even their lives. Did he ever say we shouldn't benefit from their knowledge? I'm interested in seeing what my brother can do with their alchemy."

"I just need access to the right supplies," R'Venin gave a half-smile. "And a place to put it all together."

"Your highness," Chit'Itsak rushed out of the shadows, bowing low with wings exposed. "It would be my profound honor if you allow me to assist the prince. I will see to it personally, that he has everything he needs."

"Thank you, Master Alchemist." R'Venin nodded. "Your help is greatly appreciated."

"Of course, my prince. Anything for the throne." Chit'Itsak raised his open hand to K'Rawin. "Your highness?"

"I have no objection. K'Marot, are you willing to undergo this ritual before witnesses?"

"I have no objections," K'Marot smirked. "No feathers off my calves."

"The council will gather in the healing ward in five songs." K'Marot whacked his mace on the throne's arm and launched toward the ceiling. The council members dropped to the floor, heading to the various openings, followed by their entourages.

Once the chamber emptied, R'Venin closed the distance between himself and K'Marot. "Thank you for volunteering," he said, giving him a light punch on the chest.

"Didn't actually volunteer." K'Marot crossed his arms. "More curious to see if this is all you say it is. To see if it's something we can use."

"I think you'll find there is much we can learn from them," R'Venin took K'Marot by the arms, "and the Ch'Hota."

"Perhaps," K'Marot stepped back from R'Venin's embrace. "But there is more they need to learn from us. Like their place in the world."

R'Venin cocked his head. "You've changed," he said, searching K'Marot's face. "You used to be so curious about the other flocks. What happened to make you so hard?"

K'Marot scratched at the scars along his face as his mouth shifted between pinched and pursed.

"Ahem."

K'Marot spun around. R'Venin glanced over his shoulder to find Chit'Itsak staring at them from a sunlit passageway.

"If the princes would please follow me," He bowed, raising his arms in the corridor's direction.

R'Venin gave a slight push to the small of K'Marot's back. "After you, brother."

K'Marot side-stepped and turned, copying Chit'Itsak's bow. "Age before beauty."

Chapter Thirty-Five
Divided Branches

R'Venin crossed the ward's threshold an arm's length behind Chit'Itsak, K'Marot trailing a wingspan after. Remnants of a thousand potions lingered. Their tang, like the tendrils of an invisible vine, crept through the air.

The barrel-vaulted chamber stood four wingspans wide, twenty long, and eight high. With streaks of reds, browns, and whites, the striated stone gave the room an artistic grace. Natural murals mimicked the landscape far beyond the walls.

The main hall lodged three dozen roosts on either side of the central aisle, most of which were empty. Above the nests, a long, wooden mezzanine of perches and cushions hung from thick ropes.

A handful of elderly warriors occupied the nests at the far end. With trembling hands, gaunt faces, and colorless skin, they gnashed their teeth as healers wrapped bandages, soaked in a chalky gray paste, around their wing joints. Ashen feathers snapped free like dried twigs, collecting in dusty piles.

The last stages of White Claw. Just moons away from becoming a "dead-seed."

Loitering among the roosts, male V'Jeeta worked in matching

cobalt and silver-lined apprentice tunics. Some read off scrolls as they leaned against the walls or sat on the nests. A few scrawled notes on gilded scratchplates, as dictated by the healers tending the patients, their hushed words dying to hisses.

Pillars of light poured through oculi carved into the ceiling at regular intervals, highlighting flecks of dust dancing through the air. Smaller openings pierced the darkness, casting rays onto intricately crafted solar calendars showing the number of songs before or after high sun. The natural stone floor, etched with a basket weave pattern, sloped to the center aisle and an array of drains directly below each oculus.

"Haven't been here in seasons," K'Marot murmured.

R'Venin craned his neck. He spotted K'Marot lingering in the doorway, looking around the room. As their eyes met, K'Marot pointed to his face. "The last alchemist's handiwork. Said it was the best he could do. Felt like a firebrand."

"I promise it won't hurt this time," R'Venin said, moving to walk backward.

"Sometimes growth can't happen without discomfort, my prince," Chit'Itsak said as he took a sharp turn between two roosts, heading for a pair of iron doors framed by guards. R'Venin followed, watching over the wizened V'Jeeta's shoulder as he pulled a song key from his sleeve. It resembled a small rolling pin with steely teeth dotting its surface.

R'Venin slid an arm under his sleeve, fingering the spot that once held his song key, the symbol of hard-earned authority.

Nothing like mine.

The alchemist inserted the song key, turning his wrist. R'Venin winced as the iron comb, hidden somewhere inside the door, plucked out a discordant tune. The bolt slid out of place with the final note; allowing a crack between the panels to form. R'Venin leaned forward on his toes, craning his head over the older man's crest.

Chit'Itsak stepped back, his elbow bumping into R'Venin's ribcage as the guards each took a door handle. "My apologies, Prince R'Venin." He turned and bowed with a flourish. "I didn't know you were there."

"No harm," R'Venin said, not looking the alchemist in the eye. "I'll admit I'm a little distracted. I'm eager to see your stores."

"Of course." Chit'Itsak templed his fingers, drumming them together. "It's the envy of the spires. Perhaps even the greatest Ch'Hota cache pales in comparison."

The guards pulled the doors apart, revealing a large chamber chiseled from the stone. R'Venin breathed in the scent of a hundred elements. Most immediately recognizable, some unfamiliar.

Odors of Mountain and Tree and wafts of Rain and Fire teased at his nasal slits. Their colors, textures, viscosity, and locations on the shelves of Stonetree flew through his mind. His chest expanded involuntarily, the aromas washing over him as he moved deeper into the room.

The walls, lined with shelves and cupboards, bowed under the multitudinous clay jars and glass bottles of every shape, shade, and size. A workbench stood in the center, with stacks of mortars and pestles, silver-plated measuring cups, gilded mixing spoons, and a set of intricately crafted, brass scales on one end.

On the side, closest to the doorway, shelves crammed with scrolls supported the worktop. Half of the top shelf seemed dedicated to blank parchment and scratchplates. A six-wheeled iron trolley, with three shelves, sat in front of the bench, a wooden push handle on either end.

As R'Venin opened the nearest cupboard, Chit'Itsak stepped up beside him, putting his hand on the cabinet door. "I'm afraid I can't allow that, my prince. The king granted me the right to deny access to my stores to anyone except my apprentices and me, himself included."

"My father lets you keep secrets from him?" R'Venin's brows pinched as he turned to face the alchemist.

"Not secrets, my young prince." Chit'Itsak simpered, waving away the question. "The king understands that alchemy is a delicate art. You know this, of course. The ingredients must be kept pure before they're combined. Otherwise, their potency decreases."

That's new to me.

Before R'Venin could open his mouth, Chit'Itsak held out his hands. "However, it will be my honor to gather them for you." He snapped his fingers, barking. "Kama'Zor!"

A young alchemist appeared at the doorway, bowing. "Yes, Master Chit'Itsak." He brushed wrinkles from his tunic. "What is my task?"

"Bring the cart." Chit'Itsak snipped, though his face carried a bland smile, as he turned to the cupboards. "Now, my prince, if you would, please step outside." He held out his hand toward the doorway where Kama'Zor remained bent at the waist.

"Very well." R'Venin sighed as Chit'Itsak applied the slightest of pressure between his wings.

"I don't trust anyone to procure ingredients from my stores except me." The alchemist said, nudging R'Venin toward the door. "I organized the inventory myself. It's a little complicated. My apprentices can't even find anything the first time."

As R'Venin stepped past the guards, Kama'Zor mumbled to the side. "That's because you keep moving everything."

R'Venin pinched his lips into a hard line. He looked over his shoulder to see Chit'Itsak had turned around, heading for the workbench. R'Venin spun in place, just outside the doors, and planted his feet. "Is this far enough?"

"Yes, yes." The old V'Jeeta put a finger to his lips, talking to himself, his voice barely carrying past the threshold. "Now, let me see—Healing scars. There are so many combinations. So many potential potions will do the trick."

"To go along with the incantation," R'Venin called into the room, "I'll need specific ingredients."

"Of course, of course." Chit'Itsak waved away the comment. "What are they? Do you have them memorized? If not, perhaps you have them written down." The older man's forehead raised as he tilted his head. "Would you like to give me the list? I'd be pleased to review them to make sure you're, I mean, we're not doing more harm than good."

"No need." R'Venin's brows knitted together. "With which element would you like to start? Mountain?"

"That will be fine," Chit'Itsak sighed, picking up a scratch slate from the shelf. Walking to the door, he held it out. "Scratch the ingredients on here, if you please. I'll review them and let you know if anything is amiss. I'll then need to close the doors while my apprentice and I gather your ingredients."

"Very well." R'Venin took the tablet and scratched across the surface with his claw. After a few moments, he handed it back.

Chit'Itsak took it with a bow. "Let's see." He said, holding it up to read. "Hmm. Saltriver silt, of course. Limplimb, Interesting. Irontree sap, yes. And, as I expected, Firestone." He flipped the slate over, scanning the back side, and back again. "What about this fifth element of which you so eloquently preached. It's not here."

"The Pra'Acheen say it's not appropriate to invoke the Windfather's voice before mixing the ingredients." R'Venin folded his hands in front. "And there's a certain method used when doing so."

"From one alchemist to another," he gestured back and forth. "You can tell me."

"I'm sorry." R'Venin crossed his arms. "You'll have to wait and see, just like the others."

"Very well, your highness." A thin smile pinched on Chit'Itsak's lips. He held up the tablet. "I'll just go collect your items. It'll take me a song or two. My chief apprentice, Kama'Zor, will see to your comfort."

Chit'Itsak spun around, his wings drawn tight to his back. "Get the heir anything he needs." He grabbed Kama'Zor by the arm, the fabric bunching under his grip. "Then return." He pushed the apprentice from the doorway and snapped his fingers. The guards closed the doors behind him with a thud.

Kama'Zor hurried over, pointing up. "Perhaps you'll be more comfortable on the mezzanine with your brother." The apprentice scurried past, gesturing over his shoulder for R'Venin to follow. Jumping, he flapped until he landed steadily on the platform. The wooden planks creaked under the new weight. R'Venin spied K'Marot lounging on an embroidered cushion of sunset colors.

Oh, so that's where he went.

R'Venin leaped into the air, following Kama'Zor's path. K'Marot held a silver chalice out to Kama'Zor, his lips moved, but the words died under the groaning ropes and flapping wings. Kama'Zor took the cup with a bow as R'Venin perched on a heavy wooden bench opposite K'Marot.

"Of course, my prince," Kama'Zor backed away toward the edge, then turned to R'Venin. "Would you also like some spirits while you wait, my lord?"

"Best spirits in the spires, brother." K'Marot sniggered. "No one makes elixirs better than Chit'Itsak. As disagreeable as he is, I think it's the reason Father's kept him around so long."

"Indeed." R'Venin lifted his chin, then looked at Kama'Zor. "Jitterleaf tea will be fine."

Kama'Zor turned and stepped off the platform.

"Never did care for strong drink, did you?" K'Marot leaned back, crossing his arms.

"Not really." R'Venin squatted, wrapping his arms around his knees. "Fuddles the mind."

K'Marot nodded, half his mouth turning up. "That's the best part."

"Not when you're trying to think clearly."

K'Marot reared his head back and laughed. "The only time you need a clear head around here is when you're preparing for war. And even then..."

Staring beyond the walls, K'Marot twirled his claws through the cushion's flaxen tassels. They sat nearly motionless, tilting to the platform's subtle sway with only the muddled conversations rising from below to break the silence. Wingbeats announced Kama'Zor's return just as he landed between the brothers.

"Your tea, Prince R'Venin." Kama'Zor held out a silver tray with twin chalices, wisps of steam rising from one. R'Venin took it, holding it to his lips with long breath through his nose, the corners of his mouth pulling up.

If there's one thing I missed from the spires, it's this.

"And your drink, Prince K'Marot." Kama'Zor lowered the tray to K'Marot's eye level.

K'Marot jerked his head to a low table beside him. Kama'Zor set the cup down, his eyes darting to R'Venin and back.

Kama'Zor then bowed and stepped off the platform. Moments later, the sound of creaking hinges filled R'Venin's ears. He looked over his shoulder just as Kama'Zor disappeared beyond the doors.

R'Venin held his tea two-handed, sipping as he crouched on the perch. His face glowed from the light reflecting from within, and let the cup's warmth fill his mouth and hands.

A loud grunt exploded from the chambers far end, echoing in the round. K'Marot stood quickly, dropping his chalice onto the cushion, and passing R'Venin without a glance. Holding a rope with one hand, he leaned over the edge, causing the platform to tilt.

R'Venin angled forward, gray liquid spilling from his cup. Regaining his balance, he dismounted the bench and joined K'Marot at the cable. "Is it his last breath?" R'Venin craned his neck around K'Marot for a better look.

In a roost, with a healer on either side, an elderly V'Jeeta lay on his back. He wore an ivory-colored linen tunic, stained with splotches of sage and moss. His wings, arms, and legs, spread at awkward angles, held in place by a half dozen apprentices. He fought against the bondage, arching his back with what little strength remained in his withering frame. Like a snowfall, ash-colored feathers drifted to the floor, muffling the feet of those holding him down.

"Worse." K'Marot pulled his wings tight over his shoulders.

There's only one thing worse than dying in the spires.

"They're taking his infected wing talons to slow the spread." R'Venin groaned as he draped himself with his wings. Peering down the room, he saw a healer inserting a pair of claw-tooth iron tongs into a large clay bowl of fire crystals.

"He'll be seedless in a quarter moon," K'Marot whispered. "No more sons to shout his songs."

Another apprentice approached from below, carrying a translucent sack made of spinners thread. The bag—its folds undulating with each step—emitted wisps of smoke from a bulge in one corner. R'Venin took in a shallow breath through his nasal slits as an acrid scent wafted to his nose. K'Marot sniffed at the same time.

"No one will tell me what's in the bag." K'Marot ran a finger under his nose. "They just say it's known only to Chit'Itsak."

"It's dreampetal powder," R'Venin whispered, looking around. "It's a powerful sleep drug. He won't feel the pain while they take his talons."

K'Marot nodded as they watched the apprentice put the bag over the old V'Jeeta's head. A puff of white smoke escaped as a healer pulled a drawstring, tightening the sack's mouth around the man's neck.

"Breathe deeply, old warrior." The other healer soothed. "Let P'Phet take to you to paradise for a few songs."

The bag expanded and collapsed quickly, then slowed until the older man's head and body went limp. "Bind him down," A healer said, untying the drawstring and lifting the bag far enough to uncover the old man's mouth. He then pulled the fabric off the patient's nose and pointed to the nearest apprentice. "Keep this off his mouth, but make sure he inhales through his nose every third breath."

"Have you ever watched someone lose their talons without the powder?" K'Marot asked, his eyes fixed on the procedure below.

"Once," R'Venin said hoarsely. "Just after I started branching. It was one of Father's generals. After we lost a brutal battle, Father suspected him of spying for the Ch'Hota and had him de-taloned. My mother had brought me with her to gather the silk she needed for Father's fertility elixir. Father was here when we arrived. I tried to hide behind my mother's wings when they held him down, but Father made me watch. How about you?"

"No," K'Marot said, never taking his eyes off the events taking place below.

The healer retrieved the tongs from the bowl of crystals, now glowing red with white-tipped teeth. A trail of smoke plumed from the instrument as it took a bite into the chalky talon. The odor of burning bone floated to them. R'Venin clamped a hand over his nose and mouth, but K'Marot took a noseful and leaned further out.

Twisting the fiery tongs, the healer tugged on the diseased talon. Blood trickled from the joint just as the root started to show. A crack developed along the length from where the tongs bit. Suddenly, the bone shattered, splintering in a thousand directions.

"Hurry," the attending healer said over the noise of a dozen apprentices talking to each other. "Grab it by the root before it infects the blood."

With the smell of burned flesh, a sizzle of roasting meat followed the sight of glowing tongs digging into the man's wing joint.

"He's never going to fly straight again," K'Marot muttered. "Probably won't bear the weight of his armor and spear either. Better to let him die."

"Even if he can't fly—." R'Venin tilted his head to put his face close to K'Marot's. "His life has value. Potential. He can still contribute. If he dies, all his experience—his wisdom—is lost. What good will that do anyone?"

K'Marot moved his head back. "Is that what you've been learning out there? To coddle the weak?"

"I've been exposed to viewpoints different from ours, yes," R'Venin said, pushing away from the edge and sitting on the bench. "Let me pose a scenario: You're flying over the forest, and you're seven songs from the nearest village. The sun is falling, and you spot a stranger flying between the branches. He's alone, and his wing is lame. It's slowing him down. He's struggling toward the village in the distance. Up ahead, you spot a branchclimber in their path, but they don't seem to see it. What would you do?"

K'Marot turned around, leaning on the rope. "I suppose the stranger is Ch'Hota?"

"What does that matter?"

"It matters because P'Phet says V'Jeeta looks after their own." K'Marot sneered. "And only their own."

"What if it's a Pra'Acheen?" R'Venin asked with outstretched hands.

"No difference." K'Marot shrugged. "Unless they're of use to me, I don't see why I should help them."

"How do you know they aren't 'of use' to you? All you know is that they're in danger and don't know it, and you're in a position to warn them."

"Alright. I'll play along. Let's say I warn them." K'Marot pushed away from the rope. "They avoid becoming a meal and make it to the village. Now what?"

"I don't know." R'Venin laughed, grinning wide. "That's the point. I don't know what will happen next. We can't see beyond our eyes. We don't know what else is out there. We don't know how our choices will affect the world beyond our reach. Perhaps the stranger turns on you and attacks. Perhaps, by warning them, the branchclimber sets its eyes on you for a meal. But how does that change the principle?"

"Maybe I'll just let the worm fly right into the branchclimber's mouth." K'Marot laughed through his nose. "Everyone's done something worth getting them killed."

"Like the general Father had de-taloned for treason?"

K'Marot nodded, folding his arms. "I think he deserved what he got," he mumbled as his eyes burned like the tongs. "Spies and traitors should be clipped and thrown from the spires with a grindstone around their necks," he added with more vigor.

R'Venin looked at the floor; his mouth downturned. "Turned out the general was innocent. It was his personal guard that gave away our movements. He was prone to lying with evening hostesses and, with a little probing, sleep-talked."

"I hope he was clipped. He betrayed his flock and his King."

"Unknowingly."

"Stupidly," K'Marot barked. "No one is free from the consequences of their mistakes, whether they had ill intent or not."

"Is there no room in your hearts for compassion? For mercy?"

"Mercy is for weaklings."

"It is the weak who need mercy, and something only the strong can provide."

"You sound like a Pra'Acheen. Or worse, a Ch'Hota." K'Marot

turned his back to R'Venin. "I wouldn't want to be you if Father hears you talking like that."

"Interesting you should say that."

"Why's that?"

R'Venin moved up behind K'Marot and put a hand on his shoulder. "Because you used to tell Father how much you wanted to be like me someday."

The iron doors creaked open below. Chit'Itsak strode past the guards with his fingers steepled. Kama'Zor followed, pushing the cart laden with jars and bottles filled with a dozen ingredients.

K'Marot moved out from under R'Venin's hand and jumped away from the platform, turning to hover in the air. He locked eyes with R'Venin. "Much has changed in nine seasons." He said.

K'Marot dropped to the floor before R'Venin could respond.

Yes. And you don't even know how much.

"Prince R'Venin," Chit'Itsak's oily voice carried through the chamber. "At your leisure."

K'Marot walked away as R'Venin dropped to the ground. "I'll go see what's keeping Father," he said without looking back.

And I'll be here, petitioning the Windfather to heal more than your face.

Chapter Thirty-Six
Alchemy and Treachery

R'Venin dropped to the ground as K'Marot disappeared down the hall, landing behind Kama'Zor facing the storeroom. The guards gave him sidelong glances as they bowed their heads. He took a half-step toward the doors, peering through the narrowing gap. A puff of air, laced with fragrances both familiar and foreign, blew in his face as they groaned shut.

"Shall we prepare for your demonstration?" Chit'Itsak's voice came from the central aisle. "While we wait for the king to arrive?"

"Of course." R'Venin kept his head craned toward the doors as he moved away.

What would I give to spend a full sun alone in Chit'Itsak's storeroom?

In a few strides, R'Venin stood at the cart's side. He examined the containers, picking them up one by one and holding them up to the light or under his nose.

"Why are there so many extras?" He looked back and forth between the master and the apprentice.

Kama'Zor averted his eyes from the handled end, staring at a spot on the floor with rapt attention.

Chit'Itsak stood at the opposite end; his attention focused on straightening an amulet hanging from his neck. The emblem looked alien, though he learned to revere its meaning from his seasons as a hatchling. Four circles, woven from silvervine, each bearing a symbol of alchemy. The missing element seemed to stare at him behind the intersection of mountain, tree, fire, and rain.

It should be right there. In the center. The symbol for Windfather's voice.

"Hmm?" Chit'Itsak mumbled as tugged at the hem of his tunic, spraying bits of Mountain in the air. "What was that your highness?"

"Why are there so many elements here?" R'Venin gestured to the cart. "I only needed four."

"Not to worry, my prince." Chit'Itsak waved his hand in the air as if backhanding an insect. "Standard protocol when I work with an untested potion."

"It's not untested." R'Venin's brow furrowed as he picked up the jar labeled Firestone, pushing it in Chit'Itsak's face. "I've made this potion—and performed the incantation—hundreds of times. I assure you—it works."

"But I haven't proved it, my lord." The Alchemist took the vessel and returned it to the cart. "You may be the king's first son, but I am his master alchemist. It is my duty and privilege to oversee the healing of all his warriors. Especially his sons. I take that responsibility very seriously. So, I assure you I'll err on the side of caution to ensure no one puts our warriors at undue risk. Would you administer a potion based solely on the word of another?"

R'Venin snorted. "Yes." He said, shaking his head. "Under the supervision of one who has. It's called learning." His eyes shifted to Kama'Zor. The apprentice's gaze darted between R'Venin and Chit'Itsak, and then quickly turned to the containers of elements, adjusting them, so their labels all faced the same direction.

Chit'Itsak gave a tight smile, though it never reached his eyes. He stepped around the cart to put himself opposite R'Venin and raised a finger, opening his mouth to speak, but his eyes flew to the entrance over R'Venin's shoulder.

"Your majesty," Chit'Itsak moved away from the cart, bowing at the waist. "Once again, you honor us with your presence."

R'Venin turned to catch sight of the royal guard spilling through the doorway, forming an inward-facing wall along the central aisle, their swords at the ready. Several jumped into the air, taking positions on the platform with spears pointed at the floor. Moments later, K'Rawin strolled into the ward, his eyes locked on R'Venin. K'Marot followed at his flank, staring at a point on the room's far end. The eight clan leaders followed, in order of rank, with only a pair of personal guards each.

"Are you ready, my son?" K'Rawin asked.

K'Marot crossed his arms as the king approached.

"Have you prepared your elements and this... incantation?"

R'Venin came from around the trolley, bending at the waist in front of K'Rawin. "Chit'Itsak and I were just discussing the materials I requested, Father." He turned sideways and gestured to the laden cart.

K'Rawin side-stepped R'Venin and approached the miniature wagon. Kama'Zor moved off to the side and took a knee, head bowed, between two royal guards. "Why so many?" He picked up a topaz-colored decanter, swirling it around. The viscous liquid within sloshed from one side of the flask to the other as if in slow-motion.

"As I was telling the high prince," Chit'Itsak exposed his wings' undersides. "It's our protocol when trying a new potion. I simply wanted them available if something were to go wrong with this experiment."

R'Venin rolled his eyes. "That won't be necessary, *Master Alchemist*." He over-enunciated the title. "As I said before, I've done it many times. I don't see how doing it in front of the council will be any different."

Chit'Itsak shrugged and backed away. "By your leave, my prince."

K'Rawin set the bottle back in place. "Then let's begin."

"Yes, Father." R'Venin nodded and looked at K'Marot, gesturing to the nearest roost. "Have a seat, brother."

"Will I need to disrobe?" K'Marot asked, walking around the king as he returned to his place in the aisle.

"Only if there are scars you'd like healed under your tunic." R'Venin turned to the cart and retrieved a brass pot from the lower shelf.

"Just these." K'Marot presented the side of his face as he sat, adjusting his swords to point behind him.

Settling the bowl on top of a large clay jar, R'Venin opened several containers, sniffed their contents, and relocated them to the lower shelf, making room on top. He examined the rest, arranging his desired materials, in order of use, behind the bowl as he identified each one. Firestone for fire. Seawater for rain. And limplimb for Tree. All he needed was the mountain element.

"Saltriver silt. Where are you?" He mumbled as he flipped the tags over. Finding the labeled container, he opened the lid to expose the dark umber paste. He raised it to his nose and took a quick whiff. His brow knitted over his eyes as he took another, slow and deep.

"Is there a problem, my lord?" Chit'Itsak approached from the side.

"Are you sure this is saltriver silt?" R'Venin held up the jar with one hand, displaying the tag with the other.

Chit'Itsak leaned in and sniffed, a broad smile spreading across his face. "Oh, absolutely, my lord. That is the purest sample of saltriver silt this side of Razorbriar Canyon. Perhaps you're accustomed to the Ch'Hota samples. Their refinement process lends to a... well, less-refined product."

"But it comes from the same quarry, yes?" R'Venin took another lungful. "South of Copperleaf. In the unclaimed territories."

"Where else?" Chit'Itsak held up his palms, waggling his head.

"*Search again.*" A voice whispered in R'Venin's ear.

R'Venin withdrew a sample of the muck with his claw and licked it off.

Could he be right?

R'Venin took another, larger sample, running it around his mouth behind pursed lips as he stuck his nose in the jar.

"Are you in need of a meal, my prince?" Chit'Itsak sniggered. "Should we wait for you to finish sampling everything before we begin? We could summon a banquet from the cook halls, though I don't see how a full belly will affect the outcome of this particular experiment."

Quiet laughter erupted from the council, but a narrow-eyed glare from the king silenced them. "R'Venin?" He growled, his head still facing the clan leaders. "Why do you delay?"

R'Venin met his father's gaze, boring down on him.

Don't embarrass me. That's what he's thinking.

"No delay, father." R'Venin placed the jar in line with the other three. "I'm ready."

K'Rawin held out his hand, gesturing for R'Venin to proceed.

R'Venin took a deep breath, willing the tension in his wings to release, and picked up the jar of Firestone. Tipping the crock, he shook out three rocks—black as a cave on a moonless night—into the bowl. Returning the pot to the cart, he uncovered a small bowl of fire crystals, took one with a pair of steel tongs, and touched it to one of the lumps. Smoke rose from the point of contact until the surface turned to ash, spreading like gray mold. He returned the crystal to its bowl, laying the tongs across the rim.

R'Venin picked up the pot and raised it to his face. With eyes closed, he hummed the incantation. "Nisha'an ko the'ek ka'ro." He took a slow lungful of air and blew softly into the smoldering stone. He repeated the process four more times as the bowl started glowing from within. Waves of soothing heat met his face.

Setting the pot down, he unstopped a bottle of viscous amber liquid. The container rippled in the light. Observing its contents was like looking through slow waters. Tilting the urn, he poured half the contents. Starting in the center, he watched it spiral out until each lump of Firestone had three stripes. The goo sizzled, and then spat dirty yellow smoke into the air.

R'Venin reached with a hand and wafted the billow toward him and sniffed. At the same moment, he could hear deep, nasal inhalations all around him. Though he ignored the audience, an easy smile stretched across his face as he breathed in the aroma.

From the next jar, he pulled a handful of flat, slender leaves. They appeared freshly plucked, as instructed, and supple to the touch. He weaved the blades into a square the size of his palm and set it atop the smoldering pot. He then took another handful, twisted them into a rough length of twine, and hammered it on his thigh, fraying the end.

As the smoke waned under the woven lid, he grabbed the jar of saltriver silt.

"*Search again.*" The thought poked at his mind. R'Venin held it up to his nose and sniffed.

This is the right element. Surely Chit'Itsak knows what he's doing.

"*Search again.*" The image of the lowest shelf flitted at the edges of his thoughts.

Murmurs filtered through the ranks as the clan leaders talked behind their hands. R'Venin looked over at K'Marot, who held up a hand to his mouth and yawned. "Any sun will do."

R'Venin glanced at K'Rawin. The king stood motionless, but his eyes were narrowed and pinned to the right. His head cocked slightly, listening to the whispers behind him.

I don't have time to search again.

R'Venin scraped his brush across the contents and set the jar down. Then lifting the woven cover, he scooped a glob of the sticky paste and moved to K'Marot.

Holding the potion up, he held out his other hand. "I promise this won't hurt."

K'Marot nodded, turning away. R'Venin held him by the chin and dabbed the concoction across all three scars.

K'Marot blinked, wiping paste off his eyelid. "How long until it starts working?"

"It's almost immediate." R'Venin crouched beside the roost, setting his brush on the floor, focusing hard on K'Marot's face.

K'Marot tilted his head from side to side, his neck cracking. Then his scarred eye twitched. Then again. "What is this?" He flinched away as if dodging a stave and held his hand up to his face like a claw. "You said it wouldn't hurt." He pulled at the neck of his tunic, craning his head as if to escape an invisible stranglehold and howled. "Aargh!"

"R'Venin, what's happening?" K'Rawin barked, stepping closer. "What have you done?"

"Is this how Pra'Acheen alchemy is supposed to work?" Chit'Itsak asked from over R'Venin's shoulder.

"I don't understand." R'Venin spun back to the cart. "I've done this incantation hundreds of times."

"Perhaps you're not as gifted an alchemist as you claimed." Chit'Itsak oozed under his breath, but loud enough for R'Venin to hear.

Apprentices swarmed K'Marot, struggling to pin him down while the other healers applied salves and balms. R'Venin caught sight of his face reddening and the scars opening wide. K'Marot's screams filling the chamber. He thrashed against the weight of a dozen men, cursing to the sky.

"*Search again, R'Venin.*" The thought stabbed R'Venin through the hearts.

R'Venin glanced over Chit'Itsak's shoulder, ignoring his narrow-slitted eyes, and caught sight of Kama'Zor's averted gaze. The apprentice looked aghast, his eyes darting between the cart, Chit'Itsak, and the fray surrounding K'Marot. He lifted his foot a handspan off the floor and tapped a crock on the lowest shelf.

R'Venin looked back and caught a smirk pulling at the corner of the master alchemist's mouth. "You did this." He pointed his finger and yelled.

"Did what?" Chit'Itsak's eyes widened as he held out his hands. "How could I have done this to your brother? You selected the elements. Added them. Mumbled nonsense. It is you who have betrayed your flock with unsanctioned alchemy."

K'Marot's profanity-laced agony rumbled through the chamber.

R'Venin shoved Chit'Itsak aside, rushing for the cart. He bent over and reached for the unlabeled jar Kama'Zor tapped with his foot, letting the lid fall to the shelf. It held another dark umber paste, identical to the previous mountain element. He raised it to his face, the fragrance rising to his nasal slits.

This is pure silt. I smell it now.

He grabbed the container labeled saltriver Silt and inhaled. K'Marot's howling pounding in his ears.

What did I use?

He took a quick noseful of each jar, going back and forth between them.

"What's in here?" He said to himself.

"That's silt." Chit'Itsak balked over his shoulder;, his silky voice laced with contempt. "Just as your list prescribed, my prince."

"No." R'Venin's brow knit tight, taking another breath of each jar. "It's more than that. There's something else. It's..."

His eyes flew wide as he spun around. The jar labeled silt tumbled from R'Venin's hand and shattered on the floor as he grabbed a fistful of Chit'Itsak's tunic and pulled him neb to neb. "How could you?" He growled, shoving him away.

The master alchemist backpedaled, his arms and wings flailing wild as he tumbled into an empty nest.

R'Venin tore a handful of paste from the vessel still in his hand and dropped it on the cart. Lunging for the brass bowl, he smooshed the pure silt into the contents and kneaded them. Heat spread quickly through the concoction, warming his hands to the point of blistering. Then, cupped palms, he carried the slime to K'Marot.

"Get off him," R'Venin yelled. "Get out of the way."

The healers and apprentices rolled off the nest but kept hold of K'Marot's arms and legs, stretching him like fresh sweetsap. R'Venin dodged around K'Rawin, who hadn't budged from his position; standing over K'Marot with arms crossed, his mouth pinched tight.

R'Venin fell beside K'Marot, smearing the hot sludge into his face and neck. He whispered the incantation. "Nisha'an ko the'ek ka'ro."

K'Marot's thrashing abated instantly, dissipating with the heat. He closed his eyes as his breathing became slow and even.

"I'm so sorry, brother." R'Venin choked between incantations. "I should have been more cautious."

Murmured conversations grew around the scene. R'Venin looked up, finding a hundred eyes darting in his direction. He locked onto one pair.

"Father. I..." R'Venin started.

K'Rawin raised a hand. "Explain." He said as the tumult faded to silence.

R'Venin drew a slow breath.

Will he blame me?

"One of the ingredients was tainted." R'Venin sighed. "K'Marot was poisoned."

Unintelligible words erupted from all directions, drowning out Chit'Itsak's words as he shuffled closer to the king. R'Venin lifted K'Marot's head off the nest, grabbed a cloth from a pail of water at the roost's side, and wiped his face. The rag became stained with what looked like dung after a few strokes. An apprentice carried another pail from the nearby roost and handed R'Venin the soaked towel.

"Explain." The king repeated. Chit'Itsak opened his mouth to speak, but K'Rawin cut him off with a wave.

"The silt..." R'Venin took the third towel from another apprentice. "The saltriver silt, that I was assured was pure, had been laced with freshwater mud. By itself, it's harmless, but when you mix it with irontree sap, it becomes corrosive. It opened K'Marot's wounds instead of sealing them."

"It was your mixture that did this." Chit'Itsak barked from the side, then turned to K'Rawin. "My king. Please accept my humble apologies. I should never have yielded to the prince's enthusiasm. I think I've proven myself over the seasons as more than capable of healing our warriors. I mean no disrespect, but I've given my hearts over to the study of alchemy. My devotion is more than mere dalliance or a hobby. Can your son say the same? My knowledge of alchemy is unrivaled in the spires."

K'Rawin nodded and faced Chit'Itsak. He let his arms drop, took his mace from the hook at his belt, and tapped it against his leg. "Then how do you explain how quickly R'Venin identified the corrupted element and resolved it? Are you suggesting he intentionally caused K'Marot's wounds to reopen? To what end?"

Chit'Itsak blanched, his eyes widening as he backed a feather's depth away. "Your majesty?"

K'Rawin moved to the roost, looking down at his sons. "Even as we gaze, K'Marot's scars are disappearing with each swipe of the cloth. Is there something special about the fabric? Explain, master alchemist."

Chit'Itsak's mouth formed the beginning of words, inaudible under the slosh of water and shuffling feet.

"Are you incompetent?" K'Rawin's words hung in the air.

"Of course not, your majesty," Chit'Itsak balked. "I was Master Vig'Yaan's chief apprentice for twenty seasons before he flew to the eternal tree. He taught me everything he knew."

"A fraud, then." The king stepped away from the nest, circling his master alchemist.

"Your majesty!" Chit'Itsak put his hand to his chest. "After these many seasons, after everything I've done to preserve you and your seed, how can you ask me that?"

K'Rawin stopped behind Chit'Itsak, his back as stiff as the spires. "A traitor?"

"Never, my lord." Chit'Itsak spun around and fell to his face, his wings up and exposed. "I have only ever sought to serve you and your greatness. I improved the treatment for—."

A rumble stirred on the outskirts of the room. K'Rawin sneered, his grip tightening around his scepter.

"—your condition, my lord. Is it not more potent than my predecessor's?"

"If your loyalty isn't in question," K'Rawin resumed pacing around his servant. "Then we're back to competence or chicanery. Did you not say you would assist my son yourself?"

"Yes, your majesty."

K'Rawin circled, tapping his scepter on his leg in rhythm with his stride. "Did you delegate that assistance to one of the other healers? Or one of your apprentices?" He waved his mace at Kama'Zor. "To your chief apprentice, here? Kama'Zor, is it?"

Kama'Zor nodded as he bowed his head and exposed his wings' undersides.

Chit'Itsak licked his lips. "Of course not, your majesty."

"Then, who prepared the elements for my son?"

The master alchemist swallowed hard. "It was I, your highness. I prepared them." He suddenly pointed his finger at his chief apprentice. "But Kama'Zor was in the stores with me. And, I admit, I wasn't watching him closely. He had plenty of opportunities to pollute any number of elements when my back was turned. Admit your crimes, you filthy weak-winged traitor."

Kama'Zor's eyes widened. He fell to his knees, exposing his wings further. "No, your majesty. I would never..."

K'Rawin circled Chit'Itsak again, his scepter keeping a steady tempo. "So, my faithful alchemist," He growled. "Which is it? Did you make a mistake, or did your apprentice do it behind your eyes? Was it hubris or inattentiveness that led to the disaster my first son corrected?"

R'Venin finished cleaning K'Marot's face. The scars, gone but for pale stripes of new skin yet to be tanned by days in the sun. "Father," he said, letting K'Marot's head roll off his arm and onto a pillow. "If I may?"

K'Rawin pursed his lips, nodded, and returned to a spot between his guards. He crossed his arms, tapping his shoulder with the scepter as his eyes shot fire in the alchemists' direction.

R'Venin walked passed Chit'Itsak and stood before the chief apprentice. "Kama'Zor."

The apprentice looked up, his eyes wide, his shoulders visibly trembling. "What is the punishment for accusing your superior regardless if it's true or false? What can be done to you by even uttering the words?"

Kama'Zor swallowed. His wings held high but shaking. "At best, exile. Forced to beg for food or flee to the borderlands." His voice barely penetrated the first ring of onlookers. "At worst, I could be clipped and cast off the Spires. Unable to fly to the eternal tree upon my death."

"What recourse do you have to prove a false witness?"

Kama'Zor's head dropped. "None, my lord. I have no voice against a superior."

R'Venin pursed his lips and moved to stand before Chit'Itsak. "Master Alchemist," he said, meeting the eyes of the crowd. "What is the punishment for accusing your superior, regardless if it's true or false? What can be done to you by even uttering the words?"

"You know our custom, my lord." His voice was quiet but hard. "It is as my fool of an apprentice has said."

"What recourse do you have to prove a false witness?"

"None, my lord." He glanced up and met R'Venin's gaze. "But what witness lies at your feet? Kama'Zor has accused me of nothing."

R'Venin turned away from the alchemist and folded his hands behind his back. "I accuse you."

Hissed conversations surrounded R'Venin like a den of whispers.

"Your majesty, how can you allow this?" Chit'Itsak's voice rose in pitch. "Have I ever been anything but loyal to you?"

The swish of metal brought R'Venin's attention around to find the alchemist bowing before K'Rawin, his arms held out. The royal guard on either side pointed their spears into Chit'Itsak's face and held their shields in front of the king.

K'Rawin pushed their shields apart and pointed his scepter at R'Venin. "Continue," he growled, his eyes locked on his physician.

"I accuse you, Master Chit'Itsak," R'Venin moved, putting himself between the alchemist and his apprentice. "I accuse you of tampering with the elements, of sabotaging K'Marot's treatment and casting the blame on Kama'Zor. Do you confess or deny?"

Chit'Itsak's jaw dropped as he put a hand to his hearts. "I most certainly deny. My fidelity to the king is beyond question."

"Kama'Zor," R'Venin spun on his heel. "Did you handle any of the elements, while you were alone with Master Chit'Itsak, inside the storeroom?"

"No, my prince." Kama'Zor looked up, shaking his head. "He took containers off the shelves, prepared them at the workbench, and then had me place them in the cart."

"Did you know what was in each vessel?"

"Yes." He leaned slightly, peering around R'Venin. "As Master Chit'Itsak handed me each ingredient, I opened each lid and inspected the contents, so I knew where on the cart they belonged. He's particular about how he wants the elements arranged."

"I noticed that when I was foraging for the ones I'd asked for." R'Venin said, looking over his shoulder. Chit'Itsak was still kneeling before K'Rawin in a beggar's position with his eyes on the floor. "Tell me about the jar on the bottom shelf. Why wasn't it labeled like all the others?"

"I wondered that myself. When I asked, Master Chit'Itsak told me if I didn't know, I wasn't qualified to be his chief apprentice."

"Deceiver," Chit'Itsak hissed. "He lies to cover his deceit. Every container I gave him had a label scratched with my own claw. He must've switched the tag to the contaminated silt when I wasn't looking."

"Then how did he poison the vessel?" R'Venin turned. "You told me that no one is allowed to handle your stores but you."

"He must've had it on his person when he followed me in." Chit'Itsak risked a glance up to the king.

"How would he have known what elements I planned to use to taint them?" R'Venin threw out his arms. "I didn't even tell you until I wrote them on the slate. Are you calling him a seer?"

"Certainly not," Chit'Itsak spat. "There are no seers on the Granite Spires. True seers are a myth."

"Then tell me, Master Alchemist..." R'Venin overemphasized his title again. "...how does a lowly apprentice that you say is incapable of finding anything without your help, with no foreknowledge of the potion, and no access to the list, have the foresight to bring the precise element that turned the cure into a curse?"

The murmurs throughout the chamber grew like floodwater spilling over a dam.

"Face your accuser, alchemist," K'Rawin growled, using his scepter to raise Chit'Itsak's face and push it around.

Chit'Itsak shuffled on the floor until he knelt before R'Venin. His wings up and exposed, his arms outstretched, and his eyes burning.

"I accuse you," R'Venin breathed, getting down on one knee, "of poisoning the heir apparent and laying false witness against a subordinate. Do you confess or deny?"

Chit'Itsak's mouth pinched as he fought against the words. "I confess. My prince."

With a lightning stroke, K'Rawin sideswiped Chit'Itsak's wing. The snap of bone quickly followed by the alchemist's howls. His shoulder joint spasmed, tugging at stretching flesh as the broken limb fell limp to the floor. A second swipe brought down its twin. K'Rawin stepped forward, standing on the splayed feathers, and raised his mace with both hands, eyes targeting Chit'Itsak's head.

"Father! Wait!" R'Venin stood, holding out his hands.

K'Rawin's eyes blazed. "You expect me to let him live after what he did to my son? Your brother?"

"In death, he learns nothing." R'Venin took a half-step back and bowed. Chit'Itsak clawed at the floor, wailing.

K'Rawin jabbed a finger down at the injured V'Jeeta as he glared at the crowd. "He becomes a warning for those who would betray me." He then turned on the spot, pointing at the onlookers.

"There's another message here. One stronger than fear," R'Venin spoke with confidence.

"Mercy?" K'Rawin sneered. "Your brother told me about your conversation."

"Mercy saved my life. Mercy allowed me to learn the cure for White Claw. Mercy brought me home to cure our people. Fear didn't do any of that," his first son insisted.

"And if I let you show this traitor mercy, then what? Would you allow him to remain in his position as Master Alchemist? Grant him clemency for his crimes?"

"No, father." R'Venin bowed, holding his hands to his hearts. "I would recommend demotion. Assign him as an assistant healer in the dungeons."

Chit'Itsak suddenly stopped moaning and locked eyes with R'Venin.

"One can learn much in the service of other outcasts," he said to Chit'Itsak.

"Very well." K'Rawin stomped on Chit'Itsak's broken wing and spun on his heel. His guard closed ranks around him as he stormed off.

"Father, I have one more request," R'Venin called as the king reached the threshold.

K'Rawin stopped in mid-stride, glancing behind him, his wings tight to his body.

"Allow me to heal him."

"You would do that?" Kama'Zor whispered. "You would heal a traitor?"

Without taking his eyes away from K'Rawin, R'Venin nodded. "I would heal any child of Vi'Jeet if it meant bringing peace to the spires."

"What of the cure?" K'Rawin said over his shoulder. "Are you still confident you can heal our people of White Claw?"

"Yes, father." R'Venin caught the eyes in the room. All fixed on him.

K'Rawin strode from the chamber, but his voice echoed from the corridor. "Then do as you please."

The council members filed out in the same order they entered, flanked by their guards. Once all but K'Marot, Kama'Zor, Chit'Itsak, the healers, and apprentices, left the ward, R'Venin exhaled.

He pointed to a pair of apprentices. "See to K'Marot's needs when he rouses. He'll be hungry. The rest of you, get Chit'Itsak on a roost, face down. Quickly please."

Holding out his hand, Kama'Zor took it and stood. "Thank you, my prince." His voice trembled like his hands. "Thank you. I pledge my spirit to you. I am your servant until death."

"I accept your pledge." R'Venin shook his hand. "And I need your assistance. Do you think you can find the elements I'll need to fix wings?"

Kama'Zor let a guilty smile spread across his face. "Better than Master Chit'Itsak," he whispered.

"Excellent." He squeezed Kama'Zor's shoulder. "And then I'll need your help to prepare the cure for White Claw."

The Tears of Vi'Jeet

Ka'Ala leaned against a column, her form a dark silhouette against the perforated stone. She stared toward the northern horizon as she toyed with a curtain between her fingers. "After that," Ka'Ala sighed, "I was all alone."

"Just a hatchling?" B'Luren said, kneeling at the organ. A music scroll fell from her hand, unraveling as it tumbled off a pillow.

Ka'Ala craned her head, nodding as she met the princess's gaze. "A season or two older than Ja'Ven. I knew how to fly; shift my colors. Hunt. Not much else."

"By Windfather's grace, you survived on your own," Queen P'Vrit spoke from her seat at the center table.

Ka'Ala released the drape as she turned around, leaving it to dance with the evening breeze. "Indeed." She snaked her way between tables and cushions, returning to the pillow beside P'Vrit. "He was my only companion for more moons than I care to imagine."

Music returned to the chamber. Ka'Ala glanced over to see B'Luren giving the capstan one last crank on the handle and then crossing the room to join the others.

"Perhaps that is why you're so attuned to his voice." P'Vrit reached for a pitcher, refilling a trio of gilded chalices on the same tray. She set the carafe down and pushed the plate closer to Ka'Ala.

Ka'Ala took the goblet nearest her, nodding her thanks. The scent of wine swirled in the air under her nasal slits. She took a sip as B'Luren grabbed a cup as she circled P'Vrit, settling onto a cushion.

"A gift I would spend the rest of my sunrises to acquire." B'Luren breathed into her goblet.

"I did." Ka'Ala laughed through her nose, then stared into her glass, her smile fading. "But I can't imagine my life without his voice in my hearts."

"To have the Windfather as a constant companion…" P'Vrit trailed off as she took the third glass and raised it. "What greater treasure would there be?"

The others tapped their cups to hers as the sound of metal doors scraped against wood. Ka'Ala twisted around when the veils hiding the vestibule billowed into the chamber. She shifted her colors back to match the queen and princess, and then the doors groaned open.

Nau'Ka Ra'Anee entered the chamber, parting the curtains and holding a scroll tied with an emerald ribbon. "May I enter, your highness?" She said from the other side of the veil.

"Come in." P'Vrit waved her hand.

Nau'Ka pushed through the fabric and took a knee.

"A summons from the king, your majesty." Nau'Ka bowed her head, exposing her wings' undersides.

P'Vrit glanced at B'Luren and nodded as she took a sip.

The princess got up, setting her goblet down and weaved through the tables. When she got to the servant, she took the scroll from her outstretched hand. "Thank you, Nau'Ka."

Nau'Ka stood and backed out of the room, bent at the waist. The doors thudded behind the veils as B'Luren carried the scroll between the tables.

"What does it say?" P'Vrit returned her chalice to the tray.

B'Luren stopped midstride, unraveled the ribbon, and let the scroll fall open. "We've been summoned to the sacred pools."

She kept reading; her eyes widening as her lips moved. Suddenly, her hand flew to her mouth. "He did it." She whispered between her fingers. "R'Venin did it."

"Did what?" P'Vrit stood, crossing the room.

Ka'Ala heard B'Luren's hearts singing as she stood and followed the queen.

B'Luren held out the scroll for P'Vrit. The queen took it and quickly scanned the page, her song rising to a triumphant crescendo by the time she finished reading.

"He never doubted, did he?" The queen's eyes misted over.

B'Luren and P'Vrit pulled each other close, laughing through tears, and then pulled Ka'Ala into their embrace. For the length of a song, Ka'Ala let the royal ladies make her a part of their celebration. On an unspoken signal, the three each took a step back while holding each other by the hands.

"Glory to the Windfather for favoring my first son." P'Vrit sang to the ceiling. "This day will bring peace to our flock, and all of Pirth'Vee Grah."

Ka'Ala squeezed the queen's hand.

"R'Venin convinced the king to let him heal the White Claw," Ka'Ala breathed, "Didn't he?"

* * *

Three songs later, Ka'Ala followed behind P'Vrit and B'Luren as they descended a carved staircase in hooded robes. P'Vrit wore her cowl draped across the top of her head, held in place by her crown. B'Luren wore hers the same, carrying the scroll, bound with a scarlet ribbon matching their cloaks. Slits on either side of the floor-length gowns opened to the hip with each step, exposing bare feet and legs. Togs kept the robe from revealing everything from neck to knees.

Even in this heat, I don't see why protocol dictates against a modest tunic, Ka'Ala thought. *Not even a breechcloth. Why is it so hot down here?*

Breathing heavily, Ka'Ala fanned her face. Her neck glistened like a jeweled choker melting toward her chest. Damp footprints along the stone path evaporated before her eyes. A sudden draft blasted open the slits of Ka'Ala's robe, giving her temporary relief.

Stone steps turned, fell, and rose as if the architect couldn't decide which direction to take from one sun to the next. Ka'Ala ran her hand along the jagged and pock-marked wall, as she squinted to see by the light of recessed fire-crystal sconces.

Behind her, a score of the kings' wives and concubines in identical robes trudged along like a royal train of sap. With their heads lowered, their eyes were hidden behind garnet veils.

The royal guard, split between their entourage's lead and trailing edge, rattled like endless cooking pots falling off shelves. Spear tips and shields scraped the walls and ceilings at frequent choke points along the path.

"How old is this staircase?" Ka'Ala said under her breath. "It looks ancient."

"Windfather carved many of these tunnels," P'Vrit whispered, smiling over her shoulder. "With rivers of liquid stone. During the first suns of Pirth'Vee Grah. The first kings carved the steps. This is the only path that leads to the sacred pools. It is forbidden to pass by her tears from the sky."

"Whose tears?" Ka'Ala hissed in B'Luren's ear from behind.

B'Luren paused a half-step. "The fourth daughter of Be'Tee. The Mother of Fire."

"Of course." Ka'Ala fell back in place. "Vi'Jeet."

B'Luren's shadow sharpened as they came around a bend. Ka'Ala looked up to catch the front guard disappearing into an oval of blinding light. Raising her hand, she squinted as another gust hit her in the face like the blast of an opened kiln. The sound of rushing water from the other side of the opening filled her ears.

B'Luren turned her head and spoke just louder than the din as they reached a landing. A wingspan beyond the final step, the tunnel sloped down into a luminous chamber. All she could see was a dazzling glow off the floor. "Don't say a word, not even if someone addresses you directly. Mother will speak for us."

Ka'Ala nodded as B'Luren crouched and disappeared straight into the light.

Windfather, be with me, Ka'Ala thought as she took a breath.

Always, daughter. He breathed. *Always.*

She bent at the knees, her wingtips brushing the floor as she bowed her head to clear the opening. Squinting against the light, she followed the red blur of B'Luren a wingspan ahead. Keeping B'Luren in her field of vision, Ka'Ala focused on the chamber coming slowly into view.

An enormous dome stretched out like the sky. Ten evenly spaced columns, carved to resemble pillars of fire and adorned with silvervine and precious gems, rose to the apex, branching like vines between oculi of various shapes and sizes. The shadows dusting the tops revealed gaps between the dome and its supposed supports. The largest opening gleamed like the high sun. The shaft—polished smooth like a reflecting glass—led to the unseen sky above.

Tiered levels, surfaces etched in various patterns, divided the room into rings and segments. Hundreds of gilded perches projected at regular intervals, concealed between half-moon shaped alcoves, with curtains that shimmered like Silver Silk.

This has to be twice the size of the Hiding Falls.

The floor seemed vast as a prairie. The four tiers, each one ten wingspans deep and one high, rose toward the middle, hiding something in the center.

Between the two columns opposite the tunnel from which she'd emerged, a pair of waterfalls spewed from the eyes of a massive sculpture thrusting out from the stone face of a woman. Her wings spread around the cavern, symbolizing a protective mother gathering her brood. Despite rushing waters, the statue's eyes were as unyielding as they were beautiful. An expression like the stone from which she protruded.

The Tears of Vi'Jeet.

Before she knew it, Ka'Ala had flapped past the row of pillars and up to the third terrace behind B'Luren. She flew to the highest level, twenty paces from the roar of water, and where the falls led into a basin twenty wingspans in diameter. The falls churned the pool to mist along its edges, making the surface roil like the ocean during a thunderstorm. The pool swirled toward an opening near the center, a natural drain—with another waterfall disappearing below the bath.

She followed B'Luren to the terrace's edge, turning a half wingspan before the lip, and fell in line with the others circling the drop-off. She looked off the side after a few more paces and caught sight of a crowd huddled at the pool's edge. The king stood in the center, surrounded by warriors she recognized from the cliffs upon their approach. Next to the king, shoulder to shoulder, stood K'Marot. Both were gazing intently at a V'Jeeta hunched over a wagon. Ka'Ala's hearts skipped.

R'Venin.

R'Venin looked up at the same moment, smiling. He raised his hand high above his head when their eyes met. K'Marot followed his brother's gaze, his brow furrowing as he glanced back and forth between R'Venin and Ka'Ala. The dark symphony played again in Ka'Ala's mind.

"You are safe. But be wary," Windfather breathed.

As she refocused on R'Venin, his heartsong grew in her mind. Even from a distance, she caught his eye, taking her in from tips to talons.

Oh, Windfather. Is it wrong to tempt his gaze? Do I dare? Would Ja'Naam forgive me if she knew?

His hearts are free, Windfather breathed.

With her hearts racing, she set her weight on one leg and extended the other through the slit in her robe. As she did, his song changed—lowering in pitch and rising in tempo—then turned sorrowful and back again.

* * *

R'Venin swallowed hard as his gaze lingered on Ka'Ala, half-concealed in the scarlet robe, the way it draped across her shoulders. The gown exposed his favorite parts of a woman's neck and teased to reveal the pouch flap across her abdomen.

Ja'Naam carried my seed there. Ja'Ven's egg hatched there. It's been less than a moon. How can I even consider... But if I don't, what would Father say? What would he do? To her? If I fail to take her as my mate?

"Is there a problem, son?" The King slapped R'Venin's shoulder and followed his gaze. He started laughing. "Oh, I see, a distraction worthy of my heir. But now's not the time for distractions, is it?"

R'Venin dragged his gaze away from Ka'Ala. "No, Father." R'Venin cleared his throat. "I'm ready to proceed. Kama'Zor? Let him through, please."

The chief apprentice squeezed himself between a pair of royal guards. "Thank you, your majesty. Everything you listed appears to be here."

"Of course, it's all there," K'Marot growled, his eyes still focused on the women lining the upper terrace. "My warriors are loyal to a fault." He turned to stare at Kama'Zor. "Unlike some."

"Forgive me, Prince K'Marot." Kama'Zor took a knee. "I meant no insult."

"It's not Kama'Zor's fault, Chit'Itsak sabotaged your treatment, brother." R'Venin stepped between the two. "He's done nothing to earn your distrust."

"Yet." K'Marot sneered and moved away, absentmindedly rubbing his cheek where his scars once appeared.

"Then, let's begin." K'Rawin turned sideways, opening a hole through the crowd by pointing his scepter at the falls. "You may command anyone here to assist you. Except me, of course."

The council and entourage laughed at the king's jest as if on cue.

"I'll need the wagon closer to the falls." R'Venin leaned into the wagon's back end. Kama'Zor picked up the wagon's tongue, pulling to no avail.

All eyes stared as several whispered behind their hands.

"What are you waiting for?" K'Rawin bellowed. "Do as my son tells you, or I'll have your wings for sunshades."

The clan leaders gestured for their guards to assist. Within moments, the wagon creaked to the edge and into the pool a few wingspans from the billowing water.

We've already got the eruption from a ground spout. The falls come from a natural spring somewhere behind the dome's face.

"Carry the stalks of limplimb to the falls," R'Venin shouted over the water. "Braid them into a ring that encompasses the upper and lower falls. Kama'Zor, you and the other apprentices will recite the incantation with me. I'll tell you so we can proceed as soon as the ring is in place."

As the stalks hit the water, those braiding turned their faces away, gagging and coughing. A few onlookers covered their noses with a pair of fingers, while others moved further from the water. A few clan leaders even flew to other terraces to watch.

R'Venin took in a noseful and nodded. He then waved the others into the water as the scent of rotting flesh, laced with the anal spray of a stinkstripe, filled the air. Drawing them into a tight circle, he whispered into each of their ears. Then they whispered back. He repeated the process until each one knew the words correctly. He looked over his shoulder as their loop neared completion.

"Gather around the ring," he said, wading from the shallows. The stalk-bearers, knee-deep in the water, ignored his approach. "Evenly spaced," he said, pointing to spots around the pool. "With your wings aloft and arms out. Those not part of the incantation can remain in the water but must be outside our circle. I'll finish the ring before we begin."

He walked up behind a warrior, tapping his shoulder. The man dropped the unbraided ends into the water and walked away, taking a breath once he'd cleared the water's edge. R'Venin took the strands—breathing through his mouth—and wove the ends together before setting them back in the pool. He stepped back, measuring their spacing, and gestured for the apprentices to move closer. Once they were all in position, he raised his wings and started reciting the words.

"Saph'ed pan'jon ko cha'anga."

The apprentices copied him, and then together, they repeated the phrase four more times. As they did, the loop of stalks spun around in the opposite direction of the lower falls, building up speed until the water within the coil was still as a morning lake.

The crowd gathering just beyond the water gawked and pointed fingers, not bothering to hide their conversations. The foul odor had disappeared as if frozen like the surface.

"You'll want to be out of the water for this next part." R'Venin strode away from the depths, followed closely by Kama'Zor, dripping across the stone as he exited the shallows. The other apprentices made their way out of the pool to the closest dry spot they could find.

"What next?" Kama'Zor shook out his robes next to the wagon.

"The electhium." R'Venin patted a sack from near the front end. It was the size of a child's roost—one wingspan in length and twice that in circumference. "Take an end. We'll hover over the center and pour the contents between the falls."

Kama'Zor nodded, taking a corner. It didn't budge, so he jumped onto the wagon's rail and tried again with two hands. It hardly shifted.

"I'm sorry, your highness." Kama'Zor wheezed. "I lack the strength. Perhaps with a few others..."

"Two must do it." R'Venin sighed. "No more."

R'Venin looked over to K'Marot, leaning against the back of the wagon and staring up into the dome.

"Brother?" R'Venin moved closer. "K'Marot, will you help me?"

K'Marot rubbed a hand against his cheek, then leaned away from the wagon. R'Venin kept pace as he moved toward the front end. When each hand gripped a handful of the sack, R'Venin nodded.

They rose slowly off the ground with labored wing beats, moving toward the ring like a poorly coordinated dance between waring branchclimbers. Once between the falls, R'Venin kicked out against the bag with his foot talons to no effect. K'Marot also swiped at the sack, gaining a finger-sized hole. Again R'Venin kicked, then K'Marot, yet the bag remained mostly intact.

"Warriors!" K'Marot bellowed between labored breaths. "Slice the belly of this beast."

K'Marot's guards approached the pool's edge, lifting their spears to eye level and drawing back.

"Make sure... you're not... in the water... when the electhium falls," R'Venin shouted.

The guards backed out of the pool and loosed their spears.

The first spear pierced the bag, a hand span from the bottom. Yellow crystals trickled from either side. The water below exploded with each nugget. Bolts of lightning shot through the air and sparked across the surface. The second spear grazed the bottom, opening the sack as if gutting a freshly caught runnerhound. R'Venin and K'Marot pulled against one another, splitting the bag in two and sending the brothers flying opposite directions.

The crystals tumbled into the pool, launching plumes of lightning to the sky. A column of foam followed, extruding like fresh clay from a press. Everyone watching backed away from the expected splash zone, but the sparking fluid remained within an invisible cylinder. The foam expelled its gas until there was only a thin layer resting within the ring. Those closest to the water closed their eyes as they could not avoid inhaling lungfuls through their nasal slits, waving the air toward their faces. It carried the odor of fertile soil. The kind only found when chasing sleepbreathers into a burrow. Sweet and appealing, inviting inexperienced hunters to their deaths.

"Now," R'Venin landed by the wagon, gulping lungfuls of air and turning to Kama'Zor. "The final ingredient. Amycite. Once we start pouring it in, I'll need a dozen or so people around the ring to help me fan the column to the right until every last V'Jeeta who needs the cure flies through. All they need to do is take five deep breaths, and the potion will take effect. If we stop, if the vortex dies, then so does the cure."

"What about those who can't fly?" Kama'Zor wrung the water from his sleeve.

"They can be aided by those who can. The fumes won't harm the unaffected." R'Venin adjusted a sack, wrapping a handful of fabric around his hand. "Or they can walk into the pool. The electhium has dissipated. There's no more danger."

R'Venin hefted the sack over his shoulder and turned. "Father, it would honor me if you would be the first to receive the cure. Lead the way to peace across the land."

K'Rawin pursed his lips, nodding. Then without a word, he let his scepter thunk to the ground. "Bring my armorists. Get me out of this."

R'Venin smiled and looked over at K'Marot. "Everyone grab a bag. Let's make a chain."

One by one, the bags changed hands until they reached R'Venin. Slitting each sack open with his talon, he poured the pink dust into the water. No odor escaped the circle. The surface appeared smooth as glass, but an invisible current swept the powder to his right. A plum-colored smoke trail rose from the spot directly in front of R'Venin. It grew like a vine and followed a path around the circle. When it reached its starting point, it climbed upon itself, making a second layer. Then a third and fourth, until it reached the dome's apex. R'Venin grazed his hand through the mist. Tiny trails swirled around his fingers before returning to the cloud.

With Kama'Zor on his left, a circle of apprentices and healers surrounded the ring, waving their right wings in sync. Through the mist, R'Venin could only make out the others' shadows, keeping time with their rhythm.

"This is the last sack." One of the royal guards approached, carrying the bag over his shoulder.

"Thank you," R'Venin took the pouch and sliced it open, glancing back. "Father, are you ready?"

"Of course." He stood at the water's edge, stripped down to his breechcloth. Both of his wing talons were like chalk. His skin sagged off his rib cage, and the feathers previously covered by his armor bore the telling signs of advanced White Claw, ashy and dried out. His eyes focused on the water. His mouth pinched in a tight line.

The surrounding council glared at the king through narrow lids. Smirks and sneers toyed at their lips. Their wings stiffened as an armorist held out the king's scepter.

Their loyalty is contingent on their fear. R'Venin thought. *If this doesn't work...*

The king pushed it away, shaking his head.

K'Rawin took a step and leaped. After one flap, he collapsed into the water. Murmurs died as quickly as they started as his guard took up a protective circle around him. Though mostly hidden from view because of the entourage, R'Venin could still see him struggling to his feet.

No one in the chamber moved. A few dared breathe.

R'Venin shifted his weight as if to leave his position but stopped himself. "I believe it would be beneficial if we recite the incantation again." He tossed the last empty bag to a nearby warrior. "Kama'Zor, will you join me?"

Kama'Zor made eye contact. "Yes, your majesty."

"Saph'ed pan'jon ko cha'anga." R'Venin started.

"Saph'ed pan'jon ko cha'anga," Kama'Zor added his voice.

"Saph'ed pan'jon ko cha'anga." The other apprentices came in.

"Saph'ed pan'jon ko cha'anga." The healers mumbled, catching on with the rhythm.

"Saph'ed pan'jon ko cha'anga." Every person in the circle sang out in full voice in sync with their wing beats.

K'Rawin leaped one more time, his wing joints popping with each beat. He grunted through every movement until he crossed the invisible barrier. His flapping ceased as the vortex carried him higher, his shape relaxing as he reached the apex.

K'Rawin's shadow then spasmed, flinched, and spun as he seemed held in place by strings. Suddenly, he pulled his wings in tight and fell.

"Father!" R'Venin shouted, not hearing any other voice calling to their king. Then to the circle. "Don't stop, no matter what."

K'Rawin pierced the vortex, shooting over their heads like a wandering star. The royal guard, the council, and the harem let out gasps of wonder as he flapped hard, gaining altitude and weaving between the columns at a speed R'Venin had never seen his father achieve.

As quickly as he left the vortex, he landed within the circle of his guard. Between the escorts, R'Venin could see his father shaking. The warriors stepped away, revealing their king in the throes of gut-busting laughter. The man now standing in the water, shaking his fists in triumph to the air, could have passed as R'Venin's twin.

His skin, no longer sagging, but tight over muscles that had weakened with age. His feathers, dark and soft like fresh bark. His eyes, still razorbriar sharp, carried a twinkle R'Venin hadn't seen since he was a hatchling. And his wing talons, gleamed like obsidian knives, their tips sharp enough to pierce any armor.

"Father?" R'Venin sloshed through the water. "How do you feel?"

"How do I feel?" K'Rawin tipped his head back and laughed over the din of the waterfall. "I could rebuild our armies in one season myself. Tell my harem to prepare themselves. I could seed every pouch in this kingdom."

The council and entourage laughed and applauded.

"Then let's get the rest of our people with White Claw in the vortex," R'Venin shouted, a broad smile on his face. "As long as we keep the vortex going, we can cure everyone. We can stop this plague. End the war."

R'Venin turned away, jubilant, and hollered to the masses. "Everyone. Gather the infected. Bring them here. Go. Now."

"Start with the First Tower." K'Rawin's voice boomed. "We'll cure the rest of the spires after the festival."

"What?" R'Venin spun around. "I don't understand. We have the cure. We just need to keep the vortex going until all those who suffer from White Claw fly through."

"That will take more than three suns, R'Venin." K'Rawin strode in a circle, testing the newfound strength in his body. "We'll cure our clan first."

"But we have it here. Now." R'Venin pointed over K'Rawin's shoulder. "If we let the smoke clear, we'll have to start over. Procure the elements all over again."

"We can always buy more. At any time." The king took R'Venin with both hands on his shoulders. "We cannot postpone the festival. If we do, we risk offending P'Phet. See to healing our flock. Then, after the celebration, we'll talk about healing the rest of the spires. Agreed?"

R'Venin gripped his father's arms, his wings perking up as he bowed his head. "As my king commands."

"Good." K'Rawin patted his cheek and then turned back to the crowd, pointing to the terraces above. "Now. We have two suns to prepare for the festival, and I expect every warrior and courtesan in attendance. I want my harem prepared to receive eggs immediately. Go."

R'Venin turned away, heading for the water. He glanced across the pool to see K'Marot circling toward the king, the younger prince avoiding R'Venin's gaze as he moved.

* * *

The dark symphony rose in Ka'Ala's mind as the king and K'Marot put their heads close together. K'Marot nodded as K'Rawin pointed around the dome, gesturing with both hands. The king's heartsong blared strong and steady like a war march.

What's in your hearts, your highness?

Ka'Ala caught sight of movement in her periphery. On the other side of B'Luren, P'Vrit stepped to the ledge and knelt, her wingtips meeting over her head. Holding her arms out, she took a deep breath.

"It will be our honor to carry the king's seed," P'Vrit shouted over the falls. "This is a joyful day. We will prepare immediately."

Ka'Ala heard a new melody in her mind coming from the queen, harmonized by B'Luren.

Her song belies her words.

Below, the king nodded and waved his hand to his guard and council. He seemed to be giving orders as his attendants redressed him in his armor. Everyone around the pool filed out except for R'Venin, K'Marot, and a few handfuls of V'Jeeta. The ones wearing matching tunics of cobalt continued fanning the column of smoke as members of the council removed their armor and formed a queue in the water.

P'Vrit stood and walked away from the edge. B'Luren followed with Ka'Ala who trailed behind, as did the other wives. The queen veered away from the drop-off, heading for the lowest level of alcoves in the walls.

Before they took ten paces, B'Luren stepped away. She turned and grabbed Ka'Ala by the arm, pulling her out of line.

Ka'Ala opened her mouth, but B'Luren raised a finger to her own lips, and she led her around one of the columns out of sight from the pool.

"What's going on?" Ka'Ala whispered.

"No one can catch us speaking." B'Luren breathed. "Mother is the only woman allowed a voice here."

Ka'Ala peeked around the corner, catching a glimpse of P'Vrit descended the tiers. "Why aren't we going with her?"

"Because we're not mated. We won't receive an egg. We can only watch."

Ka'Ala leaned around the column with B'Luren. Across the dome, the queen jumped off the second terrace and flew toward a veiled alcove. Landing on a perch jutting out below the opening, P'Vrit leaned forward, seemingly speaking through the curtain. The fabric parted, revealing a plump woman in a robe of fine silks seated on a bed of cushions. She wore bands of gold around her neck, like a wide choker. Then Ka'Ala saw the chain, leading off the back and into the wall behind.

The other wives perched at separate alcoves, each housing an egg mother similarly tethered.

"They're prisoners?" Ka'Ala hissed.

"Shh." B'Luren put her hand over Ka'Ala's mouth and nodded.

Ka'Ala put her hand to her chest.

I couldn't imagine such an existence.

P'Vrit's egg mother reached behind her, bringing out a basket, and placed it on the nest between her legs. The other woman handed the queen a cup from within and pointed to the falls. The other wives received identical vessels and instructions.

With cup in hand, P'Vrit flew from the perch, leading the others in a loose formation toward the pool. Upon landing, they scooped a cupful and carried it back.

"What's the water for?" Ka'Ala breathed in B'Luren's ear.

"It's for a fertility draught."

P'Vrit's held out her cup to the egg mother. The woman leaned close as if to inspect the contents. With no visual reaction, the woman then pulled a hand-sized vase from the basket, tipping powder into the queen's mug. P'Vrit then extended a wing within the nook. The egg mother yanked a feather from the underside and used it to stir the potion.

"What'll it do?" Ka'Ala asked as the egg mother pushed the cup to P'Vrit's lips, tipping it back until it seemed drained. P'Vrit fell forward, taking fistfuls of a pillow as her whole body shook.

"It'll force her pouch to open early." B'Luren's voice sounded husky. Ka'Ala faced her, catching the glimmer of wetness under B'Luren's eyes.

"She's not ready to pouch?"

B'Luren shook her head. "She hasn't been in a few seasons," she whispered. "She hasn't hatched an egg in five. And none have survived since me."

"Why has she not been made a brood mother?"

"She's too young to lay." B'Luren watched the queen with watery eyes. "Too old to carry."

"Do the healers know why she's not laying?" Ka'Ala took B'Luren's hand.

B'Luren shook her head. "She hasn't gone to see them. If she doesn't start, Father will most likely cast her out and elevate another to First Wife."

"Who else knows?"

B'Luren squeezed Ka'Ala's hand. "Just you."

Ka'Ala watched in a stupor as every wife drank the elixir, most of whom didn't shake after swallowing. Once all seemed finished, the brood mother serving P'Vrit put her hand to the queen's face. Her mouth moved, but the words died on the wind. She bowed her head to the queen and closed her curtains.

P'Vrit turned, making eye contact with B'Luren and Ka'Ala, then stepped off the perch and floated over. Her legs buckled as she landed. B'Luren lunged forward, taking the queen in her arms in an embrace. From her place at the column, Ka'Ala could see P'Vrit take a fistful of B'Luren's robes as she stood tall, her face showing only strength and dignity.

The other wives followed from their perches, falling into line behind P'Vrit in the same order as when they'd arrived. P'Vrit headed for the exit, releasing her grip as B'Luren cut in behind the queen, who gestured for Ka'Ala to join her. The two women followed the queen, hand in hand, toward the staircase.

K'Marot was there, leaning against the wall, his eyes fixed on

Ka'Ala. "I'll see you at the festival, sister." His dark symphony grew in her mind.

P'Vrit marched to the stairs. The other wives followed; their eyes on the floor as they passed K'Marot. Once the last wife disappeared into the dark stairwell, K'Marot closed the distance. The falls echoed through the chamber, as well as triumphant shouts.

He took a step closer and held out his hand to Ka'Ala. "May I escort you, my lady?"

B'Luren dragged Ka'Ala across the threshold and turned, shielding Ka'Ala from K'Marot's gaze. "It is improper for anyone other than the queen's guard to escort us to and from the sacred pools. You know that. Besides, your father has decreed his wives prepare for seed. We need to help them get ready."

K'Marot sneered and pushed between the women, taking the stairs two at a time, and disappeared around a bend. His voice boomed from above. "I look forward to seeing you at the festival, my lady."

Ka'Ala stared after him, her hearts thrumming, then turned back to B'Luren. "His heartsong..." Her voice quaked. "It scares me."

"I may not hear his song," B'Luren turned, leading Ka'Ala up the stairs. "But he scares me too."

Chapter Thirty-Eight
Weaving Branches

*H*ere we are again.

R'Venin sighed. Standing before the alcove, with a drape in either hand, he stared at the objects just delivered; carbon-feather armor, as black as Ka'Ala's feathers, glinted on their pegs. Flecks of fire-crystal light danced like stars across the polished surfaces. From the shin-guards to the helmet, every engraved embellishment hailed the armorists' three-moon artistry.

From the post supporting the helmet, a pendant draped across the breastplate. Rubies formed a familiar shape. The four-pointed star. The elements of alchemy. He traced the patterns with a finger, lingering in the void between them.

Mountain. Tree. Fire. Rain. But not the Windfather.

The curtains swished together as R'Venin let go and turned from the armor, taking in his room. A roost of thick blankets. A shelf of scrolls and scratchplates. A short table surrounded by cushions. Atop sat a brass service set with matching decanter and goblets.

On the table, held open by the cups, the scroll that accompanied the armor laid open. The message scratched with the king's own claw. He glanced down, not focusing on the words scrawled into his mind.

A gift equal to the honor you bring to me. I am proud you are my heir.

The setting suns, twelve feathers off the horizon, drew his vision beyond the balcony. As he stepped into the evening air, his tunic swayed in the breeze. The unseen chorus of rock-dwelling creatures, large and small, fell silent as the royal guard patrolled the veranda below. A din rose from the banquet hall. Clattering dishes mixed with chattering voices into a fervor of preparation.

Is the cause of their excitement the same as mine?

He shielded his eyes as he peered toward the horizon, tracing the jagged line that rose and fell in the distance.

How can one have sick hearts for two places? Two homes?

He moved to the falloff and knelt. Head bowed, he held out his arms, palms up, and closed his eyes.

"Great Windfather. The day has ended, and I kneel before you with hearts overflowing with gratitude. Thank you for opening my father's mind to the cure for White Claw. Thank you for healing so many, and for opening the skies for many more. I share this day with those I hold most dear. I wish..."

Tears spilled down R'Venin's cheeks. He cleared his throat and took several deep breaths.

Blowing out his lungs, he continued with a shaky voice. "I wish... I wish Ja'Naam could have lived to see it. I wish Ja'Ven could have met his other flock. I hope they're happy flying amid the branches of the eternal tree. I hope she's proud of me, and... I hope she'll understand that I... it's not a betrayal-."

A knock on the door cut R'Venin short. He sighed, getting back on his feet.

"ENTER!"

A trio of V'Jeeta women—adolescents given the length of their trailing feathers—in servants tunics bustled into the chamber.

"Your Highness," they bowed in unison. The one on his right

spoke. "The queen sent us to dress you for the festival and your mating ceremony."

R'Venin glanced toward the alcove.

She's been a true friend and will make an extraordinary mate.

"Where are S'Evak and Pra'Bandhak?" R'Venin turned back, peering over their heads. The only others in earshot were the royal guards flanking the door. "My stewards."

They stared at each other, whispering between themselves.

"We don't know those names, my prince." The one in the middle said, giving the others sidelong glances. "Perhaps they flew to one of the other spires after the kingdom thought you dead."

So much has changed.

R'Venin nodded. "Please enter."

They burst into stifled giggles as he waved them in. They immediately went for the alcove. Two tied back the drapes while the third opened a chest just inside, retrieving an ivory tunic. Embroidered with Silver Silk, it shimmered like spinners web. She carried it over, keeping the hem off the floor, and held it above her head. The other two tittered while they removed pieces of armor from their pegs.

R'Venin turned his back, untying his tunic.

"She is so lovely, Your Majesty," the girl said as R'Venin shrugged off his water-stained tunic. "The two of you will have strong and beautiful hatchlings."

He put his arms through the holes of the proffered garment. "Yes. She is," he mumbled to himself. "Just as beautiful as..."

She came around to face him as he started doing the ties at his waist. "Allow me, my lord," she said.

"No, thank you." R'Venin pushed her hands from the strings at his waist.

The girl recoiled and fell to her knees. "My apologies, your highness. I meant no offense."

"No, I'm sorry." R'Venin held the robe closed with one hand and lifted her by the arm with the other. "I'm accustomed to dressing myself. I can handle the tunic, but you may help me with the armor."

"Of course, your majesty," she gave a quick curtsy and rushed back to the alcove.

Finishing the sash, he turned to find the other two girls holding his breastplate. They assembled his outfit for the length of three songs, chattering about the approaching ceremony and the gowns custom-tailored for B'Luren and Ka'Ala.

With the helmet tucked under one arm, R'Venin turned to the girl holding his crown. Even though he bent at the waist, she had to stretch to get the circlet on his head.

Lastly, the tallest of the three carried the pendant over; her eyes never left the glittering token as she moved like sweetsap.

"Quite distracting," R'Venin laughed through his nose. "Isn't it?"

Her face flushed as their eyes met. "Yes, my lord." She held it out. "It's beautiful. I don't think I've ever seen anything so precious."

"A gift from my father." R'Venin took it from her, letting the chain dangle as he held it. "For bringing the cure to White Claw home with me."

"My greatfather suffers from White Claw," the youngest servant said from the nook.

R'Venin turned to face the voice. "Did he receive the cure?"

She faced the floor and shook her head.

"How far along is it?"

"His wings lack the strength to carry him. He hasn't left his roost in a moon."

"Are you not from the first tower?"

"No, my lord," she said to the floor. "We're third tower. But people are saying you will summon the healing clouds again after the festival. Is that true?"

"Yes, it's true." R'Venin stepped closer and lifted her chin. "The king has promised to make the cure available to everyone on the spires. After the celebration. Your greatfather will fly again."

She held his hand to her cheek, laughing through her tears. "May P'Phet's greatest blessing fall at your feet."

Is peace between the flocks too much to ask?

* * *

Ka'Ala stared at the three V'Jeeta figures in the reflecting panel. P'Vrit and B'Luren beamed from either side of the woman in a floor-length robe of pure Silver silk. Behind her painted face, foreign eyes stared back from the polished surface. The soft glow from fire crystals sparkled off the braids of silvervine woven into her plumage.

The organ played a cheerful tune from the other side of the queen's chamber. Ka'Ala locked eyes with her reflection as mother and daughter fiddled with the veils cascading between her shoulders and spread them out on the floor.

"I don't even recognize myself," Ka'Ala whispered. The stained lips of her doppelganger moved as she spoke. She ran her hands down the front, smoothing non-existent wrinkles and rubbing the material between her fingers. "This would've fed me for twenty seasons in the Bluewoods. I can't thank you enough."

B'Luren, in a matching robe and maquillage, clutched her hands at her chin. "You look stunning," the princess beamed, bouncing in place. "If R'Venin's hearts don't sing when he sees you, then he's as blind as a sleepbreather."

"If his hearts sing half as loud for me as they did for Ja'Naam," Ka'Ala looked away, "I'll consider myself blessed."

"His hearts *will* sing for you." P'Vrit put an arm around Ka'Ala's waist. "As strong as yours sing for him."

"I hope so." Ka'Ala bit her lip as she made eye contact with herself again. She tugged at the high collar of her dress; her hand shifted in color to match B'Luren's. Wrist-length sleeves hid the rest of her natural pallor.

"Windfather has told me it will be."

"Then it shall be," Ka'Ala said, putting her arm around the queen.

B'Luren came around to the queen's other side, framing her in shimmering fabric.

P'Vrit's calf-length gown matched her eyes. Green as conifer needles, and embroidered with silvervine, it hugged tightly from the high collar to her waist, then flared out in pleats to the floor. A ruby-encrusted crown sat atop her head. Across her belly, she wore a white sash tied in the back. A distinct line from her pouch slit pushed against the fabric. She covered it with her hand.

"Will you be able to pouch an egg tonight?" B'Luren put her hand over her mother's.

P'Vrit slid her hand out from under B'Luren's and replaced it on top. "Yes. I think so." She patted B'Luren's hand. "Everything will be as Windfather decrees."

P'Vrit removed her other arm from around Ka'Ala and put it on B'Luren's belly. "And next season, you will pouch your first. I'm looking forward to becoming a greatmother."

Their heartsongs burst into a rapturous melody as they took hands and put their foreheads together.

Ka'Ala absent-mindedly rubbed her stomach.

May the Windfather bless us all.

* * *

"ALL HAIL THE KING!" A herald shouted at the portal. "All HAIL THE HEIR." His lone voice echoed off the barrel-vaulted ceiling ten wingspans above.

An ensemble of drummers, pipers, flutists, harpists, and horn-blowers blasted The Spire's March from an alcove in the banquet hall's third tier as K'Rawin strolled down the aisle in layered robes of emerald and white, accented in silver. He raised his scepter, pumping his fist with the rhythm, as he turned in circles.

R'Venin followed on the king's right in his ceremonial attire. With a quick sidelong glance, he caught K'Marot, his face unreadable, trailing on his left. Identical to the king, he wore no armor over his robes.

I wonder if Father will insist that I be his second when he mates.

Flanking either side of the path, hundreds of V'Jeeta dressed in their finery sat wing-to-wing on cushions. Trails no wider than a forearm wove through the squat tables packed between the central aisle and the walls. The king beamed as the crowd rose to their feet, clapping and chanting.

"ALL HAIL THE KING! All HAIL THE HEIR."

From the far side of the hall, a monumental staircase drew R'Venin's eye. Three wingspans wide at the base, they narrowed to a landing before splitting off and rising to the second terrace and then switching back to the third. Framed between columns rising into the arches overhead, a wizened V'Jeeta in a chalk-white robe over a juniper tunic held a scroll in one hand and a spool of silvervine in the other. His wings trembled like his hands.

Just aged. R'Venin thought to himself, focusing on the cleric's wings. *Not afflicted.*

A handful of clerics, dressed in similar garb, positioned themselves behind him before the doors to the sanctuary.

Below the minister, a trio of warriors waited on the highest steps. From the tread just below the landing, Ati'Kruddh, Lord of the Fourth Tower, watched the royal family approach in a wardrobe as opulent as the kings. Like the spire he ruled, he stood tall and still; only his head inclined as he made eye contact with K'Rawin. The next step down, an older warrior resembling Ati'Kruddh made eye contact and waved to people in the crowd. His feathers showed early signs of White Claw. The youngest of the three, arrayed in a white tunic and black armor, stood on another step lower. Though he wore a pleasant smile, his posture was erect and solid like his straight-backed father.

You must be B'Ahz, B'Luren's intended.

As K'Rawin led R'Venin and K'Marot up the steps single file, the assembly returned to their cushions, and the music ceased. Wood scraping against stone filled the space as the king reached the landing, stopping on the last tread. K'Marot moved behind and above R'Venin, so both husbands-to-be were on the same level.

The cleric cleared his throat and bowed to K'Rawin, pointing his scroll toward the crowd. "Your majesty? Would you like to address your guests?"

The king nodded and turned. R'Venin and the others on the steps faced the hall.

"We will remember this festival on scroll, on stone, and in song." K'Rawin's voice thundered through the hall. "My son, R'Venin, High Prince, Heir to the First Tower, and it would seem our new master alchemist..."

The assembly chuckled along with the king. K'Rawin waited for the laughter to die. "...takes his first wife."

Most in the hall rose to their feet and cheered. The king let the ovation grow before signaling them back to their seats.

"Also on this hallowed occasion, the clans of the first and fourth towers will unite with the mating of B'Ahz, son of Ati'Kruddh, and B'Luren, daughter of my first wife, Queen P'Vrit."

The gathering erupted into another round of applause, though a smaller group left their cushions.

"After the binding ceremony," K'Rawin's voice became softer, "we will give thanks to Windfather and P'Phet for the silk harvest and celebrate fertility. ALL HAIL P'PHET."

"SPEAKER FOR THE WINDFATHER," the crowd replied in unison.

"Pu'Rohit," K'Rawin faced the cleric. "I return the hall to you."

"Thank you, Your Highness." Pu'Rohit bowed, his wings trembling as he pointed them skyward and exposed their undersides. He cleared his throat again. "Bring forth the intended."

Music filled the room with a fast-paced, lilting ballad. Pipers led the melody, the flutes harmonized, as no less than two dozen girls flew through the main entrance carrying sacks of fine-spun cloth. They circled overhead in two layers of opposing rings, dropping handfuls of wishflowers. Spectators got to their feet and reached for them, holding them to their mouths, and whispering secret desires. Every hand and wing kept the petals in the air, swirling like a winter maelstrom.

"MY KING, I PRESENT TO YOU," the herald shouted over the joyful ruckus, "QUEEN P'VRIT, AND LADIES B'LUREN AND KA'ALA."

At his word, the petal-bearers left their circular formations and glided down to the central aisle. With wings outstretched tip-to-tip, they formed a bower as petals fell like winter kisses.

Starting at the opposite end of the hall, guests bowed, held hands to their hearts, and exposed the undersides of their wings like a half-speed wave approaching the shore. As if following the crest, their quills billowed out, spraying petals on the guests like a wave crashing against a rock.

R'Venin curled his talons over the steps' lip and leaned forward, focusing on the gaps between the girls' feathers. Flashes of green and silver peeked through the openings. He led his target through the arbor, like spotting for a river-crawler ready to break the surface.

As they approached, his hearts beat twice for every measure from the musicians. Craning his neck, he glanced at K'Rawin. The king inclined his head toward R'Venin as their eyes met, then returned his gaze to the aisle.

K'Marot slapped R'Venin's wing. "Focus, brother," he mumbled. "Father will shower you with more praise later."

R'Venin laughed at himself and then caught sight of B'Ahz. The other husband-to-be seemed to be having trouble swallowing as he fidgeted with his collar. Suddenly B'Ahz froze, stiff as winter tears like Ati'Kruddh behind him. He lowered his hand to his breastplate and took a quick breath.

That's the look of a man who sees incomparable beauty.

R'Venin followed his gaze as the music seemed to retreat to the other side of the world.

With their wings undersides exposed, three women knelt at the bottom step. R'Venin quickly passed over P'Vrit and B'Luren to the vision bathed in light.

"My King," P'Vrit's voice commanded reverence throughout the hall. "If it pleases you, I bring my daughters to be mated to the warriors of your choice."

B'Luren and Ka'Ala lifted their heads. B'Luren gave a demure smile to B'Ahz with a slight head tilt. Ka'Ala's eyes remained hidden behind their lids for a moment, then opened slowly like the sunrise. She swallowed and licked her lips as her emerald irises locked onto R'Venin's.

R'Venin's hearts skipped along with his breath.

"Fear not to take her into your hearts, my son," Windfather breathed.

"It pleases me." R'Venin startled as K'Rawin's voice boomed. "B'Ahz, Warrior of the Fourth Tower, I give you my daughter, B'Luren. B'Luren, come to your husband."

B'Luren climbed the steps to murmured adoration from the

gathering. B'Ahz took her hand as she reached his level.

"You look as breathtaking as ever, my lady." B'Ahz cooed with an easy smile. "I look forward to many seasons with you by my side."

"Thank you, my lord." B'Luren gave a slight curtsy.

"R'Venin," K'Rawin's voice had a happy growl, "Heir of the First Tower, I give you the Lady Ka'Ala. Ka'Ala, come to your husband."

With each step, R'Venin's hearts thumped harder in his chest. Ka'Ala's gaze never left his as she seemed to float to him. He reached out his hand as she was three steps away, guiding her to the place at his side. "You... you look..." he stammered, then took a deep breath. "You look glorious."

She turned her face fully to him, her smile wider than he'd ever seen. "Thank you," she breathed and swallowed.

"Let us begin the bonding ceremony," Pu'Rohit said from behind. R'Venin and Ka'Ala turned on the spot, facing the cleric. K'Rawin, K'Marot, and the others lining the stairs did the same.

"By the rites laid down by P'Phet," Pu'Rohit said, holding his scroll and spool aloft. "I bind these couples together. My lords, pluck a feather from each wing of your respective wives."

Ka'Ala turned to R'Venin and exposed her wings' undersides. He pulled at a small tuft, one that was already loose, and repeated the process on the other. Ka'Ala's eyes widened as the feathers shifted from dark umber to ink-black in his hand.

"I almost forgot. Someone's bound to see," she mouthed, her eyes darting to K'Marot though the younger prince seemed intent on avoiding her direction. "What'll we do?"

Over Ka'Ala's shoulder, he watched B'Luren flinch as B'Ahz yanked a large feather from her wings' leading edges.

R'Venin stared at his cupped hands for a moment, then cupped her hands in his. "I'll draw double of mine."

"But if we don't use a feather each," she breathed, her lips not moving. "Will the ceremony be valid?"

"We'll figure that out later," he mouthed and tilted his head slightly toward the hall.

"Now, take feathers from your own wings," Pu'Rohit said.

R'Venin ignored the discomfort as he shoved Ka'Ala's tufts into his wings and dislodged four of his own. He couldn't read anything from B'Ahz's stone face as the warrior plucked himself.

R'Venin held up the four brown feathers and gave Ka'Ala a wink and a smile.

"Ladies, with a claw, remove a handspan of silvervine from the spool. Tie each of your feathers to those of your husbands, in separate bundles."

Ka'Ala received her thread first, being closest to the spool.

"Once you're finished with that, each of you holds one in your right hand."

R'Venin held a pair of feathers in each hand while Ka'Ala tied the silvervine around the shafts. B'Luren and B'Ahz finished theirs, holding their symbols out for the cleric's inspection. He nodded approval, turned to R'Venin and Ka'Ala, and nodded again.

"Well done. Now, Lady B'Luren, hold out your feather, like so..." Pu'Rohit twisted and handed the spool to one of the other clerics, then held his right hand out like a cup. He then let the scroll fall open. "While facing each other, recite the petition."

As he stole a glance, R'Venin could only see the back of B'Luren's head. But he caught a glimpse of the feathers in her open palm peeking over her shoulder. When he looked back at Ka'Ala, he found her gazing up at him; her eyes sparkled like veridian pools. B'Luren's voice faded away. A strange melody drifted into his mind, growing louder as the ambient noise in the hall faded. From the corner of his eye, he could see the musicians above, their instruments under their arms.

As he studied the lines of Ka'Ala's face, a halo of light appeared around her head, growing until it clouded his vision to everything but her. Surrounded by a glowing mist, her eyes faded from green as her feathers matched his armor's darkness. Ka'Ala signaled no awareness that she'd shifted to her Gir'Agit form, a tapestry of midnight and pearl. He felt her hands in his, the twined feathers having disappeared from his grip.

For a moment, nothing existed beyond her wings.

"I will be an honorable man in the eyes of the Windfather, and a loyal husband to you." As if in a dream, his thoughts filled their surroundings like an ocean's roar. "I will protect you and provide for your needs as my own. I will hold you in my hearts until they stop beating."

Warmth spread outward from his chest, his skin fading from tan to pale as the surge cascaded down his arms. She squeezed his hands as the heat collected in their fingertips, building like a pyre. Their hands glowed, identical in color and luminance.

"I will be a virtuous woman in the eyes of the Windfather, and devoted wife to you," Ka'Ala's voice filled the space though her lips never moved. "You can trust your hearts to my care. I will be your comforter and your counsel. I will fly beside you so long as the winds blow."

Then, just as slowly, her colors shifted back to V'Jeeta. The mist collected and disappeared behind her head.

"Very good." Pu'Rohit's chuckle made R'Venin look around the hall.

Ka'Ala touched the back of R'Venin's hand—the one still gripping the feathers—in hers. "Are you alright?" she breathed. "What's wrong?"

R'Venin mirrored her gesture. The heat in his chest rose again as he touched her skin. "I don't know," he whispered. "Nothing, I suppose."

"Well done, Princess B'Luren. Well done." Pu'Rohit turned, facing R'Venin. "Now for the High Prince and Lady Ka'Ala. As with them, Lady Ka'Ala will go first." The cleric held up the scroll, angling it toward Ka'Ala.

"R'Venin, son of K'Rawin..." Ka'Ala licked her lips as she held up the matching feathers bound in silvervine. "I, Ka'Ala, daughter of Ka'Alee, submit myself to you in accordance with the rites and teachings of P'Phet. I swear a spirit oath to place myself under your wing, and to be a faithful and obedient wife."

"Now, my lady," the cleric pointed at R'Venin's right wing, "Insert your feathers into his undersides, making sure you pierce the skin."

Ka'Ala chewed on her lip as she stepped closer and took hold of R'Venin's wing. The scent of clouds rose to his nasal slits. He drew in a lungful as he eyed her plumage, sparkling like the sea off the Bluewood coast. A moment later, she looked up into his eyes.

"Did that hurt?" she whispered, her hand lingering on the spot.

His hearts thrummed in his ears as he cradled her elbow with his hand. "Completely painless."

"Now, Your Highness..." Pu'Rohit turned to R'Venin and cleared his throat, waving his scroll. "Ka'Ala, daughter of Ka'Alee."

"Ka'Ala, daughter of Ka'Alee..." R'Venin held up his twin feathers. "I, R'Venin, son of K'Rawin, do accept you in accordance with the rites and teachings of P'Phet. I swear a spirit oath to take you under my wing, and to be a faithful husband."

She exposed her wings' underside, staring into R'Venin's eyes. He never lost her gaze as he pushed the shafts into her skin with the tenderness he'd only reserved for one other.

"Did that hurt?" R'Venin breathed.

"Not even a little." Her eyes spilled over as her voice broke.

"My king. My queen." Pu'Rohit raised his hands over the couples' heads. "My lords and ladies. Let it be known throughout the spires that these men and women are now, and until the wind dies, mated in the eyes of P'Phet and the Windfather."

Lively music rang out from above. King K'Rawin jumped off the staircase to the applause of the entire hall. He glided down to P'Vrit. She clapped and laughed through her tears, her gaze fixed on B'Luren as the new couples descended the steps.

From the aisle, K'Rawin raised his hands, quieting the crowd. "Bring the food and spirits," he shouted over the music. "Let merriment fill every hall and hallow. Let the songs of thanks reach Windfather's ears. And let dance make the spires quiver in tune. Let the festival of fertility begin."

Applause rattled the vaulted ceiling as trays emerged from the threshold, passed from person to person until every table bowed under tiers of food and drink.

P'Vrit took K'Rawin's outstretched hand. He led her away from the banquet hall.

Can't even wait until after the feast.

R'Venin turned and offered his hand to Ka'Ala with a slight bow. "May I escort you to a table, my lady."

"Lead the way," she said with a low curtsy. "My lord."

Chapter Thirty-Nine

The First Dawn

"It's beautiful here, don't you think?" R'Venin said as he shrugged off the ivory tunic within his changing area. One wingspan in diameter, his half-stretched wings brushed the screens separating him from the roost and balcony. He kicked his helmet into the rest of his armor, piled in the corner, dropping his robe on top. "What do you think of the view?"

"Yes." Ka'Ala's voice shook. "It's breathtaking."

R'Venin turned, catching her shadow, compact and immobile as a statue on the fabric between his alcove and hers. He moved closer, tracing her silhouette on the fabric. "What did you think of the banquet? My mother told me she made sure to have a wide variety of dishes since she didn't know what you liked to eat. I described the Ch'Hota dishes you seemed to favor when you ate with us. I think the cooks made a passable version of redblossom soup."

Ka'Ala cleared her throat, her outline growing and changing, followed by the rustle of clothing. "Everything was delicious. After a lifetime of scavenging in the wild, even the food I bought around my shop in Willowlimb was palatial by comparison. You know I'm not a picky eater." The delicate shape of her dress appeared on the curtain, hanging from a peg.

"I know," R'Venin laughed through his nose. "And I told her as much, but she wanted to make sure you felt welcome."

Ka'Ala's moved closer to the screen. "When we fly back to the spires, I'll be sure to thank her again. Your mother has been so kind. Your sister too."

R'Venin moved closer to the screen. "She's your sister now."

Ka'Ala sniffled. "My sister," she whispered as the shadow of her head drooped. "After losing... so many..."

R'Venin bowed his head.

Her hand pushed against the fabric. "After losing someone you love..."

R'Venin put his palm to hers. "It's good to feel close to someone again."

His hearts raced as they pressed their hands together, fingers nestling into valleys made in the fabric like wax in a mold. He moved closer, touching his forearm to the cloth. Ka'Ala did the same. The heat of her skin adding to his. They remained there, motionless, for the length of a song until R'Venin cleared his throat.

"Ka'Ala?"

"Yes?" Her throaty words barely penetrated the veil.

His hand slid from her palm, tracing down her arm. "Will you join me on the balcony?"

She took her hand from the screen. Her shadow disappeared as her footsteps retreated into the opposite corner. "I'll meet you there in one song."

R'Venin parted the curtain and stepped from the changing alcove in nothing but a breechcloth.

Our First-Moon aerie.

The roost, a grotto behind the Dry Falls, faced Eastward. The walls, smoothed by hand over a thousand seasons, flowed like the river that once ran high overhead—a mural, depicting a vast needle-leaf forest, covered every surface.

Framed by gossamer curtains, the night sky filled the opening to their abode. The trickle from the dried-up waterfall meandered to a stalactite and dripped into a shallow basin off to one side of the entrance. Gentle breezes drifted into the hollow, carrying the scent of sunburst petals and dust.

Within the grotto, a nest of fluffy blankets and cushions took up most of the space, while a copper pan of fire crystals swung from a hook above the bed, its perforated surface letting points of light dance around the room.

R'Venin moved around the nest in a hunched posture, his wings brushing against the walls. He knelt at the basin. Strips of cloth laid along the edge next to a pair of bronze cups. Taking a swatch, he soaked it in the water and washed his face, neck, and shoulders. He then filled both cups, placing one next to the pile and draining the other in one swallow.

He took a deep breath and stepped beyond the cave opening. A shiver ran the length of his body as the night air blew across his damp skin. His hearts thrummed in his chest as he moved to the ledge. He looked up at the moons, The Three Mothers, and then out to the horizon. The dawn was still a half-sun away.

A splash of water behind him made his wings perk up. He closed his eyes, focusing on the sounds.

Rapid dripping. Wet cloth slapping on the ground. Metal scraping against stone. Ka'Ala's breathing, muffled in a cup, and padded footsteps getting closer.

R'Venin flinched, laughing, as a pair of cold hands touched his lower back and slid to his sides. Reaching across his abdomen, he took her hands and pulled them around himself, squeezing her arms. She nuzzled her head between his wing joints.

"Our first dawn approaches," R'Venin swallowed hard, staring into the distance. "We must..."

"It's still many songs away."

Her hearts thrummed against his back.

"Tradition says... before the suns rise..."

R'Venin's hearts beat thrice for every one of Ka'Ala's as he lowered his wings to lay upon hers. He turned his head, raking his fingertips on her arm. "Do you think Ja'Naam would approve?" R'Venin asked, his voice deep and husky.

Ka'Ala took in a deep breath. "If she'd been the one who survived," Ka'Ala said, hugging him tightly. "Would you want her to fly alone for the rest of her days?"

"Of course not," he breathed. "I'd want her to find someone that made her happy again."

"Do you think she'd want the same for you? To be happy again?"

R'Venin's chin fell to his chest. "Yes."

Ka'Ala's wings lowered under his, tightening around his arms, the tips closing together over his feet. She took another deep breath, blowing it out slowly before taking another. "Do you think you'll be happy with me?"

R'Venin's head came up slowly. Raising a wing, he pulled Ka'Ala by the hand under and around to face him. She folded her wings in on herself like a shawl as she moved, her face tipped to the ground with eyes closed.

She moistened her lips as he took her by the hands and held them out. She spread her wings open like a curtain, revealing a lithe figure covered in nothing but a breechcloth and bodice. They shimmered in the moonlight unlike anything he'd ever seen. She chewed on her lip as he stepped between her hands, pulling them around and behind him. Their wings crushed on each other's, weighing down on one another as if they stood within a cyclone of winter's kisses.

She opened her eyes. Pearly irises, glowing like the three mother's above, stared into his. Her face glowed under the moonlight as he lifted her chin with one hand, snaking the other to the small of her back. She opened her mouth, letting out a breath as he cupped her face.

He leaned down, brushing his lips on hers. "Yes."

END

About the Author

I grew up in the small, rural town of Boring, OR with my six brothers and sisters. After graduating from High School in Gresham, OR, I attended BYU-ID and received my Associate's Degree in Pre-Med. After that, I returned to Portland, OR, and attended Portland State University, where I earned my Bachelor's Degree in Biology/Pre-Med before changing my career track to Architecture. I completed my second Bachelor's Degree in Architecture at Portland State University before achieving my Master of Architecture Degree from the University of Utah in Salt Lake City, UT. After graduation, my wife and I moved to Phoenix, Arizona, where we adopted four children over the next eight years. I currently live in the Salt Lake City area, where I am an Associate Member of the American Institute of Architects (AIA) and the League of Utah Writers. My other interests include movies, singing, and motorcycles.

You may visit Nicholes P. Adams at: www.nicholaspadams.com

More titles by Nicholas P. Adams

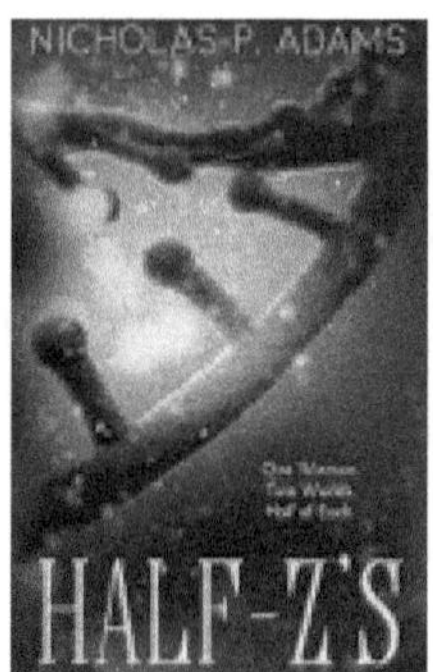

My Amazon Page:

My Newsletter:

My Goodreads Page:

Acknowledgements

I wish to personally thank the following people and groups for their contributions, inspiration, knowledge, and other help in creating this book:

To my wife & kids for being my greatest strength. To my parents for their steadfast belief in my abilities when I doubted myself. To my siblings for being my best friends in the entire world (with extra special thanks to my youngest brother for being my greatest fan). And to my extended family for their love and friendship over my entire lifetime (and a special thanks to my cousin Charlie N. Holmberg who personally welcomed me into our local writing community with kindness, grace, and infectious zeal).

To my writer's Group, Brian C. Hailes, Rick Bennett et al. patiently providing the monthly feedback that helped me identify and replace poor writing habits.

To Epic Edge Publishing for the amazing cover and interior layout that turned my manuscript into a work of art.

To Yassine Sey for his outstanding conceptual illustrations that helped me visualize my characters.

To the Herriman Chapter of the League of Utah Writers, their tireless work in bringing talented presenters from the larger community made aspects of the literary world less scary.

To my ARC Readers, too many to name, for their brilliant critiques that helped me trim the fat and hone the plot.

And to Callie Stoker, the Manuscript Doctor, who gave me the initial encouragement I needed to turn an exercise into a full-length novel. And to my editor, Deborah DeNicola of Intuitive Gateways, for polishing my manuscript into a finished product ready for publication.

Other Titles Available from
EPIC EDGE PUBLISHING

| Illustrated Novels | Graphic Novels / Comics | Childrens Picture Books | Anthologies | Non-Fiction |

Blink: An Illustrated Spy Thriller Novel
by Brian C Hailes

Defender of Llyans
by Brian C Hailes

Avila
(Available 2022!)
by Robert J Defendi
& Brian C Hailes

Devil's Triangle:
The Complete
Graphic Novel
by Brian C Hailes
& Blake Casselman

Dragon's Gait
by Brian C Hailes

KamiKazi
by John English
& Brian C Hailes

If I Were a Spaceman:
A Rhyming Adventure
Through the Cosmos
by Brian C Hailes
& Tithi Luadthong

Here, There Be Monsters
by Brian C Hailes
& Tithi Luadthong

Don't Go Near the
Crocodile Ponds
by Brian C Hailes

Skeleton Play
by Brian C Hailes

Can We Be Friends?
by Edie New
& Cindy Hailes

Cresting the Sun: A Sci-fi
/ Fantasy Anthology
Featuring 12 Award-
Winning Short Stories
by Brian C Hailes,
Rick Bennett
& Nicholas Adams

Heroic: Tales of the
Extraordinary
by Blake Casselman,
David Farland,
Michael Stackpole
& more

DIWM: The Dynamic
Female Figure
by Brian C Hailes

DIWM: A Study of the
Human Form
by Brian C Hailes

Passion & Spirit: The
Dance Quote Book

DIWM 2020 Annual 1